Voices of Hope

Voice of Hope

Volume 1

The Hub Collective

The Hub585 | New York

The Voice of Hope Program is an 8-month mentorship program that focuses on empowering teens through authorship and entrepreneurship while fostering a space of community, agency, and hope. The Voices of Hope Program is designed to engage youth in learning while giving them the social gift of hope and restoring their self-efficacy.

Copyright © 2022 | The Hub585 Inc. | Voices of Hope Vol. 1

All rights reserved.

No part of this publication may be reproduced, distributed, or transmitted in any form or by any means, including photocopying, recording, or other electronic or mechanical methods, without the prior written permission of the publisher, except in the case of brief quotations embodied in critical reviews and certain other noncommercial uses permitted by copyright law.

For permission requests, write to the publisher, addressed "Attention: Permissions Coordinator," at the address below.

Any references to historical events, real people, or real places are used fictitiously. Names, characters, and places are products of the author's imagination.

Prepared by Ebony Nicole Smith Consulting, LLC | ebonynicolesmith.com
Editor: Atossa J. McCrary | Boss Lady Press
Book cover designed by Jason Tyree | Creatiworks, LLC | www.creatiworks.com

Printed in the United States of America.

First printing edition 2022.

The Hub 585, Inc. – Hope Center
111 Chestnut St.
Rochester, NY 14604

www.thehub585.org

ISBN: 979-8-218-03900-4 (paperback)

Contents

Life of Royalty – Royalty Harvey 1

My Story – Gregory Harvey 14

The Voices of My People – Rashmond Lopez 22

The Man in Her Basement – Nhaziah Bedell-Scott 30

To Unravel a Realm – Jemeah Scott 36

Touch! – Kenneth Santiago 302

Crown of Requisite – Dylan Arce Carrion..............................334

Author's Bios 400

Synopsis of Stories

Life of Royalty by Royalty Harvey

Life for me and my family changed when we lost our dad. I didn't think I would be able to live after his death because I still needed him. But I learned that I can still chase my dreams when I set my mind to whatever I want to do. I overcame sadness and depression to become the young, black, and beautiful lady I am today. My story is proof that even if life is hard right now, you can be happy, one day.

My Story by Gregory Harvey

Being a fighter came easy to me at the age of four. From then on, all the problems I faced taught me how to be a better fighter and protector of my family. Eventually, the defender in me would take me places I'd never seen before.

The Voices of My People by Rashmond Lopez

Two stories. Two Cities. Two different times to tell HIStory. Follow Jeremiah as he navigates life as a young boy trying to survive the great depression. Then, journey with Frank as he experiences life as a fighter pilot during World War 2.

The Man in Her Basement by Nhaziah Bedell-Scott

As the night comes to an end, Amy lays down to rest only to be awaken at 3am. Trying to go back to sleep, hungry strikes. Instead of fighting it, she indulges but not without intervention from her family and friends. However, there was one person she wasn't expecting to be in her house at that time.

To Unravel a Realm by Jemeah Scott

Four unlikely friends are forced to evaluate their familial loyalties and the views that they hold of the world that they live in– as they rush against the tide of darkness – putting together the pieces that the dead left behind, in order to instill a peace that they aren't sure can ever return.

Touch! by Kenneth Santiago

Struggling with himself, Correy's grip on life is held together by his introverted personality and by being an extreme germaphobe. A year after breaking up with his ex, his attempt to live a "normal" life is halted by an invisible evil that threatens to kill all humanity. On a quest to warn the world before it spreads, Correy finds he Is already too late and must save those who dare to listen.

Crown of Requisite by Dylan Arce Carrion

Cecilia Columbus is the illegitimate daughter of Christopher Columbus who is sold as a slave to Commander Leo to be raised by other slaves. While living as his ward, she is informed of who her birth father is. This revelation encouraged her to join the army with a determination to change the Spanish Empire. Along the way she finds that with power and the craving for change comes soul-crushing truths that make the end goal that much more necessary, even if it takes unthinkable sacrifices.

Memoir Writings

- *a historical account or biography written from personal knowledge or special sources*

- *an essay on a learned subject*

Life of Royalty

By Royalty Harvey

Here lay some pieces of my heart. First piece is my mom, Miesha. Mom is dark-skinned and short, with a Coca-Cola body and cute brown eyes. She is thirty-two years old, going on thirty-three, with two jobs and attends Monroe Community College. This school is for students to go there to study and learn about different things they never knew of, so they can get a better-paying job. Right now, my mom works at Seabreeze amusement park and at Rochester City School District school, a school numbered fifty. Mom goes to church on Sundays, wearing a button-down or a dress, depending on how she feels. She loves church music, and her favorite gospel artist is Tamela Mann because she can sing up a storm. Although my mom's favorite color is red, she's got a shiny blue Acura. She gets bored easily when her mind is not occupied.

    Four other pieces of my heart are my brothers: Cardan (Dan Dan), Micah (Kih), Deshawn (Nunu), and Gregory (Baby Greg). Two of them have the same mom as me, but one does not have the same dad. The other two share the same dad as me, but not the same mom. As the only girl out of all my siblings and the youngest, my brothers are very over-protective of me. Most of my siblings are good at football, boxing, and basketball, and Micah is good at track. My brothers are fine and as they're sister, I can say that. Girls like them because of their personality, the way they carry themselves, and how they dress themselves up.

My dad's name is Gregory T. Harvey. He died on October 13, 2020 and was a very nice guy who always took care of others and his family. My dad was in love with dogs (bullies) and loved music. He was actually a songwriter and rapper, too, but didn't have a chance to publish his music before he died. He never showed the pain he was going through; he always kept it to himself. His favorite color was red, and he always made his kids play a sport to get their minds working. My dad always made sure we had an education. He always cared for his kids and wife, making sure we always had clothes and shoes to wear, a car to get around with, a roof to live under, and an education. My dad was a really good cook, who he tried to cook different things instead of the basics. His favorite dish to cook was seafood mac and cheese along with barbecue-like ribs, steak, chicken, shrimp, mashed potatoes, and grilled corn on the cob. People would know my dad was cooking when they walked past the house and it was smelling delicious. Some people would ask my dad to make them barbecue, mac and cheese, potatoes from scratch, and other foods.

My grandparents don't take disrespect from anybody because they respect everyone. My grandma works in a Kodak building and makes good money. She is tall and thick, and my grandpa is short with a big butt, and neither of them loves their body size. One thing I love about my grandparents is that they have always been there for us when we were down; they even let us live with them for a year after my dad passed away.

My aunt Christa met a man named Eddie, and they have been together for some years. I like them being together because they are both smart college graduates. My aunt's boyfriend is always there to talk to my brothers about boy things, and aunty is always there to talk to me about girl stuff that I don't know about. Aunty is thick, meaning smaller with big arms and legs, and her boyfriend Eddie is short like Kevin Hart. They both have brown eyes.

Now that I told you a lot about my family, let me tell you a little bit about "Princess" Royalty. I am twelve years old going on thirteen. I have four brothers and am the youngest and only girl out of my siblings. I love to dance and draw. Once in a while, I used to do boxing, and I liked it. But I stopped once my dad passed away. I am sad a lot about my dad passing away, and what I'm going through now is very hard because he and I were very close.

Since he's passed, I've learned how to do hair, and I'm learning piece by piece how to do nails. I had three dogs (bullies). I was taking care of them, but two of my dogs died. They were a boy and a girl named Mikey and Tiffany, so now, I have one more dog left: a girl named Betty.

Math is my favorite subject because I love it and am good at it. I also love music: both very hyper and very calm music.

Life of Royalty

Memories in My House

Once, I lived in this blue and white house on Reynolds Street across from a school called School Two with Baby Greg and Nunu and my parents. Let me take you back to the memories we all had in this house before my dad died and we moved. We all used to sit in the living room and have family talks, like *How everybody's day was? What did we do? How was school?* Sometimes, I would say my day was okay or bad or good because my day was not always great. But, I knew while living in my mother and father's house, I was not allowed to get phone calls home saying I did anything bad or was not listening to the teacher. My dad knew I was capable of doing anything when it came down to it.

We also used to talk about what we could do to make our family better and stop everybody from arguing. Everybody in the house used to argue because we were in the house together for so long, and everyone thought they were the boss. There were only two bosses in the house: my dad and mother.

My dad's brothers always came over to play games like *Madden NFL* and *NBA2K* and watch shows like *Power* and *Empire*. My uncles were sore losers, so they would get mad when they got their butts kicked, and the winner would always brag about how they won. It would always start more stuff because they were already mad. When they kept teasing each other, it made them argue and say they wanted to fight.

Boxing

Life of Royalty

Baby Greg started boxing when he was like seven or eight years old. When we used to go to the gym, I saw a lot of new people who I would have liked to be cool with so we could help each other out. Once he started getting into boxing more, he liked learning more about it and how a lot of effort had to be put into the sport. After I saw my brother boxing, my other Kih, Nunu, and I wanted to try it out so we could know how to protect ourselves, even if we knew we couldn't always protect ourselves from everything.

When I first walked into the gym, it stank because everybody was putting in hard work. I started boxing at eight years old, and my other brothers started at eleven and fourteen. When I boxed after school, the first thing I would do was grab a jump rope and jump for thirty minutes. Then, I would wrap my hands up, put on all my guards, and hop in the ring. I learned that it doesn't matter if you lose or win because you will always be a winner at the end of the day. I would get tired fast since I was not in the right shape, so I would cry when I first started working out. I felt like everybody was pushing me hard even though I was a girl. I noticed that everyone pushing me showed me how to be strong and get through anything. No one stopped me or made me think I was nothing and couldn't do or be anything.

At nine, I started to get good at boxing. While training with my coaches, TJ and Q.I., I became the best of the best, but I wanted to quit and do other things like dance. I felt like I needed to do more girly things because I thought I'd start being rough and acting like a boy, which was not okay. Still, my dad never let me quit. He didn't want me to feel like I could just give up on everything in life. I would never be anything if I just gave up on everything. My dad would sit me down and tell me that I'm a powerful, black girl and I could do anything I put my mind to, that I should never give up chasing my dreams. If I quit, nothing would ever matter, and I would not care about anything because I gave up on the sport I liked.

School

I started to do badly in school because I was hanging out with the wrong group of friends who didn't mean me any good. I was always the person to get caught and in trouble for something I hadn't done alone, but my friends would never get in trouble for it. I would get a phone call home, get grounded, and have a talking-to. I never learned my lesson. I would off of punishment and do the same thing, even though it was never good for me. But, I always went the bad route because I wanted to be popular and be the owner of the school. I always knew I wasn't the owner; I was just a kid. I would talk back to the teachers because I never liked someone telling me the right thing to do. I always wanted to have the last word, even though I always knew I would never win the battle. Grown-ups are always right, even when they are wrong. I never liked my teachers or principals because when I did start doing well, they would always bring my past up to my parents and say what I used to do.

But, they did tell my parents I had changed school, and now I'm the school helper and a role model. I changed my behavior around because I was tired of getting in trouble, having to sit through in-school suspension, and meeting with the principal. I showed people the right thing to do when I changed my life around.

Learning Beauty

When I was ten, I was in my room thinking about who was going to do my hair, but instead of someone doing my hair, I just decided I would do it. I hadn't gotten my hair done that weekend, and I couldn't find anyone to do my hair. I just started doing cornrows, and it took me some time to get them right and neat, but I did it. The next time I tried to do them, they didn't come out the way I wanted, so I got very upset, stopped, and took a nap. When I woke up, I took a deep breath and ate something; then, I tried again. Finally, I got the look I wanted. I was very excited and proud of myself because I didn't think I was capable of doing something like that.

I started to get more into hair when I watched people on YouTube doing hairstyles that I wanted to try on myself and my mother. She didn't want me to do her hair because she didn't think I knew how. All she thought was that I wanted to play around, but I wanted to show her how I was into hair and how I was going to be somebody one day. I always tried to do nails, too, but I didn't think it was my thing at that age since it would never come out perfect and I felt like it had too many steps. Plus, I just wanted to focus on one thing at a time and would try again later. I still never can get the beads right for nails, either. I put too much or too little.

Now, I will do my own hair and go get my nails done at the nail shop. I used to try different colors on my nails and get my toes done with matching colors. I like acrylic nails with a little bit of thickness and at a medium length.

Dad Does My Hair

When I was eleven, I stopped boxing because Covid cases were going around and the gym had closed down. My father and I started going on daddy-daughter dates. Sometimes, we'd go out to dinner or go to get our nails done. We would even go grocery shopping. I was happy to do that because he was there for me. From the day I was born all the way up to eleven years old, he and I had a close relationship. I could always count on him and tell him something without him getting too mad at me. We would have rap or singing battles, and my dad even did my hair for the first time when I was ten. He had me looking like a powerful, young, black lady with a beautiful afro when I'd had two messed-up ponytails. Mom had been rushing to work and didn't have time to do my hair because she got a ride to work and didn't want to miss a day.

When I went to school, everybody was asking me who did my hair because it was cute. I told them my dad did it, and everybody was shocked because they'd never heard of a dad doing his daughter's hair.

I remember my dad used to always pick me up and put me on his shoulder when I was younger. He also used to work out with me on his shoulder, throw me up in the air, and catch me.

Hard Times

Sometimes it was hard, and we needed help with money, so my dad would ask his mother for it. My mom would be afraid to ask because she didn't want anybody being in her business. My mother always wanted to be independent and do things for herself most of the time. In order for my mom to make money, she had to get two jobs, and my dad had to hustle for what he made because he didn't want a job. All the money that my parents made went to putting clothes on our backs, food in our stomachs, and a roof over our heads. Every time we went out of town and went to the mall, my parents would always use the money on us and never get themselves anything.

One day, I was crying because my dad and I had to scrape up the money for us to eat because my mom only had a couple dollars. We had to go around the house and find change, and my dad promised us that we would never have to scrape up money ever again.

My Brothers Growing Up

My brothers barely came over to hang out or check on us because their mother always put things in their heads. She never wanted my dad to be around or to do things for his two sons. She never wanted my dad to be the father he was, and my dad was very strict. He really didn't let us go places or do things because he was overprotective and didn't want anything to happen to us.

My brothers really started coming over a couple months before my dad died, and he was very happy to see them. He'd been tired of begging them to visit and was also tired of telling them they could at least call and check on him since anything could happen any day. They would feel more hurt if they never came over or called their dad. When my dad died and we started living with our grandparents, they started visiting more for a while. We were kind of healed and found a new house to move into, the house across the street from our grandparents.

    My older brother, Dan Dan, found a girlfriend who'd graduated from college and was in her twenties. She came over one day with my brother and said she had a prize: she was pregnant. The only thing U could say was congratulations because I would finally be an aunt. I'd always wanted a nephew that I could spoil and treat as if he was mine. I love babies, and some babies love me. Kih ended up going to school but got kicked for bringing something violent, so he messed up his dream of a career in football and basketball. He fought his case and had to keep going back to court. He did well with going to court to get his case closed, and now, he is able to go back to school and finish his final year.

Eddie Becoming Family

    My aunt Christa was living with my grandparents for a couple of years until she found a friend. When she went to college and stayed in the dorms, they became more than friends. After a while, she was bringing Eddie to all our family events, and everybody got to know him and started liking him more. He and my aunt found an apartment and moved in together, and sometimes, I will go over and do little things with them like play games or get talked to about real life, things I needed to know.

When my aunt got the call that my dad passed away in the house and they couldn't bring him back to life, Eddie was always here for the family and everyone else. He always helped out when we needed something or when we were having a family problem. He and my aunt are planning on getting married next year, and I will be the flower girl for the wedding. They want to get married because they are going to be together for life if God is willing and he doesn't take any more of our loved ones.

Grandparents without Dad

Ever since my dad died, my grandad has stayed to himself now and doesn't talk to anybody, which makes him very stressed out and sad. He is always locked up in his room and doesn't like celebrating anything because it will never be the same without my dad. Everybody has to force my grandad to get up and do things now. If we don't, he will sit in his room all day and be depressed and sometimes cries.

My grandad is very sick and often needs help because he can barely walk. He has to shoot himself with needles and take a lot of medicine for his diabetes. My grandma is a very hardworking woman and very independent, and she really doesn't like being around a lot of people or letting new people come inside her house. She believes in God, and if nothing comes up with family problems or work, goes to church almost every Sunday. My grandma is in her sixties but still looks good. Grandma recently found TikTok, and now every time she sees a new TikTok dance that she likes, she will learn it and show it to us at family get-togethers. She does them so well, knows all the songs, and doesn't miss a beat. This is a way for my grandma to get her mind off of my dad's death. A way to take my grandad's mind off Dad is to drive him around to places he wants to go and to talk to him about things he would like to speak about

Life Now

Everybody in our family is doing better. Since my dad's death, we all learned that we have to stick together as one whole and that we all can get through life together. We are all getting help. Greg, Deshawn, and I are in the big brother and sister program. With that program, we go on outings, and they pay for everything. People from the program come and get us two days a week. My mother also has a therapist so that she can talk about her problems. Micah and Cardan, Dad's sons, don't have anybody to talk to because they don't like sharing their problems and they don't think they need help. My aunt and my grandparents had a therapist, but I guess they didn't need help anymore because they started doing well afterward.

They still hurt from my father's death because he was such a good man and always helped everyone out without wanting someone to give him something back. I feel like mentally everybody is doing well, and sometimes every person can have their ups and downs, but they are all doing something with their life no matter what. They are doing things to keep themselves occupied. Fiscally everybody is doing okay, but they still have their dreams and bad things on their mind, like how my dad had passed out, how they had to see him sit inside the house dead on the floor, and how my brother said Dad was going to come back to life because he is a superhero and is strong.

My Story

By Gregory Harvey

My Story

My name is Gregory Thomas Harvey III. I just turned fourteen, but I'll take you back to when I was a baby in a women's womb.

My mom's name is Miesha M. Green, and my dad's name is Gregory T. Harvey Jr. I was born on February 28, 2008, at 12:36. I am my mom's second child, but I am the fourth child out of my dad's kids. I was a young kid who was trying to hustle at the age of four and went through things at twelve and thirteen. To get through the pain, I listened to Rod Wave, KB Mike, Toosii, and many others because the music spoke to me.

At four, I was a kid all about my money. My dad taught me how to get money on my own without asking for it. My mom taught me the steps on how you get a job. So, my dad and my mom had two different mindsets, but they were on the same track. My grandma helped me out and got me my first bank account to save money. My grandad was the first man to help me get a job. My first job was me helping him out.

My Story

I told you about my good side; now let me tell you about my bad side. I get my bad side from the part of my parents that likes to fight, and my mom's side just gets me in trouble a lot. When I was four, I didn't care who you were. I was ready to fight. I had a bat that I'd gotten from ABC Head Start. I used to hit people with it and punch people in the face with my hand just to play around. My mom's side would get me into trouble for something that I shouldn't even do.

Since I told you about my good and bad sides, let me tell you about how I got into boxing. I was at number two school park, where I used to go to school until my mom took me out because I didn't learn anything. I was at the park playing with my brother Deshawn and my uncle Robert, whom I call my brother. I went to get on the swing sets, and as I was swinging, a nice, pretty, brown-skinned girl came to sit next to me. I started talking to her to get to know her so that the next time I saw her I could say hi. While we were talking, her older sister called her three brothers over. They began talking about how they were going to get me, and they called their sister over before walking toward me.

I thought, *What's going on?* They pushed me onto their gate and started beating me up. Punch, kick, boom, bam, pow. They really got me and beat me like I stole something. I was on the ground after, and I saw my mom walking. I ran to her before she took me back to the park to gather up my brothers and me.

She said, "Y'all know what the fuck to do."

That was the first time I heard my mom say a curse word. But when a mother or father says that, it means you better get them before I get you. I was ready to go GBG: get back gang. This is something my family says to let each other know we got the other's backs.

We got the slow one first: punch, kick, boom, bam, pow. Then, we went to catch the second one. He was fast but not faster than me, so we got him, and he got the beating. Punch, kick, boom, bam, pow. If you'd seen me when I was a little five-year-old kid, you'd know I was fast. The second one was about eight and ran fast, too.

By this time, I was in football, so I knew how to do a little of the moves. I had a flashback of my dad saying, "Treat them kids like something you want and go get it."

So, I tackled him, and this boy got the same thing the others got: punch, kick, boom, bam, pow. My mom said, "Let's go."

Then, their older sister said they got a mom, too.

The way my mom answered sounded like Tupac: "Go get they mom then. I ain't scared. My house is right there: 183."

We lived on 183 Reynolds Street. When I tell you we were outside all night, we were outside all night. My dad had to tell all of us to come back inside, and when I say all of us, I mean my sister, brother, uncle, aunts, and my mom.

After we came in, my dad called me into his room and asked how it felt to get jumped. I said I was embarrassed, so I was ready to learn how to fight. When I walked out, I thought, *How am I going to learn how to fight?* So, I walked back into that room and said I wanted to do boxing.

He asked me, "Are you sure?"

My Story

"Yes. I am like a superhero."

Later, my dad and I searched for a boxing gym. We went to try different gyms. The last week we were looking, we went to a gym called Fight Faction on 121 Lincoln Ave, Rochester. That was when I met my coach. His name was coach Tj, and he introduced me to coach Q. My dad signed me up, and around two weeks later, I was in the gym boxing, working out, and more.

When my dad asked me if I liked it there, I said, "Yeah."

During that time, I was playing football and basketball. But boxing and football stuck out to me more, so I quit basketball. I continued playing street basketball because I was getting better. After two or three months, I was in the ring boxing the people I was working out with. We kept on fighting each other until we were ready to fight another gym.

At that time, I was seven years old, and it was time to go to another gym to fight. My dad took me to Future Boxing to spar, and I fought twelve rounds back-to-back until my dad had to tell them to let me get a break. If you knew me, I wouldn't say I got beat up, but that day, I got beat up.

After, my dad said I needed a break, and they said they were done. Coach Jahson said I was a good boxer for my age. A couple of months went by, and I had my first real fight. The fight was me versus Tag. I was ready, so I got in the ring, went to every ref, and bowed down.

Round One: I started to play around to see what Tag was going to do. Basically, all we were doing was testing

My Story

what points we could get from open shots. Round Two: I knew what I could hit because he would leave his guard open. I knew what to do. We started going back-to-back, and we both knew we were tired. Round Three: it was the best man who'd win. We both were tired and leaning on each other.

When the final round was over, it was time to see who the winner was. I got on one knee, and they said, "And the winner is: Baby Greg!"

I got a trophy. Just because I got that win didn't mean that I'd get a break.

A year later, their coach Jahson died, and they didn't like how the other coach was teaching them, so my dad told them they should come to our gym. We got in touch with one of the kids' dads, and they started coming over one by one. Later, we saw we had the whole gym over.

I became eight, nine, and ten, going out of town to fight at the Jo's and Silver Gloves. At eleven, I stopped boxing because Covid came, and they had shut down the gym. I couldn't do anything. I then started online school.

October 13: my dad died. He woke up and just passed out. I couldn't wake him up or anything. He was just passed out. I had faith that he was going to get up, so I sat there and watched him, dying on that floor, seeing what they were doing to him. No one wanted me to see him like that, so they were trying to get me out of there. But I didn't want to leave the man I loved on that floor.

That was when he was pronounced dead. When they said that, I began punching things, yelling, and doing all types of things.

Right before he died, he was like, "You got to stop trying to argue with your grandparents because they are all right."

When his birthday came up in December, we did a balloon release and rapped all his songs. Let me tell you something. The people who you call your family come to give you their respect when you're dead and gone.

After I turned twelve, then thirteen, I thought, *When is this going to be over?* I wake up in the morning around 3 a.m., checking on everyone, making sure they are good, but I ain't good myself.

I'm now fourteen years old, and I'm not doing anything but rapping, helping out my grandparents, and trying to keep the family together. But, if you don't want to get right, then you are in my way, and I'm not telling you to get out of it. I'm just telling you to get to the back because we are going up.

Fictional Writings

- *The category of literature, drama, film, or other creative work whose content is imagined and is not necessarily based on fact.*

- *A narrative, explanation, or belief that may seem true but is false or fabricated*

The Voices of My People

By Rashmond Lopez

ash

Story #1: Jeremiah and the Great Depression

My name is Jeremiah. My parents named me Jeremiah because it is a biblical name that means God is high. I was born on March the third, 1919 in New Orleans, Louisiana. Growing up was hard for a person of color like me, especially living in the south. Growing up I lived on a farm with three generations of family—my grandparents, parents, my sister, and me. I grew up on a farm in Cameron Parish. There weren't a lot of people who lived in Cameron. My grandfather had fifty acres of land on which we grew crops like: corn, tomatoes, carrots, string beans, wheat, and cotton. The years of 1930 to 1931 were the years of the drought, which meant crops didn't grow as much, and some nights, I even went without eating anything. It was a hard time. Some called it the Great Depression. I called it depressing.

The Voices of My People

Every day, my sister Sarah and I'd wake up at six o'clock in the morning and would have to feed the chickens, cows, pigs, sheep, horses, and our dog. Sarah would go inside the chicken coop and then check if the hen had laid any eggs; if she found any, she would collect them in a basket and bring them to Mom. Then, after I'd fed all the animals, I would help milk the cows and pick the crops if they were ready to be picked and eaten.

After all our chores were done, we would have to walk thirty minutes to go to school. One day, as we were walking, a couple of our friends, Theo, Clara, Isaiah, Posa and Purle caught up to us, and we all walked to school together. Our school was a little one-room building that was worn down with holes and scratches on the wall. We all had one teacher, Mrs. Brown, who had been teaching in this so-called "building" for about twenty-seven years. She carried reading glasses on her head. Her hair was usually in a bun, she liked to wear dresses, and she taught all of us, even though some of us were in different grades.

When we got home from school, we did our homework, which was usually one page of questions of what we learned in class. When we were finished with our homework, we went outside in the field and played with our gray and white bulldog, King, who was almost three years old (fourteen years old in dog years). After an hour or two of playing outside, it would get late, which meant I had to help my mom and grandma cook and prepare a delicious dinner. While the food was cooking, my dad, Earl, usually walked in the door from work on the farm, looking very tired and usually out of breath with blisters and calluses on his hands. He would have so much sweat on his body you could ring him out like a mop. Then, he would talk about how good the food smelled and how he couldn't wait to take a bite.

Before we ate dinner, we prayed over the food, and then you could eat. When everyone took their first bite, all you could hear was moaning and groaning because the food was so good. My dad said my mom and grandma cooked so well that you could taste every spice, mineral and juice they put on the food.

After dinner, I helped my mom do the dishes, which usually took five to ten minutes. When the dishes were all done, I would lay out my little sister's and my clothes, so we'd have something to wear the next day. After our clothes were done, we laid them out neatly on our dresser, brushed our teeth, prayed, and went to bed.

Every Sunday, my family woke up at 7 o'clock just to prepare for church, which started at 9 o'clock. Just hearing my grandma hum church songs while making breakfast made my day. When we arrived at the old weather-worn, clapboard church with only four windows, I went to the front of the church and took a seat next to my grandma. The ceiling fan rattled overhead but still couldn't hold back the assaulting southern heat. The choir members stood up at the choir director's cue and started singing my mom's favorite church song, "Swing Low Sweet Chariot." The song was led by Mattie Jenkins, the best singer in the church, but I thought she was one of the best singers in the whole Cameron parish. While Miss Mattie sang softly on the left side of the small church, Deacon Birdy stood tall and lanky with wisps of hair on the sides of his head and an upper lip wearing a pencil-thin mustache. His papery brown, gnarled hands passed the offering basket around. On the right side, Deacon Johnson wobbled from side to side with every floorboard complaining underneath him. He wheezed as he passed the offering basket along each aisle.

After the Deacons prayed over the offering, Reverend Rufus McGee rose from his seat and walked up slowly to the podium, his gaze looking over the audience as if he could see into the depths of our souls with his piercing, dark brown eyes. He was a man of stature with hair of lamb's wool, a strong jawline, and a very nice and fit body for a man of fifty-three years. He had all the single and desperate women in church fanning themselves because of his natural beauty. Although the women would say, it was partially from the heat. The women in church would go as far as to cook homemade meals or desserts to gain the attention of Reverend McGee.

A little while after Reverend McGee was done gazing over the church, he started to preach about perseverance and standing up for what was right. One thing I hated about when Reverend McGee preached was after every sentence, he would pause and say, "Ha." But not only that. He would also stomp his feet while doing it. It sounded like Decan Johnson was taking steps, and it was annoying, especially when I was trying to sleep during service. I was not supposed to, but give me a break, I had to wake up at seven in the morning for God's sake!

After church was over, which usually lasted until 12 o'clock, all the families who gathered would go home and cook their best dish to share at the church picnic. The picnic would always be at the park and started at 3 o'clock.

When we'd get there, I would go to talk to some of my friends I'd walk to school with, Theo and Isaiah, since they also went to the same church. We would talk about our fat Deacon Johnson and how he started mini earthquakes with every step. Also, we would chat about how lucky Reverend Rufus McGee was to have all those desperate women drooling over him. We thought he needed to pray for them to stop being so desperate to get a man rather than getting a job or taking care of their kids.

A little while later, we would all grab some food. There were collard greens, corn bread, fried chicken, barbecue ribs, string beans, corn, mac 'n' cheese, peach cobbler, apple pie, and lots of other delicious foods. After we ate, Theo, Isiah, and I would throw around the football. Then, we all went home. On the ride home, I couldn't wait for it to be Sunday again.

Story #2: Frank in France

"Ray, wake up! Wake up!"

I woke up in the heat of battle, but I was daydreaming about my wife, Corinthia, going into labor. I stood by her side, helping her stay focused on pushing the baby out, not the pain it was causing. When I woke up from my dream, the planes were spiraling down, and all I could see were fires that started from the aircraft we had shot down. The plane was picking up speed as the minutes went by, so I had to pull the handle upward to get the plane back on track to protect the cargo or carrier plane.

Once I got the plane back on track, I told my gunner, Slim from Tuscaloosa, Alabama, to fire at the bogies on the left. Slim, who was on top to get ready, was tall and skinny as a stick with a light-skinned complexion and light brown eyes. He hailed from a family of fourteen: eleven boys and one girl, of which he was the baby. Slim would always tell us the story of how his mom cried when he had to board the bus for boot camp, and he always told us how he couldn't wait to go home so he could finally taste his mom's homemade cooking again.

On the right of Slim was a person built like a military tank, whom we called Juggernaut. Juggernaut was from the northside of Philly, where they'll cut you before blinking twice. Juggernaut was tall with a neck that looked drawn on because of how big it was with a very cocky, solidly built body to back up that overgrown neck. He was an only child and never knew his father, so it was just his mother and him growing up, but all his mother was looking for was a good time and a tall drink. She often left him with a neighbor, whom he called Uncle Solomon. Juggernaut had a huge scar on his back from a brutal street fight he had when he was nineteen. After he recovered from the fight, he and Uncle Solomon determined the best way Juggernaut could keep his life from being snuffed out in the streets was to join the Air Force. He was always looking forward to checking up on the grizzled old man who played a major part in his upbringing.

Together with Frank, these three had each other's backs and successfully completed sixteen missions without loss of planes or life during their various escort missions of supply planes. These three were an unstoppable force. Frank was one of the best pilots in the whole force because of his ability to stay focused through intense times. Slim and Juggernaut were one of the best shooters because of their ability to aim with near-perfect precision.

While I was escorting my cargo plane, two enemy German planes came at us—one from behind us and one in front of us. Slim took out the aircraft in front of us, and Juggernaut took out the one behind us. It was all safe flying until we realized that one of the German planes wasn't fully taken out and shot at our plane and damaged the back wings badly. Juggernaut made sure he took the plane out completely this time, but the bigger problem was that our plane was having trouble flying, meaning that it might be our first failed mission! Throughout the ride, you could feel the plane going up and down like a car on a roller coaster, out of control.

We were flying over the Lot River, less than a mile away from our base, about to safely and successfully deliver our cargo plane. That was when a German ship started shooting at us, and our plane started to go down, and this time, there was nothing I could do about it. Luckily, we were close enough to get bailed out by our allied planes who surrounded the cargo and supply building. Our plane landed on the plane tarmac, and our mission had successfully been completed for the seventeenth time. All I was thinking about when the plane started to go down was my wife Corinthia and my unborn son, and that was all I thought about until we finally won the war in May of 1941.

The Man in Her Basement

By Nhaziah Bedell-Scott

The Man in Her Basement

At 3 a.m., Amy wakes up to go downstairs and heats up her TV dinner, and while she's waiting for her dinner, her best friend talks to her about how eating at 3 a.m. isn't healthy. They change subjects to her relationship with Amy's ex and how she's happy that they broke up.

Suddenly the microwave beeps blaringly, and her best friend vanishes. As she is taking out her dinner, her ex appears and starts talking about how she got framed for animal abuse. He also starts talking about how she shut the door on her close friends and family, that she has issues and should consider kicking the bucket because she'll never be good enough. Amy gets furious and throws a glass cup at him; he chuckles.

Just then, he disappears, and Amy comes to her senses. She knows she needs to forget about his negative energy and words. She then trudges in exhaustion to the couch, plops herself down, and turns on the TV, worn out. She starts picking at her food and eventually eats it. Enervated, she drags herself up the stairs and into bed.

The Man in Her Basement

Amy cannot sleep because she keeps tossing and turning, thinking of her ex's thoughts.

The voices in her head echo, "You'll never be good enough. You'll never be good enough."

As she reads the 6 a.m. symbols on her alarm, she suddenly hears a thud from downstairs. She doesn't bother moving because she figures that it is her ice machine. Then, she hears it again, and from that point on, she decides to investigate what or who's making all that racket. She leisurely walks down the stairs, and somehow, a raccoon made its way into her house. It appeared to be rummaging through her fridge and spilling all the ingredients for her famous lasagna, which she'd been searching for, for a long time. Of course, she shoos the little rascal away and is a little furious that it made a mess.

Just as Amy is cleaning up, her mother appears and says, "Oh man, look at the mess you made. I guess this is yours to clean up, and you ain't got any help, so maybe you should consider, you know . . . picking up the broom and dustpan."

As she starts sweeping, aggravated by her mom, her power goes out; things get worse from there. She begins to hear something from her dark, eerie basement, and unlike every other person, Amy decides to go check it out. For some odd reason, the door closes behind her, and she isn't feeling too brave but is confident to face whatever is down in her basement. She relaxedly walks down the old wooden stairs and finds out someone was, or rather is, living there. She gets a little creeped out and does not want to go any farther. But, of course, she doesn't really have a choice, considering the door is locked behind her, and she left the

The Man in Her Basement

spare key somewhere in her basement. The thing is, Amy doesn't really go into her basement unless she needs to get her gardening stuff or her old recipe books.

Suddenly, she gets attacked by someone, and a battle breaks out. What appears to be a guy grabs her from behind and starts choking her. She manages to hit him in the stomach with her elbow and hide behind one of her shelves under the dim light. The person cannot see her, and Amy has a very good plan. Amy puts her plan into action. She pretends to leave her basement by closing and opening the door, and she hears a noise and goes toward it. She sees the man rummaging through her stuff, and she carefully steps back but accidentally knocks over a box full of glass. The man turns around with a grin across his face and blood splattered on his faded denim overalls.

At that second, Amy doesn't think to run. Then, she comes back to her senses, runs to the door, and doesn't notice losing her phone on the way up. Amy runs up the stairs and into the bedroom and hides under the bed, sweating and breathing hard like she's just run seven miles. She reaches for her phone, realizes it's gone, and thinks that her life is over and that she regrets doing hurtful things to people in her corner.

She suddenly hears the stairs creak. As he walks up the stairs, she sees his shadowy figure approaching her bedroom and gets scared. Then, she hears her freezer make a noise, which attracts him downstairs.

With sweat and a few tears on her face, Amy says to herself, "Maybe all hope isn't lost, but I just couldn't find mine."

The Man in Her Basement

She determinedly tiptoes down the steps with a screwdriver in her hand, peeks around the corner, times her attack, and stabs him. But she misses. Instead, she's stabbed in the arm and starts to bleed out but doesn't give up. With all the strength left in her, she kicks him in his face and runs into the basement to get her phone; then, she tries to get back upstairs. She is caught when he sees her trying to come up and chases her back into the basement. She makes a noise just to distract him and quickly dashes to her bedroom to call 911.

"Okay, the police will be at your location soon!"

Amy sighs in relief but still comes to her senses and remembers that there is someone in her house. Still, with the courage she has, she goes downstairs, determined to tie the guy up and let the police lock him up once and for all. Desperately, she grabs a hammer, tiptoes downstairs, and hides in the closet waiting for the perfect time to attack. Then, she hears police sirens and peeks out to see if he ran away.

She can see him trying to escape through the side door when suddenly her best friend appears and tells Amy to think about ending everything. Maybe, then, she could finally relax. Still, Amy hesitates and holds back but thinks, *Maybe, I could turn him in and end this right here, right now. Maybe, she's right about this, but karma is real . . . So, I don't know if I want to do this.*

"I believe in Karma, so I think I'll choose the easy way out instead of the hard way."

Her best friend says, "Well suit yourself because if I were you, I'd whack him in the head with that hammer and end that nonsense once and for all."

The Man in Her Basement

Suddenly, she disappears, and now it's all up to Amy. She walks toward the man and is about to hit him when she wakes up, checks her clock, and sees that it's 2:50 a.m. She feels that she is sweating, so she goes to bathe, but before she turns the water on, she hears a loud noise from her basement.

"I wonder who that could be," she thinks.

To Unravel a Realm

By J. Scott

Chapter 1

The suns rose before he even had the chance to wake. Aniklo sat up, the light glaring in his eyes, chancing a glance out at the beautiful expanse of water that could be seen from his window. The sliver of the rocky beach stories below reflected the glare of the high and low sun, but not as much as the barely visible barrier around their world, tinting the air a lighter blue that only the elders could remember was once naturally richer, that only the elders had ever had the pleasure of existing outside of.

After seeing the time, he sprang into action, bustling into his ensuite to speedily ready himself. He combed a hand through his dark, curly, shoulder-length hair, putting on the standard uniform—a blue, long-sleeve shirt that flowed and straight-legged pants with pockets. He didn't even bother to accessorize. After dressing quickly, he grabbed a cashi fruit from the kitchenette connected to the dorm that he and Maryn shared. He peeled the soft yet spiky skin open and took a glance over at Maryn's door, saddened by the fact that he had already left without him. Maryn always moved his Do-Not-Disturb sign into his room when he wasn't there.

"As if he would wait for me," Aniklo mumbled under his breath, huffing as he grabbed his bag and made his way out the door.

The workers' dormitories resided in a long hallway. The amarite rock, which served as the foundation basis for the large building, showed through the thick glass that armored the walls. The sitting area for the workers sat opposite Aniklo's destination.

His sneakers squeaked as he came to a stop at the end of the hallway, pulling a flat card out and pushing it against the padlock of his floor, barely managing to steady himself as he tripped over his feet upon entering.

A room full of his fifty colleagues was already at their rows of workstations. The light from the wall-length windows glared in his eyes. As he discreetly hustled to his seat on the room's far side near the view, Jessik came striding in seconds before their boss went to her separate workstation. Her deep blue monochrome outfit slightly contrasted from the rest of the already seated workers, heels clicking. As she moved to center herself, she faced everyone with a bright smile, a smile that Aniklo always thought could cut glass.

"Good to see that you were all able to make it on time," She began.

Aniklo's tan neck flamed red as Roan, the man sitting next to him, huffed in amusement and laid back in his chair with his arms stretched behind his head. Jessik ignored him, her expression turning serious.

"As you already know, if you have checked your comms when you are supposed to, the usual protocol of sending your tasks of what latitudes you will be assessing for mistic damage hasn't been sent." She raised her manicured hand with a crystalic pointer in it, swinging it in the direction of a crystal sitting on the table. Her motion brought the projection within it to light. The map of their world was displayed before them, the energetic mistic boundary surrounding it color-coded, with the inflamed parts already circled on the board.

"At around 12 o'clock this morning, a strange combustion of energy was let out from the mystic barrier twenty miles away from the shore of the Outer Rim, and a few other formerly known dead zones adjacent to and across from that spot have risen up."

A chorus of murmurs rang out across the room, Jessik cutting through with her authoritative voice.

"Though this phenomenon is unprecedented, we will be taking care of this threat as we usually do. I will be splitting you into teams . . ."

The curly-haired boy's focus trailed off, his hazel eyes skimming through the ripples of the water. He was trying to see if he could spot the pulsation of untamed mist catching on the waves like a fish the way it usually did when surges like this needed mending. Still, he had never witnessed anything as big as what was happening now.

"Aniklo, you will be partnering with Maryn on the combustion near the Outer Rim's mistic border."

Their eyes met across the room. Maryn's dark skin was made vibrant by the tint of the suns; his chocolate eyes hardened, as if concerned. After their gaze of recognition, Maryn looked away.

"Since we are dealing with uncharacteristically large outbursts, you will be doing a different protocol from before. Instead of just sending out a reactionary code that smooths over the combustion, you will have to send out a tracker and assessment charm to decipher the exact center of the outburst and what sort of mist usage caused it to rise. Once the results come back, write a reactionary code to dispel them. These larger ripples in the walls require more specificity to take care of the issue."

After this display of confidence, Jessik's professionalism now bled into her worry as her eyes glossed over her underling, the wheels visibly turning in her head.

"I understand that with this work comes the knowledge that these combustions in our walls are reactionary, the knowledge that they are an imbalance caused by the mistic force fields reaction to our use of its resources. I personally was slightly alarmed at seeing these alerts, but it made me even more determined to make sure we all do a good job at stomping it out. We must also remain cautious about our improper use of mist. This work, this prevention of surge-ups, is integral to the stability of our society. It is integral to the safety of our people, and it takes intelligent, focused, dedicated, and tactical people like you to be able to tackle these problems. I trust that in next week's time, things will be sorted out. Now get to work." She clapped her hands, and the room was set in motion.

Aniklo looked over at Maryn again, who had his head down, focused on his screen before him, which apparently already had a map of the possible area of their specific outbursts. His palms grew slightly clammy as he tried to muster up the courage to walk over.

"You're pathetic, you know that," Roan cut into his spaciness, his haughty voice drilling a hole into Aniklo. "Fawning over that Outer Rim scum as if he belongs here."

Anger sprung up in Aniklo, almost desperate enough to pummel Roan until his pale skin turned purple and green. "You're the one that's pathetic, Roan. All you do is shut people down as a way to compensate for your lack of skills. If Maryn didn't belong here, he wouldn't have outranked you in last week's assessment during his first week here." His voice rose unintentionally, causing others in the room to tune into their conversation, including Jessik.

"Arguing will not help solve society's problems, boys. I suggest you both get to work before I make you." She barked on her way into her private office.

Reluctantly, Aniklo backed off, heading to Maryn's workstation. The other boy had already started listing possible hotspots that would serve as coordinates to shoot initial assessment charms.

Maryn was all lines and angles, a shell of practicality and sure calibration, and when his focus turned to Aniklo momentarily before darting back to the map, Aniklo practically melted.

"So, um—so I see that you already worked out possible coordinates."

"You need to stop this, Ani," he practically whispered amongst the chatter of other groups.

"Stop what?" He knew what Maryn would say next, but didn't want to hear it, didn't want to hear another way that he had failed Maryn yet again.

Maryn huffed at his laptop, unsure what to say. "I get that you have this mission to make me feel included or welcome or whatever, but I don't need you picking fights with the most idiotic asshole in the Corps just because we knew each other when we were younger."

"It's not that. I'm just tired of him getting to spew his nasty opinions and getting away with it."

"It's exactly that," he said, finally turning away from the screen and focusing his attention on Aniklo, eyes razor-sharp and insistent. "You said you feel guilty. When I first got here, you said that if you knew that I was coming, then you would have met me at the docks. You follow me around—"

"I don't follow you around."

"You follow me around like a puppy, asking for me to come down to the market with you."

"It's not following if we live together. I'm just trying to make sure you're okay."

"We are *assigned* to live together, but that's beside the point. You insist on pushing something, and you need to let it go." He huffed, brows screwed together. "We're not kids anymore."

Maryn's words stung. Aniklo looked away briefly to hide his conflicted emotions and noticed Ria and Kreena, the pair adjacent to their station, obviously turned toward them, soaking in every word of their public, private conversation. He gave them the stink eye, and as they turned away, he moved in closer to avoid the girls' prying ears.

"I'm not trying to bring up the past because it's obviously behind us, but is it a crime that I still care about you as my friend? That I want to make sure you're okay after all the shit that you—"

"I'm fine," Maryn said, shifting to his workstations, closing himself in his corner to analyze the screen. His voice was stern and final. Despite the sting and the need to prove Maryn wrong, he kept his mouth shut, knowing that it wasn't wise to push the guarded boy beyond this point, even though trying to change Maryn's mind might alleviate the growing pit in his chest.

After a beat, Maryn spoke up, "I figured out where we need to send the assessment charms."

"Already?"

"Yeah, the eye of the surge in the walls is big, so it wasn't exactly hard to spot."

"Then I'll go prepare the assessment charms," Aniklo said, sitting up a little in his seat, ready to dash out of this situation as soon as possible.

"I can do it. You go do something else," Maryn muttered before turning to head to the lower levels of the Corps.

Aniklo watched him go, that familiar pang of resignation to his loneliness clearly written across his face.

"You look like you need this, sweetie," Kreena said, passing a piece of wrapped candies his way.

She had effectively snapped him out of himself for the moment. Kreena was like most of his other colleagues, older and wiser with much more experience, a stark contrast to both Aniklo's and Maryn's youth. Unlike the others, Kreena actually made an effort to make him feel included. Her smile and green eyes were more welcoming than ever.

"Thanks, Kreena." He popped a candy into his mouth, feeling its sugary sweetness dissolve against his tongue. "I think I'm gonna take my break early."

"That's okay, sweetie. Take your time."

Desperate to get away from it all, he fiddled with his work comm, a thin crystalline bar attached to his wrist. After bringing it to life, he pressed a few buttons on the projection, started his break, and headed out of the room. He re-entered the glass-lined hallway to take the elevator that seemed to zip at the speed of light, landing on the main floor lined with similar amarite and glass walls. He ignored the barely used sitting room to the side of the main entrance and the welcome desk that was uncharacteristically vacant; then, he stepped out into the open air, the view of the rocky beach and flowing water behind him, the sounds of the nearby market a beckoning call, a promise of escape in the crowd full of bodies and noises and scents.

Subconsciously, he pulled at the precocious vines that plagued the solid amarite apartment buildings on the way to the market, as was his usual routine. He breathed in the ocean air as the slap of the waves against the shores grew duller. Once he reached the first shop, the smell of incense and joking salesmen, the clang of workers smoothing out amarite in their sweltering shops, the sight of fish and fruit and bread and people of varying heights all filling their baskets with necessities that assaulted his senses.

The thrill of the mundanity of the marketplace, their island's melting pot of everything necessary, was more like home than anywhere else. He weaved through the crowd, waving to his favorite worker at the bakery stand, whom his mother always made him buy from. He managed hellos to other shops that tried to draw him in until he finally reached the slight crevice between a fruit juice stand and a jeweler, where he was just skinny enough to slip through. Just sharp enough to notice.

The crevice became bigger after he took a few steps in; the solid stands on both sides created a dead-end alley against a vacant apartment building. He pulled himself onto a forgotten garbage can, grabbing a rickety ladder just strong enough to climb up a few stories until he reached his destination: an opening at the top of the dilapidated, old building that gave him perfect access inside of this forgotten sector of the isles.

The room had missing chunks in its walls that showcased the mile-long stretch that spanned the market, and an opening in the ceiling that gave way to the light of the sun. It illuminated the plushy cushions and table that Aniklo had somehow gathered there. This little uncovered corner of the world was completely his. Not a room lent to him by the corporation that had employed him right out of school at just because of his mother's genius. Not the home across the waters that housed the memories of his lopsided childhood. Here, amongst the crowd of people below, a sea of unobligated invisibility: a sentiment which he longed for yet similarly despised.

    Aniklo had always been a pleaser, a reassurer who said everything would be okay even when it obviously wouldn't. The weight of his emotions, the ones that he sometimes didn't let himself feel, would always be there, a dragon inflamed by its acknowledgment. On this morning, despite the comfort of his world away from reality, his chest still flooded with a heaviness, with a myriad of emotions and a vacancy that seemed to be resurfacing. He thought he had gotten over the emptiness. He had always imagined when Maryn came back, things would return to normal. Maryn wasn't supposed to make him feel this shitty.

    He dug into his bag and pulled out an unassuming bottle, but with a flick of his fingers, it came alive. The liquid formerly masqueraded as water transformed into mist in its purest form, a cloudy translucent substance that danced around his coveted bottle. Without a second thought, he uncorked it, coaxing out the mist with his hands, and gathered the cloud to his face. He breathed it in, felt it absorbed into his bloodstream, into his psyche, feeling it smooth away the aching, solid fire in his chest until he felt stable again.

    Opening his eyes, he looked down at the bottle just in time to see the charm that disguised the mist and kept the bottle replenished sizzling away, leaving it devoid with a shimmering mist on its outer surface. *There was supposed to be more left*, he thought. He was supposed to make it stretch until next month at least, but it was gone. He had to go get more.

Through the haze of his high, he swiped a hand across his personal comm on his left wrist, typing a special code on the keypad that surfaced a holographic, dark red card. The card's gilded white design around the edges alluded to the complexity of its code. It always waved before his eyes before going still, the words on the card magnifying before his eyes.

A message to all those looking for a thrill, looking to encounter the formerly unattainable, to see what is hidden, but what should be available for all, and witness the wildest mech fight of all time. Snitches not allowed. Come at your own risk.
Date: Tonight.

The inner market's ticket, hidden behind a passcode on his private comm, was his true attempt at escape, a getaway he'd accidentally acquired when scouring the commweb during an insomniatic night. It was an accidental discovery that, if found by his workplace, could easily mark him as a criminal and lead to his deportation to the Outer Rim.

He didn't know where the heavily charmed slice of illegal code truly took him when he followed the directions it gave the day before every meet. Who was behind the concealment of the loud mech fights and chattering people trading goods that could easily get them in trouble during the light of day? How had The Watch never been able to find them? But, the allure of having access to the mystique of the inner market was too addicting to worry much about all those things. It made him question how right the council was about the danger of uncertified manifestations of mist.

Every visit pulled at strands of the fabric of absolution that his mother and his job gave to him.

He only went when he needed to, dipping his toe into the underbelly of the isles when his mist bottle emptied out or when he just had a deep urge to be defiant. It seemed that tonight would be one of those times.

***

Maryn took the elevator down to the second floor, the plans and the coordinates to send out the assessment charms in hand. But, he couldn't think about anything else except the boy whom he had left behind. Maryn knew how Aniklo's brain worked, knew how personally Aniklo could take things, and pushing him away was harder than he had expected. He had told himself, when he came back on the shuttle from the Outer Rim a week ago, things would be different. He vowed that he wouldn't get distracted, that he wouldn't get Aniklo involved, especially not now. Especially not when he was so close.

A flash of the other boy's face came into his mind: his full lips that used to always be gathered into a large smile, his hands that would animatedly move when he spoke, and his eyes. Those hazel eyes were always searching for him, analyzing his every move. He wondered if Aniklo's eyes truly saw him, all of him, the way they used to, or if he had done a good enough job hiding himself away.

When he finally pulled himself out of his thoughts, he realized that he had been standing there motionless like an idiot for longer than necessary. Scolding himself for his lack of concentration, he moved into the open floor, heading to the vat of pure mist that waited for him in the center of the room. A few other workers were there, doing their own charms, and Maryn blended himself into the crowd, getting an amarite capsule from the premade piles stacked in the corner.

Navigating around the pure mist, stirring and alive, searing and malleable, was a dangerous procedure, but something that he had grown used to. Heavy tongs lay beside the pile of capsules, and he picked them up, stepping over the pumps lining the walls and stretching across the floor like vines. He made sure to stand a few feet away when he carefully dipped the capsule into the mist, coating it fully so that it could soak up the mist's agency. This process was routine, and he pulled the charged capsule out of the mist, swiftly imprinting the code from the comm on his wrist into the assessment capsule while its manifestation was still fresh.

Once the code for the capsule's destination was set, the orb sprang to life, made mobile by the mist within it, and Maryn watched it fly out the open window to its destination.

"Very well done, Maryn."

Maryn jumped, turning to see Jessik standing behind him, a little bit too close to the vat of mist that still lay broiling in the middle of the room. Maryn didn't know what to say as he watched the woman watch him.

"I'm glad to see you are adjusting well to the ways of the isles. I'm sure things were somewhat different back on the Outer Rim."

He hated this. He hated the talk, the belittling of his knowledge solely because of where he came from, where they had forced him to go. He could feel his eyes forming into slits and tried to force his posture back to normalcy, back to a delicate composure that didn't hint at his wariness. He knew people like Jessik; people with practiced performative demeanors saw more than they let on, more than he would ever know.

"I'm trying my best. I'm just glad that I was given the opportunity to be back."

Jessik prowled closer, effortlessly navigating her high heels through the wires below. Her voice lowered, in a way that hinted at the prospect of their next words being important, like a shared secret. "I just want to make clear that I don't believe the way the council deals with people that are out of control is always . . . effective. Especially when children are forced to suffer the sins of their parents, forced to be stripped away from all that they've ever known. I used to know your mother, and I never would have guessed that she would react the way she did after."

She paused, her eyes pointed, probing for more insight, before seeing that he wouldn't give any and growing somewhat bashful.

"I said all that to say despite your attachment to the Outer Rim, I value your expertise. Your intelligence. And I'm sorry that you had to go through all you did to get here." She smiled a sad but almost warm smile, one Maryn knew to be practiced.

He tried his best to do the same, tried his best not to succumb to the weight of her words, the weight of what they could mean.

"I can see that you will be a useful member of the Synthesis Corps. Just like your father." She patted his shoulder and turned away, leaving the shattered pieces of Maryn's facade behind.

After waiting a while longer for Jessik's departure, he made it to a bathroom, letting a wave of nausea take him over, his face over the toilet seat, ready to retch. Afterward, he wiped his mouth, schooled his practiced veneer into place, and pushed the heavy pit of dread and emotion down, down, down into a box that held it all. He tried not to think of his father. His father. The man who had died in the very room where their conversation took place, the man whose body particles probably stuck to the vat of mist that brewed within the very building where he worked. But he couldn't think about that. All he could focus on was breathing, and remembering why he had hustled to come back to the inner rim in the first place.

The weight of the encrypted card that gave him access to the underbelly of the catacombs was heavy in his mind, and the knowledge of how close he was within the personal comm on his wrist allowed him to return to reality and brought him comfort. All he had to do was go to the night market.

Chapter 2

Aniklo knew better than to sneak out of the dorms when all his coworkers were in the common room. The last time he tried that with the excuse of checking out a new shop at the markets, the nosiest of them had decided to tag along, effectively thwarting his chances of visiting the night market. This time, he would be smarter.

When the clock reached 11, he slipped out of bed, fully clothed in a dark turtleneck and black pants topped off with black thick-soled boots. On his way out of his personal dorm and into the shared living room, he donned the most important piece of his outfit: a cloak, thick and heavy with the weight of all its charms. It rendered him unrecognizable to anyone who saw him. The cloak fastened at the front of his chest and had ample pockets and armholes, providing substantial mobility. The coat ladened in mist swung as he walked, rendering him an unseen anomaly of the night.

He checked for Maryn's trademark Do-Not-Disturb sign before setting out, feet moving on autopilot out of the building and into the streets. Hood up, he bypassed the opening of the main market, glancing momentarily at the adults wrapped in their own cloaks on barstools who tried to fend off the slight chill of the night air and would almost get hit by the night shuttle that traveled around the isles. The whoosh of its smooth engine blew up his cloak slightly. His already fast-paced heart skipped a couple beats as he righted himself and cut down the alley between the apartment building lying against the border of the markets.

Steady and as ambiguous as a ghost, he tread the alleyway lightly, barely able to skirt around a couple huddled together in the near darkness, until he finally reached his one-hundred-and-ninetieth step.

190 steps, turn to see, the walls fall away to set you free.

The rhyme that he received when he first got his access card rang in his ear, and he flashed the card on his comm to the wall. Sure as the seas to the south, the walls shimmered in a wave from the top of the building to the ground beneath his feet. Once it reached him, he was promptly snatched away. His feet and body seemingly fell through the ground of the streets and into a blinding light. In the free fall, as the mist that activated the portal prickled on his exposed skin, he always closed his eyes. He waited for his feet to lightly touch the ground to open the landscape of the rocky walls that encased the night market: a wild scene to take in.

The path to the underbelly is different for most, but unique for those like you.

A gas mist with floral undertones covered the expanse of the cavernous gathering, veiling the crowd in a dream-like stasis. Crowds gathered at the many different stations. Veiled people perused, desperate to collect the most common illegalities available: forbidden herbs, putting one in an eternal state of bliss at best and killing them at worst; charms used for an array of personal mist manifestations, not aligning with the Corps' general usage; chips infused with mist to give access to more facets of personal comms; and so much more. The shopkeepers had the most outrageous disguises. Some decked in realistic animalistic guises; others had floating heads with no visible bodies or vice versa. All trying to draw you to the promise of the unusual in the products they sold.

Aniklo strode through the crowd, breathing in the mystique and rebellion on this casual stroll. His blood pumped through his veins as the mist formed around him. This was part of what he came there for. Not the fortune-telling, or the herbs that were bound to get him caught, but the promise of a high he'd get on the power, the feeling of his life and the pressures of monotonous existence funneled into a capsule in his mind. All the importantly, unimportant things went to that place when he was high. It would all flow out of that capsule afterward, corroding his brain, flooding him like a tsunami once the barrier was gone. It was so much so that the real him didn't exist.

He swerved through the crowd toward the far end of the room, until he arrived at his usual vantage: a spot slightly past the last most popular vendor along the edges of a large pit. A group formed, looking excited at what was below. The rowdy throng of onlookers shouted. Some exclaimed extremities. Others triumphantly guffawed as they all watched the mechs within the pit go at one another.

The two eight-foot monstrosities, built of pure rugged amarite and other ghastly materials, fought brutally in the middle of the dugout. They clashed barely a foot away from their audience, painted to match the outfits of their masters, controlling their creations with wild waving limbs at the pit's side away from the crowd. The mech on the left swung a beefy arm, planting its fist directly into its opponent. Time seemed to stop as the crowd waited for the eruption bound to shake the earth when the beaten mech hit the ground.

Once it did, it broke into pieces, shattering the core that connected it to its master's control. This yanked the crowd back to reality, all of them ducking to avoid the shrapnel flying out of the confines of the arena. An almost deafening cheer emitted from the onlookers. In the moments after a mech fight, Aniklo always wondered what percentage of the crowd was screaming because of the excitement or the pain of being stabbed by loose chunks of amarite.

"And the Deltha wins!" the announcer yelled over the crowd's voices and shopping vendors from a stand above the arena.

Deltha, the owner of the winning mech, pumped their fist while the mech mirrored perfectly. The loser gathered the heart of their broken creation, cutting through the crowd to regroup in an unused market corner. The remnants of the inanimate amarite dragged behind them as if hanging on an invisible string. Next to Aniklo, a burly man who smelled heavily of herbs and urine marched past him in a huff, loudly cursing his bad luck at betting incorrectly.

After collecting their earnings, Deltha strutted toward their usual vending station. Their shiny pants and secure boots squeaked slightly, dramatic shirt billowing, but not enough to distract from the new mods on their animal-themed mask. The realistic fox mask and slightly furry skin were a standard part of their build, but this time, they had found a way to put makeup on the fur, a thick eyeliner applied to draw out Deltha's lively, blue eyes. Despite Deltha's showy disguise, their personality alluded to sincerity and a trustworthy sureness, which was what originally drew Aniklo to them.

In a second, they slipped a casing the size of their palm out of their pockets and thrust it upward. With that action, the casing expanded and created a stand with a variety of goods popping out of the tightly compact space: bottles containing fluids and slimes of many colors, trinkets, incense, charm sigils written out on paper, and much more.

They shouted to their mech by their side, "I told you that when we're done with matches, you have to stay near me."

The mech grounded out a sigh as it made its way over and tried its best to blend in with the dirt walls.

Aniklo watched all this in amusement as he strode over, and when Deltha saw him, a switch flipped as they transformed themselves from triumphant victor to proficient vendor of odd assortments.

"I didn't expect to see you back here so early."

"Whose to say I didn't come back to see someone else."

Deltha's let out an incredulous snort. "You are such a bad liar, even with that mysterious cloak of yours. We both know that I'm the best around here."

"Well, if that's the case, then I'm gonna need another replenisher," Aniklo said, lightly clanking his bottle on the table. Deltha's formerly perky ears poked through their dark red, and their layered, long hair sagged.

"You used too much this time. The charm should have lasted longer than that."

"I know, but all I need is a little bit more."

They stared at him, a paternal sternness brewing behind their foxy eyes.

"I've seen people slip into bouts of unreturnable psychosis after taking too much of this. You seem like a good boy, and that is why I try to make sure to give you the right amount each time, but if you take more than you are supposed to, then I can't help you."

"I know. Things have just been getting really bad lately. But I have control. I can control it."

Even though the cloak hid his true features, he could tell that the urgency in his voice spoke volumes. This was pathetic.

Deltha took the uncharged bottle from his hands, and after some hesitation, dipped it into a cauldron next to them, only dunking it enough to coat the cauldron's sides in the brewing mixture. Once they pulled it out from their hold on the bottle's stopper, the mixture grew rock hard on its surface. Uncorking the top, the bottle was immediately filled with mist previously invisible in the air, and once full, it turned back into fake water, perfectly hiding in plain sight.

Deltha then turned their attention to cradling the bottle, staring into the very visible shimmers laced on its surface and trying to trace its lines.

"Do you want to know why I sell the things I brew? Especially the pure mist?" They asked, knocking Aniklo off slightly. They didn't exactly have a conversational relationship. An amicable one, yes, but never chatty. Personal was too dangerous.

"Why?"

"Because I'm familiar with the drowning feeling that can happen. That takes hold when you live to work, you live for others. The council boasts about giving us everything we need, ensuring that even those with the lowest paying jobs can make ends meet. But it's not just about making ends meet." Deltha paused, as if they weren't even sure what to say, or why they were speaking. "It's not just about surviving. It's about living, about being free despite existing in a cage. You can drive yourself crazy thinking about the prospect of never escaping here, and I feel that in you."

They finally turned their attention away from the bottle's lines and onto Aniklo's intent yet distraught face, giving the bottle over.

"I can feel it, and I want it to be a little less bad."

That thought, that warmth and slight ache that came with the recognition that, at least for a moment, Deltha had *seen* him, actually taken the time to squint her fox eyes through his cloaked façade. It was almost too much to hold in and almost distracted him on his way out the door.

Almost pulled his attention away from a boy that confidently sliced through the masses.

Chapter 3

Just one glance at Maryn told Aniklo the other boy was ill-prepared for a trip to the night market. His mask was plain, and the charms on it didn't seem to be doing much in the way of hiding his recognizability, but he seemed to be on a mission, cutting through the crowd, insistently searching for something. Aniklo knew better than to rush up to the other boy, so he waited until he was farther away to see what was going on.

But Maryn didn't go where Aniklo was expecting. Instead of heading to the mob of vendors or waiting by the gates to see the next mech throwdown, he walked over to the cave's far left side, which was vacant save for a few couples huddled against the walls. Those pairs were too far gone to really notice him while he looked down at his wrist comm. Aniklo watched Maryn stand there staring at the wall, wondering if he was already intoxicated and needed help. But that train of thought was derailed when Maryn pressed a hand into the wall, and slowly, inch by inch, slinked into it, disappearing. Aniklo, too intrigued by what he'd just seen to gather up any common sense, looked both ways and followed.

Pushing through the wall was a more unpleasant sensation than expected. His bones seemed to snap out of place and move back together at the pull of passing through solid rock, but unexpectedly, it was more uncomfortable than painful.

The walls were made of the same rough stone as the exterior market area, but the passageway was dark and narrow. A small light flickered at the end of the tunnel, his hand almost disappearing before his face. He heard a shift in the darkness.

"Maryn?" he called, wincing slightly at how different his cloak made his voice sound, but before he ever heard an answer, a fist emerged out of nowhere and connected with his face. The force knocked him back against the freshly solidified wall. Dizzy and exhausted from the pain in his jaw and back, he looked up in a daze to see Maryn crouched over him with a taser baton. The sparks brought more frightening light into the passage.

"Who are you, and why did you follow me?"

Maryn inched the taser closer to him, and he instinctively cowered near the wall.

"Mars, it's me, Aniklo." He rushed out, pulling down his hood to reveal himself. Realization sparked on Maryn's face, the façade's power on Maryn stripped away. Maryn instantly defused the sting of the baton, pointing it away from Aniklo.

"Wait, Ani? Are you okay? Why are you here?"

"I saw you from a distance and decided to follow."

Mars stood there for a second and watched Ani pitifully moan as he stretched his sides, and after a beat, he offered a hand to help him up.

"Thanks," Aniklo said, straightened his cloak, and tucked some loose hairs that had fallen out of his ponytail off his face. Maryn was mesmerized for a short second, the two of them looking unsure about what to do next. How to proceed from their little hidden space.

"If I knew it was you, I would have never hit you, but you following me in here was a bad call. What if I had bad intentions and was in here for something evil and dangerous?"

"Well, what are your intentions? Are you here for something evil and dangerous?" Aniklo was partly teasing, but a small part of him wasn't and was scared to know the answer.

If it was anyone else, Maryn would have been irate that someone dared to joke at a time like this. Since it was only Aniklo's pretty face he was searching, all he did was sigh in defeat and say, "You are too fucking nosy for your own good. We can't go out the way we came."

With those words, Aniklo finally felt the gravity of his situation hit him. He was stuck in this narrow pathway. "You mean we have to go deeper! I don't even want to be in here."

"Then, you shouldn't have followed me. Look, you can stay here and be stuck until someone else wanders in, like in another few years, or you can follow me to where I need to go."

Maryn almost felt bad for his harsh tone, but the more reasonable part of him wasn't. Aniklo's lack of impulse control hadn't changed, proving that he was right in not involving him in the first place.

"I only came because I saw you staring at a wall like a lunatic. I thought you were drunk or something."

"Well, I'm not." He swiped a hand over his comm, illuminating a slender rectangle with red and white squares within it. Two square each on each row of a rectangle created a pattern of red and white. Hesitantly, Maryn took the first step onto the stone that aligned with the red one on his map.

"What are you doing?" Aniklo knew there was no other way out, but the unknown reality of what lay ahead was the kind of exhilaration he tended to want to avoid.

"I think the flooring is laced with traps. Step where I step."

The ponytailed boy sat still, watching the other boy navigate the checkered stones on the floor, and finally, because he was scared and because it was Maryn, he followed.

The light of Maryn's taser stick had turned warm and less electric, wobbling as the two trekked down the long hallway. The deeper they traveled into the darkness, the more it felt as if the walls were closing in on them, the pitch-black becoming thicker.

"You know I'm not a fan of dark places."

"You're afraid of the dark but not of the night market," he murmured.

"What exactly are we heading toward?" Aniklo asked after a couple more steps.

"You'll see when we get there," Maryn said back.

Seconds later, Aniklo tripped on a groove in the flooring between the rocks, lost his footing, and began to fall into one of the unsafe parts on the ground. Without thinking, Maryn swooped in, grabbing Aniklo up inches before his foot touched danger and dragging him toward himself.

"Thanks." Aniklo huffed breathlessly, turning his glance away from the floor to look at Maryn, who was standing breaths apart, his hand still encased around Aniklo's waist. They stood in this stagnant space of time, flickers of illumination still in Maryn's hand, shining on both their faces. It made Maryn's face seem softer than it had become with age; the tight curls cut short on his head glowed as if on fire. Aniklo could barely breathe as he looked up at him, sighing when Maryn moved out of the little bubble they had created to step to the next block. Taking the other boy's hand to hold him steady after he tripped.

"Careful," he said, palms growing clammy in the other boy's hand from the close call. Neither of them let go.

The rest of the way went smoothly, their hands intertwined to steady one another. Ani knew asking more questions would just lead to their easy flow being messed up, but that didn't stop his brain from buzzing with the possibilities. This felt more exhilarating and riskier than the night market, and even though this was Maryn, his Maryn, he couldn't stop thinking of the worst. Was he taking him to perform a wild ritual, or dig up a dead body, or even worse, kill Ani and then dig up a dead boy and then use both their corpses as a part of his wild ritual? Before his brain could conjure up more wild ideas or he could muster up the courage to ask, Maryn stopped, facing the left side of the wall.

He rose his unlinked hand, huffing, "Here we go," before slamming his fist into a particular brick in front of him. They both waited with bated breath for several seconds, squeezing the life and circulation out of each other's hands until Aniklo couldn't take it anymore.

"You dragged me all the way out here just to punch a stupid bri—"

The floor unexpectedly warped as the mist connected to the ground apparated into the ether, and before the two had time to react, beams of light spread from the indented stone broke across the wall until it created a silhouette of a walkway. Then, the silhouetted door collapsed in on itself.

The two were static, transfixed, and temporarily paralyzed by the blinding light until, out of the blue, the light cut out, allowing a room with mist etched into the wall's mortar to take shape. The small room was barely the size of a broom closet and devoid of anything except for a singular, ornate box on the floor. The loose mist encased within the room burst out and brushed over the two briefly like a gust of wind.

"Is this what you came down here for?"

Maryn didn't answer but instead tentatively approached the box, allowing himself this moment of vulnerability to hold Ani's hand like a lifeline. He reached out to rub across the expertly carved letters of his dead father's name ingrained on the box.

On contact, all hell broke loose.

The box shot open, releasing a potent wave of energetic agony that seeped through the two of them; the shockwave of energy surged so strongly, it seemed to rattle their bones and grab at something deep inside them, clutching at their hearts, sapping their ability to react, to move. The ripples of potency were unlike any sort of mist the two had ever been exposed to before.

Time moved like molasses as the shockwave burrowed into their bloodstream, piercing every area of their bodies, inside and out, like a knife. Then, it landed at their joined hands and gathered there, refusing to move.

Aniklo heard screams during their terrifying agony, and he wasn't sure if they were coming from him or someone else, something else. All he knew was from that moment on, his innards didn't feel like just his anymore. They had something else in them, something wrong but familiar at the same time.

They both jerked back into their bodies to discover themselves weakly tangled together on the floor, their hands glued to one another by the mist, strange markings now inked onto their skin. They both coughed some of it up, its gooey flaccidity sinking into the stone.

"Maryn, what did you just do!" he wheezed, looking down at their tangled hands. Brown skin melted into tan.

"I don't know! I—"

The room was closing in, the far wall smashing their feet, soundlessly threatening to crush them.

"We need to—we need—" Aniklo's voice was a rasp, slowly feeling the world fade around him.

"We need to leave," Maryn screamed as he crawled forward and dragged Aniklo's almost paralyzed body out of the small closet, bringing the box with him. At the same time, the wall shut into place right behind them. The cold stone slapped against Aniklo's prone cheek, snapping him back into focus. His breaths were labored and deep.

"Our hands," Aniklo said in wonder, panic, and desperation.

"This wasn't supposed to happen. This wasn—"

Aniklo tuned out of Maryn's shocked rambles, transfixed by something moving at the end of the tunnel. Down the long hallway in the opposite direction, a glow covered the whole width of the walkway. It moved rapidly, and before they knew it, it was seconds away from crashing into them, closing in just as the small nook had seconds before.

"Move!" Aniklo screamed, legs crying out as he mustered all of his strength and pulled Maryn by their joined hands the way they came, desperate to escape. He could see the rock wall entrance growing closer and closer, and just as they were about to pass through, Maryn fell.

The glowing wall behind them seared Maryn's skin in the second that he remained on the ground, and he let out a cry. With all his might, he pushed Aniklo and himself through the rock wall to safety.

The first thing they heard when they passed through the crowd was a chorus of deafening screams. The night market had erupted into chaos, bodies spewed on the floor, crawling toward the exit. People dogpiled in a desperate attempt to get out first. From their vantage point, hidden behind the corner of a torn stand, all they could see were stampeding people.

Someone manning their mech swept a large hand across the dogpile, knocking everyone over to get out first as if they weighed no more than paper.

"What the fuck!"

"Our hiding spot won't last forever. We need to leave. We need to leave now!" Aniklo could barely keep his hyperventilating in check, and despite the searing pain still coursing through his body, he swung his arm around Maryn's hip when they stood, taking some of the weight off his injured foot. But, he still winced in pain.

"We need to run in the opposite direction toward the mech pits. We can head behind the shops and around the pit. There's a tunnel that leads back to higher ground," Aniklo suggested.

"On the count of three. One. Two—"

A person was hurled across the room. A sickening crack rang out when their body connected with the wall. They landed right in front of them, blood spewing out onto them. Aniklo could do no more than scream, effectively paralyzed.

"Come on. Three," Maryn wheezed, thrusting them out of their hiding spot. That was when they saw the cause of the chaos. A large humanoid-shaped cloud floated in the air, and like a bullet, sliced through the bodies of people at the exit. They collapsed to the ground, spewing up the gathering of mist that had pierced into them before seizing on the ground, chunks of their bodies melting into a vapor and adding to the mass of the humanoid cloud. While it gathered near the entrance, the boys stepped over bodies, hearts beating out of their chests, breath labored, the ache of the box's contents still coursing through their veins.

The cloud was now moving across the room in their direction, slicing through people as it floated. It ensured no one was left alive. It set its eyes on them as Maryn fumbled while slamming his hands into the stones, unsure which one triggered the exit.

"Hurry!" Aniklo shrieked as it passed through the last living, standing person in the room, the space silent except for the whimpering of the mechs, the choking of the massive amount of people on top of each other. They still seized on the ground, and Aniklo screamed as Maryn finally found the right stone, allowing them to pass through the walls.

The pathway was lined with torches. The sound of their panting breaths echoed against the walls as they limped forward, and after a few feet, reached a staircase that led upward, their hands still painfully melted together. They finally reached a hatch at the top of the stairs. Maryn reached up to push it outward, and they climbed up to the open streets to see that the chaos wasn't over.

They landed in a familiar place in the middle of the general market, right across from the bread shop and a popular restaurant. People sitting at the stands were skewered by smaller manifestations of the humanoid mist clouds. Pedestrians who'd been enjoying the nightlife ran desperately for their lives.

"Come on. We don't have time to look." Maryn pulled the other boy up, hissing at the added momentary weight on his leg. They limped, watching the people run around them, feeling the weight of the eyes of the onlooking, cloudy black humanoids, and stepping over people who had fallen during their attempts at escape.

Once they reached the outskirts of the market, the humanoids hung back in the shadows, their eyes beady, expectant. Predatory.

Adrenaline was a spike of courage that pulled them to move faster, even as they cleared the streets and struggled to make their way through the empty entranceway, into the elevator, and eventually to their dorm. They were a bundle of nerves and stress when they finally shut the door behind them.

Chapter 4

Aniklo sunk into the wall against the door, gasping for air. "Maryn . . . Maryn, what is going on?"

"Listen, Aniklo, you have to stay calm."

"Stay calm. Stay calm! We just watched people die!" The reality of the situation was finally catching up to him; tears flowed freely. "Everybody died, Mars. Everybody died!"

Mars grabbed his face with his free hand, making Ani concentrate. "Not everyone is dead. We won't be able to figure out what happened if we don't calm down."

"You knew this would happen. You knew—"

"I didn't know! I had never been to the market before, and I only went to find what our fathers left behind." He let go of Aniklo's face after the outburst, settling down beside him next to his own bedroom door and staring off into space.

Aniklo tried his hardest not to think of his father, nor Maryn's. Their death was a constant memory associated with the end of his happy childhood, but now it had been dug up in the most unexpected moment possible. "Our fathers? Maryn, what are you—"

"This was never supposed to involve you, Ani. I never wanted you to get involved."

"Maryn, what does any of what happened tonight have to do with our fathers?"

Aniklo could see that Maryn's face had settled into something fake and bland. The other boy had shut down, stoically boiling like a kettle with the lid barely fastened.

"We need to find a way to wipe the traces of whatever hit us in that cave off of us." He sprang into action, moving to the other side of the room to the drawer next to his bed. He unintentionally dragged the other boy with him, their hands connected, as he quickly emptied everything out onto the floor.

"Maryn, what is going on?"

He didn't answer, fiddling with the back of the now empty drawer. Something clicked within it after a few yanks, and desperately, he pulled out a dect sized chest, clanking it on the ground. After whispering a few words Ani couldn't understand, he lifted the tightly sealed lid, revealing a collection of odd trinkets.

"Maryn, what did we get ourselves into?"

Maryn ignored him, rustling through the small chest with one hand.

"Maryn!"

"Just wait," he said, yanking out a cylindrical bar that surged to life once he made contact with it. Aniklo shrank as far away as he could get from it in panic.

"Relax, Ani. This bar is meant to absorb the traces of the mist attached to us. We need to make sure that we don't get caught. The Watch will probably be wandering the streets, itching to find whoever was involved and escaped, and we left a trail behind us after we got hit in the catacombs. All you have to do is touch it." His voice was now steady and smooth, as if attempting to tame a wild animal.

Aniklo stayed stock still, eyes squinted, and body closed in on itself from his defensive perch on the floor.

"I'll explain everything once you let me place the bar against our hands."

Aniklo glared down at the bar, then looked at Maryn before finally nodding.

He finally took the bar, feeling a buzz connect to his hand on contact, a vapor seeping from his skin into the bar. The blob that was their connected hands loosened until they were completely separate, but the ghost of that connection was still tangible. Now that their hands were somewhat separate, runic markings appeared on their arms, from the formerly mushed hands all the way to the crook of their elbows. The ache they both felt subsided; the injuries that the two of them sustained numbed away. They were but only a whisper of themselves.

"It didn't take it all away. It just moved the connection somewhere else," Maryn said in wonder. "It usually can heal anything . . ."

Aniklo desperately wanted to ask where he had gotten this magical bar, where he had gotten all of the trinkets that shined in the chest. Many things still sat exposed on the other boy's floor, but the only thing he could say was, "My back feels a little bit better since I picked up the bar."

"Yeah. It's seeping some of the stinging out of you, but you still need to be bandaged up." Maryn then moved to get the first aid kit out of the bathroom. With the short distance he'd gone, a new string of runic carvings etched on both of their skin.

Maryn set to work in the silence, rubbing cream on the punch wound he had accidentally inflicted, his gentle touch like a memory, a continuation of the past. The silence was filled with questions but also intentional. Aniklo then wrapped the burn wound still faintly there on Maryn's back. After that, they both turned to the arm with the raw insignias painted onto he skin, glowing slightly like a living tattoo, identical to one another on their right arms.

The anxiety and intensity of their situation, somewhat quelled by the knowledge they were more disconnected and bandaged, rose up in the silence of Maryn's messy room.

"What happened down there, Mars?" Aniklo tried again and searched his eyes, trying to decipher the truth within the other boy's statuesque composure. He watched it slowly crumble, only slightly, once Mars realized there was no getting around an explanation.

Gingerly, he pulled a flat cartridge out of the still open chest, and once it spread across his palm, he pressed its center. The light within the cartridge expanded around the entirety of the room's bare wall, creating a screen full of hundreds of numerical data charts, pictures, and letters splayed out next to each other. Then, the glow expanded when a hand swiped over it.

Aniklo's eyes were wide, soaking in his father's scribbled signature on some of the documents laid out in the spread. He pieced together what all this could mean, his brain on overdrive as he soaked in the diagrams, skimming the writing of both Aniklo's father, Castille, and Maryn's, Miho. Side by side stood this collage of work material he'd never had the pleasure of seeing. Never had the pleasure of knowing existed. After both their fathers died under mysterious circumstances, Aniklo scoured all the written documents the Synthesis Corps hadn't taken from their his father's study. None of the documents looked like this. Mars watched on and admired what was encased in the cartridge, while also scanning Aniklo's reaction, waiting for the other boy to speak first.

Aniklo could see that this was all data gathered for a specific project. The diagrams mapped out the intricate pieces of an ornate conception. He could tell that the intense dedication in the cluster of information was new, fresh, important. The ache of a pondering that he had locked away long ago, the questions that he always had about his father's side, which he never got to know. It seemed to be all there before him, biting away at his emotional wherewithal.

"What does it all mean?" he finally asked, his voice a weak whisper.

Maryn was solemn, opting to look at the data before him rather than turn to Aniklo when he finally chose to speak. "When my mother took me with her to the Outer Rim, she first claimed she did it because it was the only chance she had to decipher all that remains of both of our fathers' life work. She said their other occupations were just cover-ups for the real shit they did for the Corp, the stuff no one else could know about."

"She made me spend hours painstakingly trying to come to meaningless conclusions, doing tests with mist she barely knew how to control. All because she felt the cartridge must have more than what it seemed to have or something, that he must have left some fortune for her, a failsafe in case things went wrong." He paused, wiping a hand over his face. "Eventually, she gave up, claiming that maybe there was nothing left to be deciphered, and she moved on. But I never did."

"At first, I thought all that he left behind were data charts and definitions of symbols written in messy lettering, but I came across a pattern. A hidden layer of data on the card spelled out the complexities of harnessers. And not just the harnessers we use for routine fixes on the mistic boundary we do at work. He left details of real harnesses, contraptions that could commune with the mist, capture its ability within itself in a more profound way than we do now. The way the native Ponsns did before the worlds were merged."

He began to move the configuration of the data around, focusing on a group of documents. The dashes and dots lining the pages Maryn zoomed in on were a sucker punch to Aniklo's gut.

Aniklo could barely breathe. "Morse code," he said before Maryn could even explain.

"That's how I found out about the night market. I went to every possible combination, looking for more, thinking I would somehow get lucky and find the harnesser mapped out in these pages. But, it didn't turn out the way I intended."

"So, it still exists. They really figured out how to make a harnesser."

Aniklo was always told the knowledge of true harnessers, ones connected on a more innate level than the fabricated versions in the Corps, hadn't survived the shift of the mistic boundary centuries ago. He thought the history of native Ponsns' way of connecting with the mist was dangerous and locked away after New Ponsn was formed, and the council began its reign.

The pit in his gut, pried open by this new information, was undergoing a harsh expansion. The possibility of what it truly meant for their fathers to formulate something so forbidden under the Synthesis Corps' nose was too much to bear. When he was younger and their deaths were still fresh, he held on to a wild suspicion that it hadn't been an accident. But, when he accepted that job at the Corps, he forced that suspicion away, too scared of the danger of that defiance, what that meaning could hold. This knowledge, this raw information, ripped at the fabric of the illusion that was his own life's narrative, a stifling, a suffocation.

Maryn nodded. "It has to exist, Aniklo. I thought I would find something more specific about his work there, so I examined the original data charts some more, and the puzzle pieces all came together."

"This doesn't make any sense." Aniklo almost didn't want to believe there was more to the story than what he was told, what he had grown comfortable believing, or had at least worked to accept. He didn't know which reality would be the most painful.

"It makes perfect sense." Maryn's voice had grown softer, his brows furrowed. He had no idea what to do, how to comfort Aniklo after dumping this all on him. He could see the astonishment in Aniklo's glassy eyes and almost felt bad telling him the truth, but it was too late now. He zoomed on to another page deep in the cartridge's files.

"This is a letter left on this device from your father."

If you are reading this letter, it means that you are here, you have succeeded. I can't go on anymore. We have reached a peak level of clarity, something big, something dangerous. You have everything that you need. I must go now. I love you all.

The letter was the same wording, the same writing etched into Aniklo's brain, the words Castille had left on their kitchen table the night before he died. But, more was there than what was on the note he had memorized. Aniklo was lightheaded, his body shaking as he forced himself to read on.

I'm not doing this because of what they will tell you, because I have gone insane or am mentally unstable. I'm doing this because dying this way will be much more bearable than what the Corps will do to me when word gets out.

The letter ended abruptly, the ink on the digitalized paper blotted out, the rest of what was said muddied and trickling down into corrupted code. Aniklo felt numb and physically ill at the same time.

"Someone was after him. He knew he was going to die. He—" Tears flowed from Aniklo's eyes in waves.

Maryn grabbed for a box of tissues, which Aniklo took willingly. He gave the other boy a moment of silence to collect himself before speaking again. "I think they both did. Everyone thought my dad was just a scientist studying the effect of mist on the weather and yours a runic researcher. But it seems like, based on some of the journal entries written here, they were looking into something deeper."

Aniklo became partially absorbed in his memory. Flashes of the pain he had felt after hearing the news of his father's "suicide" left a blatant scar in his brain. He remembered the way Maryn had held him in his room as he cried for days, the way his mother and two brothers, Katam and Tauro, had retreated in on themselves. Maryn's parents, Miho and Selene, had been the ones to take care of them all, holding them all together the weeks after his death. But that flimsy glue would all fall apart weeks later, after Miho's accident at the vat in the Corp.

This pain, this shock, had been a scar on both of their lives, which marked the end of their childhoods, and now, it felt clearer than ever, it was not what it had seemed. Aniklo wanted so desperately to trust Maryn, to buy back into the secret scheming the two of them had done to process their grief, but one thing was holding him back. "Tonight, at the catacombs . . . If it's true the clues you saw in the documents led you there, then why did they leave a box there to hurt us?"

"Tonight made no sense. I have put so much effort, so much time into this." He turned back to the holographic information, the stoic mask that always covered his face gone, leaving him hopeless and crestfallen. "I just feel. I feel . . . I've been waiting for this for so long."

Aniklo sat in the uncertain silence that followed, the cogs in his brain doing overtime. He looked down at his arm, studying the pattern of the unknown words he couldn't decipher.

"If my father really had anything to do with this curse, then the symbols on our arms would look way different. His writing looks nothing like this."

This pulled Maryn out of himself slightly as he looked between the markings on both of their exposed arms. "Then, if that's the case, someone else tampered with the room and the box."

Aniklo, having scoured all of Castille's work on ways to channel the mist using glyphs, knew this formulation meant something strange. He wasn't sure in what way exactly, but it was unmistakable. "The shape the glyphs form most likely means this is a binding curse."

"Meaning?"

"Meaning there's a window of time to respond to the rules of the curse before something happens."

"Rules?" Maryn asked in confusion. "What rules?"

"I don't know."

"Well, if you don't know, do you at least know what's going to happen?" Maryn was growing slightly impatient, and in hindsight, he knew turning that frustration on Aniklo wasn't fair, but after all that had happened tonight, he couldn't help it.

"I don't know," Aniklo said again.

"What do you mean you don't know?"

"I mean that I don't know! You're the one that blindly waltzed into this obvious trap and dragged me along with you!"

"You're the one that followed me blindly without knowing what I was doing."

Aniklo huffed dramatically before saying, "Fine. It's both of our faults then, mostly yours, but that doesn't matter anymore. We need to find the person that tampered with the box so they can reverse the effects of the glyphs. They might know more about our dads too."

"But isn't that more tedious than trying to do it ourselves?"

"Do you know anything about curses? Uncasting requires knowledge of how it was cast, what was used to harness the type of elemental mist it was cast with, and so on. If we get the ingredients wrong, we can end up in a much more dire situation than we're already in."

To quell his suspicions, Aniklo traced the beginning of a glyph on Maryn's arm, watching as goosebumps sprang up on his skin and the light of the mist encased within it brightened from his touch. Maryn swiftly pulled away, getting up from their spot on the floor to look out the window.

"We need to figure out how to cure this as soon as possible. I don't like tampering with formulations of mist I don't understand." Maryn's vantage point gave him perfect access to the streets. In the black of the night, it was hard to tell if the gooey conjurations of black mist plaguing the streets were still out. Still, flashes of their experiences, of the bodies and the people sucked into the darkness, were fresh and unescapable.

"Did opening the box cause this?" Maryn whispered underneath his breath. He had always assumed what they had been working on had been a force for good, but the crossover between the time they found the box and when the blackness rose was uncanny.

"My dad would know what to do." Aniklo was still on the floor, still observing his arm in alarm, in wonder.

"Well, he's not here anymore. They're not here anymore." Maryn's voice was hollow.

A lightbulb went on in Aniklo's head.

"But some of his research is!" Aniklo sprang up, bouncing on the soles of his feet over to Maryn's perch near the foggy window, looking him dead in the eyes with new vigor in his strong grip around his wrists.

"In the basement at mom's house, she has a draft of his runic dictionary. The watchers didn't take it away when they collected most of his other work stuff for evidence. We're bound to find something there to let us know the terms of this binding curse."

A banging rang out at their front door, making them halt.

"This is a mandatory assessment." Jessik's slick voice rang through their joint room and carried to Maryn's specific door.

"Quick, help me tuck all of this away!" Maryn whispered, piling his trunk full of oddities back into its secure position, throwing his clothes on top, and running the first aid kit back into the ensuite.

"Where do I go!"

They heard the click of the front door opening.

"Get in the bed." In record time, they got in and closed their eyes, involuntarily tangling together on the small mattress just as the click of Maryn's door opening sounded and Jessik's heels on the rocky floor were heard inches away from them.

He tried to keep his breathing slow, relaxing against Maryn's chest, keeping his limb against the other boy's hip loose. He hoped Maryn didn't sneeze from his hair splayed across his face.

"See? I told you there's nothing to worry about." Jessik seemed irritated. The tap of her toe caused rhythmic panic in the boys' ears. Why was she wearing heels this late anyway? Did this woman ever sleep?

"We are trying to track traces of everyone involved in the strange deaths last night," a deep voice almost whispered.

"I'll let you scan them while they sleep if you are that insistent on focusing your precious time on nothing."

Aniklo imagined they were having a stare-down right over their prone bodies. The freaks.

"It won't be necessary," the deep voice murmured, their hard-toed shoes leaving the room. "We are just trying to make sure the ones responsible for the havoc tonight face the consequences."

Maryn instinctively tightened his hold on Aniklo, practically smothering him against his chest.

"My workers are nothing you should be concerned about. If anything, they probably went out at some point, got wasted at the juice shop, and came back before anything happened. I practically raised Aniklo, and he owes me his career. He wouldn't cross me. Not in some treacherous way like this."

They headed out, the door clicking behind them.

"That was close," Maryn whispered, loosening his hold on the other boy.

Aniklo didn't do the same.

"They never do checks unscheduled like this." He was still breathing fast, the laden mist within him strumming through his veins. "She thinks she owns me. She thinks I owe her."

"You shouldn't feel you owe anyone anything. Especially her." Maryn paused, reluctantly rubbing a hand through the other boy's tangled, curly hair.

This touch, to Aniklo, felt like a flicker of a memory, homage to what they used to be, the closeness they used to have. But Maryn only did it once before reality hit him.

This was too much. This was something he had vowed to leave behind. Maryn pulled away, sitting up from the bed. Aniklo outlined the muscles on Maryn's back, mourning the loss of fleeting comfort.

"If they scanned us, what would they have found?" Aniklo asked.

"I don't know. That's why we need to head to the house as soon as possible." Maryn turned back to look at Aniklo, who still lay underneath his covers, raven black hair still lying on his pillow. "I think you should go to your room. We need to get some sleep. We only have a couple days off before we have to head back to work."

Aniklo didn't want to move, not after what they had seen, after what he had just learned, but the rigid line of

Maryn's back was all he needed to know. He had worn out his welcome. Flashes of the night's events flooded in, filling his brain with the monsters and the dead and the shadows watching, reminding him how much he didn't want to be alone. Despite it all, he got up anyway, the bed creaking at his departure, feet heavy, feeling the weight of Maryn's stare watching him leave. Just as he opened the door, Maryn's voice cut through the silence, and he shifted behind him.

"We'll figure out how to end this." Maryn had turned in the bed, watching from his heap of covers. He seemed small at that moment, unsure. His deep voice was reassuring, but Aniklo didn't know what to say back. This was too much, his mist-filled arm tingling with the reality of the now. But he was tired, so tired.

"Goodnight," he said back, the click of Maryn's door closing faintly behind him as he retreated to his room.

============== ==============

Nebu's sturdy booties were saturated in the mush of mistic residue littering a formerly vacant alleyway now bustling with activity. A team of low-grade watchers stood in an efficient wall around the scene, blocking perusers of other nightly activities from seeing the catastrophe. They urged them to stay away from the patch of unsanitized mist and go home. Others stood on signified posts at different intervals on the road, sensors out and ready to detect anyone with a higher level of mist than usual.

A watcher at the front of the group stepped forward.

"Civilian, return to your home until everything can be sorted. Await alerts from the comms."

"I am a mistic specialist with authorization to be here. Please step aside."

At the flash of her badge, the wall of soldiers split, allowing her to see the scene or carnage at the entrance and beyond. Medics in full protection suits descended and ascended from the portal that opened up to the night market. Those coming up were surrounded in a cloudy grey residue, their arms straining under the weight of the prepackaged body bags from below. The body bags were stacked on top of an already daunting pile within the small alleyway, against the hard walls. A pungent, rancid goo stuck to the siding and the foot coverings of those who had traveled below to see the wreckage. The same goo seeped out of the zippers of the packaged bodies.

Nebu watched the scene from the entrance in astonishment. She had been woken up out of her sleep by a call for a routine mistic anomaly inspection, expecting to see the usual case of weather fluctuations causing the mist to spring up inorganically. The solidified mist that clung to the streets and the people stacking up by the dozens, was completely unexpected.

"Who let you in here, Nebu!" her commanding officer barked to her over the short distance.

"I got here as fast as I could. Why are all the bodies being packaged this way?" She asked in frustration, eyes glued to the bags being stacked.

"Ah, you didn't get my message," the burly man murmured to himself before turning back to Nebu.

"You won't be needed here tonight. We usually would require your services in this sort of dire situation, but new developments have been made in the past couple of minutes."

"What exactly does that mean? There hasn't been an accident with people dying to a mistic surge in the last forty years, let alone a hundred! Every mistic specialist should be here on the case." Nebu was frustrated and appalled, eyeing the shorter man fiercely.

"Watch your tone," he said fiercely, his voice lower and huskier. "The reason we elected to keep this quiet is because . . ." he looked over his shoulder, as if suspicious others were watching before inching closer to Nebu. "The bodies . . . aren't exactly stable. We have decided the best course of action would be for you to study them off-site in a secure facility."

"But that's completely against protocol. If we don't observe them swiftly on-site, then—"

"This is not our usual situation. We need to make sure to keep this issue as contained as possible. We don't want to disturb the public. Come to the labs tomorrow to do a modified assessment. Then, you can convene with your colleagues."

"Could you at least give me more information on what happened here so I can research beforehand."

"That's all for tonight, Nebu. Get some rest."

At that, he turned his back, attending to the task force who were extracting the bodies from the catacombs.

She reluctantly followed orders, knowing she was on thin ice, but not before pulling out her test kit. Stealthily, she tried to get her supplies in order and take a sample while no one else was looking. She thrust sanitary gloves on the walker near the exit, and when no one was looking, she took a peek at one of the bodies. When the bag was unzipped, she instantly regretted it.

She uncovered a face, or what would have been a face before, but was now an acidic, globular mass of bubbling mush. What would have been eyes were now dripping, thin, melted sockets, the consistency of candle wax. The goo, formerly peeking out, was now spilling onto the outer casing of the bag, barely evading her hand. The pungent smell was stronger than ever, sticking to her, choking her.

She stepped back, not even rezipping the body bag up or taking the sample as she had intended. In a panic, she pushed through the crowd, hand over her nose and mouth. After a short attempt at escape, she threw up in a vacant alley a few streets down.

Nebu had been studying the medical effects of mist on the body for half a decade now, and thought she had seen all there was to see. Now, she knew deep down that she was wrong. So wrong.

The higher-ups had labeled this a routine mist release triggered by unknown causes, and she had been to hundreds of them, had collected mist, taken thousands of different types of conjurations. She'd seen people burned by the occasional burst of rogue mist. What she had just seen was a level of something that shouldn't exist. She knew this was something big.

Chapter 5

Maryn awoke early in the morning as he usually did, the vibrance of the suns a faint whisper in the sky. The light gave his view of the isles jarring clarity.

Parts of the markets were in shambles. Some stands toppled over into the walkway that typically allowed pedestrians to pass; others knocked into each other. People were gathered in huddles. Half tried to help their friends set up their broken-down shops; the other half yelled at one another. The light of the suns showcased more of the disaster than they could perceive on their frantic dash to safety last night, but the bodies, the people who had fallen around them, and the black mist were nowhere to be seen.

Maryn almost felt as if the events of last night were a twisted dream, almost wanted to believe he had just fallen asleep before going out to the catacombs, but the twinge of the mist underneath his skin, the carvings of the runes etched into his arm, was a reminder this was not a dream.

Through his doorway, he heard the faint sound of voices, and after wiping the sleep out of his eyes, he ventured out of his privacy.

Aniklo was sitting in their living quarters, a bowl of oats and sliced fruit in front of him. He was still in his pajamas, curled up on the couch, eating while talking with someone, presumably a man, through the crystal installed on their living room table. Maryn sat frozen to the spot, not sure whether interrupting would be rude.

"Hey," Aniklo said when he noticed Maryn's presence, beckoning him to join him on the couch. "I'm on the phone with Tauro. He didn't believe me when I told him you were here."

Maryn crossed the room, and when he sat down next to Aniklo, Tauro's face came into view. Aniklo's older brother had changed drastically since the last time Maryn had seen him; his scrawny body and chubby cheeks of a boy on the verge of manhood had transformed into someone almost unrecognizable. He had the same deep dark hair Aniklo did, but his hair was cut short on the sides with the longest strands curling at the top, showcasing his chiseled jawline and neatly trimmed beard. Tauro was sitting at a desk in a room that looked very similar to their own; a look of astonishment overtook his face.

"Maryn, you've grown up so fast. Six years ago, you were just a scrawny twelve-year-old, but now. . ." Tauro leaned closer to the screen, as if trying to go through it to get to him.

"Yes. A lot has changed. It's good to see you." To Maryn, Tauro was just another reminder of how so many things had changed without him. He tried not to insert a wild envy into his tight smile.

"If I knew you were in the transfer program, I would have come to the docks when you arrived, helped you out with adjusting and all that. The watchers who handle that sort of protocol aren't exactly the most accommodating with . . . ex-Outer Rim citizens."

Tauro's last words left a sour taste in Maryn's mouth, the memories of his unwelcome return still fresh. The watchers at the docks had jostled him around, some attempting to spit in his face, treatment he knew he didn't deserve.

"Tauro works at the watchers' facilities, handling paperwork and all that legal stuff," Aniklo cut in, distracting Maryn from his thoughts. "The reason why I called was to check in with him on his insight into what happened last night."

Tauro's welcoming face twisted into one of concern, his thick eyebrows drawn together.

"The two of you shouldn't have been out that late, Aniklo. You're lucky you both left before the mist surge rose up in the streets."

"So that's what they're calling it? A mistic surge?" Maryn asked in confusion.

"What else would it have been?" Tauro was intrigued, no longer sitting so close to the screen, but fiddling with things on his desk.

Aniklo could sense the tension gathering in Maryn and tried to dispel it. "He's just trying to say it seemed like something bigger. People died."

"How did you know that people died?" Tauro was like a shark, analyzing them through their crystal connection as if right in front of them.

Aniklo's palms were sweating, and he was desperate to blurt out an excuse, but Maryn was first to respond.

"It was just a guess. We saw bodies laid out from my room. My window has a clear sight of the market."

"Your window . . . so you both were in his room, in the middle of the night, after getting a little tipsy at a bar, and managed to hear the panic of the surge through the tightly sealed windows of the Corps from five stories up?"

"Yes! Now, would you just turn your dumb detective brain off for five seconds? I'm just calling to check in with you, and you get all accusatory. We both know you're too dedicated to your job for your own good. You barely even come home anymore."

Tauro was looking down, fiddling with his hands underneath the desk. "I don't need the guilt-tripping from both you and Ma."

"Whatever," Aniklo responded. Maryn just watched on from the sidelines, absentmindedly nibbling on the ripe fruit. "I'm not trying to guilt-trip you. It's just I'm always the one that has to make excuses for you and Nebu when I go visit Ma and the others. Katam and Ma both worry about you."

"I'm fine. As for Nebu, she's off being a nosy know-it-all with all of the other mistic researchers. Stirring up problems where there are none." Tauro's tone was bitter at the mention of the other woman, and Aniklo, sick and tired of their petty rivalry, chose to ignore it. He turned to Maryn.

"Nebu is Katam's sister-in-law. They got married a couple of years ago, and Nebu and Tauro have been at odds for no reason ever since." Maryn nodded, trying to picture Aniklo's eldest brother in his head.

"It's not for no reason. She's part of the reason why I never come home. She's always running her mouth about how the policies of the watches aren't good enough and how I'm such a fraud for pretending like what I do matters, and I just get sick of her prissiness and yapping and complaining." Tauro's tone was indignant, and to Maryn and Aniklo, seemed somewhat whiny and childish.

"You could come home if you wanted to. Don't make excuses just because you hate her."

"I don't hate her. We just don't get along."

"Well, you should at least try. Now more than ever."

"Whatever." He checked his watch before looking up at the boys again. "I have to go since my shift at the bureau starts soon, but I'll keep in touch. When you go visit Ma today, take the [insert port] instead of general transportation. The watchers aren't really gathered there yet, so you'll have a smoother ride."

"Why are they gathering at the general port?"

"Paranoia most likely. You know how it's rumored surges like this are triggered by something, so we've all been told to be on high alert."

"Okay. See you soon," Aniklo said.

"Love you guys. Stay safe," Tauro responded, and the connection cut out, the hologram dissolving.

As soon as Tauro was gone, Maryn turned to Aniklo, who had just taken a bite full of his softened oats.

"Did you tell him about why we're going to visit her?" Maryn was urgent, accusatory.

"No," Aniklo said through a mouthful of food, chewing and swallowing before speaking further. "I didn't tell him anything except that we're going to check up on her. And you know, I lied about us being out last night, so we're fine."

"Good."

They ate alone in silence, the jitters of last night still palpable in the new day. Maryn could only manage a couple of bites of fruit before he gave up on trying. "We should be leaving soon."

Aniklo checked the time, then walked the short distance from the couch to the kitchen. He washed out his bowl, then Maryn's, the two standing in the middle of the room, unsure how to proceed. "Tauro said it looks like most guards are stationed at the site, which is at the main strip of the market and main docks. If we cut through the more vacant side of the market, then we'll be able to bypass the main roads and go to the east port."

Maryn nodded, the glitter shimmered underneath his skin. "Sounds good. I'll go get dressed."

They showered and changed in a hurry, Maryn absentmindedly scrubbing the markings on his arm, as if he could undo the latent cluster of mist stuck to his skin. They had agreed it was best to dress in their regular attire instead of the monochrome blue of the Corp's uniform. The two, after preparing all they needed to take for their trip, put their shoes on at the door. Aniklo was shaking as he put on his sneakers, tripping over his own feet.

"Hey," Maryn said seconds after Aniklo almost fell over as he was balancing on one foot, fumbling with tying his shoes. Maryn could tell plain as day that the other boy was nervous. "It's going to be okay. I have the bar. No one will know."

"I know it's just . . . I don't know." Aniklo could still feel the effect of the small puff of pure mist from his secret bottle coursing through his veins, the small puff he hoped would be enough to cover up his jitters, but had only made him more anxious at being easier to detect.

"Just stay by me, and if a watcher scans us, run." With that, Maryn opened the door, the two cutting through their coworkers talking in the halls and taking the elevator down to the first floor. Aniklo felt as if eyes were everywhere, tracking his movement, the target on his arm in the shape of wild glyphs a dead giveaway that something was wrong. But on their way down, no one bothered them, everyone keeping to themselves. The two of them thought they were in the clear until Jessik stopped them on their way out of the building.

"I'm sure the two of you heard about what happened last night." Jessik was as clean-cut and sure of herself as ever. She had just wrapped up a conversation between her and another department head, landing her in the middle of the doorway. Aniklo's palms were sweaty, and he tried his best to nod along with Maryn.

"A couple of the techies upstairs said there was a huge surge that knocked over a bunch of stands," Maryn said in a concerned but nonchalant tone.

"It did more than that," she said, picking at her nails and staring the two boys down.

"Was anybody hurt?" Aniklo asked.

"It's hard to tell." She looked at them head-on unwavering before asking, "Are you guys heading out to look at things close up for yourself? I wouldn't recommend it. There have been a lot of fights."

"We're going to go visit my Ma. You know how she gets with these things." There was a pause as Jessik studied them.

"Hmm. Well, tell Nirima I said hello. And be careful. I wouldn't want a couple of my best getting hurt out there." She brushed a manicured hand on Maryn's shoulder before she headed back inside, sending chills down his spine.

The streets surrounding the market were more densely packed with watchers, the guards armored in more than just standard uniforms of light padding and a singular gun. They displayed the threat of their blasters and stunners on their belt hilts.

Aniklo waved to the ones he knew from visiting Tauro at the bureau, hoping to keep them at bay. Maryn kept a fast pace, desperate to head through the market as soon as possible and take this target off of his back. He knew that if he got caught, he couldn't afford to go back to what he left behind.

They opted to pass by the central entrance of the market, where loud voices rang out, and people argued over goods. The clang of stands being rebuilt and the heat from the amarite welders crowded their senses. The south entrance was barer, the watches in the area spread out, and the stands less affected by the catastrophe supplied goods. Aniklo knew this section was the recluse area, where the more rickety stands loomed over a significantly narrowed pathway, and the cobblestone roads ended halfway. He knew those who didn't have a shot at selling their goods on the main isles scraped by with the currency attained here. This area was where people came to sell when they had no other options, but luckily, most stands were empty. The shop owners in this section piled their goods into containers, taking down the signs that told what they sold.

Aniklo walked up to a particular stand, one he came to regularly. The robust, older woman who always gave him a smile was now there, packing away her jars of canned goods.

"Penoa, why are you packing up?" Aniklo asked, causing Penoa to start.

When she looked up, she noticeably relaxed. "Oh, it's just you."

Her eyes were puffy, and one hand clutched a handkerchief while the other put her rickety jars in the crates.

She huffed, then said, "I've decided to leave the shop for the time being, just until everything settles down. You shouldn't be out here after everything that's happened."

"I'm just going to visit my ma. To check to see if she's okay."

"I haven't seen Nirima in ages." She smiled sadly, taking one of the many crates that had been stacked up, a smaller one with six jars in it. She handed it to Aniklo.

"Take these. I have too many to keep anyway."

To Unravel a Realm

"I can pay you."

"There's no need for that." Her face was somber, the wrinkles setting in, her eyes unfocused for a second before recentering on Aniklo. She moved closer to the two boys, prying her bright blue eyes into them like a warning. "I feel like I should tell you that money's not gonna matter anymore. Not after the darkness that rose up last night. This was what my Nan always predicted. I never thought I would live to see it."

"See what?" Goosebumps rose on Maryn's skin, and her eyes snapped to him, as if noticing him for the first time, but that didn't deter her from speaking further.

"To see the full circle effect of the mist. The nothingness rose up the same way during the war on the outside centuries ago. The same war that cracked against the mistic boundary of old, creating this newness. Dark mist is a sign of death and rebirth. We don't have much time until we will all be engulfed."

Through the course of her speech, she began to radiate with an intensity that kept them locked in place. In the space between her words, her eyes seemed animalistic, sucking their breath away. It was as if the world around them melded into a subversion of its former reality, warping the air around them, the sparse amount of people walking by no more. Penoa became covered in fur, the tawny texture of her skin glowing with a wild captivation. She looked at them, through them, her eyes: a light, wild blue.

"I know what you have done. This is what must take place." The glyphs imprinted on their arms took on a white ambiance, the light glowing underneath their sleeves and floating in the air. Penoa inhaled labored breaths, arms stretched out slightly as if absorbing their aura, their knowledge, the information of the suns that beat down on them. "I see now. Only the strong will live."

She breathed out, and they were snatched back into the now, the people around them back in place, their arms concealed, and Penoa's skin no longer latent with patches of fur.

"I was meant to see you." She huffed, looking frail and weak. "This was meant to be."

The boys didn't know how to respond, still unable to fathom what had just happened, weak in the knees. Penoa then pulled out her walking staff that had been stashed in the corner as they took a second to recover.

"What are you?" Maryn asked.

"You will know soon enough," Penoa responded. "Go." With the swing of her staff, their limbs were made into limp noodles, their eyes closed and snatched back open. Then, they were in an entirely different place. Somehow, from the wave of her staff, they had reemerged at the ports, Aniklo still holding the crate of canned goods securely in hand. The two of them stood panting.

"Aniklo, what just happened?" Maryn was shaking, clear fear written all over his face.

The beep that signaled their shuttle's departure across the waters rang out. Only a couple of people gathered, who seemed unaware of their distress and sudden arrival beside them.

"We can talk about it later," Aniklo said, wobbling on his shaking legs. The two followed the others onto the shuttle to the animal reserve.

To Unravel a Realm

Chapter 6

The shuttle ride across the waters between the Mainland and Ponsn animal reserve usually took twenty minutes, but this time around, with Maryn by his side on the practically barren shuttle, it felt as if it took an eternity.

Since they had taken the northern shuttle, the extra fifteen minutes to drop off others at the farming district piled onto their time, which weighed down their confusion. After everyone else had left, the two of them were left to themselves in the amarite charged shuttle.

"Did we imagine it?" That was the only thing Maryn could think of to explain it. They were hunched together near the shuttle's exit, Maryn's voice hushed even though no one else was around.

"If we had imagined it, I wouldn't have these cans." The tins rattled in Aniklo's lap at the slight jolts of the shuttle skating across the water.

"But, she gave you the goods after that whole crazy vision so . . ."

"Maybe, it was the effect of our arms," Aniklo said back. The weight of the box that had contained their curse was heavy in Maryn's bag.

"This is why we need to fix this as soon as possible."

Maryn's mind then shifted from the woman at the market to the daunting reality of coming face to face with Nirima again after so long. They lapsed into a tense silence, Maryn's long leg tapping up and down and an impatient furrow angling his face. Aniklo placed a hand on his knee to stop the bouncing. Maryn turned his eyes from the view of the water to Aniklo's arm and then his face. The shorter boy tried his best to put on a confident look. Somehow, Aniklo knew this wasn't just about the market incident.

"You don't have to be nervous."

"I'm not nervous."

"Yes, you are, and it's understandable."

Maryn's face lost some of its tenseness, his eyes shifting back to the waters. Aniklo watched the contours of the other boy's face and nervously fiddled with his long sleeves that hid the reason for their visit.

"I sent a message out to Ma before we left to let her know we would be coming. It should only be her, Katam and his wife, Rioba, and their daughter, Astoria."

"He has a daughter?" Another image to discard as a false reality.

"Yeah. She'll be two in a couple of months. Both Rioba and Katam still work at the reserve, just like before." Aniklo continued to study Maryn, gauging him for the reaction he knew was boiling underneath the surface. "Rioba is quiet, but she's super sweet once she warms up to you. We always say that Astoria is the exact opposite of her mom because she'll talk to anyone."

The shuttle stopped at the docking port before Aniklo could ramble any longer, letting them out onto the lush forestation of this smaller pocket of the isles. The trees were denser than on the Mainland, a variety of greens and blues stretching high and branching out. The high grass covering the inlands was littered with vines, bleeding into the small perimeter of a sandy and rocky coast, which the water brushed onto. Aniklo led them into the trees, dodging the slight sway of them as they trekked up the hill.

"Ma said lunch should be ready soon after we get there. That's usually when Rioba and Katam come in from feeding and checking up on the animals in the reserve territory."

Maryn looked down on the pack of periwinkle flowers springing up, yet not quite in bloom. "The flowers shouldn't even be turning periwinkle this early."

Aniklo bent down, picked one, and turned it in his hand. He then looked up at Maryn before they continued their ascent to the residence. "You're right. I should ask Ma about it when we get there."

A few feet later, the trees branched out, and the path widened, the commune finally coming into view at the crest of the hill. Unlike on the Mainland, the cluster of houses at the top of the hill wasn't made of solid amarite but had wooden bases. The exterior was made with more earthy materials. From the path they had emerged from, they were caught in the back of a circular layout of homes.

Nostalgia was a deep pain in Maryn's chest, and he stopped to take it all in, take in the view of his old home base and how it had all changed without him. The edge of a large garden peeked out from the front of Aniklo's home, and he stared at the space, knowing that was where his old house used to be. Everything was different now; the trees cut back more to make room for additional living quarters for the workers at the animal reserve, the reality of what had been bleeding into it. Maryn kicked himself for thinking things wouldn't change without him.

"Are you coming?" Aniklo asked tentatively from his side, snapping him out of his head. He felt heavy, weighed down, but after a deep breath, he nodded, following Aniklo up the path and around the side of the house to the front.

When they turned the corner, the first person they saw was Aniklo's mother waiting by the front door with a toddler in her arms. When she saw them come around the house, her face turned from worry to astonishment. She walked to the edge of the porch and, as soon as they stepped up, wrapped Maryn in a big hug, smashing the toddler in between the two of them. He stiffened slightly, but eventually warmed up to it, and returned the embrace, resting his head on the top of Nirima's short dark hair.

"You've grown so much." She huffed, pulling back to observe his face, tears forming at the corner of her eyes. Her hand brushed briefly against his chin, a big smile covering her face.

"I'm sorry it's just the last time I saw you, you were shorter than me and as skinny as a twig. And now, look at you. You're all grown up! I just wish I had been there to see it happen." Her smile dipped slightly at the last words.

"There's nothing you could have done, Ma," Maryn murmured, a tight half-smile directed to her. "I turned out all right."

"You sure did." A couple of tears slipped down her cheek as she rubbed a hand up and down his arm. "I know I'm not your mother, but you've always had a place in this home. You've always been one of my boys."

A pit grew in Maryn, a feeling he couldn't really describe surging up. Was it the feeling of being loved? Of having a sense of belonging? But underneath it, he felt something more familiar; something he had grown accustomed to: the feeling of being a fraud.

The toddler, who previously had played quietly with a toy in her hand while watching the exchange, yelled, "Hi!"

"Hi, my star," Aniklo said warmly before taking her and giving her a big hug, her shrill voice laughing all the while.

"Well, what are we standing on the porch for! I made your favorite, Maryn." Nirima swept into the house, past the living room with toys littering the floor and into the dining area, where the table was set. Astoria wiggled out of Aniklo's grasp and ran around the table aimlessly just because she could.

"Come. Sit. I know the two of you must be so hungry. They don't feed you well enough at the Corp, and the markets don't always make things the way they used to. Not as fresh, especially fried foods." She rambled on, taking several trips back and forth between the kitchen and the dining room, where the boys now sat. Then, she brought out a big platter of cod, an assorted fruit basket, fresh-baked bread, potato slices with cloves, and flavorful rice.

Maryn's eyes widened exponentially as she brought out more and more food. "This is a lot," he murmured to Aniklo on her third trip to the kitchen. Astoria had at some point wiggled her way into Maryn's lap, her big brown eyes watching him as her wispy ponytail swung in between the food and his face.

"You know how she gets."

She brought out the last platter, smiling at the boys in accomplishment, before sweeping up Astoria, who had, between the second and third dish, gotten back out of Maryn's grasp. The toddler babbled something about fish, and Nirima placed her into a highchair. "All right, everyone. Dig in."

The cod melted in their mouths; the rice had a lemony taste that complemented the fish perfectly. Both of them took a little of everything, falling into the trance of good food was bound to put anyone in. Maryn wasn't used to this kind of comfort anymore, the kind of affection that came with the knowledge someone had thought of him while making something heavenly. Falling into that comfort felt dangerous. But he did it anyway.

In between bites, he caught Nirima eyeing him, as if she was at a loss for what to ask him, how to approach the difficult maze of questions for the child she let go. Thankfully, Aniklo cut through the silence.

"I thought Rioba and Katam were having their lunch break soon."

"They were supposed to, but the animals have been acting up recently, snapping at each other, trying to nip at the workers. Stuff they never used to do." Nirima leaned forward as if trying to keep a secret contained. "Rioba thinks it has something to do with the flare-ups at the border."

"Just like the flowers on the trail. They're not supposed to be changing color until a month before the solstice." Aniklo pulled the bud he picked earlier out from behind his ear and put it on the table.

"Exactly. Right now, we're trying to distill a huge mistic surge that sprung up near the Outer Rim," Maryn cut in.

"Back when I was in my prime at the Corps, the border was never as active as it is now." She tossed around a piece of fruit on her plate, contemplating what to say. "There never used to be as many surges on the Mainland, especially not ones like last night."

"You heard?" Aniklo asked.

"Niki, you think just because I retired I'd allow myself to fall out of the know?"

"How have you—"

"I kept a couple mistic scanners, down in the basement, just to keep track of what's going on, but that's beside the point. I want the two of you to know the reason I retired. I felt I could do better work outside of the Corps than in it."

That last statement sat in the air, the cogs turning in both of their brains.

"I haven't really dissected the alerts I got from the activity of last night's events, but from what I've seen, it doesn't feel like the standard surge." She continued, pausing to eat more. "But, I didn't say all that to make you lose your appetite. You don't have to worry about any of that. It doesn't involve you."

Aniklo stayed quiet like they agreed to, not wanting to be the one to spill the beans and get on Maryn's bad side, but Maryn's opinion about how up-front they should be had changed. "Actually, it kinda does involve us."

She looked up, triggered by the grim tone of his speech. "Sweetheart, just because you work at the Corps doesn't mean you have to regulate everything that goes on."

"No, that's not what he meant," Aniklo chimed in, and he pulled up his sleeve. Reluctantly, Maryn pulled up his sleeve as well, revealing the identical glyphs on their skin. The mist underneath their skin was still active and worming around. Nirima dropped her fork in shock, the silverware clanking on the floor, her eyes bugging out at the sight before her.

"What the—" She breathed, swaying in disbelief. "Where did you get this?"

They both looked at each other, unsure of how to proceed. They hadn't really planned to show her, just allude to the fact that they had things they wanted to research, but the lie they crafted prior wouldn't hold up against Nirima's curiosity.

"We went out last night to the market, and we kinda ended up drinking too much java juice at some bar, and around two o'clock, everything went crazy." They explained what the shadows looked like, the way people around them continuously dropped like flies, and how they were almost caught by The Watch when they burst into their dorm. They opted to keep the inner market a secret.

"We don't know how to uncast the curse, but Ani figured out it was a binding curse based on the formation of the glyphs. We just don't exactly know how to uncast it."

She was silent throughout their entire explanation, remaining stone-still, staring between the two boy's arms and their faces.

"If you're worried, you should know it doesn't hurt. All it does is glow when we touch," Maryn added impulsively, unsure what to say to the obviously distressed woman.

She sat back, face uncharacteristically grim, clearly at a loss for words. She eyed them for a long time. So long that the boys pulled back their arms from awkward positions on the table.

"So, you got hit while escaping the market at night. From some random, perfectly legal restaurant." Her brows were deeply furrowed, fingers tapping against the table. She knew. They knew she knew, but Aniklo chose to continue the lie anyway, nodding along perhaps too eagerly at her last deadpanned retort.

"Part of the reason we came to visit was because we wanted information on the nature of the curse and how to fix it," Aniklo murmured. "We thought some of, um . . . some of Dad's research would help. The stuff you have in the basement."

The sliver of joy left from seeing the two was partially sapped away at the mention of her dead husband. Her eyes glazed over, hands fiddling with her crumpled handkerchief on the table.

Aniklo knew it had taken her so long to get to a point of normalcy, where living without his father wasn't so much of a burden. He felt guilty for mentioning Castille, knowing his name carried the weight of his absence, that it soaked away the joy from his Ma. Sometimes, he also felt guilty for the anger coursing through his veins, senseless anger at his father for having to go and die, taking a huge chunk of Nirima away with him.

Before Nirima even had time to bounce back, the toddler burped loudly in the corner, which led to whining and calling out for her "Nana." Astoria was clearly done eating, having cleaned off her plate with half of it collected in her bib.

"I have to go clean up Astoria. We should move our conversation to the sitting room." She turned away and focused on unfastening the toddler, like she couldn't even bear to look at them anymore.

"We can help put away the leftovers." Aniklo stood up and grabbed at both his and Maryn's dirty plates.

"Don't worry about it, Dear. I've got it." Her voice cracked, and she rushed out, sweeping the toddler into her arms along the way.

The couch in the sitting room sagged underneath their weight.

"I didn't know we were planning on telling her," Aniklo said.

"I didn't really know either. It just kinda came out. I wouldn't have if I knew she would be that distraught."

"Talking without thinking is really unlike you."

"It's just . . . it felt she had the right to know." He was scanning Aniklo's face now, eyes uncharacteristically unguarded. "She never got over him."

"Did your mother get over your dad?" Aniklo chanced, turning closer to the other boy. Maryn hadn't mentioned his mother once since he'd arrived here, and Aniklo had so many questions. Was she still stuck on the Outer Rim? Was she still in contact with him? Was she the one who made Maryn develop this tightly guarded armor he barely ever took off? But, it was too much too soon. Maryn's apprehensions were back, and he was no longer making direct eye contact with Aniklo.

"She moved on, but not in the right direction."

Before Aniklo could pry any further, a siren rang out, the universal signal of a national alert. Their crystals on the table lit up and sprang to life, a holographic image plastering itself onto the wall.

Nirima and Astoria came into the room and sat down just in time to see Council Member Oraan in all of his decadence and glory. He was stationed at a deeply stained desk with a sash that covered his chest. With a window view of the waters behind him, the Isle's white and green flag hung in the background in front of the window. All five of the other council members stood behind him against the window, backing his every word. He opened his mouth to speak.

"Hello, All. I am Council Member Oraan. Here as head of the Department of Mistic Safety, to greet and assure all of you on this fine evening. I am aware some of you have heard of a severe mistic surge that took place last night between 1 a.m. and 3 a.m. I am here, with the authority of the council, and its resources and respect, to tell you that everything is under control.

"Some of you may ask what caused it, and to that, I must tell you a very harrowing truth. It has been uncovered that a secret underground syndicate of criminals has been congregating within the old catacombs. This group has been mixing and selling illegal mistic substances without our knowledge. Last night, a huge burst of mist was unleashed from their headquarters, killing many, and triggering the surge that decimated most of the market. Although we were previously unaware of these individuals, we are currently on the hunt to stomp out all those who have caused this atrocity."

His voice droned almost robotic in his authoritative state, his eyes, glassy and unfocused, posture strictly still.

"We are unsure of these people's motives, how many are associated with them, and because of this, we are in the process of establishing a system to ensure the safety of our world."

"Peace to all."

The crystalized device ended the projection, leaving the room in momentary silence, save for Astoria walking around, babbling to herself, and playing with her stuffed toy.

They all sat in the silence that the end of the broadcast brought.

"What do you think he means by setting up a system?" Maryn asked no one in particular.

"I don't know, but it doesn't sound like anything good." Aniklo was now looking down at his arm.

Nirima turned to the boys, her face determined and serious. "This is why you two need to be on guard. You need to be prepared. I know you guys aren't telling me the full truth about how the two of you became bonded, and frankly, I don't care. You're my kids, but you've grown up and gone into the world and made mistakes." She looked down at their arms and the currently glowing glyphs on their touching limbs. "Mistakes that I probably should have made when it truly mattered, but I can't change that. All I can do is make sure you get yourself out of it alive. I've scoured all of your father's research in the basement, time and time again. I practically memorized it, and I know you won't find what you're looking for there. But, you will find it here."

With that, she let go of them and pulled an ornate box out of her pocket.

"That's your special box. The one Dad charmed to be just for you, right?" Aniklo asked with wonder.

"And now, it's yours. Three clockwise circles around the clasp, and one push to the center, and it's open."

"Why are you giving this to us?"

"Because it wasn't exactly given to me directly by your father. It was given to me by Maryn's uncle, his father's brother, at Dad's funeral."

"But, my father was an only child," said Maryn.

"That's what I thought too, until I met Miho's brother, and he told me things that—" She paused.

"He told me things that made me wonder how much I truly knew about your fathers."

The overload of information made him see his mother in a new light, made him question how much more she knew. "What did he tell you?"

"I think it's best you hear it from him. After all, he's the one that made the binding spell you both have on you."

The two boys were in shock.

"How do we find him?" Maryn desperately wanted to know more and to have a clearer connection to the truth, more so than he had ever expected.

"Look inside the box," she said quietly, standing up from their huddle on the couch. "You will find everything you need." She grabbed Astoria on the way to the kitchen. "Come on, Ri. Let's make some cookies."

Aniklo watched her walk through the sliding door; then, he turned back to Maryn, who was fiddling with the box in his hand.

Tentatively, the boys hovered around the box. Within it was a coin-sized crystal, and it immediately sprouted a holographic screen of an image, a picture of Castille and Nirima. They were posing in front of the large tree in their backyard. A younger version of Aniklo, Maryn, and Tauro ran, possibly playing tag in the corner. They switched to the next picture, an image of Aniklo and Maryn when they were five months old, lying on a blanket outside with Nirima and Selene beside them smiling. There were many like this of both sets of parents, happy with their kids, as if nothing in the world could ever happen, as if they would never change.

"I've never seen any of these before," Aniklo whispered, like anything louder would blow the images away.

"Me neither."

Eventually, they reached the end of the slideshow, and . . . nothing was there.

"Wait . . . ." Aniklo turned the box in his hand. The back of the hologram for the last picture pointed to inside of the box above the crystal projecting their family photos. Aniklo moved his eyes closer, squinting to read the words *Where to Find Me* above the words *Hit Twice*.

"Should we—" before Aniklo could get the rest of his words out, Maryn reached over and tapped twice on the last holographic clipping, and the box transformed. The box's top lifted, folded in on itself, the crystal rising and detaching from the contraption. In the blink of an eye, the box had reformed, turning into a compass with the central crystal snapping back into its center, the light beam shooting out of it a highlighting north toward Old Ponsn.

"Woah." Aniklo looked at Maryn, who was inches away from him.

"Are you sure this guy is our best bet?" The other boy practically whispered.

"Who else do we have? He's literally the one that made the curse. And he's your family."

"Blood doesn't always mean anything. Especially considering that I just learned about him."

"I know you have a hard time trusting people. But, we need to figure this out as soon as possible. I'm not going back to the Mainland until we figure out what's going on with us and how to at least contain it." Fatigue from the last couple of days finally started to set in, and despite it being early evening, he yawned.

"Fine. We should get some sleep before we leave."

Aniklo got up from the couch and popped into the kitchen, with Maryn following after. Nirima was mixing the cookie batter in a large bowl at the countertop, Astoria in her highchair licking a spoon and whacking it against her seat's tray. They both looked up, Nirima smiling sadly and Astoria cooing and calling, "Niki!"

"We just wanted to let you know we're leaving in the morning. It's best we get some rest first. After everything."

"Yeah," Nirima said, moving Astoria's chair out of the walkway to stand next to the boys. "I wish you would have come to me with what you knew before you went digging, but I know this was probably unpreventable. I'm just mad at myself for not doing enough to protect you, to make sure you're safe." She was speaking again in that strange, cryptic sadness Aniklo was accustomed to when she discussed his father, but now it felt more weighted than ever.

"We'll be fine, Ma," Aniklo said, before Nirima sucked him into a hug. She squeezed tight as she always did, like he was saying goodbye forever.

"I'm sorry, Aniklo," she said to his chest.

Maryn, during their touching moment, wondered if he should question her as much as he could before he left, squeeze all the information she trapped inside her petite frame. But, he decided against it when she turned to pull him into the embrace.

After a couple more seconds, she finally let go and wiped at her puffy eyes. "Take care of each other. I'll leave you food to take with you."

Astoria let out a short scream behind them, demanding their attention, and Aniklo kissed her cheek on the way out.

The path up the stairs from the sitting room was short. Aniklo's room was the first door on the left, and they both slipped inside, just like old times.

The side of Aniklo's room reserved for Maryn was exactly the same as he remembered it the day he was ripped away from the isles. The star maps he couldn't fit at his own house were still plastered above the blue twin bed on the room's left side. The worn-out tan rug, the lampshades the five-year-old boys had worked together to paper mache, the dent in the table between their beds, which nine-year-old Maryn had put there when he had banged his head against it. His side was all there. He bet if he looked in the closet, the clothes twelve-year-old him kept at their house would be there, too. It was all the same, yet their fathers were dead. It was all the same, yet he was not.

He sat on his bed and ran his hands over the dusty covers.

"Maryn, what are you thinking?"

"You kept it all here. Everything is the same. Why?"

"It didn't seem right to change it." *Changing it would have been like forgetting you,* he wanted to say, but held his tongue, hoping the look in his eye said it all.

The two didn't talk much as they got ready for bed. Aniklo waited for Maryn to come out of the shower before going in after. It was routine, a flow of regularity in a space that felt dead and foreign, and Aniklo wanted to hold onto that comfort, that soothing, knowing it came from just being with Maryn in a time untainted by trauma and barriers. He wanted to stay in this faux safety forever, to not think about what lay ahead.

They settled into bed. Aniklo stared at the wall, waiting to hear the sound of Maryn's loud snores, unable to sleep from the tingle of the runes on his arm. When his snores finally came, the rhythm of them slowly lulled him to sleep.

Chapter 7

*M*aryn opened his eyes, expecting to wake up in the comfort of his old bed in Ani's room, but instead, he was somewhere else. He was lying in long grass, the same turquoise grass that turned a shade of wild midnight blue during the solstice. The same grass his younger self used to run away to at night, the same patch of meadow he and Aniklo had decided was their favorite spot on the island; to stargaze, to kiss, to talk, to make plans for the future, to just be.

Now, like a sucker punch to all his memories, he was here again in the hazy cover of a dream. But this time, the tingles formulated on his arm, the ones that revolved around the new runes, seemed to be floating in the air. The vibration of this curse that bound them tainted their sacred place.

He sat up, and adjacent to him, lying with his eyes closed in the grass in an oversized pajama shirt and shorts, was Aniklo. He leaned over and whispered Ani's name, wondering if the dream would snatch him awake when the other boy woke. But, it didn't.

"Why are we here?" Aniklo asked as he sat up, stretching his arms and looking around.

"I think we're dreaming," Maryn said in a hushed tone, somehow knowing anything above that would be too much for the dream to handle.

The two heard giggles from somewhere across the meadow, already knowing what they would see when they stood up.

It was them, the younger them, cuddling together on a blanket in the grass, pointing at the mistic barrier that lay in full view above them.

"It would be so dumb to name a star that." Aniklo's younger self giggled as he adjusted himself in the crook of the other boy's arm.

"But, it would be really accurate! We have to name the stars after what they look like. At least for now. Until we can see them from outside the barrier." He absentmindedly twirled one of Ani's curls around his fingers.

"Do you really believe we'll be able to see it?" He was turned away from the sky now, their faces inches apart.

"Of course, we will! Da says every day we get closer to being able to see the outside world. I believe when that day comes, we'll be able to experience it together, and we'll go out and name the stars whatever we want." Maryn, eyes sparkling, connected the dots of Aniklo's freckles. "We'll go out, and we'll see the skies the elders saw, maybe even different ones. We'll own the stars, and we'll name a constellation after us."

They smiled at each other, a smile that turned to laughter. Laughter at hope, at the promises they made to each other, at just existing.

"Things were so simple then," the older Aniklo murmured, arms clasped tight around himself.

"Things were never really that simple. We just thought they were." Maryn's voice was dead, raspy, and strained.

The laughter began to echo, growing louder and louder with an abnormal boom. The trees in the meadow swung against the tingles in the air, and the wind picked up as the laughter morphed into something deep and haunting. The younger versions of them melted into the ground, parts of the grass turning black and some changing into a vapor, aking on the shape of shadows. Shadows that could pierce them through.

Maryn instinctually grabbed at Aniklo's arm; the runic tendrils of mist within them glowed. The glow from their arms intensified, shooting a beam into the moon. The moon had formed a mouth with a wide nose and golden eyes. A moon of Miho's face. A moon that screamed through a cacophony of havoc.

"You will own the stars! You are owned! You will own! You are owned! You will own!"

A scream sliced at the shadows, sliced at the boys that cowered in the night. Sliced at the fabric of their dream, jerking them apart and into the grassy void below. Into oblivion.

They jerked awake in their respective beds, both gasping for air. Maryn looked over to Aniklo to find him looking back at him, eyes wide and slack-jawed. The cord of light that had formed between them in their dream still stretched across the expanse, still connected them, faint and slightly shimmering like the light of the moon coming in through the window.

"What was that?" Aniklo panted out.

"I think it was the curse. It somehow has access to our memories, and it . . . twisted them. Made them feel real again."

Aniklo pondered over the dream, the feeling of the black grass, the exhilaration of sinking through the ground still vivid and fresh. He hadn't had a dream about the two of them that felt that strong in a long while.

"But, it didn't feel like a dream. It felt like a warning. Like it was trying to tell us something."

After soaking up Aniklo's wistful murmurs, Maryn got up, and the tendrils between them stretched as he put on his day clothes.

"What are you doing?" Aniklo could barely wipe the sleep out of his eyes.

"I'm getting ready to leave. It's almost sunrise, and we'll make good time if we go now." Maryn didn't want to talk about the dream. Didn't want to think about the inner meanings of it or about what they were before. Didn't want to look at Aniklo, disheveled and guardless and soft. The tether between them was practically an ache, terrifying and strange and real. But he didn't want to think about it because soon, it would end. It had to. Aniklo, still half asleep, had been looking at him for a solid minute, around the room, out the window, and back at him, the way he always did when he stalled getting up.

"Okay," he finally said, getting ready at the pace of a slug, the tether shaking between them.

They stealthily made it out of the house—passing a man, who Maryn could only guess was Katam, in the living room, snoring with Astoria nestled in his lap. Before leaving, they had grabbed the food and a note wishing them good luck left by Nirima and left their own thank-you note for her. Eventually, they passed the cluster of houses for the workers at the reserve and crossed into the thick trees that were the passage to Old Ponsn.

The tether between them was still unwavering, stretching as they made it through the trees, the compass tightly clasped in Aniklo's hands. They walked through their meadow, flashes of last night's dreams playing in both of their heads, while the long grass tickled their thighs. The cord connecting them increased its glow slightly, as if it remembered, too. They could hear the rattled calls of the gigantic creatures prowling within their encasements somewhere on the isles, their murmured roars of many tonalities a welcome to the day.

Their thoughts were then veiled by the sound of the small waterfall that pounded into the river near the meadow. Their trek led them adjacent to its spray, to the left with thicker shrubs. Maryn cut through without hesitation, the sky slowly tinting itself in a lighter shade as they progressed.

After at least an hour of walking, Aniklo finally broke the silence.

"I think the dream was trying to tell us there's something deeper going on than just an entanglement of mist joining us. That there is more to everything . . . the dark shadows, our bond . . . That maybe we would be free, like the untainted version of us wanted."

Mary stopped momentarily, a stray branch slapping him in the face. He wanted to buy into Aniklo's optimism, but didn't allow himself to, to fall down that rabbit hole again. "What makes you think the dreams are anything but just a dream? Or, at least, if it's tied to the bond, why not a weird combination of our subconscious?"

"We were in it together, Mars. People don't just have dreams together and remember everything that happened as if it was real. It had to mean something. This bond, this tether between us, it has to mean something."

Maryn didn't talk for several minutes, picking up his pace through the trees. He didn't turn back to Aniklo until he had broken past the veil of dense foliage, coming to a stop at the divide between the reserve lands and Old Ponsn. The river separated the two conglomerates of land rushing into the ocean, which expanded toward the beyond. Maryn had his back to it, his eyebrows scrunched and lips set, as he looked down slightly at the other boy.

"We can't stay this way, Aniklo. This was never a part of the plan, and if we don't figure out how to disconnect ourselves, they'll find us. It will be over before it even began."

"I know you have painstakingly put the pieces together about your Da for so long, about both our fathers, but what if this is a part of that puzzle." Aniklo had moved closer, looking into his chocolate eyes in earnest, trying to get him to probe the fog within him away.

Mary huffed, rubbing at the bridge of his nose. "Your curiosity will be the death of you. The death of us. We need to be on the same page when we go in there or else . . ."

"I know. We go in, find the guy, ask about the bond, and how to —" Before he could finish his sentence, a dart whizzed through the air, piercing his neck in a matter of seconds. Maryn stood in confusion and shock as Aniklo grew weak in the knees. He could barely catch Aniklo before he was shot as well; the two toppled to the ground near the river, unable to stay coherent as the world involuntarily faded to black around them.

===

Tauro shielded his eyes against the barely risen sun, opened the door to the Watcher Bureau, and froze. He had never seen this many people at The Watch headquarters. They were packed like sardines. Half the officers he knew tried to comfort civilians, but one woman near the front desk at the head of the crowd caught his eyes.

"My son is missing! Our family members are missing! The markets are in shambles, and you're telling me you have nothing to tell us, besides the measly two words the Council released last night!" Her voice was shrill, and Tauro followed it, opting out of going to his corner desk and finally cutting through the crowd to see her face.

Ashen and distraught, the woman's eyes were red and puffy, hands swinging in the air and nearly slapping the people huddled around her, waiting for answers.

"We are doing everything we can to alleviate the stress of this situation." Rivera, head of the office, said behind the general front desk. Tauro knew his boss to be consistently calm and collected, but today, his desperation and exhaustion showed through the blanket of comfort that his steely voice cast. At least thirty people crowded into the main section of the small room, the other regular officers pulling away others to help thin out the crowd. But, Rivera was alone against the most eager of the bunch. "The tragedy brought on our city was caused by deviants of the law—"

"You people should be focusing more efforts on finding our children, our siblings, our loved ones, instead of putting all of your search energy into harassing the public for a small group's crime!" The woman was ballistic, stirring up the crowd surrounding her, and Tauro's hope to aid Rivera was slowly losing its vigor.

"Well, it can be deduced this 'small group' may include many of the missing."

The mob let out a cacophony of objections, the distraught lady at the front, the loudest of all.

"My son is seventeen! He's just a boy, and you're telling me my baby boy was a criminal!" The crowd got rowdier at that, and during their time of redirection from Rivera's word, Tauro snuck in beside the disgruntled man. At seeing Tauro, Rivera sighed in relief, and he said to the crowd, "I will be back with you shortly," before dragging Tauro along with him into the back room.

"What's going on, Rivera?" Though Rivera was Tauro's boss and double his age, Tauro never shied away from asking questions, testing the limits of his authority. Luckily, today Rivera was too overwhelmed to correct him.

"The mystic researchers are still working on analyzing the autopsies from the surge last night. They are doing the assessments upstairs while we're trying to keep everyone at bay until things blow over." Rivera wiped a hand across his sweaty forehead. The passage of his hand cast a deeper shadow underneath his eyes.

"Why are they at our facility? And last night, didn't you say everything was going to be handled by the higher-ups?" Tauro asked.

"You don't need to worry about that. All you need to do is join Cynda upstairs with supervising them."

"Supervising them? Why would they need to be—"

"For once, Tauro, do as you are told without question." Rivera hissed, huffing one more time before putting a hand on the door and heading back into the chaos. "They're on the third floor. If you see anything out of the ordinary, let me know."

With that, Rivera was back at the front. Still confused, but knowing not to continue further questions, he headed for the elevator in the back of the sitting room. He passed his holographic key card against the sensor and was granted access. As soon as he stepped into the heavy contraption, he was whizzed up to the third floor.

Tauro had only gone to the upper floors a handful of times, mostly to look in the archive of evidence files for cold cases, but that was all on the second floor. The third floor was mainly a mystery.

Jitters followed him as the elevator opened up to a room full of the dead, rows and rows of bodies all on white dissection tables. The tinted windows, spanning the room's right side, cast the lifeless in a white light, the rows covering the whole third floor.

The sound of Tauro's boots against the old tiles had caught the attention of the huddle of ten workers, four of them being his colleagues. Cynda and Olin were the only two he ever bothered to associate with, their youth matching his own.

"What are you doing here, Tauro?" With a sway of her soft dark mane, Nebu turned away from the group, faced Tauro, and eyed him with her trademark look of disdain.

"What are you doing here, Nebu? This isn't exactly your field of expertise, or your regular workstation."

"Well, it's technically your field, although you're certainly not an expert in it."

"Enough, you two! We don't have time for petty arguments!" A stout man with thick glasses and straight dark hair stepped out of the group.

"You were all gathered here because you are useful. Not in the regular sense of the word, because this is not a regular situation. We are dealing with a mistic anomaly that involves a manipulation in both the atmosphere, and the bodily functions of many casualties. This is a niche situation requiring a unique group of people. Because the Corps and the Council have some suspicions with our departments, things will have to work differently than normal."

"The investigators downstairs are blaming this on the dead," Tauro butted in.

"Right now, we are not authorized to determine exactly what's happened. We can only do a thorough autopsy and assessment of the mist that overtook these people. We'll send the report over to the council heads. Then, it's out of our hands." The burly man, whom Nebu knew as Dr. Aja, solemnly turned to glance at the rows of bodies.

There was a silent pause between the group. Tauro had never taken on a job he couldn't see through. The thought of involvement with an evaluation as a bystander without knowing if people would be brought to justice unnerved him.

"Each of you will be splitting into groups of two: one mistic investigator and one watcher. Bodies laid along the floor have anti-deterioration charms on them since not all could fit in the freeze boxes—"

"So, there are more?" Cynda said, looking out to the rows with disdain.

"Five groups, with two pairs each, will work through the people here, and then, we will talk about the others." Dr. Aja paired Nebu and Tauro together, then, the others.

The begrudged couple unzipped the first body bag, and the sight before them was unlike anything they had ever laid eyes on. The bobular corpse's sex was undecipherable, their bones protruding out of skin softened by the oozing mist that sprang from their body's center. There was a hole in their torso, evidence of a strong force tearing away at their insides. Their face had dripped, the cartilage of their nose sprouting through their nostrils, and their teeth had rotted, the residue sitting in the gooey cavern of an unstable mouth. It was hard to tell where their tattered clothing began and melted skin ended. Puss and blood scattered and mixed into the melted concoction that was formerly a body. That was formerly a person. The glossy white eyes were the only thing left completely in tack, staring lifelessly into the two standing over it.

Tauro, who was standing to the side watching Nebu work, had to turn away, barely able to hold in his breakfast. Nebu was more prepared, having already had her unwilling glimpse drilled into her psyche. She tore away more of the bag that covered the corpse, her gloved hands finagling with the strings of melted flesh that stuck to the covering. Nebu could deduce the body had either had worse damage than the first one she had seen, or somehow, the mist instilled within it had settled and run its course.

Soon, Tauro had recovered, hunched over the bodies in slight fascination.

"I've never seen mist manifest itself in this way. When it's harnessed and solidified, it usually crystalizes or turns into a distinct liquid. It's never so . . . mushy," Tauro said. Through the cases he had covered, he had been forced to see disgusting sights and had picked up medical lingo and mistic knowledge here and there, but what he said was sincere.

"Step back," Nebu said harshly, before turning back to observe the body. "You say all these words as if you know what they mean, when we both know you don't."

She took samples of the tainted skin near the hole in the corpse's body, cutting off the heavily infected particles to store for later. Tauro had to gather all his willpower to ignore her and not throttle her on-site.

She selected a circular disk from the tray on her workstation, pressing a few buttons on its top surface, which caused it to spring forward and hover perfectly over the body. It shot out a beam, scanning inside and out, before the disk floated back into Nebu's hand.

"What does the scan say?" Tauro asked, watching the gadget.

"The cause of death is obviously an overload of mist in the body. Their identity, unfortunately, is undeterminable because of the amount of deterioration, which is extremely rare." It seemed Nebu was willing to put aside their differences to play the know-it-all, looking from him to the device in confusion.

"The thing that stands out to me most is that this sort of mist manifestation isn't in the system. No one in my field has ever logged it in or identified it before."

"Maybe, this is where I come in," Tauro said, looking to his work comm, which scanned the database of his previous cases. After scanning the test sample Nebu had just taken, the comm vibrated, but after a second, it came up blank. "It doesn't have a match."

They both looked at the body, pondering their next steps.

Nebu pulled the sample out and looked between it and the body. "Maybe, we should move on to the next body. Then, I'll be able to—"

A loud scream rang out across the room. A few rows over, Cynda sat stunned as the arm of a dead corpse reached out toward their partner. It all happened too fast for a reaction; the corpse grabbed at the screaming woman, pulling her into its melting flesh with brute strength. She sank into its torso, her own skin sizzling against the cadaver's body and the forming black hole of mist that sprung to life after the unexpected animation.

Tauro, Nebu, and the rest all watched in horror as the corpse's abyss engulfed their coworker into its stomach, its skin stretching to accommodate the new body. With lightning speed, it sat up some of its bones left on the table, its eyes inhabited by the same mist that swirled within its torso. The corpse had somehow come back to life, and everybody scattered.

"Everyone, stay calm!" Dr. Aja screamed, before pulling out a gun and directing a bolt of energy through the revitalized corpse's gut. On contact, the creature let out an otherworldly scream, high and piercing, skin flakes and gooey mist residue spewing across the room. The screech paralyzed them all, shooting a strong visible cord of energy through the air. This made other dead bodies, which lined the room, move within their bags, ripping at the material and breaking free, newly alive and peeling, searching around desperately for people to engulf.

Everything happened too fast for Nebu to even think about moving, clouds of the dark vapor burning at her skin, peeling away at her legs, finally jolting them into action.

Tauro was the first to react after the shock of the burning mist wave skirted across his skin. Before it could pierce him or Nebu, he grabbed her and ran to the nearest window, only a few feet away, and shot several bullets into a corner of the glass to shatter it. The shots sprang Nebu to life. She bolted out, ignoring the screams of her colleagues being attacked, blocking out the pain of the dark mist attached to her ankles. The ground connected with her feet at a breakneck pace.

She looked around, first spotting Tauro beside her, who had clearly broken his ankle in the fall. His foot contorted at a grotesque angle. Only two others had escaped, Olin still lying on the floor. Cynda's engulfed corpse was hanging out the window, body turning to mush on the spot as the dark mist began to set in.

Nebu turned to Dr. Aja, moaning on the cobblestone with a head bleeding and a bent leg.

"You said the people were dead!" she screamed.

The disgruntled mob who'd gathered on the first floor turned their attention to the screams coming from the streets. The bulk of them tried to make it through the dense crowd to the exit, but by then, it was too late. The mist-inhabited dead had found a way downstairs, some of their bodies dripping through solid floor and coating the crowd in dark, slimy, mist-infested flesh. The more solid monstrosities were finding a way to man the elevator and swallowing the crowd.

The sound of glass shattering rang through the air once more. Everyone on the streets turned to watch the dead envelope the protesting civilians and officers through the window of the watchers' headquarters. The civilians, lucky enough to escape, ran and briefly missed the fattened dead. Unexpectedly, when the dead walked outside, they stopped, their flesh breaking down as the mist that powered them sank out of their systems, gathering and solidifying in the air for all to see, before disappearing into the dirt.

Their disappearance didn't stop the chaos. The injured people in the crowd were decomposing, their bodies liquefying under the dark mist's influence. Many came out of the streets half-conscious and tried to get away from the pain, the anguish of their slow deaths. The screams turned to choking gurgles as their insides shot out of their widened mouths. Those who could endure the pain stumbled through the street and crashed against houses, begging for help, begging for relief.

Dr. Aja, who had been standing near the door, was now covered in the putrid flesh from a woman who had collapsed against them. The two of them slowly melted together on the streets. Others, including people who had come out of their homes to investigate, met the same fate; children screamed over the sludge that was now their dead parents before melting into them. People left unharmed ran for their lives, including Tauro and Nebu.

The two limped along, barely able to dodge the crowd, blocking out the deafening screams to duck into an alleyway. She let go of Tauro and pulled out an almost transparent cube out of her cloak. With a few whispered words, the cube expanded, passing through them with tingles before stopping before expanding a meter and blocking them off from the outside world.

"Where did you get a room cube? The Watch would deport you if they found out." Tauro rasped, tensing at the pressure that he had to put on his ankle to avoid leaning against the electric mist surrounding them.

"How do you even have the energy to mutter on about The Watch at a time like this! We need to go!" Nebu was manic, her cloak slightly torn from the acidic air they had narrowly escaped. Her hands were cut, and her hazel eyes had grown wide in her brown face.

"It's fucking dumb of you to trap us in here then." He panted, finally leaning against the wall to get off his broken ankle.

"Shut up!" She yelled in frustration, also panting as she yanked off her bracelet. She twisted the crystal on it three times clockwise, another three times counterclockwise, then quickly set it on the ground before them. Tauro was too distracted by the room cube to notice.

"The residue of this room cube better not be trackable, or I swear —" He didn't get to finish his sentence. The bracelet generated a vortex underneath their feet, yanking them away from the scene, the room cube contracting and falling through behind them.

Chapter 8

The smell of stir-fry was the first thing Maryn detected when he was brought back to consciousness. He felt the soft couch cushion beneath him and the tether on his arm, a sign that Aniklo was close. Memories of Ani falling limply flashed before his eyes, the reality of the situation hitting him. He was shot . . . by who? He kept his breath steady, not daring to open his eyes, hearing the pitter-patter of heavy feet getting closer and closer. A grunt sounded, barely a couple of feet away from him. Shifting, the sound of a sip, and then, he felt the weight of eyes on him, boring into his performance and making his heartbeat even faster. If he could just pretend long enough for the person to leave.

"You can open your eyes now. I don't want to hurt you," A deep voice said.

Having been caught, Maryn opened his eyes. A man sat in a chair adjacent to the love seat the two boys were perched on. He was an old man with deep wrinkles, bronze skin, and thick salt and pepper brows. His wispy hair was the color of his eyebrows and his beard. Maryn, though still groggy from his involuntary sleep, could see this man's resemblance to his father and to him plain as day: his almond piercing eyes, wide-set nose, and full lips a mirror.

Unlike Maryn, the man didn't wield his features into stone; they were soft yet strong. His warmth matched the warmth of the room, a decently sized living room with intricate tapestries. Drawings occupied the wooden walls, a small wooden table in front of the two seats was littered with candles, and a peephole in front of Maryn gave a slight view of a kitchen, pots simmering on the stove.

The man had a palpable energy radiating from him, the imprints of it reminiscent of the room's welcoming tones; his eyes alluded to wisdom. But, Maryn never trusted warmth since, more often than not, it had been a lie for him, and this man's warmth and resemblance to him was still not enough to explain how Maryn and Aniklo got here.

"If you didn't want to hurt us, why did you shoot us?" Maryn challenged. Aniklo shifted closer to him, still fast asleep on the couch.

"That wasn't my doing, but I still apologize. We have been on high alert since the night market attack. I'm sure you can sympathize with the severity of our reaction, considering you saw what was unleashed." He took a sip from his tea beside him. Maryn's eyes narrowed to slits.

"There's no need to feel threatened." He looked at Maryn head-on, unfazed by his stare. "The only reason why I know is that I can sense the dark mist on you. It lingers from that night, not enough to hurt, but enough. Enough to know."

"What else do you know?" Maryn's eyes were still slits as he studied the man, wrapping an arm around Aniklo, unsure where this was all going.

"I know Aniklo's mother sent you to see me, judging by the fact she transferred the compass to you." He nodded to it sitting on the table before them. "I know the two of you must be here for answers about your fathers, your bond, or both since you have the box from the catacombs in your pocket. I know you need my help, and I'm willing to give it to you. But, you won't be able to muster up the strength to get over that stunner that hit you earlier unless you take our replenishers."

He dug into his pocket, pulling out bandages. They were green, a leaf-like material with a jelly side on the back. The jelly on the bandage stayed solid, and the man put them on the table as an offering.

Maryn eyed them warily, but after feeling the ache in his limbs cry out for relief, he patched one to his arm. He felt the effect of the healing mist slowly sink into him, smoothing away the stiffness left over from the stunner.

"While you two are patching yourself up, I'll be in the kitchen finishing lunch."

Maryn shifted on the couch so that Aniklo was flopped to a more stable position and smoothed a patch onto his arm. He jerked awake, clutching at Maryn as he looked around the room in haste.

"Calm down," Maryn whispered. "We're at the uncle's house, the one we were looking for."

"We got shot! We got—"

"Listen. He knows we were at the inner market. He knows about our dads and the bond. We're safe now, but I still don't trust him, so whatever you do, don't eat anything."

Aniklo warily looked around, still holding onto Maryn as he took in his surroundings, and saw the older man still working in the kitchen.

"Did he at least say why he shot us?" Aniklo whispered.

"He said something about it not being his fault, and everyone being on high alert . . ." Maryn's voice trailed off as the man came around the corner, three bowls of food balanced on a tray. He laid the two bowls out before the boys, wooden spoons balanced within them. The blend of vegetables, rice, and a sweet-smelling sauce was enticing.

"I hope the food and the bandages are enough to make up for my people's resistance to newcomers, especially since everything has been very tense of late." The man took a break to eat the food, moaning slightly, as the boys watched him eat in stiff silence, still having not touched their bowls.

"You should really try it, boys. It's tasty," The man said, a slight smile on his face.

Aniklo shifted on the couch before saying, "We appreciate the food, but—"

Maryn interjected, "Cut the crap. We came to this side of Ponsn with no intention of harming anyone, yet you shoot us on sight, and drag us here unconscious, and now you want to feed us? We want to know why you set up the bond that cursed us."

"Eager and abrasive, just like your father." He smirked fondly, pausing to take a sip of his tea, which had undoubtedly gone cold by now, before speaking again.

"To understand what's going on with your bond, you have to know who I am and how I knew both of your fathers. My name is Hyanth. Miho and I grew up together here, at the epicenter of Ponsn. We both have strong ties to the earth, to the mist, since we were brought up learning how the elders communed with it before the war. They used the mist to take care of the land before the equilibrium the elders and the mist had created was tarnished by war, and the world shifted.

"In our youth, we learned rituals outlawed by the Council out of fear of the mist in a less controlled form. The two of us were positive you would stay here forever, in what you outsiders call, 'old Ponsn,' taking care of the land. We wanted to keep a semblance of the equilibrium from times far away intact."

His eyes were distant, voice hushed as he continued his recount of a facet of his life long passed. Maryn hung onto his every word, soaking up a side of his father he never really learned about.

"The peace we had here in the epicenter changed drastically when amarite was seen as an essential renewable energy by the Council. Before, it was mined in small chunks to be melted down as a sealant around houses to protect against acid rain. But after they discovered it was a relatively stable harnessing mechanism for encapsulating mist, everything changed. They started cutting back on our community's supplies, agreeing that the epicenter's maintenance wasn't enough to guarantee all the resources we needed. Our people were forced to turn to the mines for work." He paused, eyes glassy, then took another sip to clear his throat, followed by another bite of his food.

"What do the mines have to do with our fathers' deaths?" Maryn asked.

"Not much, but they have everything to do with why Miho left. Both sets of our parents died in a mining accident a few seasons after the mass excavation of amarite was sanctioned. A quarter of our older population was gone in a single day, and we were only fifteen. He ran away after that, and I didn't see him for another thirty years."

"He always said we were his only family," Aniklo murmured in between the pause that followed.

"I think a part of him died along with his parents, and it took him finding out he was working for people that didn't have his best interest at heart to realize he had to come back."

"So, it's true. What they were both researching was what got them killed. The harnesser." Aniklo remembered that work used to be almost everything to his and Maryn's father. They were both seemingly so hopeful and dedicated, always boasting about their progression toward something greater, something that would revolutionize their way of living. But, the details of their work were always behind thick veils of secrecy. Now, the two boys thirsted to know why.

The older man nodded solemnly. "Miho was always too smart for his own good, and too trusting as well. I think when he started to move up the ranks at the Corp, he made it known that he thought using amarite the way they do on the Mainland wasn't right. Like an idiot, he divulged harnessing techniques we learned of as a child to make something that tapped into the mist endlessly. The way the old world intended." The old man wiped his hands across his face, sighing emptily.

"I don't think I can ever forgive him for opening up that can of worms, using that sacred information, which had been passed down generations, through decades, in such a public way. Especially considering how the Mainland criminalizes our culture. After our world shifted and the Council took over in the name of peace across Ponsn, they criminalized the magic that exists within the mist.

"It's an existence pure and unaltered by society's shapings and wishes for convenience, an existence connected to the earth and its flourishing state. But though Miho was a fool, he was also impeccably intelligent. If we lived in a better world, things might have turned out differently. The mist wouldn't have fallen into such a state of corruption." Hyanth was somber and teary-eyed, taking slow bites of his food.

"So, that's it?" Maryn asked. "You put that curse in the catacombs for us to find as revenge? As a way of getting back at our Das by hurting us?"

"I wasn't the one who put the curse there. I only found out about it after it was too late, after they both died. They only told me things when they came to ask questions about my runic knowledge, the lore surrounding harnessing in the old world. I didn't even know what they were making until they brought it to me, put it in my hands as I watched it come alive. The orb . . . When I held it, it felt like holding raw life in my hands. At that moment, I thought this must be what gods feel like when they mold reality into being. The day I held it was one of the last times I ever saw them alive."

"When was the last time?" Aniklo asked, teary-eyed and itching for answers.

"It was a couple weeks before the season changed that year. He came alone, babbling almost incoherently, about how everything was going to end, how people were following him. He said it was only a matter of time, and he was coming to say goodbye. I didn't know Castille had already died. I didn't understand it until it was over." He sighed heavily.

"That last time, he brought this." Reaching toward the table, he grabbed a lever under it. A portion of the top flipped up, revealing a wooden box almost identical to the one they encountered in the catacombs. The boys froze on the couch, hesitant to reach for it.

"I found the box in the catacombs long ago, but it never opened for me, and it was addressed for the two of you. You two are the ones they wanted to solve the puzzle, to possibly shed light on a facet of the harnesser they left with me in the box before you now."

He nudged the box toward them, Aniklo grabbing it up in awe. He looked to Maryn who had a nervous face but gave him a nod. Aniklo opened it, revealing a fractal piece of see-through rock. The runic patterns etched into the piece and dusted with a bright powder matched perfectly with the ones on the boys' arms. *It was meant for us* was the only thing ringing in Aniklo's head. Without much delay, he yanked the piece from the box.

The reaction the boys had to the shrapnel was completely similar yet completely different from when they first bonded. A pure energy connected to Aniklo's palm was within the harnesser, surging into his bonded arm and connecting with the tether that joined them. An instantaneous, indescribable burst of overpowering warmth took over. Maryn could only describe it as being on fire while being the fire, as a duality of cognition, a solidification of the tether. Maryn knew all the excitement and fear he felt at that moment couldn't just be his; it had to be Aniklo's, too.

The energy from the harnesser turned their vision white-hot and rendered them motionless. When their sight cleared, the first thing they saw was the Hyanth's room as a hologram shot from a piece of the harnesser's shrapnel still encased in Aniklo's hand.

It was Miho and Castille, their fathers in the lab. The lighting was dim, and their workspace was in disarray. A strange glowing liquid splattered across and burned through the center table behind their heads. Magnification charms and more sat in leftover, empty petri dishes. The two men were in a worn-out state, bags under both of their eyes, looking directly out at the three of them like they could see for real.

"We regret we must ever make a video like this, but if you two boys are watching, that means you followed all the clues." Miho choked out and stepped back to cover his face.

Castille picked up where he left off.

"We chose the two of you to be the harnesser's default wielders because it takes a significant level of intimate trust to support the energy and to reveal its secrets. You two have always been close, always looked out for each other in a way we could never replicate, so when— *if* everything goes wrong, then it will belong to you."

A single tear slid down Miho's face as he moved back into frame, and he coughed to hold back a sob.

"We've seen things no one should ever have to see, and we know it's not going to end well for us, for any of us, if what's going on at the Corps continues. But, we need to try. We need to trust you can find a way to change the fates. It's too late for us, but it might not be too late for you."

The screen then faded out in intensity, and from their father's end all of the names of everybody jumbled together as they tried to get in their last goodbyes on the screen, saying their last I-love-yous before the hologram cut out.

The boys sat hanging at every word, the tether between them rustling with raw emotion, too much for them to handle inside. Aniklo couldn't stop the tears from falling, or the overwhelming emotions from creeping in. This was too much; it was all too much.

"It worked. We finally have something," Maryn said through his awe.

"I knew this piece was meant for the two of you."

The rest of Maryn and Hyanth's words melted into the background for Aniklo, the weight of his father's desperation gathering in Aniklo's gut, in his hands, in his tears. The weight of the dead he had seen only a couple of days ago and the reality his life would never be the same was almost too much to handle. Before, it felt like a morbid dream dulled over by excitement from Maryn's recognition. But, seeing their faces made it reality, made its effects terror, made the job he had dedicated himself to a trap. It truly made nothing safe.

Everything was too much.

Out of breath, he got up, almost tripping over the table, desperate to run away. He crossed the room to the front door, opened his escape hatch, and breathed in the fresh air. His bottle of mist was only a grasp away, and he uncorked it, feeling the familiar relief as it entered his bloodstream, dulling away some of the buildup within, slowing his breathing. He sank to the floor against the walls of the wooden house.

Maryn came out after a few minutes and sank down against the house beside Aniklo. They sat looking at the expanse of green surrounding the house; the slope of the hill that Hyanth's house rested on reached down into the trees. The glimpse of the mountain ranges that encased the Northeast side of Ponsn rose up before them. After a long lapse of silence, Maryn finally spoke.

"If you're not up to it, I can take you back to the house. Let Ma know what we figured out."

"It's not that," Aniklo croaked out, wiping the flow of tears away from his red cheeks. "It just caught me off guard to see him . . ."

"I'm sorry." It was a hushed murmur, but it was there.

Aniklo turned to Maryn, runny nose and all. "I don't want you to feel bad for me, Maryn—"

"No, it's not that. This is different for you than it is for me. I had years to come to terms with everything, and you had only a couple of days."

After a pause, Aniklo wiped snot away with his long sleeves. "It didn't even feel real until a few minutes ago. And now, it's him, and it's our jobs, and my whole life just . . ." He didn't really even know how to finish the sentence.

Maryn reached out, grasping the other boy's hand. "If I could take it back, I would."

"I don't want you to."

It was like one of the thousand nights and days they shared in their meadow, an analysis of faces, a confidence in knowing there was no such thing as being alone. Yet now, it was terrifying because there was no longer such a thing as choice. The tether, ever-present, vibrated in the short distance between them.

There was a rustle in the trees, a wild gust of wind snapped them out of their private moment. To the east, down the path leading into an open courtyard, were shouts. The boys stood up at the commotion, turning to return inside right as the old man came out. A girl came sprinting up the path, calling for the old man.

"What's going on?" he asked.

"It's Nebu. She and another man just fell through her portal in the clearing. The two of them are badly injured."

"Nebu? As in my sister-in-law Nebu?" Aniklo asked, but there was no time for clarification. Hyanth was already racing off with the girl, and Aniklo and Maryn followed after.

=====

The portal had spit Nebu and Tauro out violently, their already exhausted bodies crashing rather than falling softly the way she intended. Tauro screamed out, hitting a nearby branch at the edge of the clearing, roughly slamming to the ground, and having Nebu land on top of him. His broken ankle crunching further.

A girl with light brown hair and wide blue eyes gaped at them from her perch in the clearing, her sandwich poised only an inch from her mouth as she stared on in awe.

Nebu rolled herself off Tauro and turned to the girl. "Fina! The bodies came alive! They were dead, but then they attacked and—"

Fina was awestruck, looking between them before cutting off Nebu. "I'm gonna go get Hyanth," and she sprinted into the trees.

Tauro finally gained his composure, fighting through the pain to mumble, "What have you done, Nebu?"

"This was the only way to get us out alive," she said with great exasperation. "The mist is still clinging to us, and there are people here I know will help."

"You just turned us into criminals, Nebu! The Council is on the hunt for anyone who uses the mist like you just did for us."

Nebu used all her remaining strength to turn to the other man, retorting with venom, "Put your rigid moral code aside, and use your brain for once, Tauro! The Council is stuck in their spire tower, and they have no idea what is going on! We just tried to do an autopsy on the living dead, Tauro, and most of our coworkers are gone! It was either leave or be eaten up completely by what was attacking us!"

Fina came sprinting through the trees, along with a crowd of people. Hyanth was the first to reach them, and surprisingly, Aniklo and Maryn shortly followed. Tauro turned to Aniklo first, as Hyanth ducked down to examine the swirling pocket of darkness that had begun to encase Tauro's leg.

"Tauro? Nebu? What are you doing here?" Aniklo asked, wiping off some of the sweat building on Tauro's forehead with his sleeve. To Aniklo, the two of them looked terribly ill. Tauro's tan skin had turned chalky.

"It's like the mist from the market," Maryn said from the sidelines. He watched Hyanth gently remove the clothing covering their wounds, which showed the black ick struck to them, worming itself underneath their skin. It slowly advanced its veins like a labyrinth, spreading more and more by the second.

"We need to get them to the pit now! Fina, help me lay out the mats." Hyacinth stepped forward and pulled tiny scroll-like mats out of his pockets that when flicked out, elongated into a gurney.

"Help me get them on," Hyanth said to the others, and Maryn and Aniklo obliged. Once they were secured, a veil of mist encased the mats, making them go peacefully limp.

Fina, Aniklo, Maryn, and Hyanth all chipped in to carry the matts south toward the edge of the clearing. Aniklo and Maryn were wary about what lay ahead.

"What happened to them? Where are we taking them?" Aniklo asked while dodging a branch.

"Nebu said they were attacked by dead people. I have no idea what she meant, or if she was just delirious, but based on the dark mist stuck to their legs, it seems pretty serious." Fina answered.

Bile rose in Aniklo's throat, the lingering effects of the comforting mist he'd inhaled slowly slipping away.

They reached another clearing before any other questions could be asked, but this one was different from the other. A strong, calming energy reverberated throughout the air as they stepped through the tree line, the whole field veiled in a fog.

"What is this place?" Maryn asked in awe. The boys almost lost sight of the others in the thin veil.

After several bated breaths, the group broke through the heavy fog into clear air. Meter-high pillars in a circular configuration sat around the clear air pocket and loomed over the two boys. A powerful vibrance reverberated out of them, dark runic markings carved into the rock.

"This is our sacred pit. It's been here for millennia, a place of majesty that helps collect the mist. The rocks are almost like harnessers, but they've been here for longer than even our people. They can only do so much, but hopefully, they will be enough."

The group set the bodies down in the center of the pit. The markings surrounding the area glowed brightly from the center, extended wide across the ground, and reached into the static rock, veiling everyone in its vibrance. Aniklo and Maryn felt the essence of it reverberating through their tether as they set Tauro down.

"Everyone step back," Hyanth ordered as he moved over Tauro and Nebu's prone bodies. The pitch-black coiling on their skin rose into open air, more pronounced than ever, as if attempting to break the opposing light it felt gathered around it.

Hyanth mumbled a few distinct words, pressing his hands against the glowing earth.

"What is he saying?" Maryn asked Fina, who was currently standing beside him.

"He's calling to the earth, calling to the mist to gather within him," Fina responded from the edge of the pit, where they had all gathered.

Suddenly, Hyanth's hands were as iridescent as the markings in the dirt beneath. He rose his hands, silent and authoritative, into the air toward the sky above them, toward the midday suns that greeted his acknowledgment, and then, with a superhuman speed, he slammed his charged hands onto the dark mist on Tauro and Nebu's skin. A squealing resounded through the pit from the skin on skin contact, and Hyanth's body shook slightly as he pressed to exterminate the black leeches within.

"It shouldn't sound like that." Fina's voice was warped by the energy that gathered around them as the group watched on in awe and with a wild fixation. But by then, it was too late to move to the safety of the mist cloud behind them. The reverberation of power reached a high pitch, that final precipice. Hyanth's hands were jerked away, a wild explosive white invading the pit, throwing them all away from the pit in its fury.

Chapter 9

They all, Tauro and Nebu included, were yanked back into consciousness and left gasping for air when the hold of the white light was released. The six of them were sprawled in the dirt, faces covered in a blanket of light when the suns' midday beams had shifted slightly. The pillars surrounding them and the carving beneath voided of their former surge of power. Tauro was the first one to speak.

"My ankle is back in place." He rasped, jerking and wrenching at his ankle, the soreness still present.

Hyanth grunted as he sat up, his formerly pristine clothing sullied. His confidence in the situation seemed to be stripped away, the wrinkles on his scrunched-up face aging him a decade.

"I thought I would have more time. I thought it wasn't this bad."

Fina moved toward Hyanth, smoothing a hand over the older man's arm. "Pa, what's going on?"

He looked at the drained group of people, at Maryn and Aniklo, weak from the blast and collecting their bearings while leaning against a dormant pillar. He saw the faint traces of black veins still visible on Nebu's and Tauro's injured legs. He stared at the swirls of black that had transferred underneath his skin, still present in the wake of his attempt to banish them. A grave epiphany fell over Hyanth.

"Between the large surge that took over the catacombs a couple of days ago, and what I just saw when I touched those two's legs, I think the mystic boundary is . . ." He took a raspy breath, his eyes impossibly wide as he still continued to stare at the veins of black forming under his skin. Fina stared intently as well, the gravity of her father's panic enveloping the both of them.

Hyacinth continued, "I think our peace that has been preserved around Ponsn is coming to an end."

He stood up, stumbling slightly, Fina quick to keep him steady. "I thought we would have more time. I thought things wouldn't have gotten this bad so soon."

Tauro stood and paced wobblily back and forth a couple times in the pit, his heart beating fast. "I don't know what just happened, but I think it's time for Maryn, Aniklo, and I to leave." He moved toward the two boys, who were still crouched in the dirt.

"I'm not going anywhere until we all figure out what just happened." Aniklo was now level with his brother, determination gleaming in his eyes.

Tauro sighed, swaying slightly, his brows furrowed. "Aniklo, don't fight. It's dangerous here."

"From the looks of it, Miho just saved your life. The least you can do is stay until we explain."

Tauro paused, soaking in Aniklo's words. "Explain what?"

"Hyanth is my dad's friend and we think he might have some insight into the conditions of Da's death," Maryn confessed.

His words knocked the air out of Tauro's lungs.

The pit was silent for a beat, Nebu's face lighting up for a second. "Wait . . . so you're *the* Maryn? Aniklo's Maryn that got deported?"

Maryn nodded slowly, too exhausted to correct her.

With his acknowledgment, she smiled and went on to say, "Nice to finally meet—"

Tauro interjected, "Everything that there is to know has been revealed. I've spent years combing through the case files pertaining to both of our fathers' deaths. Trust me when I say, there is nothing else that we can do." Tauro stared at a fixed point on Maryn's face, desperate to keep his breathing calm, to keep the feeling that his head was seconds from exploding at bay.

"I think we should move this conversation out of the pit," Fina said, cutting through the small space and drawing attention to herself and her father. Hyanth was now visibly hyperventilating, opening his mouth as if to say something before coughing wetly. He slumped more against Fina like holding onto his lifeline.

Tauro, unsure how to proceed, said, "I appreciate what you've done, but I want no further involvement in whatever illegal shit you guys get up to here in the epicenter—"

"My father's hurt, and you might still be hurt too. It would be in your best interest to follow." Fina's voice seemed almost electric, the sway of the fog outside the pillars clearing at her tone.

Until now, she had just been a bystander in the passing events, but with her father incapacitated, she stood forward, demanding their attention. With great effort, Fina gathered her father into her arms bridal style, moving out of the mist. Her voice carried toward them at her departure. "Follow me back to the cottage so we can plan our next move."

With the punctuation of her demand, the group made their way toward Hyanth's house by way of the passage through the thick trees, buzzing with the prospect of what they had all walked into, what they had all seen and felt. Fina moved at a faster pace, desperate to get her father back to their home, but the others went more slowly.

After a while, Tauro pulled the three others back, standing in the middle of a walkway and blocking their path.

"Nebu, how well do you know these people?" His eyes were almost slits as he eyed the three of them; then, he turned to Maryn, "And why did you drag my little brother out here?"

Nebu was the first to respond, her hands struggling to put her thick coils into a low puff that would avoid the reach of the trees. "I did the research required for my job here. I also spent a lot of time on my practicum, taking experiments to gauge the differences between the mistic air quality here and on the Mainland."

She had finished putting her hair in a puff, turning her steely eyes to Tauro, her hands resting on her hips defensively. "I consider Fina and her father close friends, and if you weren't touched by the mist, I would have left your ungrateful ass at the scene."

To stifle an argument between the two adults, Maryn interjected, "I didn't drag Ani out here. We came because we had to. Because of what happened in the catacombs the other night—"

"You two were at the catacombs! You're a part of the people who set off the mist!" Tauro's eyes were wide, a finger pointed.

"Don't believe everything you hear, Tauro. Everyone there isn't bad like the Council says," Aniklo said in their defense.

"We almost got eaten alive by the living dead because of what happened there, so don't try to downplay the severity of the situation!" Tauro was irate, eyes bulging and his deep tone stern.

Despite Nebu's shock at their admission, she was quick to jump to their defense. "Stop yelling, Tauro! There are other ways to deal with this besides attacking the boys."

"What they are involved in is illegal, Nebu! All of this is illegal! If anyone from the Mainland found out what we just did, especially with all the crazy stuff going on, they could—"

"The only reason we were there was to follow a lead," Aniklo found himself blurting loudly.

His words snapped Tauro and Nebu out of their intense stare-down.

With eyes flicking between Aniklo and Maryn, Nebu asked, "A lead for what?"

"A lead that had to do with what my father left behind for us," Maryn almost whispered. A pained expression settled over Tauro's face. He flapped his hands in exasperation.

"This again. I understood you two would make conspiracies up when you were younger and still freshly grieving, but you're basically adults now. You need to grow up. Neither of them would want you wasting your lives to connect dots that lead to nothing."

Aniklo's face was bright red, his blood pumping through his veins at breakneck speed as he tried to contain his frustration and anger. Years of underestimation, of belittling of his gut instincts, were at the surface, and he just wanted to scream at the highest pitch possible until Tauro's ears bled. Maybe, then, the older man would actually stop to listen.

After taking a few deep breaths, he spat, "A couple nights ago, the dots led to something, Tauro. Something big, and if you weren't always so quick to dismiss us, then you would see."

Aniklo pushed past Tauro, moving as fast as he could to get away from it all, and left the others to walk silently back to the cabin. He didn't care if Tauro decided to come or not.

Aniklo cut through the trees, tripping over roots, desperate to get out of the dense forestation that surrounded the misty pit. He spit into the clearing where Tauro and Nebu had fallen and moved up the hill, only stopping when he reached Hyanth's front door.

Fina had already arrived with Hyanth, a withered form on the couch, weak and still hyperventilating. The sunlight coming in from the windows glistened against his sweaty face, and he moaned in pain as Fina examined his hands with thick gloves on. Traces of the black mist he had helped to extract thrummed underneath his palms, the skin splitting from the force of the dark energy worming beneath it.

"What's wrong with him?" Maryn asked from right behind Aniklo in the doorframe, making Aniklo jump.

All four made it back, and Aniklo moved to sit on the couch beside Hyanth. Nebu and Maryn looked on in the center of the living room, and Tauro stood back in the ajar doorframe as if ready to leave at a moment's notice.

Hyanth's energy and focus had deteriorated drastically since standing in the pit, his half-lidded eyes weary from exertion.

He rasped, "It's too late. I thought it would be better, I thought . . ." He sputtered out to cough, hacking up a ball of black onto his grass-stained shirt. He wiped a heavy hand against his face to clear away the residue, but all it did was smear the back ick further. With great effort, he looked up to Fina, who was looming slightly over him.

"The walls might not hold."

Fina's face was grave, a single tear sliding down her cheek. "It's okay, Pa. It will all be okay."

They all watched as she unwrapped a yellow, waxy cylindrical ball sitting on her lap. She rubbed the substance on her gloves, and a light reverberated through the fabric.

"Rest now," she said before touching her gloved hand, which had been set alight, to his forehead. The energy from it made him go limp, the swirling of the black still lingering on his skin stilled.

"What did you do to him?" Nebu asked, moving closer from a reserved stance, gazing at the motionless swirls underneath his skin. Hyanth, with his eyes closed and body completely still, looked as good as dead.

Fina looked to Nebu, her face hard. "Help me get him to his bed" was all she said, and Nebu, knowing where to go, promptly gathered his feet. Fina heaved underneath his arms, and they walked through a door attached to the kitchen's far side and out of sight.

Maryn sat on the couch beside Aniklo, feeling the heat of Hyanth's body like a blueprint on his back, a taunting reminder all of his hopes were quick to leave him.

Tauro then moved from the doorway to stand in front of the boys. "Now's our chance to leave."

Tauro's words snapped Aniklo out of his shock, and he harshly whispered back, "Hyanth is literally dying in the other room because of what he did for you in the pit, and you want to go now?"

Tauro felt a weight; a tingle of worry mixed with guilt grew in his stomach, but he pushed through that to urgently whisper, "You don't understand, Aniklo."

The girls came back to the living area before Aniklo and Maryn could respond. Fina's light-brown hair was swept out of her face, her features hard. In the short time since they had been gone, she had changed out of her dress into a tank top and flowy shorts that showcased her muscular frame, her eyes scanning the room. Her arms were crossed as she looked between Tauro and Nebu. The four didn't know what to say in the painful seconds they were under Fina's observant eyes.

"The mist you guys carried through with you today . . . We can't let it spread any more than it has."

"Is Hyanth dead?" Maryn asked, already somewhat resigned to the possibility.

Fina sighed, crossing the room to sit on the chair next to the love seat where Aniklo and Maryn were. She rewrapped the energy ball, picked up the chunk of the harnesser still resting on the table, and fiddled with it in her hand. She spoke slowly, forcing the words out through sheer will.

"No. I had to put him under a trance to stop the dark ichor from taking over him completely, but it's only a matter of time . . . It's only a matter of time for both of you. That's why we need to do something to readjust the timeline."

"The timeline for what?" Tauro asked.

Fina paused, looking up from the harnesser to face the room.

"A couple of centuries ago, when the mist first shifted the bounds of what was considered Ponsn territory, the elders were tied closer to it than we can imagine. The mist before was a lifeline to a deeper knowing, as they would call it. People could draw out an estimate of the future. In the second war, when the mist's bounds brought in the neighboring clans, they saw us mistic manipulators as a threat."

"The elders of that time gave a disturbing prediction, the prophetic downfall of Ponsn as a whole. They were told a dual force of mist would emerge, something dark, something deadly. It wouldn't stop until it decimated everything. Pa always said the timeline for the dark mist was supposed to be centuries from now. We were supposed to have more time to create a true countermeasure to fight against it. But now we're here, and it is coming."

With the others, Nebu listened, sitting on the carpet in front of the coffee table to rest her sore leg. "Dark mist has risen up before. The mist can take millions of different shapes and elemental formulations. How is this different?"

"It's never been this big, has it?" Tauro asked, a deep part of him almost resigned to Fina's words, despite the danger and confusion they held.

Fina was looking at him now, nodding. "Yeah. It's never been this parasitic. Every conjuration of mist in the database has been healable through a trip in the pit, through the conjuring of a masterful wielder who could handle the mist's weight. But, this was unquenchable. It didn't submit like it should have to the light; it chose to devour." The whites of Fina's eyes were large, despite her insistence on keeping a steely composure.

Aniklo was packed with questions, confusion, and a deep sense of regret. "This was all our fault, wasn't it?" he asked in a hushed tone, staring into the harnesser. It glowed under the setting suns' light from the window. The whole room was alight with the effects of the golden hour, the vibrant red electrifying every word. "We set this free when we went looking. This is what they left behind."

Fina turned to Aniklo, a knowing look on her face. "This wasn't all your fathers' doing, Aniklo. As I'm sure my Da told you, people were after Miho and Castille after they found out what they were brewing, what they had miraculously managed to replicate. Our best bet is to find the harnesser they left behind. It's the only lead that Pa ever talked about—"

"A harnesser?" Tauro asked, his face paled, and he turned to his brother and Maryn. "Is this what you guys were on the hunt for?"

At Tauro's words, Aniklo's eyes were glued to the fraction of the harnesser that Fina still held, knowing the gravity of its depth, knowing what it had in store for them.

"Tauro has the right to know," he said to Fina, and in confusion, she gave the harnesser over to Aniklo.

In a flurry of intense light, the holographic image from their fathers played out before Tauro's eyes just as it had before, the tether between Aniklo and Maryn fueling its release. Tauro took it all in, the desperation in their cracking voices, seeing Castille in a level of clarity he had never been able to replicate since his death. All of his searching, all of his regret, all of his determination he'd thrust into his career seemed pointless at the knowledge a facet of his father's reality was out of reach. Yet, it had been in clear view this whole time.

He couldn't hold back the well of tears that began to flow. The message cut out after a few short seconds, and the harnesser's energy was slightly defused. Its remaining light further emboldened Aniklo and Maryn's tether.

"I've never seen anything like it," Nebu said in awe. "Can I hold it?"

Aniklo handed it over, and she studied the glyphs on its surface, noting the string of light that still existed between Aniklo and Maryn. All Tauro could do to dull the pang of shock coursing through him was turn to his brother.

"How did you find out about this?" Tauro's voice trembled, his eyes wide and still glassy.

"My mother had a chip of old research from him," Maryn answered. "It led me to the catacombs and then here, and now . . ."

"It's never done that before," Fina said in awe, a glimmer of hope in her eyes. "There was always the concern from Da that it didn't work. But now that we know it responds to you two, it will be so much easier to find the rest and use it as a counteractive measure against the dark mist."

"Isn't there an easier way to replicate the abilities of the harnesser without having to search for the other piece?" Nebu asked, looking to the three boys. "I know you guys are on the hunt for what your fathers left behind and all that, but we're kind of on a time crunch here. Can't we create a new one or look for the other harnesser once everything is safe?"

Fina was contemplative, her face grave. "Pa always said harnessers cost soul sacrifice and resources we no longer have. They are dangerous, risky, and take decades of manipulation and resources to bring to fruition. If it weren't for us blocking the sensors the Council set up to track our mistic harnessing a few years ago, we would have found a way to cultivate something like it sooner, but now it's too late. We need the full insight of the elders back, and the harnesser is the only way I know to make that happen."

"After what happened on the isles, The Watch will be on an even higher alert," Tauro said in a hoarse tone, his eyes still red. "They'll know you fixed our leg. They'll sense the strange mist Aniklo and Maryn have floating between them."

"That's why you need to work fast," Fina said, a revitalized vigor in her voice. "Our best chance is to collect the harnesser and use ley line energy to counteract whatever darkness is brewing on the Mainland. It's the only thing I can think of doing. It's all Da ever mentioned."

"What if the Council takes care of it before any of this is necessary?" Tauro asked.

Nebu interjected, "Really, Tauro? After all we've learned, you still want to wait around for change when all they're doing is criminalizing the wrong people? After Castille's message, you're still willing to count on the Council to get things right and capture the right people!"

"I'm just being realistic! The Council are the people in charge of our world! If they really are affiliated with the Corps, like my dad hinted, the Corps is one of the only known powers that could control whatever mechanism it takes to create such twisted mist. Then, the chances of them stomping us out the way they did our parents are high."

"This has moved way beyond the risk of getting caught, Tauro," Aniklo said. "Even though I know you would rather not be, you're in this now. You're affected now."

"This is what he would have wanted," Maryn spoke up, determined, yet wary. "This is what they both would have wanted."

"I'll be damned if I just sit around and do nothing while the world is engulfed in darkness all around me," Nebu said, looking to her injured leg, still encased in the stagnant black veins. "Especially knowing the darkness is in me, too."

Fina now turned to Tauro. "I can find a way to brew up whatever it takes to mask the effects of the mist underneath your skin, and to mask the effect on the bond between Aniklo and Maryn. But, our only option moving forward is to find the pieces we need to heal my father, and the both of you. My main priority is to keep the epicenter safe. We have methods set up to protect us from the mist for as long as we can, but if you want a chance to make a difference on the Mainland, then this is our best option to do so. All of you have access to the inside, and that's a resource we in the epicenter have never had the privilege of utilizing effectively."

Just then, an old crystal glowed on its perch over the fireplace, the fuzzy illumination emanating from it not as strong as the one back home on the reserve. The Council Member Oraan from the day before was back. A formal announcement blared.

"We are in a state of emergency. The outbreak set in place by the vandals in the inner market has now caused further damage on the Mainland. This dark mist is now tormenting our streets, taking lives at rapid rates."

A picture of the events of earlier that day sprung onto the page, the onslaught of gelatinous bodies put on display for all to see.

"The terrors on the streets are nothing to take lightly. We are conducting extensive research at this time to evaluate the cause of the surges and reanimation of the dead, and are on a search to rule out all suspects in this atrocity."

The screen then switched to a picture of Tauro and Nebu, their official, on-file portraits on display for all to see.

"These two are suspected of working with the rebel group that set this all into motion. They were seen at the site of today's attack, and traces of an illegal portal were tracked back to their mistic signature just hours ago. Anyone able to find them will be rewarded."

"Safety zones are being set in place in the markets for all those who seek protection and need supplies. Task forces will be scouring the streets for those in need."

The Council Member's face then hardened to stone as he stared threateningly into the camera.

"The task force is also on the lookout for those who have strange and illegal mistic signatures on their person. If you are a part of this malicious group, it is best you turn yourself in as soon as possible, because we will find all of you. We will exact justice on those who commit crimes against our world by breaking the laws of mistic regulation. The punishment will be far worse than being sent to the Outer Rim. Rewards will also be given to those able to identify anyone else affiliated with this terrorist group besides Nebu and Tauro.

"Stay indoors and stay safe."

The public service announcement ended, leaving everyone in shock.

Tauro was never the type to break the rules, always desperate to keep his hands clean, and this plan wreaked of dirt, wreaked of risk, but Tauro knew now that this was, like Aniklo said, beyond the laws of their society. This to him: was now life or death.

"We need to move fast," Tauro found himself saying, shocking everyone in the room.

"Alright then. Since Aniklo and Maryn are the ones with access to the harnesser's chip, the two of you will take it back with you to the Corps, and see if you can locate the rest of it there." Fina then turned to Tauro and Nebu, her game face and authoritative voice demanding their attention. "The three of us will do the groundwork. Before Ponsn included the Mainland, the elders would gather mistic energy from different potency points of the isles. This served in energizing their rituals to the max and truly tapping into the mist. Now, these points extend outward, to different parts of the Mainland. It will be our job to track them, and collect each of the seven mist clusters from the ley line convergent points needed to open the harnesser to its full capacity."

"How do we know where the ley lines meet?" Nebu asked.

"We have an informant who keeps track of the mist alignments. We'll be stay at his safe house between trips to collect the convergent energy."

"If they find out what we have, what we are, they'll kill us, won't they?" Aniklo's words were barely above a whisper, but their magnitude was akin to a shout. Maryn almost thought he felt the other boy's anxiety through the beam of mist that connected them, felt the itchy scratch of terror in an intensity that could not just be his own.

Maryn then put a hand on his arm, the one covered in the glyphs, and Aniklo turned to him, eyes as intense as a burning fire. "We're going up against the very people our fathers were afraid of." Aniklo then thought of his mother, thought of the grief and latent heaviness evident in her voice when she had given them the compass, given them the instructions to come here. Had she known what she was doing when they left? Had she known the danger they were in?

Tauro watched their exchange, feeling the burning reality of their rapidly shifting world in his bones. "This . . . they want us dead . . . there's no going back from this." A flash of his old life, the satisfaction of his detective work, the heady feeling of justice he was a part of all floated in his brain, disappearing like a fog, a distant memory.

"The only way out of this is to get through now," Nebu spoke up. "We need to get ourselves together, get some rest, and end this as soon as possible. There still might be a chance we can clear our name, and I won't rest until the dark mist is stomped out."

Nebu, standing before them, despite her short stature and ragged dress, was the picture of confidence, the tight coils that stuck out of her low puff caught against the last light of the suns.

Fina stood up, collecting the three bowls of her father's stir-fry that lay cold on the table and said, "Nebu's right. We don't have time to get caught up in what it all means. We eat, we sleep, and we leave in the morning. Everything else will fall into place."

The rest of the night passed in a blur. They ate the leftover stir-fry in silence, the food lining their stomachs, a nice distraction from what lay ahead. After dinner, Tauro fell asleep on the couch, the events of the day weighing down his jumbled brain. Aniklo and Maryn were taken to the back room by Fina to look over her father's notes, and Nebu was left alone to her own devices.

The woman slipped out of the cabin, the cover of the trees on the hill a rustle that resembled the static of her mind, the conscious pull of the now. Nebu, veiled in darkness only interrupted by the light of the moon, crouched behind a bush and swiped at the personal crystal comm on her wrist. Panic was already flooding her gut, but before she could convince herself otherwise, she tapped on the holographic icon of her sister's signal.

After only a second of waiting, light illuminated her dark features, and Nebu's sister's visage hovered in the space before her. Rioba's eyes were puffy and wide, her thick locs tied back in a messy ponytail. At the sight of her other half, she sighed in relief.

"Nebu. You shouldn't have contacted me."

"I needed you to know I didn't do anything wrong. I was just there and—"

"I know, Nebula." Rioba sighed, her voice thick and heavy, tears falling down her face. "I know you aren't the monster they painted you to be, but it's not safe for either of us if we keep in contact."

"I just wanted to say I'm sorry." Nebu's voice cracked, and she looked away, desperate to hold back her tears. "It's just . . . after everything that's happened, after everything you did to get us here, I messed it up." Her tears began to flow, and she looked into the holographic image of her sister's eyes, a light blue that contrasted the brown of both their skin. Nebu felt like a child again, desperate to be held and comforted by Rioba, desperate for her soft voice to tell her everything was okay.

"I don't blame you, Nebu. I don't blame you for anything. We did what we had to do before, and we'll do it again."

Images of their life before their escape to the Mainland flashed before Nebu's eyes: the toiling of her little hands in the farming district, the way she had seen the workers beside her drop from exhaustion, the beating of the hot suns against her bruised skin. All of the suffering of her youth tied into one flash of memories that felt centuries away from the present. Nebu was always thankful for her sister's desperation to get them out of the cyclic struggle that was working in the farming district. She admired Rioba's intelligence, but in the back of her mind, she always knew their lucky streak would end someday, and she knew that someday was now.

"Nebu, things are getting bad out here. Parts of the market are on temporary lockdown, and the black mist is surging up at random times, snatching whoever it can. But, your biggest concern will be staying away from the watchers." Rioba's voice was calculated, her soft eyes yet desperate. "Whatever you do, don't let them catch you. Don't let them see what you are."

The thrumming of that deep knowing, the hidden reality trapped in her torso, trapped beneath her skin, was a constant vibration brought alive by Rioba's words. This secret had been a nagging weight, a feral desire buried under years of fear, under precautions of what had happened to those before who had been found. "I would never tell a soul. I would never let anything happen to us, especially sweet Astoria."

"I know you wouldn't. Just be careful."

"I will. I love you."

"I love you too. Stay safe."

The call was disconnected, leaving Nebu alone in the void that was the quiet night.

Chapter 10

*A*ll that Maryn heard when he opened his eyes was screams. He was hiding in a closed wooden crate, the air filling his lungs too slowly from his crouched position in the sullied alleyway, heart beating at the speed of light. The streets were littered with blood, people slashing at one another in a last-ditch effort to steal, to take, to grab any little crumb they could to stay alive. The ocean of bodies he saw from the sliver inside the crate was never-ending, trials of red dripping from the main road and catching on his bare feet, catching on his soiled, ripped pants.

It was all too loud, the deafening, debauched screams of horror, a scar that left only numbness in its wake. His mother had left him to die there, standing in the lines with angry people unable to get their rations from the state. The onslaught of anger led to the wielding of makeshift weaponry, and then, to death. All he could do was hide with the ration of bread he had managed to steal in the chaos. Hide away to let it die away, let the riot peter out and everyone go back to their own separate parts of the slums. He was in this body again, in this prison again, and all he could do was nothing at all.

Suddenly, the wooden crate was yanked away, and his ripped shirt was grabbed roughly by a scrawny kid twice his height. Before Maryn could even react, he was jerked upward, a knife held against his throat. The kid before him snatched the bread away, a rabid look of panic evident in his eyes. Two were towering over him: bone-skinny, dirty, wild, and out for blood.

"Give me your money." The kid tightened his hold on the knife, the sharp blade digging deep.

Maryn cried out, closing his eyes against the pain, against the tears.

"I don't have any money!" Maryn squeaked insistently, snot dripping. The older Maryn reliving the nightmare knew how this would end, knew how it all would come crashing down, and there was nothing he could do about it.

"Finish him off!" The kid standing back venomously spewed, ravenously eating the bread with moldy cheese they had managed to scavenge somewhere else. But Maryn paid no mind, the terror of the moment all culminating into memory as the knife was yanked away from his throat, and with a crank of his arm, the boy holding him stabbed the knife into Maryn's gut, the white-hot pain all-encompassing, the screams an echo of the ones around him.

Just like when it happened the first time, the Maryn trapped in this haunted body, in this haunted reality, *watched his assailants casually walk away as he was left slumped against the rickety crate. The knife impaled within him, his blood mixed with the excretions of watery bile and the red the streets already held.*

At that moment, all those years ago, Maryn remembered wondering whether or not he would be joining his father so soon after missing him. He wondered if he would die there, in a dirty side street of the Outer Rim, without the comfort of his absent mother, without ever seeing Aniklo again, without being able to escape. The suns were a vortex above him, swirling in his state of delirium, his father's voice carrying through the chaos and urging him to get up.

"You will own it all," Miho's timber voice echoed, drowning out the commotion all around him. A shadowy version of Aniklo appeared before him, the Aniklo from the now, his face trapped in the alley walls. And then, there was screaming, screaming from the sun, from the walls, from his cut throat, the ebb of white-hot pain in his torso never ceasing, the blood turning obsidian and thick. The cloud of darkness burned him, engulfing his surroundings, taking over the alleyway, and swallowing him.

Maryn jerked awake and sat up abruptly in his bed, not quite able to catch his breath. In a panic, he checked his torso to only see the hint of a scar, the hint of what he had just relived instead of the sharp knife he had felt seconds ago. It took him a second of looking around to remember where he was: the tight space that housed a queen-sized bed, a guest room in Hyanth's home. Aniklo still lay fast asleep beside him. The memories the dream took on were crisper than he had ever felt, something he wished desperately to never relive.

It took him a second to calm his breathing, and after lying wide awake for a while, he got up before the suns did, detangling himself from Aniklo and stepping outside into the morning air. It was crisper here, as if life buzzed more vibrantly with every breath, the exact opposite of what his life used to be before his return to the isles.

Inhale. Exhale. A taunting reminder that this vibrancy was a gift that would be snatched away from him. This peace, his peace was never meant to last.

The door creaked, and he knew it wasn't Aniklo, feeling through their tether that he was fast asleep still. It was Tauro.

"You're up early," Tauro said, sitting down next to the younger boy, a cup of something hot in his hands.

"Always am." He paused, clearing his throat to scrape away the scratchiness, trying to mask the terror that still coursed through his bones. He hoped the look in his eyes didn't give him away. "You helped yourself to coffee, I see."

"The old man probably won't mind." Tauro took a sip, staring out into the trees from their spot on the steep hill before turning to Maryn.

"We didn't get a chance to talk that much yesterday. About you, how you've been . . ." He trailed off, studying Maryn's face for any sort of emotion, wondering.

"What are you trying to get at, Tauro?" Maryn cut to the chase, defensively dodging the intrusive feeling questions always gave him. He knew the dance Tauro liked to do, the game that conversation always seemed to be, and he didn't want to relive another moment of his past.

"I want to be honest," Tauro said, his eyes fixed on Maryn's exposed arm, and then on his face. "You were like a little brother to me, and I never really got over the feeling I failed you when you left, the feeling I failed both you and Aniklo by letting the two of you get separated. I know that even as kids, you saw each other as your other half, but now it's real. You are really two halves of a forced whole." Tauro noticed the glyphs sparkling on Maryn's arm and the energy shifting underneath Maryn's skin and scrunched his brows. "I don't know how to feel about it. I don't know how to feel about any of this. I don't know if I should blame you for dragging him into this or not, or pity you for getting yourself caught up in it in the first place."

"I didn't ask for this, Tauro," Maryn softly murmured.

"But, you don't mind it. The closeness that Fina alluded to. This was your father's doing. Both our fathers' doing." A small part of Tauro felt resentment of being somewhat left out of Castille's vision. A part of him wanted to be more central in it, instead of just an afterthought, an accidental and small yet essential piece to the puzzle. Maryn saw the grievances in Tauro's composure, in the slant of his crooked mouth and his tense posture. Maryn was familiar with the strange phenomena of being the brunt of misplaced resentment.

"Look, I know you're looking for someone to blame, but I never wanted Aniklo to get involved. I would never, ever knowingly put him into a position to be hurt."

Tauro paused, soaking up Maryn's conviction, assessing the vulnerability in his eyes. "I'm sorry I didn't believe you before."

"I don't blame you. It might be easier if I didn't believe me either." Maryn sighed, running a hand over his face, thinking over all the mistakes he'd ever made and the ones others made he'd been forced to pay for. Before the catacomb's events, Maryn had always seen his emergence from the Outer Rim and discovery of the truth at the end of his father's breadcrumbs as a miniscule price to pay, a quick close to a chapter left ajar. Now, after all that happened, his perseverance felt burdensome, the clues a taunting that weighed on his psyche.

"I just want this all to end" was all Maryn could muster. "I just want to know the full truth." He looked down, picking at his callouses to avoid looking directly into Tauro's eyes.

"Promise me," Tauro pleaded, reaching to grip Maryn's shoulders, their eyes now aligned. Tauro gulped before continuing, "Promise me whatever happens after we leave the epicenter, you will do whatever you need to make sure you both walk out of this unharmed. Promise me you'll do whatever it takes to make sure Aniklo walks out of this alive."

There was a heaviness to the silence that followed, the boy and the man staring each other down. Tauro, looking back on this moment, would feel bad for pressuring the boy into such an unfair dilemma, into another situation where Maryn would have to put himself behind the needs of someone else.

But, there was no turning back when Maryn responded:

"I promise."

"Good," the older man said.

Tauro eventually released him, a flurry of warm hues springing up across the tree lines and puncturing the gray remnants of the night. The two watched the rise of the suns in uncertain silence.

===

Fina, Aniklo, and Nebu eventually awoke shortly after the suns rose. After breakfast and a quick wash, Fina gathered everyone in the living room while she packed three bags.

"Nebu, Tauro, I have bags packed for us filled with supplies and dried rations. Everything else we need will be at the safe house."

She handed the bag over to Nebu and Tauro, who she had lent a change of more practical attire to wear on their journey. Nebu traded her heels and soiled dress for a monochrome, fitted pants and shirt set similar to Fina's, while Tauro wore Hyanth's clothes, which were pretty similar. Cloaks that framed their faces were the final piece to their disguise.

Fina then turned to Aniklo and Maryn and picked up the piece of the harnesser that rested on the coffee table. "All we have left to do is to hide the harnesser."

Aniklo and Maryn remembered her vague explanation for their bond the other night, her voice echoing in both their ears as she stepped toward them.

"As far as I know, bonds like this were created as a test of compatibility, something necessary to channel the full-fledged integrity of a harnesser without the same level of stress that it costs a single wielder. The manifestation of it on your arm is a prototype, something Hyanth fashioned with his limited knowledge."

Fina had turned from the notes splayed out on Hyanth's desk in his room. She'd been full of ideas to look at their arms, a fixed expression of awe present.

"All I can say is what you have, in some form, is sacred and dangerous."

"Is it deadly?" Aniklo had asked, skimming the drawings and glyph formulations surrounding them on the small room's walls, waiting with bated breaths for her answer.

"Things like this are different for every pair. I've heard stories, passed down from centuries ago. Some people died from not being compatible enough to support the bond, to support the weight of its connection, but that usually happens at the site of the first contact. The two of you made it this far, so only time will tell."

"What about the dreams?" Maryn had asked, almost unsure.

"Are the dreams real? What are they like?"

"They're confusing, like memories meshed with a harsh fantasy," Aniklo answered. "We've only had one."

"Hyanth always said dreams are a connection to the divine mist. They're meant to guide you."

Currently, Fina had the harnesser balanced in hand between the tether of light that connected the two boys. "In the notes, it said the people connected to a harnesser could encase it within their bond, making the bond and the contraption connecting them in this plane shift to another." Fina's brows were scrunched as she looked at them. "I don't know exactly how this is supposed to work, but maybe if you think about the bond taking the harnesser away, it will."

Aniklo and Maryn, looked to each other, then back at the harnesser. Maryn closed his eyes, feeling the thrum of energy that reverberated outside of him, sensing the way it was entangled within the bounds of the harnesser fragment. With a shared intensity, Maryn and Aniklo imagined the harnesser seeping into the tether. After this vision, the light between them expanded, encasing the harnesser, bathing the room in a mysterious tingle of energy. With a snap, the harnesser disappeared along with the visible evidence of their bond.

"Woah," Aniklo and Nebu said in unison.

"Are you sure this is safe?" Tauro asked.

"It's what Da would have wanted us to do." The reminder of her da was enough to spring Fina into action. She swung her bag over her shoulder, a feeling of determination evident in her stature and confident composure. "We don't have much time, so we should get moving."

After taking one last glimpse back at her father and the home they shared, Fina guided them out of the boundaries of Old Ponsn, trekking their way back to the reserve. The young woman, unbeknownst to the rest, had never traveled outside of the epicenter. Her fast pace through the trees opposed the butterflies growing in her stomach. She passed by the two people watching the epicenter entrance, only saying a quick goodbye before they left the bounds of Fina's home.

They were all silent, a nervous bundle of jitters that threatened to combust if they didn't continue forward, if everything didn't go according to plan.

"After we make it through to the docks, we go our separate ways," Fina said after a long lapse of silence. Fina's thick, light-brown braid swayed in the wind.

By then, they had practically made it to the backyard of the reserve's houses. After riffling through her bag, Fina pulled out a band very similar to their personal crystal comms, but the shiny piece that fueled it was much larger. The crystal encasing the cylindrical metal piece served as the base.

"We communicate through these crystals." She handed them each a set, and then turned to Aniklo and Maryn, but before she could speak, a loud voice projected through the area.

"All citizens of the reserve. All must come to the clearing near the docks to be scanned." A blaring siren was issued through the air, stunning the group.

"Watchers never come to the reserve," Nebu objected in confusion.

"It doesn't matter. I have another way for us to get to the Mainland." Fina motioned to the east.

"An underwater passageway leads to the Mainland. It will be a long walk, but we can make it by dinner."

"Then, I guess this is goodbye," Maryn said, the gravity of their situation not lost on him. Over the past couple of days, his search for answers had expanded past the scope of what was explainable. The fact that they would have to return and act like nothing happened was an almost unbearable thought.

Tauro and Nebu looked at Maryn and Aniklo.

Tauro was the first to wrap his brother in a hug. "Stay safe, little bro," he murmured into his hair, before turning to Maryn and hugging him just as fiercely.

He looked Maryn in the eye after their embrace, a reminder of the promise hanging between them. Tauro squeezed Maryn's shoulder in encouragement as they pulled apart.

Nebu hugged the two boys next, telling them to stay in contact and say hi to her sister for her. Reluctantly, the group went their separate ways.

Aniklo and Maryn broke through the veil of trees, momentarily blending in with the people heading to the docks. They diverged from the crowd on their way to the family house.

Katam, Rioba, and Astoria were on the porch, speaking with a trio of watchers. The two boys approached with caution, observing the scene in front of them.

The watchers, who usually wore dark blue uniforms and combat boots, were now decked in padded armor over their normal uniforms. One of them crouched near Rioba, running a scanner over her dark skin. The scanner, thankfully beeped green, and the watcher who wielded it turned to their two colleagues.

"Log that House 475 C is clear."

"Aniklo. What took you so long? You said you were only going for a short walk," Katam said. Aniklo had always known Katam to be a bubbly, optimistic man, but those traits seemed to be sucked away from him as he regarded the two boys. His slanted eyes turned beady like he was trying to tell them something.

The watchers then turned to the approaching boys, who were now at the foot of the front porch. A flurry of anxious anticipation reverberated between Aniklo and Maryn, invisible to all but them.

"What's going on here?" Aniklo asked.

"Given the fact that your brother and sister-in-law are wanted criminals, we are authorized to take special tests. We must ensure the rest of the family isn't involved in the rebel group's agenda."

The woman who had just scanned Rioba turned to the two boys, stretching out her scanner, which oddly resembled a loaded stunner. The scanner's beam stretched over the two, probing for any signs of loose mist. The seconds it took to scan them felt like eons, the anxiety kindling underneath the surface, poking at their tether, which they both hoped was truly hidden away. Aniklo forced himself to stay still, to summon the best poker face he could muster. After the longest seconds imaginable, the scanner turned green.

"The two of them are also clear." The head watcher instructed the others to lock in Aniklo and Maryn's statuses. Aniklo had to try surprisingly hard to hold back his sigh of relief.

"What next?" one asked.

"You go join the others in the search. This island still hasn't been scanned completely. I still have work to do here." After the other watchers on the scene dispersed, the head went inside the house as if she owned it, leaving the family to their own devices.

Katam rushed to hug the two boys, Rioba following shortly after with her daughter in her arms.

"I'm so glad you're okay. Both of you. Especially after everything," he said. After his embrace, he gestured at Rioba and Astoria. "Maryn, this is my wife, Rioba, and my daughter, Astoria."

Rioba was quick to rush in for a hug, her long dark locs tied back in a thick braid. Her face and eyes had an uncanny resemblance to her sister, but she was taller and willowy, her arms strong and skin darker from hours spent under the beating sun.

"It's so good to meet you," she said to Maryn. She released Maryn, and despite their unfamiliarity with each other, he immediately knew her warmth and welcoming attitude was real.

"You, too." Maryn said with a slight smile.

"So sorry we couldn't welcome you home when you first came back." Katam's voice was hushed as he leaned into the huddle the family had made. "The animals have been really erratic in the fields, and the reserve needs all the help they can get. But, if we would have known you were coming sooner, we would have taken off."

"It's all right, Katam," Maryn responded.

"Where's Ma?" Aniklo asked.

Katam and Rioba turned to one another; Astoria's babbling filled her parents' silence.

Rioba whispered, "She's inside being questioned by some Corps officials. They're new ones in charge of tracking this mistic calamity since all of the credentialed specialists are all . . ." Her soft voice trailed off, her thin brows pressed together.

There was an unspoken contract the group made at that moment while surrounded on all sides by watchers, a distance away but still looming.

"I just can't wait for all this to blow over," Katam finally said after the short pause.

"Love, you know it's not going to be that simple. For any of us. Tauro and Nebu, after what everyone is saying they've done . . ." Astoria, who had been somewhat quiet throughout this whole exchange, was now growing fussy, begging to be put down. Upon release, she waddled in between the four adults, before attaching herself to Maryn's leg.

"Everything will work itself out," Maryn said, wanting desperately to believe it.

The front door opened, Nirima stepping out with, to Aniklo and Maryn's surprise, Jessik. Their boss was dressed pristinely as ever, heels devoid of any mud despite the soft grass below them. Upon seeing the two boys, Nirima let out a noticeable sigh of relief.

"See? I told you they would be back soon."

"That you did, my friend," Jessik said back, a tight smirk plastered on her face.

"What are you doing here, Jessik?" Aniklo asked, trying not to be too obvious about his shock.

"Oh, dear Aniklo. Me and your mother, as you already know, go way back. I decided to come on this required . . . exam to make sure your family is coping well with the news of yesterday's events." She put a gentle, manicured hand on Nirima's arm. "I can't imagine how hard it must be for you. I know you and your late husband tried to raise your children with good values, and for two of them to go off and do—"

"Yes, well, I know for a fact my son Tauro is a good man. Whatever your scanners have detected must be some mistake. You of all people should know readings can be wrong sometimes."

Jessik's smile tightened at Nirima's interjection, her hand slipping away to fluidly fall to her side.

"Well, the readings you had taken when you were in my position at the Corps may have sometimes been faulty, but I pride myself on exactness." The syrupy sting of her words left a sour expression on Nirima's face. "I will make sure to look out for your kid, and all your children, no matter what happens in the coming days."

She then descended the stairs, turning her back on Nirima before she could utter a response, ignoring Katam and Rioba to home in on Aniklo and Maryn beside them.

"Another reason I came on this search was to ensure you two will return to work. Our streets are on high alert, the air distorted, and we need as many hands on deck as we can get to stomp out the undesirable energy."

Aniklo's throat was dry, his palms sweaty, and he desperately wanted to respond, but Maryn beat him to it. "We were planning on coming back by tomorrow."

"That will be impossible. We're closing off the docks for leisurely travel tonight. You must take the next shuttle back with me in the next hour." Before anyone had a chance to respond, she turned back to Nirima, who had not moved a muscle.

"I enjoyed visiting your quaint little house and seeing you and your family again after all these years. I wish you well."

"I wish you well," Nirima parroted blankly, watching Jessik walk away toward the docks.

"Bitch," she muttered under her breath, turning to her family. "People like her are the reason I left the Corps."

"Ma, they can't just—" Katam began, but was cut off by Nirima shushing him and rushing everyone into the house.

"You need to be careful what you say now, Katam," Nirima said urgently after she had shut the door. Her anxiety was finally allowed to leak through after everyone had made it back inside, her brows creased tightly together.

"Ma, this is insane, they can't just shut everything down. The reserve depends on produce and supplies from the market to take care of the animals."

After Katam's words, everyone began talking over each other: Astoria shouting just to shout and pacing in circles at their feet.

Nirima gathered them around her in the living room, one hand on her hip and another rubbing the bridge of her nose.

"Everyone, listen," Nirima finally said, catching their attention and bringing them to silence. "We need to be careful from now on. And I mean careful. And when it comes to this situation with the borders, it's likely best that we comply. Aniklo, Maryn, go back to the Mainland, and do your job. That's the only way we'll know what's being said and what changes will come."

"But, Ma, we won't be able to get back if—" Aniklo was cut off by her hand on his shoulder.

"Don't worry about that. We'll find a way to see each other again soon. I promise." She then pulled a couple of bags off the couch.

"I packed a bag of stuff for you two. Some of the things you may need. And in the other bag, there's some food since I know how the rations at the Corps can be."

"I wish I had more time to get to know you again, Maryn," Katam said with teary eyes. "but I want you to know you're still one of my little bros. We'll be looking out for you both in any way we can."

Maryn pulled the crystal comm Fina had given him out of his pocket, putting it on the coffee table. "This is the best way to contact us. If anything happens."

"Where did you get that?" Rioba asked with wide eyes.

"From my uncle, Hyanth. It's safe."

"How did it go?" Nirima asked in a hushed voice, unsure if it was safe to ask. Aniklo and Maryn both looked to each other, then at the rest of the group.

"Let's just say things could have gone better . . ." Aniklo then looked at Rioba, contemplating whether he should speak his next words until he finally did. "He helped, um . . . he has a lot of knowledge about—"

"I know," Rioba said, her eyes glassy. "I spoke to her last night."

Katam had a look of confusion etched onto his face. "Wait . . . you spoke to—"

"I don't want to know any more," Nirima interjected, taking a deep breath to calm her nerves before continuing. "I vowed I would never get involved in this a long time ago, and now that you are, I did everything I could to set you on the right path to finish it."

A swirl of emotions were in her eyes as she looked at Aniklo and Maryn. "If I would have known this burden would fall on the two of you, I would have taken care of it before all of this ever resurfaced. I've given you everything I know, and now, it's time."

Aniklo didn't notice he was crying until he felt his tears dampen his shirt, and he urgently swept them away, sweeping his hair out of his face right after.

"I'm sorry, Ma" was all Maryn could think to say.

"The whole point about what she said was that you shouldn't be," Katam spoke up, rubbing a hand on Maryn's back. "But, now it's time for you to carry the torch."

After Katam's words, Aniklo forced himself to pick up his bag still resting on the couch, slung it over his shoulder, and turned to hug his family members. They all huddled in an embrace, Aniklo picking Astoria up to kiss her on the cheek, doing his best to hide his sobs.

"This isn't the end, Aniklo," Nirima said with conviction, the two of them the last to let go. She was the first to pull away, taking Astoria out of his hands and wiping his tears. "This isn't the end."

Aniklo couldn't stand to look at his home, his family, his niece any longer, and after he said his last goodbyes and wiped his snotty nose, he burst through the doors and made his way to the docks.

Maryn, despite the isolation he had been carrying for almost a decade, was reluctant to take his bag and follow Aniklo out the door, but when Nirima shoved it into his hand, he grabbed it before it hit the ground.

"Take care of him" were Nirima's final words. The three adults in House 475 C watched the other two walk away, heading toward the crowd at the sea's edge.

====

The only way to describe the ride back to the Mainland was to call it stiff. The walkers were more like statues than shuttle occupants. Jessik and an couple of other Corps officials spoke on the opposite side of the shuttle while Aniklo and Maryn stared out into the waters. Both wondered if this would be the last time they would see the family.

Toward the end of the ride, the head watcher's voice boomed across the shuttle's confines:

"Listen up, everyone. The shuttle will be depositing us at the docks in approximately ten minutes. Because the Mainland is compromised, you will need to be on high alert. Team one, you will be escorting the Corps workers back to their workplace. You will be moving in a diamond formation with any workers in the middle of it. Team two, you will be heading back to the stations to be redistributed.

"Everyone, although there are uncompromised people on the streets, you are not to engage with anyone outside of our circle, whether they look sick or not. Do not touch any mushy shapes, bones, or other things along the way to your location. If you do any of these things, you will be left behind. I repeat. Do not touch anything that looks compromised."

The shuttle whirred to a stop, the watchers associated with team one gathering around the Corps workers. They all prepared for what they would encounter on the streets.

The shuttle doors opened, the sight before them a blurry memory of the one Aniklo and Maryn had seen on their last trip to the night market. Except, it was more like what they imagined the aftermath would be. Skin particles that resembled slime were smeared on buildings, and a few straggling, immobile dead showed through the formation of the watchers guarding them. Aniklo had to hold back the urge to throw up, trying desperately not to focus on the bones littering the streets.

Beside the gore on the walkway, a few heavily veiled scavengers were walking in formation, all heading in the direction of the general market.

"These damn idiots." One of the watchers in team one mumbled in the formation. "Hey! Go home to safety. We will be supplying homes with the goods shortly!" He shouted.

The head watcher stopped the formation to watch the scroungers scatter, dodging grime to cut in between houses and get away from the cluster of watchers and workers.

"You shouldn't have scared them away, Conner," The watcher beside the man insisted. "They could have been infected."

"Everyone quiet! Let's keep moving. Keep the formation tight and your mouths shut," The head watcher instructed as they were pushed along down the residential streets lining the Outer Rim and into the working district.

When they reached the market entrance a couple streets away from the Corps, it was blocked off. A wave of soldiers wielding stunners and armed to the teeth stood guard, the tattered destruction of some skinny stands still visible behind the wall of defense. His home, their home, brought to ruin by darkness.

"Where is everybody?" Aniklo asked.

Jessik whispered back, "The streets near the docks were cleared out yesterday evening. Most are in shelters inside the market bounds, and others deemed unfit for shelter are nervous about being scanned for mist. So, they're still wandering the streets. We've tried to gather everyone who can help at the Corps."

The echo of her heels cracked loud as shotguns in the silent streets.

They were feet away from the entrance to the Corps when the darkness struck. Thick mist rose from in between the cracks of the cobblestone streets, making themselves known through the rifts in the soil, a clouded humanoid wave readying itself to strike. A crackling static and ripples emanated through the air, the only noise it originally made until finally it let out a shrieking roar. Particles of the dead and old flesh left behind became animated, possessed by the dark mist, ready to strike.

"Move!" The guard yelled, Jessik rushing to the front of the group to signal for the Corps' heavy doors to open for them. A delay for the signal to go through stretched to infinite seconds, the mist and animated flesh advancing rapidly. A couple of the guards who moved out of their diamond formation to defend were the first to be picked off, skewered by the blackness. A few others sliced at the animated bodies. The beasts attacked by slathering some of their infected skin onto its assailants, causing the guards to cry out.

All Maryn and Aniklo could do was watch on, huddling as close to the door as possible until it finally began to open. The group desperately made it past the entrance, Maryn pulling Aniklo through the open door seconds before it shut.

"Are you okay?" He looked Aniklo over, a hand on his shoulder, another smoothing down his hair that had gotten blown around by the thick air.

"I don't think I'll ever get used to this." Even the simple comfort of Maryn's touch couldn't make Aniklo take his eyes off the sight from right outside the window: the dead skewered bodies of the walkers who had been charged to protect them, smears of fresh blood on the glass, the rush of black seeping into and out of the earth, the lives continuously ending before him. He wanted all of this to end.

From the horrified look on Maryn's face and the twinge of feelings Aniklo sensed through their tether, he knew Maryn felt the same.

Their conversation was cut short by the loud whir of a pure, metallic-charged mistic wall sinking over the windows of the entrance way, tinting the outside world a dark hue. Other people filled the room besides Jessik and the officials. A couple of groups who perhaps had just made it in from their separate locations watched as they were slowly being closed off from the world. There was protest, murmurs of confusion. Despite the risk stagnancy brought, regret tangled knots inside Aniklo's gut, and he wondered if continuing their search for answers was the right thing to do.

"Everyone, this way," Jessik said, beckoning stragglers huddled in the entranceway to the lift as she stepped inside of it. Once some of the officials and stragglers, including Aniklo and Maryn, made it to the lift, it started slowly upward. They were all scrunched into the mobile contraption, the hyperventilating of others like panicked music in Maryn's ears, as they continued to ascend. But instead of landing on their usual floor, the passed it, and they all watched as they passed the fifth and headed to the sixth floor.

"Why are we moving to the top floor?" A girl's shaky voice behind Aniklo asked as the lift whirred to a stop.

"That's where everyone else is gathered." A man with graying, straight, shoulder-length hair, who Aniklo vaguely recognized as the head of the transportation development floor, swung the door open in front of them, revealing the contents of the room.

Thousands of people were crammed into the large room that was essentially the attic of the Synthesis Corps. Aniklo had only been up here before a couple of times, but the walls and all the equipment and files from before were gone. The entire sixth floor was open for all to see. The space was lit by mistic light orbs, which were stuck to the walls to distract from the darkness created from the Corps' new boundary.

Besides the rows of people existing within it, everything was empty except for a long shelf along the far walls, where dormant amarite projectors lay stacked on top of one another. Within the sea of people, Aniklo saw some faces he could recognize from several departments, and despite the cramp, he could see circles taped on the floor the size of large desks spread all throughout the space.

Maryn quickly grabbed Aniklo's arm when they were forced to integrate into the packed space as everyone swiftly pushed their way out of the lift. After standing on his tippy-toes to see above the crowd, he spotted the leaders from each department gathered near the amarite-laden shelves.

Jessik and the other officials from the elevator joined the others, cutting through to head to the front.

"Why do you think they have us gathered here?" Aniklo asked.

"I don't know . . . this wall around the building, it has to be exerting an extreme amount of mist. The power source will only hold for so long," Maryn said just before a whistle cut through the air, bringing the murmurs to a slight halt and catching some people's attention, but not enough for complete silence.

"I need everyone's attention, please!" A deep voice boomed from the front. The crowd of people, finally silent, directed their attention to the front of the room. Jessik's face appeared above the crowd, presumably by stepping on a stool, the rest of her body blocked by the sea of heads.

"I'm sure you all recognize me as the head of the Mistic Border Regulation Team. I have spent decades studying the capabilities and power that lies within the mist, just like most of you. I'm sure you know the current mist is unlike anything our settlement has seen. In the wake of one of the most unexpected and tragic events, I stand before you to tell you that you have been ordained as the saviors of the Mainland and of the general Ponsn area.

"A horrific disease has plagued our streets, something evil brewed up by the scum of our lands. With your expertise, we hope to eradicate this threat. We will be using the same technology we use to heal the ailments that rise up on the borders, to take out the dark mist appearing from the earth. We will put an end to the hold it has over our streets."

A small cluster of people clapped after she finished talking, which led to the whole room erupting in applause. Jessik clearly bathed in the applause before quicky silencing everyone.

"From now on, The High Council has decreed that the Corps' workers will be quarantined here while working to stop the dark mist until it is eradicated. We have put up a mistic wall of our own for your own safety and to keep everyone and everything undesirable contained."

The room's atmosphere changed from excitement to confusion, and one by one, people began calling out, questioning. When could they see their families again, how could the Corps guarantee the safety of people they care about outside?

Jessik took it all in stride. Eventually, she made a statement:

"The walkers outside are dedicated to rescuing everyone in need and bringing them to the shelters set up at the market. We are all trying our best to address the situation in the most plausible way. From now on, we at the Synthesis Corps are no longer serving the needs of special interests. For the time being, we all have one common goal:

getting everything back to normal. Your work, once all of this is said and done, will be rewarded generously."

After she was done speaking, Jessik stepped down, and the man with silver hair from the elevator stepped up.

"Hello, everyone. I am Winther Nowar, head of the Comm and Technological Regulations and Development Department. The crystal amarite workstations behind me are what you will be using to evaluate and stomp out the mist. In a single file, you will come to collect the amarite stage you will use. Afterward, you will be paired into groups of five. Each group will be focused on a singular spot of the isles where dark mist has sprung up, and you will work as a team to regulate that area."

Neither Aniklo nor Maryn could see what was happening on the far side of the room, but after Winther stepped down, the wave of people moved. People shifted as they got paired up with their teams.

"Stay close to me, okay," Maryn said to Aniklo, who he was still holding on to. The other boy nodded softly, preparing himself for the task ahead.

Chapter 11

The passage's humidity underneath the waters left the thin material of their clothes sticking to their skin. The iridescent walls were shiny, much like the amarite used to build the most expensive houses on the isles, but it wasn't as thick. The dark blue tint of them alluded to the suffocating waters a small barrier away from engulfing them. The crystals that lit the pathway were few and far between, adding more and more to the suffocation Tauro felt.

"How much longer?" he asked for the tenth time.

In normal circumstances, Nebu would have been more inclined to turn around and slap Tauro, but for once, they were on the same page. "Yeah. The humidity is really messing with my hair."

"How could you even be thinking about your dumb hair right now . . ."

The obnoxious sounds of their banter faded to the background of Fina's mind, and she didn't even bother to answer Tauro. Her concentration was too preoccupied by her racing thoughts. It had been a while since she had taken this passageway, but the distance between the crystal lights on the wall were always a guide.

Walk 'til you find crystal lights side by side.
Lest you risk being swept out by the tide.

The chant was fresh in her mind, making her speed up her pace as the distance between the lights got closer and closer. After another twenty minutes, she stopped.

The twin light fixtures marked the end of their passage and beginning of the city on the right side of the walls. Ripples of water were more visible through the translucency.

"This is it." Fina turned to the others, who she just noticed were still arguing.

"Enough!" she yelled, effectively shutting them up. "The two of you are wanted as fugitives. The disguise I gave you won't be enough if you don't get your acts together and start acting like adults. That means settling your differences and stopping the petty arguments! You're in your late twenties for crying out loud." She then turned to Nebu. "And to be honest, the only reason you're included in the hunt for the ley lines is because we see you, Nebu, as a part of our group, our people. Act like it."

Nebu swallowed, playing with a loose strand of her hair. "I understand. Thank you."

"Of course, Nebu." She then turned back to the twin lanterns, placing both into each other like she had done many times, the connectivity between them causing a rift in the center of the passageway. A blue energy pulled water into a whirlwind, swirling before them, blocking their way forward.

"Woah." Tauro adjusted the bag on his back, his brown eyes wide. "So, what now?"

"We go through. We'll need to join hands so we'll land together, and it's only a couple blocks away from the safe house. Once we get there, we'll start mapping out the ley lines."

The two women had already joined hands and secured their bags around them, but Tauro was still complacent, a swirl of nerves forming in his stomach.

"Who's to say that when we go through, you won't just turn us in for the reward? You said yourself that you could do this without us."

"Because the two are a part of this as much as I am. We all have remnants of mist on us. Turning you in would be the dumbest thing I could ever do. They would catch me, too. Besides, you're my only safe connection to the dark mist." A flicker of Hyanth's limp body flashed before her eyes, a reminder that time was short for all of them. She pushed the memory away before it could expand and consume her and reached out her hand for Tauro to grab.

They stood eye to eye, a challenge evident in Fina's gaze. "If we're going to do this, you need to trust me." After a couple more seconds of reluctance, Tauro finally grabbed her hand, and without another word, Fina thrust the three of them into the portal, through the swirling waves, and up into the open air.

===

The portal opened on the market's grounds, softly depositing them in the northern sector of the isles, the opposite direction of the Corps near an secluded area. The pathway, like all other regions on the Mainland, was overrun with leftover bone fragments. The flimsier stands, completely eaten away, blocked some parts of the market's narrow path. If someone looked closely at the desolation, they could see people hidden away in the wreckage.

Nebu guessed they hid out of fear of being caught by the watchers for illegal mistic influence. Or perhaps, the shelters on the market's side near the medistation were already overflown and the mile-long walk was too dangerous to risk. But, the group of three didn't look closely, the panic of exposure a hovering cloud above them.

Tauro and Nebu followed closely after Fina, both of then barely allowing themselves the luxury of a full breath, too caught up in keeping completely quiet as they ventured farther north. Nebu didn't even have the brain space to wonder about their exact location. The prospect of a watcher catching them kept them all on their toes.

They breached the end of the general market, crossing the streets into the run-down district near the Mainland's edge. The amarite that formed the homes was noticeably flimsier, the abundance of vines lining the homes slowly withering under the weight of the thickened air. The architectural details were stripped to barren mediocrity in these parts, the streets clear except for the residue of death: the remnants of what had happened and what could happen again.

Tauro and Nebu knew this was the housing district of the less fortunate, the people who resorted to tedious fishing jobs and scraped by with what they sold at the outer, desolate corners of the market. Tauro especially knew the watchers circulated these parts more than any other place on the Mainland. Though he didn't know if their routes had changed with the wild surges plaguing the isles, he felt in his bones there was a higher likelihood of them being caught here. The thought brought goosebumps to the surface of his skin.

Carefully, they stuck to the shadows as they moved through the streets, passing by a couple motionless transportation shuttles left empty at their ports, taking cover behind houses when a spare watcher came prowling by.

"We're almost there. Just one more street over," Fina informed them in a whisper as soft as the wind when she knew the coast was clear.

Fina let out a sigh of relief when they finally reached their designated street, leading them with enthusiasm toward a house in the middle with wooden stands that held potted plants displayed on its front lawn. She knew the house was their ticket to temporary safety, but that relief was stomped out at the sight of what stood before them. She pulled the others behind an overgrown bush a couple of houses away from their location, a troop of watchers coming down the opposite side of the street. The uniformed thump of their boots made their blood run cold.

The watchers went from house to house, zigzagging down the street, the sound of their inquiries about stray civilians ringing in Fina's ears. The beeping scanners, a familiar ring, brought Tauro to attention. The full group of watchers eventually came into view when they reached the front of their safe house. The watcher with the scanner stepped up to the front porch, extending the locational mechanism toward the front door. When it beeped two times, Tauro knew they were aware someone was in the house, knew their plan to take refuge was becoming more and more unrealistic by the second.

The walkers, knowing someone was inside, banged a heavy hand against the door, the sound reverberating down the empty street. Fina, her mindscape an echo chamber of panic, didn't know what to do, where else to go, and how to save her friend on the inside.

"We know you are here. We will give you exactly one minute to come out with your hands up," The walker's deep voice boomed into the doorway, the others behind him readying their blasters.

That was when Fina glanced back, spotting exactly what she hoped not to see. Wes, her friend, and only connection on the Mainland, prowled around the house's side, donned in nondescript clothes that contrasted their pale skin. The ends of their ponytail caught on the house's ridges as they slinked their body directly against the walls, moving in the direction of the watchers.

"What are they doing?" Tauro asked in a quiet panic, but by then, it was too late. The watchers, having had enough of the wait, busted down the door with a powerful blast from their stunners, the residue of mystic energy leaving a heavy stench of smoke in the air. After the intensity of the blast subsided, all the watchers turned their attention from the street to inside of the small house.

Wes knew it was the perfect time. He detached themselves from the house, and with a quick movement, dug into their pocket and shot a ball of light out of their hand. The contraption swirled in the air, landing in the middle of the fray. By the time the watchers noticed, it was too late. The ball of light exploded, shooting the group of watchers in all directions. The mist encased within the contraption chewed through their armor, some were forced to lie on the dirty cobblestone while others were thrown against the house walls.

Wes, after the waves of the explosion had subsided, made a run for it in the direction that the three others had come.

"Wes, duck!" Fina yelled from their cover behind the bush as she helplessly saw a watcher, whom the bomb had only slightly affected, stand up and take a shot toward Wes. He barely dodged the energy blast hurling toward them.

There was no time to waste. Fina, Tauro, and Nebu all ran from their hiding place, catching up with Wes, who was sprinting at top speed toward the safety of the cluttered market.

"What's going on!" Nebu yelled in panic, looking back to see the watchers who hadn't been badly injured bolting toward their group, blasters charged and loaded. The ones desperate enough to seek revenge shot shaky blasts that only connected with the ground and houses the group was dodging behind.

"No time to explain." Wes huffed. The group sprinted for blocks until they finally reached the bounds of the market. "Our safehouse is compromised. We need to try to outrun them."

Wes threw more bombs of light behind them, the sounds of their explosive reactions and the sizzling of desolated stands only a whisper in comparison to their beating hearts. The group followed Wes as they passed under fallen storefronts, weaving through the maze to try and lose their assailants.

Despite their efforts to escape, blasts shot in their direction, a sizzled charge scraping a huge gash against Wes' pale skin, making them cry out. Tauro and Nebu's injured legs were stifling their efforts to move fast, the ache of Tauro's sore ankle a deep pain. They were panting loudly, desperately running to unknown safety. The bombs Wes threw back as a distraction only kept their assailants at bay for a couple seconds. The ones at the front raised their shields to prepare for impact before the shock of the blast was triggered.

"We can't keep running forever." Tauro huffed, sweat dripping off of him and dampening his shirt. The cloak he had donned as a disguise shredded by the heat of a rogue blast.

"We have to try," Fina said, her voice cracking with exhaustion. Seconds later, she tripped on a rogue piece of wood blocking their pathway. Nebu mustered up the strength to drag Fina out of the watcher's path, still hot on their trail.

After a couple more zigzags through the market lanes and another reverberation of Wes' bombs was felt, their luck, unfortunately, ran out. They had reached the bubble that signified the end of the abandoned market and the beginning of the populated region, where civilians had been forced to congregate. The boundary encasing everyone expanded on both sides, watchers brought to attention by their abrupt appearance. In the second it took the escapees to realize they had reached a dead-end, the watchers who had been following them for miles closed in on all sides. They sneered in triumphant as they raised their stunners directly at Tauro and the others.

Wes, in defiance, reached into their pocket for another blast that could set them free but was stunned to realize no bombs were left. There was nothing left for them to do but stand there and allow the watchers to close in.

"What now?" Tauro asked over his shoulder to Wes, whose face had turned as white as a sheet of paper.

Nebu instinctively grabbed onto Tauro and Fina's arms, closing her eyes and preparing for the sting of being shot, but surprisingly, that sting never came.

"Stand down!" a masked watcher announced to the crowd of soldiers, his deep voice carrying across the enclosed space. "Come in with us, and you will not be harmed!"

"But sir—" A watcher beside him objected, but the masked watcher quickly raised his hand to shush them.

"Silence!" the man boomed, and after putting his blaster to the side, he pulled off his mask, revealing himself.

Tauro gasped slightly at the sight of his boss, and for the first time since he had been back on the isles, he was forced to put a face to the people before him, the people threatening his life. Rivera's face had a deep gash on the side, his thick brows scrunched together, jaw clenched and eyes steely. The older man ducked his head, searching to see their faces as clearly as they could see his.

"Tauro, if you stop running and surrender with your hands up, I will try my best to negotiate with the Council to get a better sentencing for you. I know you're a good man, and you don't deserve to be held accountable for whatever accident —"

The rumbling of the ground beneath them cut Rivera's voice short and sent everyone in the small sector of the market quaking under the power of its movement. Suddenly, underneath Tauro's feet, the cobblestones turned soft, then sandy, and in a flurry of movement, before Tauro or any of his friends could react, the ground sucked each of them away from the watchers surrounding them. Down into its depths.

===

Their pants of breaths seemed to echo audibly in the darkness they had fallen into.

"What happened." Tauro rasped in between gasps for air.

In the blink of an eye, the pitch-black was eaten by a light positioned right in front of the stunned group. Holding that light was a robed figure, the only amount of skin showing was their clawed, disfigured hand engulfed in fur and clasping an orb of light. Another paw clutched a wooden staff.

"Come," the figure said in a slick voice. "Safety is just down this walkway."

None of them moved, all of them squinting in the dim light, and after a second of awe passed, Wes was the first to speak up.

"Who are you?"

At that, the figure unveiled their hood, revealing an unimaginable face. The person's face was dominated by a reddish-brown layer of thin fur. Their noses connected to their mouths in an animalistic fashion, eyes slim and swirling. The thin sheen of fur on the person's face matched their hands, slipping back to a well-kept, curly ponytail that extended down their back. The animalistic figure eyed them all, watching their silence as they took her in with an almost predictable amusement.

"Knowing me isn't your biggest concern at the moment, Wes. You should be worried about escape, and I guarantee you, the refuge I have is much better than the one you had planned."

"How do you know my name?" Wes asked.

"I know the name of everyone who steps foot into my night market, everything that is sold, and I know who is and isn't safe."

Everyone was in awe of this strange woman's omission of her connection to the night market, but Fina wasted no time reveling in the potency of her words. She reached for the knife tucked securely in her boot, but the woman standing over them sensed it and threateningly raised her staff. Sparks of electric energy rode from staff's end as it pointed directly at Fina. The older woman's face was serene, devoid of panic or tightness.

"I get you are stressed right now, but I just wasted precious energy to save you all. Don't make me regret it."

With a flick of her staff, they were all forcefully pressed flush against the ground, and in a fluid movement, the rock beneath them wrapped around their limbs in a cage. A soft patch of soil and grassy vines quickly sprung out of the rock, gagging their mouths and snaking across exposed skin. The furry woman then stabbed her staff into the rocks underground. The slab that imprisoned them dislodged from the passage, hovered over the earth, and carried them behind the woman.

They all sat still, anticipating what was next, and despite the furry woman's quick rescue, Fina was most ready to strike at a moment's notice.

Nebu studied the woman's almost familiar face from her vantage on their hard, moving slab, analyzing the fur that blew with the wind created by their makeshift conveyor. She was enamored by the stranger who defied the laws of science and medicine.

"Spit it out, girl," the woman said to Nebu, sights never shifting from the tunnel as she willed Nebu's gag away. Staff moving left and right, the woman controlled their direction. They made some fast turns, lifting up, plunging down, and turning in, going at a pace that made it almost impossible to keep track of their location, but slow enough Nebu could still speak.

"It's just, from my research of mistic influence on the body, people with your condition can't control the urges turning animalistic brings. I've researched thousands of cases of Animoa like yours. The cases I've treated so late a stage in your condition have never been this coherent." The gag slapped back across her face before she could continue.

"You should know better by now. After seeing the way the Mainland has been quickly overtaken, the Corps and the mistic research facility aren't exactly all-knowing or capable of protecting the common people. And they aren't exactly the epitome of lawful good either." She turned to view her captives as their slab of stone came to a stop against a dead-end.

"People like me, people the council forces the mistic researcher and medical officials to deem mistic mutations, aren't doomed to a slow death the way it is perceived."

She then stabbed her staff against the dead-end wall, causing it to slide open and release them all from their encasement. They all jumped to attention, stepping away from the slab of rock melting back into the ground before them, and when they could finally see around them, the view was completely unexpected.

Behind the wall was a luscious expanse of rocky terrain, covered lines with moss and grass. The central part of the massive space was reserved for farming. Rows and rows of raised garden beds packed with vegetables and fruit were being picked by Animoa covered in fur. Trees provided partial shade throughout the cave. Around the walls of the encasement were large tents lined with thick fibers, an artificial sun beating down and casting the greenery in the space with a rich light.

"My name is Penoa. I bring you here with the promise of peace. I know what you have endured getting here, and unlike the watchers who had threatened your life minutes ago, all I wish to do is help." Penoa's voice was silky, her eyes absorbing the four of them, and despite the precarious circumstances that led them here, Nebu automatically was willing to explore.

Before Nebu could take more than a single step, Fina grabbed her arm, yanking her back.

"What if we don't want to come in?" Fina said defensively, her eyes slit and stance spread.

Penoa blinked at Fina before furrowing her brows. "What other choice do you have? To go back to the open air, where the walkers are waiting to slay you? I brought you here with both of our best interests at heart. I believe we both need more of the same thing."

The hand that controlled the casting of the orb of light was now brought out before the group, and with a flick of her wrist, the light was shifted, turning electric and crackling upon her fingertips. The orb now changed in its level of vibrance with a weighted, pulsating energy, ornate inscriptions shifting faintly along its surface. Fina, just at this sight alone, dropped her guard and stepped forward, hands skirting across the surface of the new ball of essence.

"Ley line energy . . . How did you—"

"I'll explain everything once we get situated," Penoa said, her eyes filled with slight mirth as she flicked her wrist once more. The ball of ley line energy disappeared into a void beyond Fina's grasp.

"This way," Penoa said, and with a repositioning of her cloak, she moved through the open wall into an alcove, the four others too lost for words to do anything but follow.

Something about the layered ambiance of Penoa's welcome, the familiarity and knowing extension of her gaze, made it seem to both Wes and Tauro that the space before them was only a glamour concealing something wild and untamable.

The four followed Penoa through the large cave. Their path cut through the middle of the expanse, which allowed for a more detailed look at the raised gardens and hidden alcoves etched into the walls. Animoa people of all varieties, and regular people mixed among them, watched their trek, some waving and saluting to Penoa.

They eventually made it to a large tent ornamented with beaded chains at the very end of the cave's expanse. Two almost identical Animoa with antlers protruding from their light brown hair stood posted at the opening of the tent. The girl to the left of the opening, saluted Penoa, and opened the tent for them all to enter.

Penoa's space was filled with gadgets carved from tough rock, and formerly molten amarite littered the shelf on the left side of the room along with a stone desk which blended in with the ground of the cave. The ceilings were lined with beaded chains that glowed despite not catching the light of the sun, and two couches were propped up on the left and right sides of the tent walkway. The couch composed of a rocky foundation with soft cushions to make it comfortable.

A rug of moss stretched throughout the entire floor of the tent, and Penoa was the first to step on it, walking around her desk to hang up her cloak, then back to sit on the sofa. She sat close enough for the four who had already rested on the couches to see the intricate details of her thin, tawny red fur.

"What is this place?" Nebu and Fina asked together.

"Why did you save us?" Tauro asked.

"Are you the market master?" Wes asked.

They all spoke simultaneously, the slap of her staff against her desk the only thing able to shut them up. She slouched against her desk, looking at them as she began to speak.

"Yes. I am the market master. I've been cultivating a bubble of mistic illusionary energy around the night market for the past twenty years, that is until Aniklo and Maryn came, shattering it with the contents of that box behind the market."

"How do you know their names?" Tauro jumped in defense, almost hitting Nebu with his elbow as he got up.

"As I said, I know everyone who steps foot into the night market, but I knew you before he came on my radar. I've known your whole family." The familiarity he felt in her bright eyes and steady gaze, in her build and soft hand, finally set in, and he was instantly hit with a realization.

"You're Penoa? The Penoa from the market who sells jams?" As he uttered her name, he remembered fond times when he would run errands with his mother, perusing through the crowds to buy the best fruit, always prioritizing a stop by Penoa's stand to get her newest supply of jam.

She smiled slightly at his surprise. "I was wondering when you'd figure that out, but that was just a side hustle—slash cover job, something to keep me under the radar until the time was right."

"So, what was the night market to you, then?" Nebu asked.

Her smile waned, and her posture became more structured. "It was my job to weed out all the people who could be a danger to the space of intrigue and freedom. A goal I have been working to cultivate. I've been waiting for a sign for a long time, and the events of the past couple of nights are all I need."

"A sign for what?" Fina questioned, scooting up to the very edge of the couch.

Penoa's face was alight with vigor, her eyes burning into them like hot coals. "The Animoa have been a target of medical discrimination since the beginning of the new Ponsn we know today. We were created by the shift in the mistic barrier, causing the connection to nature integral to instilling a sense of balance to humanity and the mist's relationship. We have been experimented on, mutilated, to the point of near extinction, to the point where people like my grandmother, the person who started this underground settlement, had to run away."

"And in the most recent decades, the Corps and medical affiliates have formulated deadly medicines to wipe out the Animoa for good." She sat back from her impassioned rant, leaning back to take a swig of water from a cup on her desk before continuing.

"So, to answer your question, I want exposure and acceptance for my people, and to get that, I'm going to need to take down the Corps and rewire the Council." The radical weight of her words sent a jolt through all of them, and Tauro's face contorted in disgust.

"Is that why you created the dark mist in your market? To start a revolt?"

At Tauro's accusation, the woman guffawed harshly, sitting back in her seat in disbelief.

"You think I would destroy my precious market, my people's only authentic connection to the outside world?

You think I would destroy the rest of the outside world so callously just to gain nothing from it but more hatred? I will guarantee you, better yet, I will swear on my life I never knew the dark mist would spring up in the markets until it did."

"Then why else would you need your market to fall apart for you to take action? You said yourself you were waiting for Aniklo and Maryn to messed everything up?"

"The box from the catacombs behind the inner market's wall is not what brought on the dark mist, but it's potent content is. Whatever was in there was stronger than any sort of mist I've ever tampered with, and I could never open it. But, I knew, in my bones, whatever it was would lead me to something beneficial. Something big. I never expected it to attract the dark mist.

"But now that it's here, now that things are unraveling to such a large extreme, it is time for us to act against the Corps. They, as well as the Council, singlehandedly carried out a mass genocide against the Animoa. They continue to criminalize mist worked outside of their narrow-minded intent. It's time to unravel their lies and expose them for what they are. I know you four are on a mission to do the same. That is why I brought you here."

"What if we say we don't wish to make an alliance with you?"

"If you walk out of here without my protection, you will most likely be tortured endlessly by the hands of the Council for treason. If you stay here, I will provide for you and set you up with a team to help collect ley line energy for us both. You can easily collect all we need, and we can go our separate ways."

Fina hung onto Penoa's every word, a sour taste collecting in her mouth. She could grasp the intellect and planning behind Penoa's words, could grasp the other woman had a hint of foresight Fina didn't have the fortune of tapping into. Fina didn't like walking into things that felt too easy, but she kept her mouth shut and waited for everyone else's reaction.

"They wouldn't really kill us," Tauro said, putting on a convincing face despite the confusion in his voice. The image of his boss reaching out to him before he fell into the earth flashed before his eyes. Tauro, in this time of uncertainty, scrambled for a reason to claim it couldn't be that bad. "The maximum punishment is reassignment to the Outer Rim and—"

"I admire your insistent positivity, but let's remember the predicament you were in when I saved you. You were being shot down by walkers less than an hour ago. The Corps and the council has issued a bounty out on your head. They are hunting down anyone with traces of mist on the streets. This is not a time of fairness and safety in the eyes of the law. Our warded section of the catacombs is the safest place you could ever be."

"Could you give us a moment to talk privately? A lot has been happening recently, and we would really appreciate a chance to catch our breaths and regroup." Wes spoke up, and after a pause, Penoa nodded, lips tightly drawn in.

"I will be right outside the tent."

As soon as she left, Wes started pacing back and forth. "What have we gotten ourselves into?"

"What did you get us into?" Fina turned on Wes, the taller girl standing up to loom over him. "You said when we left the reserve, you and the house were clear and warded."

Wes gulped, nervously pulling at the ends of his sleeves. "I thought I did, too. I was working on a map of the ley lines, scoping out the best passage, when The Watch came knocking at my door."

He brought a hand to Fina's arm, looking up with pleading eyes. "Please believe me when I say I did everything I could."

A meaningful look passed between the two.

"I know, Wes." Wes sighed in satisfaction, glad Fina wasn't quick to blame him for it all before he turned awkwardly to the other two.

"Good to see the two of you are okay after everything. My name's Wes." Wes held out a hand, which Tauro reluctantly took.

"I've kinda caught on to who you are by now. I'm Tauro."

"You didn't have to be so rude, Tauro," Nebu said with a pointed frown.

"I was being polite."

"No, you were being a dick."

"Whatever." Tauro got up, wanting to be anywhere but next to Nebu, and went to look at the collectibles and hangings within the tent.

Wes shrank back into the couch, his leg tapping rapidly, leaning away from the tension hanging palpably between Nebu and Tauro. Everyone seemed at a loss for words, still processing all they had seen and experienced until Nebu finally broke the silence.

"I think Penoa is right when she says she's our best bet." Nebu's voice attracted everyone's attention. "She had the power to capture the energy of the ley lines without even casting a runic circle. And despite her crazy plans about taking down the government, she has everything we need."

"As much as I hate to say it, I agree with Nebu. I didn't get a chance to take all the tech we need from my ley line research, and even if we left and went searching, we'll probably get caught."

"Part of me wonders what she'll do if she succeeds in starting this revolution she wants," Tauro spoke up from near Penoa's desk, his eyes avidly skimming a stack of paper with glyphs written on it.

"Da always said the Animoa aren't to be trusted, that their condition is a curse on the outside tribes from the mist. Not the blessing Penoa paints it to be."

"That sounds really hypocritical. Especially coming from the man who said a lot of the same things Penoa did about the world needing to change to accommodate your mistic abilities. Hyanth just said it in a less abrasive way." Nebu was picking at the back of her fluffy hair that had gotten matted down by the rocks. "And besides, the Mainland is already going to shit anyway. I want to survive this, and going outside will most likely get us killed. I want us all to survive this."

"I hate to say this, but I agree," Tauro said, nodding once, his arms crossed as he faced the group. The memory of all the watchers crowding around them brought out an icky feeling. It brewed in his limbs alerting him to the fact their attackers could have been someone he knew, and that reality struck him to his core. Despite that pang of betrayal, the daunting whiplash of the vast difference between his then and now, he knew there was no turning back. "This is our best bet right now."

Fina sighed, brushing a stray curl out of her face. "Okay. We stay. For now."

Chapter 12

*D*rowning. *Throngs of water flooded into Aniklo's lungs, into his bloodstream as he was pulled deeper and deeper under the waves. The pain in his leg pulsed from a bite, from tough jaws, a monster's sharp teeth wedged into his calf. There was no hope for escape, the bubbles of his last breaths trailing behind his prone body as he was dragged deeper and deeper below into black, inky water.*

Suddenly, the pulling stopped, the monster dislodging his long teeth and turning away. His blood fogged the water around him, the silhouette of a boy in the murky water. He knew what this was: this vision, this memory. He had played it in his head thousands of times, remembering in fine detail the monster biting Maryn's torso as he wrestled with it in hopes of saving Aniklo. He remembered how Maryn valiantly stabbed the beast and pulled Aniklo's almost unconscious body back to shore.

"Aniklo," Maryn had pleaded in the fog that was a memory, but now, it was different. They both somehow knew they were occupying a space between reality. And seconds after reaching the shore, Maryn's scrawny physique morphed into his more angular build of the present. The bite marks on his torso that had been profusely bleeding were now bumpy scarring.

As Aniklo felt the pain of his body stretching out, changing and widening to what it was now, he knew this was all another dance down memory lane.

"We're in it again. We're in another one," Aniklo said, his head still in Maryn's lap.

The mirror version of themselves, their younger fractal memories, seemed to shift to separate from this foggy reality, appearing next to them. The pain on a younger Maryn's face as he cradled a younger Aniklo, the blood gushing from his torso and from Aniklo's skinny legs, the adults running to the scene. It all appeared as a video they were only passers-by in, a memory they were forced to relive.

The older versions of the boys watched on, saw Katam urgently inspecting Maryn who was bleeding out. He was shouting about how the monsters weren't supposed to come anymore. Nirima and Selene ran seconds behind him. After a minute of coughing up black water, Aniklo and Maryn realized they were invisible to the crowd gathering around the disaster, the blue skies of that day hollow and unclear, crowding in on the isles.

Seconds later, the monstrosity that had attacked them rose from the deep and slithered onto the beach, the *group tending to their younger selves completely oblivious to its arrival.*

The fishy beast was larger than a man. Its beady eyes that shot out of its cylindrical, scaly head set on them. The beast's large fins skirted across the shore inching closer and closer in a crawl, leaving deep grooves in the sand. Remnants of their blood stained its teeth pink, and the boys, despite the urgency to get up, were stagnant. The pain of the memory the beast had caused too much, they watched until its mouth was inches from them, its teeth jutting out of their sockets, seconds away from rescraping flesh.

But, suddenly, it stopped, squealing, morphing into a whole new creature.

Its scales flaked off, its teeth shrinking, the internal mechanisms of its body compacting. Its long tail split in two, changing into the shape of a crawling man, brown and naked and afraid. The vision of the crowd tending to their younger selves bled back into a misty exterior, the rasping figure raised its head, a half-realized conjugation. Then, the figure of the moon, the figure of Miho, a slight vapor in the dulled void of the barren shoreline. Aniklo and Maryn's bones felt as fragile as lead. The wet gasps that vibrated out of Miho's shifting face struck terror in their core.

"Find me." He rasped. "Find me in the deep."

As if snatched back, the figure that resembled Miho was yanked apart, slicing neatly into a molecular vapor. Its brown aura shot through the waters, out of the reserve's territory, to the shore of the Mainland. Its screams emanated in their shared mind's eye.

The brown vapor was yanked back to the Synthesis Corps, the gush of its movement resembling a shriek as it was dragged into the vat of energy that powered the Corp. The space closed in around Miho, his booming voice withered to one of desperation. The vat was swirling like never before, the tint of brown stirring it up. Miho's labored wet rasps echoed, rising in tonality until it reached a screaming pitch, and a separate, deeper tone spoke above it.

"Find me. Own the truth. Own me. Find me, find me, find me!"

Screams of the dream snapped them into the waking world, leaving them gasping for air, desperate for safety. Sweaty and disoriented, they both shot up on their respective portion of the couch, Maryn almost violently falling to the floor.

Over the past couple of days, since their return back to the Corps, they had taken to sleeping in the living room of their dorm. They curled up on their separate parts of the couch as they waited for sleep to take them, waited for the mist that fueled their hidden glyphs to guide them. The clues they had received materialized in sparse messages, which could barely be placed. But now, after they had gotten an inkling of something, it all just felt more and more like a discombobulated mess.

Aniklo watched Maryn closely as they both tried to recover from the vivid pain and confusion of their dream. "Are you okay?" he asked.

"Yeah . . . It's just a lot, that's all."

Aniklo got up to get them both something to drink. After he settled back on the couch beside Maryn, they both stared out the window, analyzing the foggy swirls of mist that had overtaken the view of the waters: a consistent reminder of their captivity, of the fact there was no turning back.

"I thought . . ." Maryn's words seemed to catch in his throat, a subliminal blockage to keep him from sharing what was weighing him down. But after taking a sip, he turned to Aniklo and tried again. "I thought coming back to the Mainland would end this thing, this feeling that a crucial truth I've been chasing would finally sort itself out. That's what got me through my time at the Outer Rim. Knowing the truth of what happened was waiting for me here, if I only had the courage to get through."

He shook his head, the shadows beneath his eyes more pronounced as he looked down at his glass.

"Now, how do you feel?" Aniklo almost felt too scared to ask.

"I feel like he's taunting us. Nothing makes sense."

"I think . . . I think both of our childhoods ended when they died, ended when we were left to pick up the pieces of our formerly perfect worlds where nothing could ever go wrong. But maybe, everything had to go wrong for us to appreciate it when it finally falls into place."

"I wish they would stop showing us things I've been trying so desperately to forget."

"You wanted to forget us at our meadow?" It slipped out before Aniklo could stop it, and he turned away.

"You know what I mean" was all Maryn gave the other boy after a long beat of silence before changing the subject. "We should go there. The place where he ended in the dream. See what happens."

That was all Maryn could say, the fear of anyone watching holding his tongue. He was worried whether the buffering crystal he had hidden away in his box of treasures was enough to protect them all.

"You want to take it there." The weight of the only accessible piece of their father's harnesser was a conscious living thing inside the tether that connected them. It thrummed through the mist trapped in the glyphs tattooed on their arms, a constant reminder of how close they both were to getting caught. "If we take it out and we're wrong, then I don't think we'll be able to put it back in before they detect it."

"It's the only thing that I can think of. We need to try."

Aniklo knew Maryn was right, but breaking the bounds of what was and wasn't allowed within the Corps was just another nail in the coffin for his former worldview, making the danger more and more real.

"We need to wait just a little longer. Gather more intel on the floor plan to figure out the watchers' blind spots, see our best chance of execution."

A knock jolted them out of the little bubble they were in, and they knew it was time to go. A watcher used a master set of keys to open their dorm door, scanning the area with their eyes for anything suspicious before saying, "Hello, Aniklo, Maryn. You have ten minutes to be dressed and ready for your shift."

Aniklo recognized the watcher as one of Tauro's old detective friends, but her bright smile and attentive hazel eyes were hidden behind the secure enclosure of the watcher's modified uniform. Their decked-out, padded attire and holsters full of several blaster mods made the watchers seem robotic and separate from their former selves outside the mask their armor created.

"Okay," they both said in unison, keeping their heads down in the millisecond it took for the guard to move to the next dorm. The woman forced say the same structured announcement after knocking on the door.

As Aniklo swiftly got ready and headed to the lift with Maryn and many other patrons of his floor, he couldn't help but feel as if the new structure being implemented in the Corps treated him like an emotionless subhuman, as something to be used and discarded.

Their daily routine was a simple redundant pattern that seemed to extend for eons. Each day since they'd returned, they would head to the sixth floor and set up their stations. Each person positioned themselves in the circular work areas that had been outlined on the floor since day one. Today, however, was slightly different.

After Aniklo and Maryn settled into their workstations along with the rest of their group, they noticed the watchers who normally stood outside were now lining the walls. They loomed over them, standing with a static stiffness Aniklo was positive he could never replicate.

"Don't look at them," Maryn instructed softly, poking him with his elbow.

Kreena, who Aniklo had been pleasantly surprised was included in their group, slid a piece of wrapped candy over to them both. "Just eat your candy, and do your work. It will be easier to ignore them hovering if you've got something to chew on."

Roan, who had been eavesdropping from a station adjacent to theirs, scoffed, turning a haughty eye to the three in disdain. "There's no need to be suspicious if you have nothing to hide. The watchers are here for our safety. Only people who have something to hide would be nervous around them." Roan's accusatory voice had caught the attention of most the floor. Most of them now turned from the calibrations visible on their stations to watch the conversation unfold.

"What are you insinuating, Roan?" Kreena spoke up, the wrinkles on her face pronounced by her deep frown.

"I'm just saying an invalid piece of Outer Rim scum like Maryn would be the perfect candidate for a suspect involved in creating the dark mist! And Aniklo is no better! Always hanging on his shoulder!"

"You've got no business making accusations you can't back up!" Aniklo spat, his face turning bright red. Maryn, despite his nerves building up, gave Aniklo a desperate look to shut up.

Before the conversation could continue any further, sirens issued throughout the building, snapping the boys and the rest of the room out of the intense argument. A walker raised a hand, and the siren cut out, drawing all of their attention to them.

"Due to a concern that has been brought up, all workers in the first three rows near the entrance will be brought to the walkers' lobby."

After the head watcher had spoken, Aniklo's group and twenty others were circled by the watchers, forced to stand up, and funneled out of their workspace and into the hallway. Then, they were made to take turns on the lift.

There were shouts for an explanation, but none were answered.

Aniklo and Maryn just tried their best not to lose it, tried their best to keep their breathing calm. They all knew what this was about, but Aniklo especially almost couldn't handle the anticipation and dread.

This could be it. Fina could have been wrong about our bond not being detected. They could know. They could have sensed it while we were dreaming.

Aniklo's mind sent him in a spiral as they settled in the corner of the packed lobby. Maryn's hand in his was the only thing grounding him.

Kreena huffed as she was forced to strain to sit down beside him. "All this up and down isn't good for my limbs," she complained softly, turning to the two of them as they waited for the rest of the room to fill up.

Kreena, leaned in after a couple of pants of exhaustion to say, "Don't listen to what that dumb idiot Roan said about you, Maryn. Ignorant people like him have no empathy in their hearts."

"I know." Maryn was stoic, only chancing a couple of glances at her between watching the crowd come in.

"No, but I mean it. There's beauty to endurance, to uniquity." Her eyes had a knowing glint to them. The wrinkles gathering with her sad smile added to her gaze's depth. "I can sense you two know more than you let on, but just know that even with everything going on, with all the accusatory glances and pointing fingers, there is still hope."

The two boys could read between the lines, feel the words left unsaid through the comforting squeezes she gave both their arms. But before they could say anything more, they realized the room had filled, and the guards with their backs to the entrance doors faced the workers, calling for their attention.

"We realize we have neglected to do a proper scan on the workers of this facility, mostly because we thought with your respectable statuses and dedication to the safety of the isles, there was no need to. However, we have recently seen a reason to conduct a proper scan for reasons we will not disclose today."

Despite the muffled effect the head walker's mask created on her voice, there was still a detectable venom that bellowed out with her words, one of her hands poised on her blaster as she spoke. Several heads turned in Aniklo's group's direction. The three tried to ignore the attention, tried to remain neutral.

"We are giving you, those who possess a potent amount of illegal mist, a chance. If you step forward and reveal yourself, the punishment will be less severe."

No one did, the silence as they waited deafening, and eventually, the head watcher signaled to the others that lined the room, the watchers all put into motion.

Aniklo felt as if he was outside himself as he saw the watchers gather the workers into rows, felt himself being pushed into lines, and observed the head watcher scan people one by one. In a charged silence riddled with angst, the only sound was the beep of the head watcher's scanner as row one through three were found secure.

Aniklo couldn't stop the nervous tapping of his leg.

They all, in horror, jumped when the first beep of invalidity issued from row four. A girl with shaggy hair and freckles began to cry, begging that they spare her, but there was no mercy. A short-range blast issued from the head watcher's blaster, shooting the girl, leaving a searing hole in her chest, her body swaying wildly before thumping to the floor. Her blood painted the amarite beneath in its deep stain.

The crowd was stunned, some crying out as they watched the girl drop to the ground, and others holding stone still. A couple of watchers came to drag the girl away toward the exit, her blood trailing behind her limp corpse.

"This is what happens to people who don't follow the rules now," the woman who fired the shot bellowed, silencing them all. "We no longer tolerate undesirable manifestations of mist. This is a danger to our kind, and anyone who is scanned and doesn't pass will be penalized."

The rows of five continued, people filing one after another, two more workers beeping red, two more workers getting shot. Aniklo realized in the minutes that transpired, as he watched the woman with the blaster get closer and closer, that the longer he stayed here, the more danger he would be in. There was no waiting, no complacency in gathering intel. There was no turning back.

The scanner blazed over the two of them when it was their turn to be analyzed, the beam's slow process almost painful. Finally, it turned green for them, and a weight was lifted off his heavy shoulders, the worried monologue that ran through his head stifled by his temporary safety.

And then, there was Kreena.

The whole room watched the scanner go over her, knew the terror of its stinging light, but after a couple of seconds, the beam unexpectedly turned red. Her soft eyes widened, and she gasped, turning to look at Aniklo, but it was too late.

Aniklo and Maryn, with their eyes wide open, unable to look away. They watched Kreena take her last breath, saw the watcher raise her blaster to Kreena's chest and take the shot. He closed his eyes as Kreena's blood splattered over him on impact, felt the heat of it stain his blue tunic, his face, his hair.

Aniklo, at that moment, felt himself go farther away from his body, as the bile rose to his throat before he could stop it. His lunch came shortly after, slathering on his sneakers along with the blood of his dead.

Maryn dragged him to the side, barely able to hold back his own vomit. A numbness set over the two as they were ordered to go back to their rooms for a short rest to recover. The lobby was cleared of the dead as the protective barrier surrounding the building was momentarily dropped to eject the bodies like trash onto the dangerous streets, still littered with infected goo.

Once the two were safely back in their room, the door sealed and locked.

Aniklo turned to Maryn, a dead weight in his eyes. "We need to make an exit plan. Then, we go to the energy source."

Chapter 13

The group of four stayed overnight in a tent adjacent to Penoa's, the hanging cots positioned above the mossy floor plush and restorative, granting them a short respite to ready them for the days to come. Besides the cot, there was a large rock table that resembled Penoa's desk lined with a plush moss, and all the things they had gathered for their trip were securely supported by it.

Nebu was the first to wake, sitting back on a chair in front of the tent, enjoying the artificial sunset of the glamoured cave walls. The allure of the glamour gave the illusion of open space, making the stalactites on the high ceilings seem almost beautiful.

"Hey."

Nebu jumped at the sound of Tauro's voice beside her. She instinctively readjusted the bonnet on her head, pulling her shawl tighter around her. "Why are you up so early?"

"I could ask you the same thing," Tauro responded, his hands in his pants pockets.

Nebu rolled her eyes. "If you came out here to argue, you might as well walk right back inside before you embarrass yourself and me."

"Actually, I came out here to do the opposite." Approaching her cautiously like a wild animal, he tentatively sat down.

Nebu was on guard, her eyes scrunched. "I didn't say you could sit."

"I didn't ask."

"I thought you said you didn't want to argue."

"Well, it's really hard not to when you're being so confrontational!" After his outburst, he pinched the bridge of his nose, took a breath, then sighed. "I didn't come out here to do this."

"Then, what did you come out here to do?" Nebu said incredulously. "You're ruining my morning, and it's not even sunrise."

"To apologize. And to say we need to make a better effort at working together."

She softened her posture, sitting back slowly, as if this was the first time truly seeing him that morning. "Apologize for what exactly?"

"For blaming you for us being fugitives of the law or whatever. I realize now it was either getting eaten alive by the people we were trying to autopsy or escaping with you, and I'm glad I'm still alive. Because of you." Saying all that visibly pained him, but he knew it had to be done for the sake of peace.

Nebu let his response hang in the air for a beat, mulling it over before saying, "Is that all you're sorry for?"

Tauro crossed his arms, "What else do you want me to say, Nebu?"

She huffed in frustration. "It's not what I want you to say. It's what you should have said. The apology was nice. I'll give you that, but a sentence won't make me forgive you for everything you've done."

Tauro huffed, exasperated. "I've never done anything to you, Nebu. From the first day we met, you decided hating me was the only option, and ever since then, you've been a constant annoyance. With your holier-than-thou attitude, pettiness, argumentative disposition, and annoying vanity—"

"You are the most hypocritical person I've ever met. You say I have a holier-than-thou attitude when your entire being is attached to always being right. Always following the law and being perfect and judging everyone for not meeting your disgustingly high standard of existence. And the most pathetic thing about it is your lawful goodness didn't get you anywhere but almost dead." Her tirade ended with them both glaring daggers at each other.

Tauro's eyes were the first to loosen up, and he looked away. "I don't even know why I try anymore."

He moved to get up, but she stopped him, quickly clasping his arm.

"Wait."

"What is it now, Nebu," Tauro said, snatching his wrist out of her grasp, looming over her with his arms crossed.

"You're right. Just because we hate each other doesn't mean getting along isn't important. We're in this together now. As much as I can't stand you, I will make an effort to not noticeably hate you as much."

"Good," Tauro responded, not sure what being nice to Nebu truly looked like. The flap of the tent opening broke the tense moment of awkward silence between them, Fina stepping out with a smile.

"Good to see you two are finally getting along," she said, Wes trailing right behind her. Wes and Fina then sat in the two seats across from Nebu and Tauro, the group huddled together with the light of the artificial sunrise rising behind them.

"This was the only thing I managed to take with me when I left the safe house," Wes placed a disk-shaped piece of tech on the table, then pressed a button on its top surface. Before them, an illuminated holographic map of the Mainland, millions of lines crossing over at intervals on different points of the isles, sprang up. Five points of crossover between the varying lines were circled on the map.

"This is my triangulation of the ley lines for the next couple of days. The points of contingency are in a constant state of motion on the isles, so this map won't be a valid resource for long."

Penoa approached before Wes could continue on with more map descriptions, standing over their cluster of lawn chairs, a calculated yet warm smile present on her face.

"Nice to see all of you are up. Hope you all slept well." Penoa sat in one of the remaining chairs, observing the map laid out on the table. "I came to find you so we could all work out the terms of our agreement, but it seems you already started without me."

She took in the map while Wes repeated the knowledge about the triangulations.

"Interesting," Penoa said after Wes was finished talking. "So, it's what I predicted then. You're using ley line energy to supplement an ancient piece of native Ponsn tech. . . . May I ask what the tech does?"

"I'm surprised your foresight hasn't figured it out by now," Fina replied snarkily.

"Yes, well, . . . it only gives me pieces of what is to come." Her staff was perched in her lap. As Penoa talked, she ran a soft hand over the swirling globe of mist that was ever-present in her staff. "Just as your people had elders who carried on the messages from the mist, we do too. It just manifests differently."

Fina stared into Penoa's soft gaze, her sight moving from her captivating eyes to the unignorable fur that adorned her skin.

"Just remember we all want the same thing. We all want a chance at glimpsing past the veil."

"That's what the harnesser is supposed to do. That and attempting to be a counteraction against the dark mistic outbreak," Nebu responded.

Penoa looked over the group, a calculated determination evident on her face, as she fiddled with her staff absentmindedly. "It seems our goals are the same, except I don't have the patience to wait for insight from this . . . harnesser, as you call it."

She pointed back to the map. "Your map is a valiant attempt at triangulation, somewhat accurate despite the ley lines moving at such a rapid speed, but it is warped. The abilities my people have as a collective allow us to use the power of the ley lines to shield our home. The energy you picked up to develop this map is altered by what we wanted you to see, but only slightly. I can give you the real map if you make a deal with me."

"What would this deal be?" Fina spoke up.

"I assume Aniklo and Maryn are somewhere on the isles trying to track down the rest of the harnesser, most likely at the Synthesis Corps—"

"How did you know it was in the Corps?" Tauro interjected with wary eyes.

"Where else would it be? The isles are basically at the will of the Corps. The Council being only a measly group of spokespeople who officiate the Corps' decisions. The watchers' facilities and detective work are all interwoven with the mechanisms the Corps pushes out to keep them running. They are the masters behind the manufacturing of all our essential goods, and they have a partnership with anything they don't make themselves. They monopolize the market, dominate the production and selling of top goods, and only let other merchants prosper to avert suspicion."

"No other legal power is strong enough to shield this important piece of tech you are after. The Corps has a stronghold on the inner workings of the mistic system, and if it wasn't made by them, it would have been easily snuffed out by now. It takes a strong ability to block my sensors."

Wes, Nebu, and Fina all nodded along with her impassioned speech, Tauro absorbing her words with a fascination that hinted at the confusion this news brought. For so long, he had only allowed himself to think minutely, to take things one case at a time, but now, it was if the world was unraveling right before his eyes.

Penoa leaned forward, a hint of mirth glimmering in her eyes. "I can grant you access to the unaltered maps of the ley lines and grant you protection with my ranks in the coming days. In exchange, I'd like your spies on the inside to feed me information from the Corps."

"What kind of information?"

"Access to the Corps' files: evidence of the intentional genocide they have carried out against my people, access to the exact security glyphs they used to make protection charms within the Corps and the Council Headquarters, and exact layouts of the buildings, including the guard's rotation periods. I'm sure things have changed since I've been able to have a proper spy."

The group look at one another, knowing what this all would entail. What it all could mean. She sensed their hesitation and repositioned herself, planting her staff on the ground. "The government is getting overthrown whether you like it or not. You can either stand with me and have protection, or stand against me and be eaten by the monsters who want you dead. So, do we have a deal?"

The group of four looked amongst one another for a quick second, Fina scanning each of their faces before finally answering, "Of course."

"Good," Penoa said cheerfully before standing up. "You all should get prepared, then. The two escorts I've assigned to you will be ready to leave in the next couple of hours. I'll send over someone from the kitchen to give you your rations for the trip, as well as breakfast."

With a final nod, Penoa was off, and the group was left to their own devices.

"Do you think we made the right choice?" Wes asked after Penoa was out of shot.

"I think we're making the best choices we can," Tauro said back. "You're the navigator. Do you think what Penoa was saying about the Animoa warping the ley lines is legit?"

Wes' brows were furrowed as he rubbed his chin. "It would explain the way they've been able to harbor so many meetings in the catacombs for the past decade without watcher interference. If there hadn't been a mistic manipulative element set in place, then the nightlife wouldn't be as lively as I remember it."

"The only other explanation would be Animoa being in affiliation with the Corps, and that could be the most hypocritical thing they could ever do." Nebu looked almost distraught, her hands holding the side of her face in regretful contemplation. "I almost feel like a failure of a researcher, going for so many years standing by the almost deadly practice of 'Animoa erasure,' not knowing there was another way."

Wes hesitantly put a hand on her shoulder. "I felt the same way when I left the Corps. I spent many years working the scene, being brainwashed to revere the Council's rules on mistic purity. But once I found the night market, I knew I could never turn back. Knowing is freedom." Wes gave a sad smile, and Tauro witnessed one of the first true smiles he'd ever seen from Nebu.

"We can see our similarities, but we also need to see our differences," Fina's voice was more serious than ever, the hunch of her back more pronounced as she leaned. She cracked her knuckles in between words. "We can empathize with her struggles, but also stay focused on our own goals. She's being nice now, and we'll be nice in return, but we don't know her full hand of cards, so whatever you do, don't get attached."

Tauro hummed along to her words, and they all fell into an awed trance as they looked to marvel at the rising of the sun. The glistening stalactite that cut against the glamoured illusion created the most beautiful sight of false skies.

———-------

After the group had packed and eaten breakfast, they were brought away from their tents by the kitchen workers and deposited in the greenery that reached against the cave's entrance. They met face to face with Penoa and the two antlered guards they had encountered when they first arrived. Upon closer inspection, the antlered guards were similar to the point of being identical, both with golden-blond, short hair and thin, shiny fur more discretely tucked away underneath their close-fitted pants and long sleeves. The only distinction to differentiate them was one had wide eyes, and the other had slimmer ones.

"Srih, Rhys, these are the four travelers who will be joining you on your expedition. Their names are Tauro, Nebu, Fina, and Wes." Penoa pointed to each of them as she named them off, before continuing. "I know you were planning to make this trip alone, but because of last minute circumstances, they will be assisting you and will also require double of what we already planned to extract."

Penoa's emphasis on double didn't go unnoticed by Fina, her brain whirring about what Penoa planned to use the other ley line energy for, but she kept her mouth shut.

Srih and Rhys eyed the group of four, as if inspecting a package of fruit for its ripeness.

"Nice to meet you," Nebu said to break the silence, holding out a hand neither Srih or Rhys took. Their rejection left a sour taste in Nebu and Fina's mouth.

"You and Tauro are the ones the Council wants dead, aren't you?" Srih's voice was a deep silky tone, a contrast to her wide eyes and round face.

"Is that a problem?"

"It's only a problem if you make it one," Rhys responded as confidently and smoothly as his sister. His words visibly formed a rift between.

Penoa cleared her throat, snapping the static caught between the two separate groups. "I have business to attend to, so I will leave you all to figure out your next moves. I expect your end of the deal to be sorted out by the time you get back."

With that, Penoa struck the earth with her charged staff and opened an exit for them to the Animoa safe haven.

As the group of four stared into the expanse of dark catacombs, Wes materialized an orb that sparked a beam of light. Rhys had brought a disk similar to Wes', and the catacomb's map was brought to tangible light before them.

The conversion of lines slanted and slithered like living facets of the underground.

Penoa had shrunken back into the deeper safety of the cave's lush greenery. She was standing underneath the shade, her bright eyes visibly glowing and staff still in hand. The tails of her cloak swayed slightly in the wind dragged in from the outside world. She didn't say a word, but the group of six knew it was time to go.

Rhys was the first to step forward, the map clear in his hand. "We're headed to the first conversion point, which is only a couple of miles away. Follow me, and you'll be safe."

After his last words, almost reluctantly, they began their journey, the thump of Penoa shutting the door a rumble of stone behind them.

Chapter 14

The tight-knit energy on the sixth floor of the Synthesis Corporation was palpable, the workers almost silent as they kept their heads tied to their screens, tracking the trails of the dark mist dying out in the streets, ready to be terminated. The memories of yesterday's dead, of the people who had been executed over the past week since Aniklo and Maryn had been in lockdown was still fresh. The feeling of Kreena's blood sticking to his skin remained a taunting remnant of his trauma, of the fear they could somehow be next. Every other day, the walkers would pick a random group of people, hoping to select a few for the slaughter, and every other day, fewer and fewer would come back.

The cordial chatting of colleagues at lunch breaks had stopped, and with the walkers constantly looming over them as they assessed their screens, everyone knew even moving a muscle the wrong way could lead to being selected and dragged to the slaughter. No one had the gall to debate or fight back publicly. They persevered, sending the calibration of their mist termination charms to the department heads to be formulated and planted in problem spots.

Every morning before work, after the scanned selected group came back thinner than it had gone out, Jessik showed a map of where each target area where sprouting mist had been stomped out. She would praise each group for their successful charm calibrations.

Maryn wondered if what they were stomping out was actually dark mist or just undesirables who had been turned away from the shelters. Every time he went down that train of thought, he had to remind himself why he was there. He had to dig up the past, dig up the memories of his darkest hours when he was bleeding out in an alleyway at thirteen. He had to remind himself of why he scraped and fought his way up and out of the Outer Rim to get to the Mainland. *This was all to know the truth*, he would tell himself. *This was all to pick up where Miho left off.*

But sometimes, late at night, when he heard Aniklo quietly sobbing in the bathroom, when he lay on the couch paralyzed, desperate to comfort him but unsure what comfort would mean, what vulnerability would mean, he wondered if the hustle was worth it. On those morbid nights, he knew Aniklo was worth more than the struggles that seemed to come from staying beside Maryn, and Maryn wondered if he was worth more than those struggles, too.

Aniklo's hand discreetly tapping on his leg brought him back from his thoughts, and he jerked his attention to Aniklo's face.

"Look," Aniklo mouthed, pointing to his screen. Aniklo's holographic screen showed the diagnostic reports on their assessment from the surge at the Outer Rim. What Maryn found knocked the breath out of his lungs.

"This isn't right," Maryn whispered. The diagnostic reports pointed to the black ick that had gathered in the craterous hole burrowing its way into the edge of the mistic barrier. The collection of dark mist the radars pulled up around the screen was daunting, and almost surreal. The assessment's reenactment of its movement similar to the monster beneath the seas from their dream, except 100 times larger and way more unshapen. Its magnitude could only be described as a sharp cloud, chewing expertly through the barrier that surrounded the isles of Ponsn.

"What the—" Suddenly, the screen glitched out. The diagnostics of the barrier breach changed from a daunting display of mist to none at all.

"Hey!" A watcher had posed themselves behind the workstation of the two, holding onto their blaster tightly. "This is not the work you two should be assigned to."

Their booming voice gathered the attention of everyone in their vicinity.

Aniklo, red-faced with embarrassment and panic, blurted, "We were just checking up on an assignment given to us last week. There was a strange occurrence at the barrier, and we were supposed to—"

"You are supposed to be defusing the issues on the isles, not anywhere else." The grip the watcher had on their blaster shifted, the deadly mechanism now pointed vaguely in their direction, causing them to shrink into one another.

Thankfully, one of the departments heads stepped in after hearing the commotion.

"That's enough Watcher Brennan. You can let them pass," the sound of the head's voice boomed across the room, and Watcher Brennan moved on.

Aniklo and Maryn let out a breath of relief after attention was finally diverted away from them, their panic further affirming they needed to move fast. Their screens were currently turned to see a display of all points in the inner market area, where they should be coordinating charms to fight against the dark mist. But, that was only their day work. All the exciting stuff was set to happen at night.

They had decided, after watching the passing guards over the past week, to track the times when the border around the Corps flickered to its weakest point. Today was the day they would make their way to the energy source. Aniklo was more a bundle of nerves than Maryn, asking every possible question imaginable:

"What if the guards don't pass over the entrance to the energy volt the say way they have the past couple of days?" Aniklo had whispered in the middle of the night. *They both had been lying on the couch, waiting for sleep to take them.*

"They always pass over at the same time. They always have, and it's our best chance to go with this alternative," Maryn reassured him, resisting his eyes that were beginning to drift closed.

"What if the volt is turned off?"

"The volt is never turned off, Aniklo. They need it to power the mistic wall trapping us."

"*What if—*"

"*I'll understand if you're too nervous about going. I can make the trip alone.*"

"*No, we're in this together,*" and when he'd said that, he meant it.

The cord connecting them thrummed a constant reminder they were meant to carry this out as a team.

Their conversation played in Aniklo's head as they continued the monotony of their workday, wondering the effect of the work they were forced to do, knowing they were so close yet so far away.

The hours passed by as slow as thick molasses, the end of their workday bringing relief that mixed with a deep dreaded angst bubble in a cocktail within them. This is what they and been waiting for.

They walked with the others back to their respective dorms, feigning tiredness as an excuse to sneak away faster. When the door shut behind them, they hurried to collect the most important part of their scheme: Aniklo's charmed cloak. Though it was originally designed to formulate a disguise that matched the theme of the night market's animalistic attire, it also had a setting that allowed for invisibility. It had been hidden away in Maryn's chest, out of the view of the daily raids, but now, it was time for it to see the light again. They just had to wait for the clock to strike 11, and then, their commute would begin.

They sat in charged silence, playing the game of pointing out what shapes formed within the pattern of the mist swirls on the wall encasing the building before getting bored. Then, they settled into a jittery silence that left only the panic of their own minds.

"I think the way they died was both selfish and heroic at the same time," Aniklo blurted it absentmindedly, unable to think of anything else to say, anything lighter. Maryn was just a breath away on the couch, a frown shaping on his face.

"I want to think he did the right thing," Maryn answered, looking into Aniklo's eyes. "I want to think what we're doing now is worth something."

"What if it isn't? What if this danger we've been thrust into leads to something beyond our control?" Aniklo was fiddling with his hands, wondering if the expanding tightness in his chest unearthed by his words was intuition, was some form of warning to abort.

"This is what he wanted for me. This is what they wanted for the both of us. To avenge them." Maryn's voice was tight and deep, his tonality final, but his face was the opposite.

"What do you want, Maryn?" The air between them had reached a roaring pitch, their faces now centimeters apart. The milky expanse of Maryn's wide eyes generated a trance Aniklo couldn't look away from. Maryn could barely choke out a breath, could barely form a sentence, but Aniklo let out all he had wanted to say for days.

"I want you to be happy, Maryn. What if what we find just makes everything a thousand times worse? Makes the dark mist a thousand times worse?"

Maryn turned away, unable to stay in the cyclone of closeness and familiarity they had been dancing around, cultivating, and deflating over and over again. This was too much; he was too much; all of it was too much. He just had to keep going. He stood up, running a hand over his short, tight curls that had started to grow in, and looked at the clock, the time springing him into action.

"It's 11:01! We're a minute behind schedule. We have to go."

They both rushed to fit themselves underneath the concealment cloak. Aniklo settled into its cocoon and the hard feel of Maryn's back flush against his own, their steps too loud in his ears. As they made it out the door in unison, they scurried down the hallway to the stairs across from the lift.

The creaky stairwell door was deafening, and after opening it just enough to slither through, they moved as fast as they could in tandem down the several flights, down to the basement where the energy volt was stored. It was a race against time to fall in line before the guard rushing to his post reached it and blocked their path to the vault. With a painstaking panic, trying to hold themselves in tandem as they rushed, they passed the guard who was a feet away from taking his position at the vault. They made it through the door before the guard could notice their presence, but not before he could notice the door was slightly ajar.

An eternity of a second passed, the guard looking around the room, huffing about how the last guard was dumb for leaving the door open. Aniklo thought for sure the flashing light the new guard swung would somehow expose the two of them underneath the veil of the cloak.

Heavy boots, the bated breaths of the boys in the corner, and then finally the clank of the door closing, and silence.

They allowed themselves to exhale, separating from underneath the cloak and looking around. Neither of the boys had ever been to the energy volt, but it looked exactly like the flashes from their dream.

Pipes lined the room's amarite walls, the glimmer of protection charms apparent. Dust gathered around the shadowy cavernous walls glimmering from the main attraction: the thick amarite pipe that acted as a portal to the ocean at the room's center. It sucked the pure mist from the water molecules, creating a cauldron-like portal the width of a man.

This was what Maryn had envisioned when he had first been to the energy vat on the upper floors to create their assessment charm. This was where his father's fate met him. It took everything in Maryn to hold back the bile rising to his mouth. It took everything in him to reign in his sense of control, to reign in the tears threatening to flow.

"This is it." Aniklo turned to Maryn, urgent, heart beating fast. They both remembered the instructions Fina had given them, her insistence on the correct way to pull out the harnesser piece.

"Imagine the shape of the harnesser. Imagine the way it would feel in the palm of your hands. Make contact with the bond, with each other, and summon it into reality."

They did just that, getting lost in each other's eyes as they did their best to dig within, feeling the tether between them expand in an almost painful way.

The shrapnel piece of the harnesser appeared above the rematerializing tether in an almost holographic formation, before dropping solid into reality. The tech formulated by their fathers caused a shift in the air at the point of its materialization, floating rather than succumbing to gravity. The light permeated around it acting as a cord to the mist that lie within the volt's power source. Before the boys could even gather the courage to touch it, it was sucked into the pool of chemically infused mist.

"What do we do?" Maryn panicked, but not for long. The facet of the harnesser reemerged, the piece dripping in wet gelatinous mist. A holographic image of the complete harnesser formulated around the part of it they possessed. The harnesser fragment rooted in reality was energized, the glyphs cut into its surface, glowing like they had never seen before.

"Wow," Aniklo said in awe. The singular part of the harnesser, along with its holographic conjuration, landed within his open hands. Maryn moved closer to get a better look, not noticing what approached from behind.

A man, a familiar man, inched from the cavernous shadows of the volt's corner, swinging a pipe that connected with Maryn's leg.

Maryn cried out in anguish at the initial hit, falling to the ground and hitting his head on a pipe against the wall. Their attacker swung the pine toward Aniklo once Maryn was down, but the younger boy ducked before it could smash his head, the harnesser dropping out of his hand.

"Catching you guys will get me a bonus for sure!" Their assailant Roan said smugly in between wild swings.

Maryn resurfaced as Roan tried in vain to attack Aniklo.

Roan, with a swift push from his pipe, connected with Aniklo's chest quickly cornering Aniklo against the cauldron's edge of searing mist. Aniklo felt the strong heat of the bubbling energy churning behind him. With his teeth clenched, Roan tried to strong-arm him into the vat. Aniklo was forced to raise his hands in retaliation, hands raised up against the bar pushing him back.

Roan and Aniklo, in the seconds of their struggle, were eye to eye. Roan's spit from exertion dripped down his chin, his eyes crazed. Aniklo's feet slipped against the ground, his back burned by the chemically infused mist.

Maryn, after taking a couple of seconds to recover, got up, and with all his strength pushed Roan to the side, making him topple away from Aniklo and hit his head on the edge of the vat. As Roan weakly got up from the floor, Aniklo acted in a spurt of rage, lifting Roan's legs with strength he didn't know he had and tipping Roan's whole body into the steaming cauldron.

Roan's screams were loud as he was dropped into the searing mist, and the severity and danger of the situation finally set in. Aniklo stood motionless, staring in awe and horror at his colleague slowly being burned to death because of him.

The volt's cogs turned as the guard opened the door to inspect the clatter. Maryn snapped out of his shock first, swinging the cloak around them and grabbing the harnesser piece that had been lost in the tussle.

Their travel back to their room slipped by in a blur. The sound of guards flooding the vault who would see Roan's lifeless body stabbed at Aniklo's conscience. Maryn limped along up the stairs, the boys could barely stay concealed underneath the cloak as they walked quickly down their hallway.

Luckily, no one was outside of their dorm to see the door open and close on its own, to hear the panicked pants of the boy's breaths as they tried desperately to get to safety before the guards undoubtedly conducted another scan and search.

As soon as they reached the cover of their room and closed the door, Aniklo dropped to the floor heaving, his eyes wide open, hand clutching his chest.

"I did it." He wheezed out around his sobs. "I did—"

Maryn rushed to comfort him on the floor, wrapping him in his arms and rubbing his back. "We both did it."

"I did it," Aniklo repeated, his tears flowing like a waterfall. Another flash of Roan burning in anguish, another thing to add to the list of horrors he would never forget.

His hysterics had dulled down slightly after a few long moments of reveling in being comforted, in not being alone. Maryn's touch was like a dose of pure mist from his bottle, encapsulating him in a strange relaxation he couldn't describe. But, it didn't completely quell the pain from the vivid images of all the dead he had seen, nor the horror on Roan's face as he was stripped of life.

"He would have told, Ani. If he lived, he would have told," Maryn said in a calming voice after Aniklo's heaves had lessened in intensity. They stayed curled on the floor for a long time, listening to people rush back and forth outside their door. Maryn worried about how much longer it would take before they got caught.

"How much more of this do we have to do? To what lengths do we have to go?" Aniklo's voice was a whisper against Maryn's chest, but he didn't respond, detaching from him after Aniklo started breathing normally again.

The harnesser was still glowing on the floor beside them. Maryn knew there was no more time for them to panic. He pressed the piece of the harnesser they had charged along with the holographic image, which had still not dissolved back into the string of energy connected to them.

The buzzer of a drill rang true, jerking them out of the shock of the moment. Aniklo wiped at his tears rapidly, and Maryn tried to stand up, wincing in pain at the soreness of his leg.

"We have to go," Maryn said.

"What about your leg cuts?"

The door opened before they could do anything else, a watcher appearing to usher them out of the room into the flow of bodies headed downstairs. Without explanation, they were led to the lobby.

Chapter 15

Fina was covered in soot and dirt, staring at the glow of the light from the crystal in her palm. It had been a week of this: traveling under the fortified tunnels of the isles, alternating teams of three to take different passages to collect the mist needed from the ley lines. Wes, Fina, and Srih had finished collecting their third round of ley lines earlier than the others. They observed the crystals they intended to use to call Aniklo and Maryn with fascination.

Srih's long antlers atop her head were a shadow over the glowing comm, her hand securely rested on her bow in her lap, a quiver full of arrows and a blaster beside her.

"It's pretty pointless to have spies inside an organization if you don't even know how to contact them," Srih said with a smirk as she observed Fina and Wes tinkering with mild fascination, leaning back on her travel bag for slight comfort from the hard floor.

"We never intended for the mistic wall to come up around the Synthesis Corps," Wes interjected. "I worked there for many years, and this was never in the floor plan's capabilities. Their energy source shouldn't be strong enough to support both this and their charm formulations."

Footsteps came from down the walkway to the west, and the group was put on high alert, but softened their stance when they realized it was just the second team.

Tauro, Nebu, and Rhys headed toward them, a crystalized formation of the mist gathered in Nebu's hands.

"Did you guys get a hold of Aniklo and Maryn yet?" Tauro asked as the group blended together. Nebu placed the collected ley line mist next to the other ones.

"The wall surrounding the Corps is interfering with our signal, but we should be able to get through to them soon," Fina said.

Rhys walked nearer to the gathering, his antlers thudding against the wall for a slight second, his eyes sharp. "Penoa said if you guys haven't held up your end of the bargain by the first three ley line clusters, then we would have to head back before we get the other ones."

"We want to," Nebu said earnestly from beside Fina. "We're not stalling or trying to trick you. We're just facing an unexpected variable that needs time to be worked through."

Rhys held out his hand. " Let me see it."

After a slight hesitation, Wes lifted the comm crystal out of the layer of mistic charms the two had been using to inspect it and gave it to Rhys. Rhys held it in between his fur-laden hands and closed his eyes, a layer of mist seeping out of his skin and swirling around crystal.

"What is he doing?" Fina asked Srih as the rest of the group watched on in awe.

"You'll see," Srih responded.

After a couple of seconds, Rhys opened his eyes, the tendrils of energy returning back into his skin, eyes slightly glossed over.

"The crystal's not strong enough," Rhys said, tossing it back to Wes, who caught it clumsily.

"We know that already. Whatever trick you just did with the mist under your skin won't tell us anything we don't already—" Fina blabbered on.

Tauro noticed Rhys and Srih were not even paying attention, a glance stretching between the two of them, their formerly solid horns twitching slightly atop their heads.

"One thing you need to know about my people is the way the mist works within us is different than how it works in the epicenter, and in this case, I have more insight than you do." Rhys interjected, cutting off Fina's anxious tirade, turning to the rest of the group.

"Here's the plan. I know what you're saying is true, that the connection is being severed by the wall around the building. I think we could use the energy from the ley lines to our advantage," said Rhys.

"How?" Wes asked.

Rhys then pulled the disk that contained the map out of his pocket and swept a hand over its surface to bring to life the forever-changing coordinates. "It's simple really. We already collected the first three ley line batches. Now, all we need is the two conjunction points at the inner sphere, where all the ley lines connect. If we get an extra cluster of the charged ley lines and harness it from a point at the inner sphere, we should be able to use it to charge your communication device."

"Good. So, what are we waiting for?" Tauro asked, loading his travel bag on his back.

"Not so fast, Tauro." Srih was the first to speak up, lifting herself from her lax position on the ground and swiftly moving to stand beside her brother.

"The last two convergent points will be the most difficult. We're not just going to come up to the point, say a few words, and gather the mist into its crystallized form like before. We're going to have to go above ground."

The group was quiet for a long moment, the nerves building up. The comfort of the underground made them feel invincible, untouchable by the threat above, but they all knew there was no turning back.

Fina was the first to gather her wits, pulling out the protective gear Penoa had given them. "We've come this far, and there's no other options. We might as well get a move on before the darkness sets in."

And that was that.

———————

The river passage that provided a window to the outside world was traveled with great caution and bated breaths. The group had layered protective vests over their clothes, a tough second skin to veil the runes and preventative glyphs. Rhys and Srih had a hooded component to their vests with holes to accommodate their antlers. The hood somehow warped the sight of their antlers into a part of them that wouldn't be seen at first glance, something hidden away from the naked eye.

The group finally reached the end of the passage, the impasse where there was no way to go but up. Rhys turned to the rest of them, a hard set of determination on his face, while the others showed varying degrees of stress.

"I think it's best I sit this one out," Wes said before anyone else could say a word.

Rhys let out a grunt of annoyance. "Wes, we all need to be involved for the plan to work. We need everyone on high alert."

The map of the underground in Rhys' palm had been switched to mirror images of the streets above. The glow of the central convergence piece they needed just a block away, almost atop the place where the civilian refuge had been established.

"We'll split into two groups: Fina and I will go to collect the mist at the convergence, while the rest of you stay back and pick off the guards from the cover of the shacks."

"I'll come with you," Srih said.

"It's probably best you stay behind. Your fur is also noticeable, and you have the best aim of anyone I know." He looked over the rest of the group. "Stay close to me. Nobody wander off, and we should all be fine."

Rhys' composure was airtight. With that, he lifted the patch of loose cobblestones above their heads, and they breached the protection of the ground with weapons drawn, breathing in the rancid smell of death carried on the wind.

The streets were surprisingly cleaner than before. Some of the flesh and bones accrued from the dark mist consuming bodies had been cleaned away. But the stony ground was still tinted burgundy. Broken-down shacks were rearranged into piles on the pathway's side so as to not block the main walking area where they stood. The setup gave a barricade that separated their position from the civilians as well as their convergence point.

They could hear the sound of many hushed voices and of footsteps beyond the cover of the stacked shacks. The sounds bounced off the clear dome of mist encasing the area, but the group didn't spend much time looking around. They all followed Rhys, coughing as they walked, staying in the cover of the shade some of the damaged storefronts provided.

Rhys raised a hand, motioning forward, and they slinked through the streets, ducking behind stores when a spare walker came passing through. Finally, they made it to an opening in the shack barricade that revealed the civilian shelter. An enormous tent was posted in a large dugout surrounded by rubble and scrap storefront materials. The bubble of protective mist that surrounded them peaked in intensity at the top of the tent, watchers standing post at the front and the back, blasters at the ready. Other civilians in a motley assortment of filthy conditions and torn clothes moved soundlessly in a line, collecting food at a few storefronts still operating in the circle of rubble.

The group huddled behind a desolate shack at the back of the large shelter, looking to Rhys for their next move. He pulled out a cluster of rocks held together by moss, dirt, and grime; the vines sprouting out of it seized from being in open air. Whispering a few indistinguishable words, he touched the vine-littered shape, touched his chest, and then Fina's leg. At that touch, they turned invisible, blending into their surroundings.

"I can see you, but you look shiny," Fina whispered in confusion.

"That's the invisibility setting in. We can see each other, but they can't see us."

Tauro, Nebu, Srih, and Wes looked to the spaces where their voices came from in awe. The bundle of vines Rhys had whispered to were now alight, the vine which created the charm's spark shining through their roots.

"Cover us if everything goes wrong. Protect the vines." They all heard Rhys whisper, and then heard the soft patter of his and Fina's feet as they walked away.

The other four huddled in the spot listening to the departing steps from their perch: silent, eager, breathless. Srih waved her hands over the vine cluster, letting the mist from her skin seep into it, keeping it alive.

Rhys and Fina easily knocked out the unsuspecting guard toward the back of the fortified station with a sharp hit from a silent stunner. Outside the view of the open corridor, they set the armored body down before it clattered to the ground. Rhys was the first to move past the flaps of the tent and see what was inside.

Upon entering the tent, Fina and Rhys realized the rancid smell of death and decay was actually permeating from this enclosure. Mixed in rose the smell of feces and urine. The ginormous tent was packed from wall to wall with people tied up along the posts and in long rows down the middle. Surprisingly, watchers were amongst the restrained; some seeming too weak to talk, others too scared. A single person in the first room near the back begged to be set free. Most of the guards inside stood motionless at their posts, possibly with a moniker of guilt evident on their near stoic faces.

Rhys and Fina stood in shock, watching a particular guard walk up to a screaming civilian who was begging to be set free. The watcher grabbed the person's hair to yank their heads up and forced them to look directly into the guard's eyes.

"I said stay silent! You will be granted food and drink when the time comes, but it is my orders to keep anyone who resists or tries to escape restrained."

The civilian was crying, barely able to cry out, "We don't deserve this treatment. Keeping us tied here—"

"All of you wouldn't have been tied up if you hadn't been trying to escape," the guard yelled loud enough for everyone to hear. "If you keep complaining, we'll put you in with the others."

Then, Rhys and Fina snapped out of their shock and walked along the narrow path leading to a separate section of the tent. The people in the second room were in a worse condition than the first, the civilians bound abnormally, piled on top of each other at grotesque angles. Their chins were connected to a contraption hung at the wall's side near the entrance to the second part of the tent.

The sound of their moans through their gags was loud. The guards stationed in this room, clearly more aggressive, stunned people within the pile who screamed particularly loudly in comparison to the other bodies surrounding them.

Bile rose in Fina's throat as she tried to hold back her lunch, following Rhys as he tiptoed through the mound of bodies. Their target, the convergence point, pinged at the side of the room. The two arrived at their target over the point.

Rhys, as he had done a thousand times, pulled the hollow circle from around his neck and put it over the convergence, the crude markings on its wide surface made more visible by its connection to the earth. A summoning of energy that strong took two to absorb, two to master, and with great effort, Fina and Rhys placed both their hands on the hollow circle before them, crouching down and willing the point's energy to rise to validity and solidify before them. The fragment of the earth's essence released, liquified, and then materialized into a hard ball.

It took all of Rhys and Fina's energy to sap a couple of these spheres of light, hiding behind the pile of bodies and concealing what they were doing. Once they were done, they each stored one of the spheres in the vest pockets.

Rhys was somewhat familiar with the exertion that came from tapping into the ley lines, but Fina was a mess, discombobulated and dizzy, but her eagerness to leave the tent fueled her ability to stand.

Seconds after they gathered what they had been looking for, all hell broke loose. A scream rang from outside the tent, guards rushing in one by one.

"Someone's trying to breach the tent!" One of them screamed, dragging the body of the soldier they had stunned to get in.

Outside, Tauro, Nebu, Srih, and Wes held down their post, blasters at the ready, as they shot at the guards advancing on their territory. Nebu's precise aim sent her blaster's energy shooting into the approaching enemies, clinking against and slicing through their armor, while Tauro and Wes focused on picking off the guards attempting to warn the others inside the shelter, Wes' aim being less precise. Srih was huddled over the viny structure that granted the two inside invisibility, but her concentration was more and more strained, the effort to maintain the glamour becoming increasingly more taxing.

"We have to go! We have to leave!" Wes was panicking, shooting aimlessly.

"We can't just abandon them! Just hold on a little longer, Wes!" Nebu said from beside them, shooting a watcher point-blank a second later, her accuracy never wavering.

At their moment of brief conversation, a watcher came around from the side of their hidden post, dragging Wes back to grapple with him. Srih with her hands still reverberating energy, witnessed the watcher as if in slow motion pull Wes in a tight headlock, their blaster poised inches away from his skull. After a moment of hesitation, she released her concentration to wind up and shoot her bow, landing a clear shot to the watcher's head who had breached their corner.

"I'm sorry," she whispered to Rhys's creation, knowing they were no longer protected, shots firing all around them as they persisted in their efforts to defend their shelter.

Inside the tent, Rhys could feel the strength of their invisibility veil slowly unraveling, could see the watchers scoping out the people in a panic, getting closer and closer. He knew he had to act.

He shot a blast at the controls keeping the bound people at bay, the contraption sparking before losing its hold, the people within the tent finally unleashed.

Hundreds, perhaps thousands, of bound civilians screamed out as they rose from their captivity, the most angry ones diving at the nearest watcher in their sight. Dogpiles of attackers overpowered their captors with intense vigor. Watchers shot at the angry civilians no longer kept at bay, the room where the most aggressive had been stored becoming a bloodbath of confusion and chaos.

Rhys and Fina fought through the crowd of tight panic. The people trying to escape ripped through the thick tent material they had been trapped in for the past couple of weeks. The guards advanced on the four outside the tent and turned to the new surge of people desperate to escape and out for blood.

"Run!" Rhys shouted, but Wes was already ahead of them, the six sprinting through the bang of blasts, away from the civilian compound, and to the tunnel that led below. They no longer took the extra time to be discreet, ducking and weaving and leaping over limp bodies, but when they reached their open slot in the cobblestone, it was too late. Black mist had risen from the undergrowth, bleeding onto the streets directly in their path, taking a humanoid form that whizzed toward them.

Wes, being the one farthest ahead, let out a deafening shriek, impaled, his eyes wide open and the breath knocked out of his lungs for good. After tearing through Wes' flesh, the bundle of black mist charged on the rest of them, ready to attack. As a last-ditch effort to stay alive, Fina raised her portion of the ley line energy, letting the vibration of it encase her and those around her. She held energy out toward the dark mist, causing it to halt, diverting its path toward the inner compound still tormented by an ocean of screams.

After the dark mist had passed over them, Fina rushed to Wes' side, only to see their eyes had glassed over, their breath already sucked from their lungs.

"Don't touch him," Srih softly said from behind her. "It will only contaminate you, too."

Fina numbly watched the darkness crawl in the hole the mist created in Wes' torso, stuck with the horrifying image of her friend struck down meaninglessly. The other four of them stood around, silent, jittery, their adrenaline still running high.

"I know this sounds harsh, but we can't stand here forever. We need to leave before it comes back," Rhys said.

Fina, after closing Wes' bloodshot eyes, left his corpse to be consumed as the group went back underground, the hatch shut securely behind them. They all let out a sigh of relief once the cobblestone was set back into place, trying to catch their breaths. Fina, weary and ready to burst into tears, slumped against the wall along with the others.

"We should get away from this area," Rhys said after they had all caught their breaths. "The dark mist might come back."

They walked aimlessly for a mile underground to a destination Nebu, Tauro, and Fina weren't privy to, until they reached a slight alcove that expanded into a deep room. Fina set her small travel bag down, flopped down right on top of it, and leaned her body against the hard floor.

They all knew, without really saying more than a few words, this would be their resting spot, their place of regeneration after the chaos and death of their day.

After they had bandaged their scrapes and wounds, Fina pulled out the crystal comm they planned to use to contact Aniklo and Maryn, hoping now after all their sacrifice it would finally work. They all waited with bated breaths, watching the crystal synergize with the convergence cluster. After a long moment, the crystal sprung to life, instilling a holographic image of Aniklo's face on the screen, Maryn not close behind.

"Hello. Tauro? Is that you?" Aniklo's voice was fuzzy, the connection dim, but he was still there, alive, and safe. That's all the group, especially Tauro and Nebu, wanted to know.

"Yeah, it's us. I'm not sure the connection will stay for long, but I need you to know we've got four clusters of energy from the ley lines. We only have one left. But things went in an unpredictable turn somewhere along the way," Tauro said quickly, wiping away a quick tear at the sight of the two boys safe.

"What do you mean?" Maryn asked.

"We need you to get a map of the inner security system at the Corps. And to give us an idea of who has the master comm system within the building."

"I don't understand. What's going on? Why do you need—" The line was flickering out, every word stretching into more and more of a hum.

"It's important you collect this info. We can't go to the last convergence point without it." Tauro, in those last seconds, wanted to tell him the way everything in their world was going wrong, wanted to tell him he was right to question society's order and authority that was slowly unraveling into something horrendous right before their eyes. He wanted to tell him he was sorry for how wrapped up he had always been in work, tell him sorry for not making enough time for him. But, all he could say was, "I love you."

He heard the faint echo of it back as the screen got too weak to sustain itself, the mist from the ley lines trickling away, the connection lost.

"That's it. That's the last of it?" Nebu asked when the screen had completely dissolved, the light of the communication crystal extremely dull. Tauro, as she looked at him, seemed completely distraught.

"Yeah. I wish we would have had time to grab another dose of energy, but . . ." Fina's voice trailed off.

"You did all you could," Rhys said. "The people flooding out got in the way."

Fina's angular face had now taken on a look of horror, a dazed confusion. She was curled up on the floor, staring off into space. "They were tied up, piled on top of one another, unable to move as if they were . . . I don't even know what to call it. As if they were nothing."

"We're not going to be able to bounce back after this," Tauro said into the heady, stuffy air of the tunnel surrounding them. "There's no redemption from that kind a dehumanization."

"This is why we need to make our move soon." Srih had moved away from the already sleeping Rhys into the sphere of conversation. "We need to get back to the main stay as soon as possible and tell Penoa everything."

"But what about the last convergence point?" Fina asked.

"We'll make it to that. But, Penoa needs to know." She looked back to Rhys' unconscious form. "We should rest for the night. Gather our wits. We'll leave for the headquarters at first light."

Chapter 16

The unexpected call was cut prematurely, Tauro's jumbled image no longer lighting up the room. The boys were left lost, more confused than before and unsure of what to do next.

Maryn was on high alert, glancing in between their front door and the crystal dimly alight before them. It was now deep into the night, the watchers having just released them from their last scan. The adrenaline from the charged harnesser coursed through their veins, and Roan's recent death was still fresh. "I don't know if my buffering crystal is enough to block out the harnesser and the call. Do you think they would have sensed it? "

"I don't know. And at this point, there's really nothing we can do about it."

They were both weary, tired from the scan that sapped out all their energy, the adrenaline of this night's events replaced with dreariness. They sat side by side on the couch, a wave of heavy fatigue washing over them.

Aniklo yawned, the two of them sinking deeper into the couch, and in the moment of intense lethargy, Maryn felt the invisible harnesser weighing down on the space between them, dragging their conjoined consciousness deeper into its depths. In those peaceful moments in the waking realm, with the two slipping into cushiony delirium, Aniklo hung onto the idea that maybe when they woke up, this would all be over.

Their subconscious mind, the dreams they now shared sucked them in, painting the surroundings of an awning in the lush background, one which Aniklo and Maryn's families used to share. The swing set and tree house were still new and polished, poised at the trees' edge that eventually became a forest. The grass was littered with toys and other things the boys had dragged out throughout the day. Under the awning, sitting on the other side of the table, was Castille. Aniklo and Maryn were in awe, shocked to finally see a clear image of one of their fathers in a joint dream, but he wasn't the same.

Castille was a sick husk of his former self, his hair streaked white, eyes framed with more defined wrinkles, the deep tan of his skin sucked away to something haggard and pallid.

Somehow, Aniklo knew his condition was because of this place, because of this falsification of reality, a foggy vortex of a backyard that no longer existed.

"Da," Aniklo whispered, reaching out a hand to touch his father. But, his hand hit a wall, warping the shape of Castille, rippling the air like moving water before it finally set into place.

"My boys," Castille said weakly, voice strained from lack of use. "You finally made it." His face was sorrowful, eyes blinking rapidly. "I'm glad you could follow the clues we left."

"Da . . . I've missed you. I've missed you so much."

"I've missed you too, Aniklo. I'm sorry I could never be all you needed. The work. I thought we were going to change everything." He swallowed, the tears finally beginning to flow.

"Why hasn't your mother come to visit me? I thought she would find us first."

"She didn't know how."

"But the two of you did." His smile was almost bright, but it was as if his face rejected it, the wrinkles prominent and weighing it down before it could completely blossom.

He looked fragile, a second away from crumbling into oblivion, and the two boys knew their time with him was running short. Aniklo wanted to ask if he was real, how he came to exist before him in such a withered form, but he was scared of what the truth would be, was scared of hearing the horrors Castille endured to get here. He didn't even know if this version of Castille would hold up against that questioning.

"Uncle Cass, where's Miho? Where's my da?"

Castille's eyes were glazed over, his gaze disconnected. "He used to visit, but that was long ago . . . He always had to return to his section when he was here for too long." Castille began beating himself up, face scrunched up in anger. "This place is always the same day over and over again."

The two boys looked to one another, unsure what to do, how to ask what they truly needed to know. Aniklo, at this desperate time, chose the option of comforting him, "It's okay, Da. We're here now. We found you just like you wanted, and we'll take care of you. Everything will be fine."

"It's too late, Ani. What we did can't exactly be erased." Castille had turned in on himself after his frustrated rage, moving away from the table to curl up against the pillar of the gazebo, rocking back and forth, ashen and voice hopeless. *"I tried to back out, but it was good, it was too good. It all fell to pieces when they found out."*

Looking out from their spot under the shade, he noticed the bright trees had turned into a void of advancing black, patches of grass lifting into the nothingness, coming closer and closer to their slice of safety.

"Da, what do we do? Tell us what to do!"

"Finish it" was all he could say before the black swallowed him.

White pain ripped through their bodies as they were snatched awake, the tether that connected them and the harnesser painfully alive with activity, before it turned to a dull, unbreachable nothingness.

To their colleagues, it appeared the two of them had disappeared the next day. There was a thrum of exhaustion that came with working around the clock. Some workers also noticed all of the higher-ups had been moved to more serious matters, matters that had everything to do with what was going on behind the scenes.

Aniklo and Maryn, to their surprise, didn't wake up to the comfort of their dorm beds. White light was shined into Maryn's eyes before he could adjust. When his vision snapped into focus, he realized the room was a decorative lab, a high ceiling displaying the gleam of the midday sun. A large vortex of deeply tinted mist swirled in the center of the room; a wildly rancid stench came from it. Power cords laced with the mist branched out like vines against the walls, syringes, and other ghastly items sprawled across the messy space.

Maryn could only see a part of what the room stored, because as he discovered in his woozy daze, he was tied to a hard board, head locked into a singular position, arms and legs shackled and virtually immobile. The arm decorated with his pronounced runes, the trademark of Maryn and Aniklo's bond, was chained in compartmentalized sections, and a tight security brace circled his bicep.

Through the bond, Maryn could feel the grogginess of Aniklo's waking form but couldn't see him from his side of the room. Hot panic and urgency to set them free was his primary emotion.

"Hello, boys," Jessik's slick voiced resounded across the room before Maryn could even do any more scheming for escape. "Good to see you're finally awake."

"Why are you doing this to us?" Aniklo moaned, the same panic and confusion about their location coursing through his veins.

"I have to admit, you two did very well carrying out your little scheme, but I'm putting an end to that now."

"So, you found out we're bonded. What are you gonna do, kill us? Shoot us point-blank like you've done to everyone else undesirable?"

"You spout the lingo of the Council as if you expect us to actually abide by it. If I truly wanted you dead, I would have made it happen as soon as I found you at the reserve. But, I brought you back here for a reason." She set to work tilting Maryn in the contraption he was bound in, making his tied-up arm with the bond glyphs more accessible. After they were maneuvered, their gags were locked into place, making it so all they could do was scream into the buffers trapped in their mouths.

Maryn was rolled over the volt of swirling darkness, his arm positioned over it.

"I just want to make it clear I'm doing this for everyone, for the good of our world. Your mother believed in the Corps' values as well, before she found out her husband and his best friends were sneaking around. After that, she couldn't take it anymore."

She spoke to them as if this was gossip hour, while she leisurely walked the room, searching through a drawer of sharp objects. A guard who Maryn had previously thought was a statue moved to her aid. There were more of them, standing at attention around the people who upon closer inspection, Maryn realized were the department heads of the Corps. They all watched along in mild fascination and anticipation.

Jessik dismissed the guard who'd been casually inspecting the weapons within the drawer.

"Don't worry about it, Felix. I can do this next part on my own." Finally, she picked up an ax from the array of options and began to sharpen it to perfection.

Maryn began to hyperventilate through the bounds of his gag, flailing unsuccessfully to break free. Aniklo did the same, itching to help him, hearing the screech of the ax being sharpened and unable to know what would happen next.

She was done sharpening after an eon of tenseness, making a beeline for Maryn over the vault. She stood over him, ax secured in both hands, the glint of it from the light of the sky taunting him.

"I consider myself a fair person, a person of morals, so I think in this situation, it would be fair to explain what is about to happen to you and why." She set the ax down on a table beside Maryn's bed. Her voice was deathly even, the sharp angles of her face as defined as the weapon she wielded.

"I'm about to cut your arm off to take the harnesser's abilities connected to the bond you and Aniklo have cultivated. Then, I will take you away, to let your body rot like I did your father's. A fitting end to selfish scum, don't you think?" A hand brushed across his one-inch curls in an almost soothing manner, the other sweeping up to wipe away the fountain of panicked tears flowing from Maryn's eyes.

"There's no need to be afraid. Your sacrifice will aid in our freedom. Freedom from the mist that traps us here, a deathly incarceration set to extend for the rest of time if not for your sacrifice."

She then moved away from her oddly comforting stance, picking up the ax and getting into position, ready to swing. All Maryn could do was scream, looking to Aniklo who was equally helpless. Their connection intensified their fear until it was a palpable weight between them, a palpable ache.

"The dark mist will prevail," Jessik said with excitement.

Her ax swung up, and the crowd of her colleagues watched, echoing her words. The bubbling pit stirred at the sound of its acknowledgment, almost preparing for its next meal.

Time slowed down, Maryn watching helplessly as the ax swung down, the sharp slice of it audibly cutting through his skin. Intense, sharp torture washed over him, his voice going hoarse with how loudly he screamed.

Jessik didn't cut all the way through on the first slice. He felt it all, heard the snap of his bone as it cracked on the second slice, dizzily felt the searing black abyss of mist coming nearer to his skin when his arm was fully disconnected, dropping into the tub that became electrified once it had engulfed the intense cluster of the bond.

Aniklo felt a phantom pain as he watched it all take place, seeing the blood, *Maryn's blood* splatter everywhere, felt the weakness that set on as their tether was damaged, searing anger engulfing him in his moment of weakness. Maryn was unconscious, and all Aniklo wanted to do was run to him, and make him okay, but it was too late.

A couple of the others moved up to wheel Maryn away, Jessik unfazed as she wiped at the blood splattered all around her, her facade of sleek perfection in shambles.

She then turned to Aniklo's weak form, signaling for someone to wheel him over, but a large boom resounded from outside, an explosion large enough to cut through the buffering effects of the wall around the Corps. Everyone turned in confusion, all except Jessik.

"The boundary near the Outer Rim . . . I think we did it!"

"What do we do with him then?"

They all turned to Aniklo who was snotty and sobbing in the middle of the room. Jessik stepped over, looming, a spot of Maryn's blood falling from Jessik's shirt to Aniklo's cheek. She looked at him for a long beat, before turning to everyone else that awaited her command.

"I think I'll give him the present of dying with the boy he loves. It would be the nicest thing to do."

Against his will and despite his screams, Aniklo was wheeled down the same corridor as Maryn within the lab. Blurry images of others laid out on similar tables whizzed by him, people who were in several different states of deterioration, many limbless with a rank so strong it made him momentarily choke on his own bile. He was taken to where all had been left to die, and the door was locked behind him.

Chapter 17

Tauro was awoken from his slumber on the catacomb's hard floor by Srih.

"We need to be on the move in the next ten minutes."

The passage back to Penoa's safe space was entirely different from before. The hidden latch against the rock wall was no longer disguised, the pathway alight. Srih headed the group. Nebu, Tauro, and Fina took turns supporting Rhys, who had barely any time to heal from his injuries. Srih had awoken them at what Tauro could only imagine was the crack of dawn, a bit earlier than he was used to. The exertion from yesterday's events and the panic over what would happen next fresh in his mind.

When Srih opened the passage, the refuge in the catacombs had shifted from a quiet, peaceful refuge to organized pandemonium. The residential tents were down as well as the other stations. The only ones standing were Penoa's in the far corner of the large area. The nice landscape and sky illusion that used to cling to the walls had been dissolved, exposing the statue-like, humanoid rock structures underneath that lined the perimeter. Many had shapes like the ones that came to fight at the night market.

The crowd's mood that occupied the space was different, the formerly leisurely people charged and bustling around. To Nebu's surprise, more humans than Animoa were had gathered. Some humans were injured, others bleeding with the fleet in the middle of the crowd.

Penoa was in the center of it all, talking with Animoa who had the same uniform insignia as Srih and Rhys. At their arrival, she approached them, parting the crowd with just her presence.

"You guys are back just in time. What happened to Rhys?" she asked Srih in between beckoning for a medic.

"It was during the third convergence point. Everything's a mess on land. The watchers are trapping civilians just like you predicted."

Rhys was dragged to get treatment during their short exchange. Srih and Penoa, engrossed in their conversation, walked together with the three others following behind and headed toward Penoa's master tent. Tauro and Nebu watched on, soaking in the change in their surroundings, possibly scanning for people they might know in the influx of the crowd, scanning for some semblance of the normalcy they had lost just a week ago.

They quickly made it back to Penoa's tent, and she finally turned to acknowledge the three others. "I hope you found what the both of us are looking for." She extended her hand to the bag that carried the convergence pieces, but Fina didn't offer it up.

"Thank you for allowing us to travel with your team on the expedition, but we still are missing the last mistic convergence piece," Fina spoke up, pulling Penoa and Srih out of their bubble. Penoa then turned to Fina, a small smirk present underneath the mask of her fur.

"Ah, yes, I almost forgot about that." She looked to her staff. The fractal light encased within the orb attached on top swirled, the glare of it intensifying as she flicked it swiftly forward. The orb materialized their last needed piece.

Nebu grabbed it swiftly out of the air it had come from before gravity could bend it to its will. Then, she handed it over to Tauro, who had the rest of what they needed.

"Thank you," Tauro said, the group excited they had finally been able to do one thing right, had finally reached the goal they had been striving for. But, it was all shattered when Penoa opened her mouth next.

"I'm glad to be doing service with you, but we're not done yet."

Their faces dropped, knowing they had not held up their end of the bargain.

"We weren't able to—"

"You all forget I made this deal knowing how it would turn out. You underestimate my staff's knowledge. Give the crystal to me."

They reluctantly handed it over, and with a tap of her staff, it was brought to life again, the holographic message of the floorplans, fuzzy but there. With the flick of her finger, she slid the hologram from their comm crystal to the one on her staff. The projection's graininess evened out, the picture as clear as lightning in the sky.

"So, they found a way to send it after all," Nebu said.

"Of course, they did. I believed in them." Penoa's triumph was quickly stomped out when she looked deeper into the crystal, a deeper aura of black rising from the depths of its surface. An ashen mask of horror fell over her and Fina's face.

"Why is it turning colors?" Tauro asked in panic, looking between Fina and Penoa. Fina was pallid, her voice flat when she opened her mouth to speak.

"Hyanth wired the crystals so they would, to some extent, be connected to our well-being. If they change color, it usually means something good or bad."

"What are you trying to say?" Nebu asked, but her question was quickly answered when Penoa drew something black out of the crystal, another picture forming in the air.

It was a faint flash of imagery, the flash of Maryn and Aniklo's anguished faces, the flash of an ax, and the shadow of a girl, an Animoa who looked very similar to Penoa, the girl's body thin and mutilated. She was leaning against a hard wall, sitting on the floor, sagging like a doll. Penoa's face was in a wild contortion of grief she only took on when talking of her daughter, and Srih knew what this meant.

Tauro and Nebu still looked on in confused shock at what the crystal unleashed.

"I was right. They have her. We have to act now," Penoa said. Her grief transformed into determination, and with sure footing, she moved out of the tent and into the crowd. Srih followed after her.

This left Nebu, Tauro, and Fina in the tent, the crystal still resting on the table, flashing nightmares right before them.

Tauro knew from the start there would be a risk attached to this plan. But now that he had seen what he had seen, the civilians manhandled by the watchers who were supposed to protect them, the vacancy of the now dangerous streets, the people dead all around, there was no denying that whatever was in this crystal was serious.

"They're both in danger. We have to do something."

"This could be a false alarm. And we have to protect the ley line clusters—"

"My brother is in danger, Fina! I don't give a fuck about ley line clusters. I could never live with myself if I just went back to the reserve and acted like nothing is going on."

"But, what about everything we've worked toward for the past week? You're gonna risk this just to check on a nondescript vision from our broken comm?"

"We won't be able to fulfill the ritual without it, Fina. And Aniklo's family. We can't leave the Mainland without him."

"We don't even know what these people are trying to achieve right now. This is against the plan—"

A large horn sounded outside the tent, and in the distracted moment, Tauro grabbed the bag of ley line convergent mistic chips from Fina, holding it out of her reach.

"We're going to save my family whether you like it or not. You can come with us, or go back to the reserve with nothing." He pulled Nebu out of the tent with him, not even waiting for an answer.

"She's gonna be so mad at us," Nebu said, a hint of thrill in her voice.

"She's gonna have to deal with it." Tauro responded back, stopping once they were deep in the crowd. "Thanks for agreeing to come."

"Of course."

The boom of Penoa's voice cut into their moment, drawing everyone to attention. She stood in the center of the group, her ropes draped around her, staff clutched in hand.

"You are all here because you have been wronged by society, wronged by the people who abuse their power on our isles. Over the past couple of weeks, our world has fallen into shambles, fallen into a place of disaster that can only be recalibrated by profound action!"

There was an uproar of agreement in the crowd.

"Many of you pure human folk have never seen people like me, have been told we Animoa are a sick mutation who don't belong, but that is not the case. We have been beaten down, killed off, and tortured by the Corps, tortured by the people who call themselves scientists. Those who claimed to be working to better our society. For so long, we have hidden. But now, now that everything is truly falling to pieces, and nothing is being done, it is time to hold those who have wronged us accountable!

"We have all been gathered here for a reason. Whether to avenge those who have been unjustly killed or captured, or to put an end to all the lies that have been spread, all the hurt that has been caused. We wish to pave a new future on the backbones of the old days of oppression. Now is the time for action! Now is the time that we march!"

With that, the crowd went wild. Penoa raised her staff to the air, the orb attached to its top issuing lightning bolts of energy, shooting into the mechs. Through that pulse of energy, the figures were animated, brought to life to roar along with the crowd.

"Today, we march to storm the Corps. To take down the power that has caused the dark mist to flood our streets, and bring about peace. Today we march for our peace!"

And with that, she beckoned the mechs from their place. The crowd moved forward like a singular tidal wave, like a body of water, which flooded out of the Animoa's hiding place and up out of the catacombs, emerging in the streets.

Tauro and Nebu moved with the wave of people, holding tight to their bags, weapons drawn at the ready. Their part of the crowd emerged close to the Corps' strong tower, the rise of the suns to the east illuminating the path to their target.

Some walkers had abandoned their posts, sitting idly in the streets. The practiced exterior of their authority had melted away, showing who they truly were. Others more dedicated to their job fired their blasters into the screaming crowd. The people moved through the rubble still decorating the streets fluidly, and Tauro and Nebu watched in horror as the marchers beside them dropped like flies, adding to the pile of bodies that had been consistently accumulating on the ground. The dark mist was surprisingly nowhere to be seen, but the wall of watchers standing guard along the Corps' forcefield were a much bigger threat.

"Stand your ground, everyone!" Penoa screamed from the front of the crowd, raising her staff to shoot out a wave of white that temporarily stunned the guards long enough for the people to effectively advance. They crushed the watchers against the sizzling exterior of the mistic wall. The animated rock people moved through the crowd, all standing at attention, raising their fists repeatedly to crash against the barrier around the Corps. Their attempts shook the ground, cracking the surface, their fists immune to the backlash of energy the wall issued out.

The people cheered, a loud cacophony of noise and chaos, encouraging the animated rock people on as they created cracks within the wall. But the nature of those screams changed drastically in a single second.

A loud boom issued from above, loud enough to shatter eardrums. They all looked up and out, and watched in awe the mistic barrier that encased their entire world get polluted in an inky black. The sizzling of the larger barrier all around them dropped down like black lightning waves to the earth. The waves hit the ground and polluted everything it touched. The crowd that had been triumphant was now being struck by black lightning, the sky convoluted. An intense inky blackness could be seen covering the border walls of the Outer Rim.

"We need to find them now!" Tauro screamed to Nebu, barely able to hear his own voice, the ringing in his ear and the shouts of others drowning it out.

They saw some of the people who had marched beside them turn to scorched piles of hot skin right before their eyes, the black lightning dissolving all that it touched, and the residue of those people doing the same. Some were trampled; others on the edge of the crowd ran away, but Tauro and Nebu held tight to one another, cutting through the chaos where a lightning bolt had struck the barrier around the Corps, shattering the energy like glass.

Tauro was cut severely across the face, a thick gash sliced into his cheek, temporarily halting his struggle, but Nebu kept him from falling and being trampled, the inside of the Corps finally breached.

Nebu and Tauro desperately scrambled with the others brave enough to break through, knowing time was running out.

Chapter 18

Aniklo was left drained when they shut the door behind him, wanting to drift away and separate from the agony of their damaged bond and Maryn's missing arm, the thrum of Maryn's pain still palpable, the remembrance still fresh.

The tint of the room was dark, the glow of brewing cauldrons the only light provided. From Aniklo's vantage, he was almost tempted to believe he was in his room back home, the glow in the room moonlight, something pure and not evil to lull him into a detached state of mind. He could almost block out the ominous moans coming from the shadows when a voice unexpectedly snapped him out of his morbid thoughts.

"Hello?" It came from the corner of the room, raspy yet feminine and somewhat familiar. Through sheer force of will, he shook off his gag enough to murmur back.

"Who's there?" he asked. The ominous jingle of shackles resounded from the darkness, his heart racing at his inability to move, inability to protect himself from what was coming. It was only when he could match the face to the voice when everything fell into place.

"Deltha? How did you get here?" he murmured through the constriction of his gag. She, in their tattered form, limped on a singular leg, a dingy gown hanging over them. The same fox disguise, or what he'd thought was a disguise, was intact from their time at the night market.

"The same way you did. They brought me here after . . ." Her voice trickled off, forced to sit down in exhaustion. "A few have died, Aniklo."

"How do you know my name?"

"We have no time to discuss that," Deltha responded, working to untie him. He could finally sit up and almost threw up with what he saw, now in full clarity. Dismantled bodies were stacked against the walls, some appearing dead, others too weak to stand or speak or feel at all. They all looked shattered, draped against the wall. The lights he had seen at a faint glance were actually glowing cauldrons. The faint imprint of bodies slumped at grotesque angles to fit within the liquid were visible through the film of the sparkly bubbles. There were rows and rows of cauldrons, all lining the room, haunting, a prediction of what was to come for those left alive on the other side.

"What is this place?"

"It's where they dump everybody when they're done sucking the energy from them." She gave him a second to retch across the floor, rubbing his back in comfort. He recovered from his slumped posture across a former bed.

"There's no time, Aniklo." Deltha wobbled to her feet, leading him over to a couple of still chained people, dazed and moaning in pain. "Now is our chance to escape. You're the most able-bodied person they've ever brought here. With your help, we could probably bust the door down and get help."

Deltha, out of sheer force, heaved a couple of the living onto the crate Aniklo was formerly tied to, but Aniklo was too captivated by something shining in the corner of the room to help. In between the rows of cauldrons, where the wired vats of energy were all tied to, was a single circular orb. Its imprinted runes within it beckoned him, called him.

He didn't even recall moving through the rows of cauldrons full of dead people, didn't even feel the sizzle of his skin being burned by the mist entrapped within the vats of energetic liquid. All he could do was fixate on what was powering it all, knowing the dull light was shining for him. For what they had risked their lives to come back and find.

"Don't touch that!" Deltha screamed from their vantage. "It will—"

It was too late.

Aniklo yanked the harnesser, something his father had died for, out of the exposed force field that had locked it into place. A rush of tingling air and white blinding light was all Aniklo sensed for a quick moment before his vision returned to normal.

Somehow, in a wildly unexplainable way, he wasn't in his body anymore. He was a spectral I, a floating being above himself, above his circumstances, above the world itself, and right beside him was Miho. Miho's dark skin was tainted by the transparency of his body, his robes and pants suit crisp and iridescent in the light.

They were in an open expanse. The trees around them swayed in a comfortably crisp wind, the ground beneath a grassy plain that never ended. Miho smiled his warm smile at Aniklo, his almond eyes soothing, a hand on the boy's back. Maryn, despite the severe injuries he had sustained, was right beside Aniklo, the same face of shock and awe present on his face, his arm still missing, but now just a stud encased in a warm light.

"I'm so happy you guys finally made it." Maryn was crying, and he moved to hug his dad, but his body just bled through him, the fractal reality they existed in not able to sustain it.

"You won't be able to hug me here, my son. You have been brave, and smart, and the two of you have been everything I knew you could be. I have watched you all along. I have been with you through everything, and I know all that's happened has been hard." His face was the definition of both pride and worry, his deep shoulder-length curls swaying in the wind.

"But, unfortunately, the work it will take to find me isn't over." Out of his cupped hands appeared an orb of pure white light, the veins of its energy spinning in the air around it.

"I opened up a can of worms I can't close from the fractal realm I am trapped in. I went searching for power I should have never been able to attain, further corrupting the equilibrium between divinity and man." He was staring at the orb, both of the boys too stunned to speak.

"By creating this harnesser, I could tap into a controlled reality man should never have access to, that should only be left to the unknown. Power like this is why Ponsn is in isolation, why the causes of the war, between both the natives and the outer tribes, was punished. The mist gave them a chance, but it's too late." He lifted the sheer essence of the orb encased in his hand, and it floated into the air, drawing the attention of all.

Somehow, though their attention was held tight by the wonder of Miho and the energy he demanded, the boys felt a sea of eyes around them, a watching that pulled at their backs, at their core. When the boys could finally look back to Miho from the attention the orb required, he was another visage entirely, the clean attire he formerly donned now littered with earth and vines and leaves. His head an evolved into a moon orbiting the pull of the suns, a wild power that had no business taking the form of a man, but still chose to.

The voice that spoke next came from no mouth, but seemed to echo from the wild serenity around, a hollow power all octaves at once, stripping them of will and emotion.

"You need to reverse what we started, what division brings. Ponsn is to be no more, but the new world that emerges has no place for the darkness."

Though Miho had marched into something foreign and wild, the boys knew he was still himself, but an altered version, something unexplainable. "Tell Nirima I forgive her."

The orb that Miho thrust into the charged air struck them at their core, forcing its tendrils into the fabric of their bond. A shell-shocking pain knocked them back into their bodies, out of the spectral realm, which the harnesser had tapped into and attempted to wield.

They were back in the hellhole that was the Corps, Aniklo holding the dormant harnesser in his burned palms. The vats that encased the dead bubbled over and seared away the door. Maryn was awake, the stump that was formerly his arm sealed in a faint glow, his binds burned away. Deltha was the only one beside the other two boys who remained alive after the explosion, the others too weak to withstand the wave of light, their wounds encased similarly to Maryn's.

"What did you do? Where'd he come from?" Deltha questioned Aniklo. Their shock intensified as the dead bodies in the emptied-out vats rose, now white figments of energy, possessed by the harnesser's residual power. The dead figments of light walked through the locked door, searing a hole through it with their sheer existence.

Aniklo rushed over to Maryn, holding him close and helping him up, "We need to get out of here."

Reluctantly, Deltha left the room behind, joining the boys in their escape attempt. They made their way to the open floor of the Corps to see the catastrophic sight of the dark mist slowly taking control over people. It had seeped into the building, the wall now shattered away. Workers slumped over their stations became a gooey remembrance of their former visage, the swirling of the pure black hovering over them. The figures of light that had risen from the vats surprisingly ate away at the darkness, engulfing it in its depths of light.

Maryn, Aniklo, and Deltha passed through as the two sides of strange energy waged a war on one another. They joined in with the escaping workers and ran through the hallway to more chaos.

Watchers in their terrified state were shooting down anyone who seemed remotely injured as they came funneling out of the work room, people ducking and weaving as the crowd was picked off.

Before the three could get shot, the stair door opened, a perfect marksman stepping out to shoot down the guards with precision. When they turned around, Aniklo realized it was Nebu, sweaty and dirty, her hair gathered in a tight puff.

"Nebu!" he asked in confusion.

She turned to him, hugging both him and Maryn in relief. Maryn cried out when she brushed her arm against his injured one, and she looked at it in horror. "What happened to you!"

"No time to explain. We need to get out of here," Deltha said with urgency, pushing them all into the current of people headed for the stairwell.

They reached the final floor, dodging bullets from walkers who had been posted above, and finally emerged in the lobby. Soaking up the havoc of the crowd, all of them tried their hardest to beat up whoever was in the middle.

They pushed through the chaos and dashed into the streets, Nebu calling out for Tauro, who she'd left hidden at a potential rendezvous. For a moment, she feared the worst before she heard his voice cry out.

"Aniklo! Maryn!" Tauro was near the building's edge. He sprinted toward them, embracing both Aniklo and Maryn.

Tauro's embrace of his brother was cut short when the sound of a scream rang out, a loud blast issuing through the tight space. It was Jessik, who somehow crawled her way out of the fury of the crowd, a blaster in hand, aimed directly at Tauro. The blast went through his shoulder, digging in, and Aniklo and Maryn felt its impact.

What happened next felt as if it was in slow motion. The mist had infused within the two boy's bond and ignited, solidifying within Maryn's hand. He let the anger sit there, propelling the power of the mist out of his palm like a bullet and right into Jessik's chest. She fell to the floor, coughing up blood.

The others watched in awe before all four walked over her prone and desperate body, cut through the crowd, and headed out the door before the crowd noticed her there and sucked her in with all of her colleagues being pummeled.

They reached open air, the cobblestones in shambles, the flare of the mist toward the docks surging up in a profuse explosion near the market, blocking their escape. They, in a futile attempt to no longer be exposed, huddled in the closed bounds of a torn-down shop, trying to catch their breath.

"We have to find a way out of here," Maryn said with urgency, the first to catch his breath. He propped Aniklo up on his lap, surveying his wounds despite his own injuries.

"Tauro called Katam earlier. He's on his way," Nebu said back. "You have to put pressure on your wounds. Both of you." She pulled out the first aid kit from her bag, but was never able to properly assist Tauro in wrapping the wound on his shoulder.

A big manifestation of mist rose out of the gravel right outside their feeble shelter, pulling at Nebu's exposed leg with a humanoid claw of solid mist. It attempted to pull her out into the open. Tauro, with all of his strength, held onto her with his uninjured arm, and Aniklo did the same. Maryn used his newfound ability to shoot light conjurations of mist like bolts into the black humanoid blob, but what truly made it let go was Katam.

Katam, on a winged beast, landed on the mist. The behemoth's growl was strong enough to intimidate the blob of black mist, and it slipped away, leaving Nebu weak on the ground. Nebu's sister jumped off of the animal they had flown in on, pulling her sister on with her.

The three boys came out of their hiding space, desperate to leave the Mainland behind. After checking for everyone's safety, the massive wings of their salvation flapped them high into the air, the mist seeping up from the ground far out of reach.

They could see all of their small world: the fragments of the Outer Rim veiled in complete black, people like small blobs fleeing the prison state to open waters, desperate for escape when it was impossible. The walls near the Outer Rim cracked at an exponential rate, the light of the suns finally permeated the bounds of mist, and with that sight before them, the group realized maybe whatever they were trying to do was all in vain.

To Unravel a Realm

Chapter 19

They winged creature they rode eventually landed in an exposed area of the port, while the mist increased around the Mainland. The cloud of mayhem had evolved and spread at a rapid speed, marking the end of all they knew.

Nirima was no longer at the house. She waited with a large group of people, Animoa and full humans alike, gathered in the cove of the reserve's residential dwellings, a force field of mist built up around them.

Upon their landing, the force field opened, Nirima rushing to embrace her kids.

"What is going on?" she asked in their huddle, not even worrying about the other people watching on wary of Tauro and Nirima's presence.

"The city is in shambles. The black mist the Corps has been facilitating has spread too far for us to do anything about it from the inside, but we have everything we need to trigger the harnesser," Tauro responded, looking over the crowd. They noticed the Animoa huddled around the forcefield, using the mist from within their skin to fuel their shelter.

"Thank goodness you guys made it." Fina emerged from the crowd. "Have you got the convergence pieces?"

"Right here," Nebu responded.

"Good," Fina said.

"What's our next move?" Srih asked from her station at the force field.

"Can you guys make the force field move? From here, we have to trek to the epicenter."

"Can't you guys activate it from here?"

"There's no time, and it won't be the same without the energy from the pillars. Besides, the epicenter has a much more stable force field than this."

The debate carried on for a short while, people begging to wait a second or two longer for their loved ones who they had been forced to leave behind, but it was too late. To Tauro, it was disheartening that this group of approximately fifty people was all he knew for sure was left in their world.

Despite her injuries, Nebu was on Fina's side. They all had to get it together and find a way to move, even with everyone in varying states of disarray.

"None of this feels like it matters anymore." Maryn murmured from his position next to Aniklo sitting on the ground. In the short time they had arrived, Nirima had made sure to wrap Tauro and Aniklo's injuries, and she had now moved on to bandaging Maryn's arm. In between his arm and Aniklo's, the tether, visible again, throbbed as a reaction to their shared pain.

"It matters, Maryn. It does. You matter," she said to him in earnest, wiping a tear that had slipped out. "You two never got to tell me what happened with your search. What you found," she said as a change of subject.

Aniklo almost didn't want to answer. What Jessik had said about his mother tainted his image of her, making him question where she stood in all of this. After a second, he pulled out the drained harnesser, its glimmer softened.

She gasped, then moved to touch it, before thinking better of it and pulling away. "So, he finished it."

"My father said he forgives you," said Maryn.

Her face was a contortion of horror, confusion, a strand of her short pixy cut falling into her watery eyes. "How did he—"

"When we first touched the harnesser, we talked to him for a couple of seconds, and he said at the very end to tell you he forgives you."

"I don't deserve that from him." Her voice was thick, her tears fell freely. "When I was there I didn't know what the Corps truly wanted. . . . I didn't know that he was . . . that they were . . ."

Aniklo buried her head in his shoulder, comforting her like he had become very accustomed to. Despite all the questions, all the unfinished confusion rotting underneath the surface, he knew she deserved this.

"It's okay, Ma. Everything's going to be okay."

The sincerity of their moment was shattered with the boundaries of their protection, the Animoa keeping them safe knocked back with the force field's strength slipping away. A massive claw had cut through the energy and stabbed into the ground, trampling anyone in its way.

For a second, they all sat to soak in the majesty of the creature before them, its large claws and iridescent scales reflected off the sun. But, the dissolving portion of its body laced with the essence of pure dark mist made it rabid, its eyes beady and desperate to attack.

"Run!" Fina screamed, and everyone scrambled, trying to escape the creature infected with the parasitic energy.

Aniklo, Maryn, and the rest of the family ran desperately without the cover of safety, ducking through the trees along with others in the crowd in a desperate attempt to escape.

As they passed through their meadow, the giant, formerly gentle creature leaked its infection of mist through the branches, polluting the trees, the grass rotting almost exactly as their dream. But now, looking back wasn't an option. The group was gradually thinned out, the people the creature had sucked into itself becoming a part of its roar, their choir of screams haunting.

Time slowed as Aniklo held desperately onto his mother's hand before he felt her hand slip out of his own. Her body impaled by the claw of the approaching beast, her screams gathered into the chorus of the fallen who had been devoured within the beast. Aniklo could only stand there and watch his mother fade away from him, watch her die right before his eyes. At that moment, it almost felt futile, like him mattering was a lie, like all they had done meant nothing.

Maryn noticed Aniklo had fallen behind, the others too occupied with getting themselves to safety. He used all of his strength to pull Aniklo upright, dragging them both to the clearing that led to the overpass between the reserve and Old Ponsn.

Fina released the signal once she slammed against the outer wall, calling for someone to grant them entry with no answer. The creature was advancing, the group of people who had once been fifty transformed to less than fifteen.

Tauro finally noticed his mother's absence, his brother hyperventilating, Maryn's tears slipping freely.

"Ma…" was all Tauro could say, the rest of the group screaming as the rabid creature progressed, scraping its claws into the small hole they all were barely able to fit through.

"What is taking so long!" Nebu yelled, her already wounded leg was slashed open by the beast's claws shortly after, making her let out a scream.

"They won't open! It won't—"

Without further hesitation, Nebu smashed one of the ley line convergence clusters against the wall and a release of energy thinned out to a certain extent.

"What are you doing!" Fina screamed, taking the bag before Nebu could smash another one.

"We have to get in!" Katam screamed, with Astoria hysterical in his arms.

The claws of the beast almost sweeping the poor baby away finally snapped Maryn out of his daze, and he moved to solidify the tether between Aniklo and himself, smashing the spear it created into the softened energy barrier. It finally broke and let them in and away from the rabid creature behind them. Its roar still reverberated through the small human-sized opening, but its reach could no longer grab anyone.

The foliage within the epicenter was wilted, the trees rotted away, not infected by the dark mist, but slumping in on themselves as if wounded, as if they could feel the coming darkness and wanted escape.

"Everything's okay, right, Ma?" Katam looked around, expecting to see her with Aniklo. "Where's Ma?" Katam finally asked, Rioba soothing their daughter who was still understandably worked up.

Aniklo didn't even move to get up from his face-planted position on the grass, unable to even breath from the shock, not wanting to answer. He knew it was his fault.

Katam slumped against a tree as the reality of his loss hit him. "She was safe. I just talked to her a minute ago. She was safe."

Maryn sat next to Aniklo encouraging him to get up. Nebu was beside Rioba unsure of what to do with Tauro curled in on himself beside her.

They only had a second to absorb their situation before the people of the epicenter emerged from the saddened trees, weapons drawn. Fina stepped forward reassuringly, saying "Hey, it's me, Fina. I brought these people back with me. The harnesser and the ley line pieces, too. We're safe."

The people with their crossbows still had them raised, unwavering in their defense. "How do we know you're not infected?"

"That's enough." Hyanth's voice rose through the trees, his form stepping through, calm and collected, but a dull, haunted shell of his former self. He relieved the people who had come with the crossbows, never taking his gaze off of his daughter. He stepped into the circle of the wounded.

"I wasn't expecting to see you again." His eyes were sunken in, mouth pulled down in a frown.

"What do you mean, Da?" She paused, confused by this version of her father whom she had never seen before, all the affection and love she had come to know stripped away. "You weren't expecting me to come back?"

"It's too late. Whatever Miho may have had with the harnesser will be no match for what is coming for us. The suns are finally setting on our corner of the world. It might even be a mercy to let them shoot you, just to make it less painful." He pulled out a crossbow from behind his back, aiming the contraption directly at her.

"But Da, I love—" She was shot in the neck before she could even get another word out, dropping dead right before them. The rest of the group were motionless, all of them watching Fina fall to the ground, coughing up her own blood in shock, her eyes bugging out.

Hyanth put the crossbow down, calm as ever, brushing a soothing hand over his daughter's head. "I love you, too," he said, watching over her as she took her last breaths, closing her eyes when she finished gurgling up her own blood.

"What have you done!" Nebu said in shock. Hyanth turned to her.

"All of you have been exposed to the darkness. Something more black and evil than I ever imagined. You tainted the land by even stepping foot here, and I can't allow you to ruin our sanctuary, I can't—"

Tauro, in the middle of his tirade, swiftly pulled out his blaster, shooting Hyanth point-blank. The old man dropped right next to his daughter, their corpses sinking into tussled dirt.

"We trusted him . . ." Aniklo said in shock.

"What do we do now?" One of the Animoa in their ranks asked.

"We finish this. It's our only option," Maryn responded, dashing with all his strength deeper into the sanctuary.

Nebu took a couple of moments to say goodbye to her friend, closing her beady eyes that still contained the horrors of her last moments.

Before they went much farther, Rioba shot all the people who had donned crossbows in the leg before her sister swiftly gagged them with a handful of leaves. Then, they followed everyone else to go deeper into the epicenter.

The place was a ghost town, but the main central dining alcove was packed, all the residents conveniently eating, unaware of the group dashing across the square headed toward the pillars.

Maryn led the way, cutting through the trees that led to the cloudy meadow, Astoria's cries, the pants of exhaustion, and thuds against dirt the only sounds they made.

Finally, after what seemed like forever, they broke through the trees. The mist that encased the grassy, open space buzzed with a sort of urgency. The calm inside the storm of this wild environment cut into the open air, illuminating the midday suns, almost overcast by the black veins that threatened to rip the entire barrier in half.

The pillars were still where they had been weeks before, the glow of their glyphs flickering in and out. They were all gathered here, underneath the intensity of the carved hard dirt, the world open above their heads as it faded to nothing everywhere else.

The Animoa, Katam, Rioba, and a confused Astoria were at the edge of the pillars, barely within the circle. The rest stood in the middle, prepping for what was to come.

Aniklo couldn't help but think about how wrong everything had gone over a few short days, and how wrong it could go in this very moment as he pulled out the harnesser from his pocket. He looked to Maryn, whose face conveyed the same emotions, before putting their father's creation down on the ground. The glyphs didn't just light up with a dull reaction the way they had before, but were a rising surge of power, shooting feet off the ground, the outline of them puissant and alight.

"What do we do now?" Maryn asked after a few moments.

"Get the bag." Tauro brought the bag to Maryn, the pieces of the ley lines evidently carved out in the engraved slots on the edge of the pillars' boundaries. They both, in record time, put the ley line clusters into place, everyone watching in anticipation as it all was coming together. Katam and Rioba clutched each other tighter, Astoria finally calming down at the display of the lights before them. Aniklo turned to Maryn, the light from the ground's activation shining in his chocolate eyes.

"What if we did something wrong? What if we let them down?" Aniklo asked.

"In a way, they let us down by giving us this weight to carry, this cross to bear. But, they were just people. We are just people. That's gonna have to be enough."

Aniklo heard the last piece click into place, felt the reverberation of the sound waves around them, felt the itch of their skin as the air within their pillars' barrier was altered, the mist resetting, reshaping their surroundings. He looked down, then looked up, and for some reason, he was more at peace than he had been in a long time.

"We're just people," he echoed, and the mist rose, encasing them all in the white of their own creation.

Touch!
Kenneth Santiago

Touch!

What is this? What's going on?
News just came in that several thousand people are dead from unknown causes.

I remember waking up that day from an eight-hour nap. After putting on my grandpa-like sandals, I made my bed a look-alike of a brand-new bed. You know, the way they look on TV and in the paper advertisements. I walked to my bathroom and looked at my face, examining it for any blemishes or dead skin that needed to be taken care of. Luckily, I was clean if not greasy from the heat.

I put on my usual blank white shirt, black baggy pants, black FILA sneakers, and a black, fake leather jacket. But most importantly, I put on my dark brown gloves before I wore or touched anything. I made sure they were tight enough to not expose my bare skin as I diligently scanned myself to make sure every other part of my body was covered.

Before I left, I'd always scan my small studio apartment to make sure everything was perfect and fit. Not that it would really matter to anyone, but perfection is key in my world. I noticed my tablecloth was uneven. So, I sprinted over to fix it before leaving.

Leaving the safety of my clean home, I headed to the stairwell. Pushing open the door with my hip, I was fairly happy it didn't have a handle for me to touch, and with my hands in my pockets, descended the three floors of steps to the basement garage. I tried to remember where I parked with the hopes no one had gotten too close to me. I was happy when I saw no one had.

Having a Jeep Wrangler was nice, but it was too bad it got dirty so easily. Then again, everything gets dirty. Like the newish vibe to my bed, I usually go the extra mile for my car, cleaning and polishing it like my ma used to when she got me dressed and groomed for church every Sunday. I guess I can say the apple doesn't fall too far from the Catholic church tree. I can't really help it; it's a force of habit.

I continued scanning my car, ensuring cleanliness and that it wasn't ransacked. Luckily, it was all right, good heavens. I buckled up and distinctly remembered a picture falling in front of me. It was painful to see, especially considering what happened recently, but there was no time to reminisce. I had to go to work. So, I drove off pretending it wasn't there, but it stared back. I knew it was there.

Music usually drowns out emotions, but the radio was playing Black Keys' "Too Afraid to Love You."

"I wish loneliness would leave me, but I think it's here to stay . . ."

I silently sang along to it, feeling like life was poking fun at me again. While I drove past trees and

Touch!

multiple corner stores, I thought to myself how time flies by but also how slow it can be when there's nothing to get excited about. Nothing intrigued me; this was basically a daily routine for me. No stark visuals that pleased the eyes, no eye candies worth ogling.

The city wasn't big by any stretch but had a stable community. The grimy black setting of graffiti on every corner wall was visible, as well as the many disgusting cigarette buds littering the sidewalks. All I could do was drive closer to my destination and smell the fragrance of new car smell with a hint of minty, pine tree and be happy I hadn't forgotten my gloves again, which would have put a damper on my day. But, I always had an extra pair of disposable gloves in my compartment.

While on the road, I noticed a bum. Usually, I would drive off, but I felt generous that day. I pulled over and noticed he looked like a Sasquatch. I could tell he hadn't showered in a while, and it was hard to see whether or not he was awake. I thought about opening my window to give the man a fifty, but when I saw his grimy exposed hand, I thought otherwise. So, I just crumpled the bill and miraculously threw it into the bum's plastic cup.

As I was getting ready to drive off, I noticed in a brief last-minute glance the bum's sign read, "End Here." I was certainly perplexed by this, but I turned to look at my phone and didn't have time to decipher this man's conspiracy.

After a good while, I thought to myself about how his normality was different from the general ninety percent. I also thought about the bum on the expressway and whether he was asleep or something else, like drunk, or on some kind of drug.

I worked at the general hospital as a tollbooth operator. "The introvert's dream job," I would always say. But hey, who was I kidding? Work for me, generally was just asking for a receipt and payment in a little cubical box. Handing over receipt after receipt, thanking and saying farewell to many strangers. Often, I'm asked, "Why do you wear gloves and a mask?" I usually just say it's the protocol or a force of habit.

Either way, I'm in my world; everyone roams around with simple freedom of feeling and expression, while I am a conscientious objector.

The eight hours in the booth flew by, which was good because I was ready to get out of there before I even started. Before I even started my shift, I had to spray the seat, cash drawer, and everything else I knew I would be touching. Even outside the window, as I sometimes came in contact with it. I just needed to know it was pristine as can be, and no one could tell me they had done it for me. I didn't trust others' cleaning abilities.

After work, I went to the local diner for dinner. I had a random case of the munchies. Usually, I'm suspicious when it comes to public places. That day, I was feeling experimental. So, I went over to the front entrance, pulled on the lever with my brown glove, and entered the small diner that had six-to-eight people.

The checkered floor gave me the feeling of a challenge. I walked to each black-squared tile as if the white tiles were lava.

Touch!

When standing in front of the register, the cashier said, with a distant look, "Welcome to Tim's. I'm . . . Tim."

"Hi, Tim. I would like an omelet."

"Would you like our new special sauce?"

With a strange excitement, I said, "I'll take that!"

Tim turned around and shouted my order to the cook behind him. He told me I could take a seat at the counter or at any available table. He eventually returned with a plate of toast, butter, and grape jelly that came with the omelet.

As I sat down at the counter, I quickly changed my mind about sitting at a table. I grabbed my plate and walked to the back of the diner, out of the way of people and their bodily fluids. I'd chosen the back because the guy next to me had been drooling.

Once I placed the plate down, I pulled out a small spray tube of disinfectant to clean the table and seat. That done, I sat down and removed my brown gloves, and slipped on a fresh pair of disposable rubber ones. I was hungry, so I attacked the toast with butter and jelly and then stuffed it into my mouth.

Shortly thereafter, Tim arrived with my omelet. He asked me if I wanted more toast, which I gladly thanked him for. While digging into the hotbed of eggs, cheese, veggies, and meat, my phone disrupted my rhythm of cutting the rolled yellow goodness, scooping it with the toast, and lifting it to my mouth.

With a look at the message and the name of the sender, I picked up the phone. "I'm at dinner. Will be there shortly. I won't be long."

Touch!

The food wasn't five-star dining but looked edible. For a moment, I got a little excited to eat my meal.

The restaurant wasn't busy, which meant there wasn't much noise. The sounds were low whispers, the clanking of silverware on plates, and the occasional burp. There was also the voice of some late-night talk show host discussing the day's events when he was interrupted by an emergency news broadcast.

"Breaking News! There are reports coming in of fifty sudden, unexplained deaths in the Rochester, New York area. No details have been given about this astronomical tragedy in our community. Further investigation details will be given as soon as available. Please be cautious, and please reach out to law enforcement with any questions and details of this tragic event. This is . . ."

Click. The TV was turned off by someone, the line cook Tim had yelled at before. I didn't say a word as he scanned the restaurant to see if anyone objected to his decision. With none being expressed, he walked back through the kitchen door to get back to cooking.

I was very slowly beginning to take off my disposable gloves, at the speed of a snail. Before even thinking about going any further after that news, I stopped. I noticed the drooling man was still, face-planted on his plate.

I guess he was tired or really hungry, I thought to myself. Gloves back on, I dropped some cash on the table and simply speed-walked out of the diner.

I remembered feeling very disenchanted with my head leaning on the window.

Touch!

Next, I was outside my ex-girlfriend Beth's apartment, and I could hear the loud rave music and chants of the random partygoers in the complex. I was not too pleased with this reality, especially considering Beth knew who I was and what I was about. She knew I didn't do well with parties and extravagant events. I knew it wasn't on purpose, but still. She could've texted me: "Hey, having a party. Beware."

I took a moment to look at an unsent text message to Beth: "You didn't tell me you were having a party."

It had been about three months since Beth and I'd broken up after a year-long relationship. Miraculously, I managed to get through the ever-present party, and there I saw her, presumably beside her new sidekick. Her partner saw me and walked off as Beth said something to him I couldn't decipher; the loud music didn't help the situation. Beth came over, and gave me a hug and kiss on my cheek.

I got straight to the point. "Where's my stuff?"

"How's it going, Corey?"

"Where's my stuff?"

"Are you okay?"

"I will be as soon as I get my stuff."

"But don't cha want to mingle a bit?"

"No, I know no one here and rather just go home."

We stood in awkward silence, with the party music still blaring in the background.

"So…"

"Where's my stuff?"

I recalled Beth's new partner in crime grabbing her, saying something about her friends being there. She told me she would be back in a minute. After a while, I learned my belongings were in my favorite or rather former favorite spot of her apartment, the study room where I usually would be calm, quiet, noise resistant, and cozy: my own little haven.

Reminiscing on the good times there, I was able to find my box of precious vintage collectors' books of old tales. Reading was my life, my world, my escape, but these in particular stood out. They came from a time far beyond, and I couldn't risk losing these beauties.

The Vampire, His Kith And Kin by Montague Summer was a beautiful tale of bloodsuckers in a Halloween orange with bat demons. Another was *Ghostology, Products of Nature* by WM Danmar. With its phoenix-like cover of George Washington's head, it was so spooky indeed. And finally, Alexandre Dumas' *The Wolf Leader* with its Greek mythological cover, a hint of the Brothers Grimm, of which I'm sure they would be proud.

Before leaving, I stared at my former thinking chair, a cozy red couch with wooden stilts. Wanting to reminisce a little more, I sat on the chair to enjoy its ever-eternal comfy glory, thinking, *Wish I could bring this home.*

Before I knew it, I had gotten a little too comfortable and began to nod off. As I was nodding, I could almost vaguely hear the muffled party and music from outside the door, visibly not so loud compared to when the door was open. But, I heard a lot of hard thumps. Before I could register what the heck had happened, I fell into euphoria.

The next day I arose; the sunlight and the singing birds could be heard. For a moment, I had forgotten where I was. Scanning the room, I saw my stuff and instantly remembered my current predicament. So, I got up, picked up my box, walked toward the door, and mentally said *Goodbye* to my old thinking chair.

Outside the room, I distinctly recalled seeing everyone or close to everyone on the floor knocked out. Thinking they all had gotten high and drunk, I carefully maneuvered over everyone's motionless corpse. Right before I could go straight out the door, I saw Beth in her room. Like everyone, she was motionless. Beth always loved to have a good time, but somehow, she always seemed to end up in a comfy place every time she got a hangover. I thought about just leaving, but I walked over to her, looking at her vulnerable state.

"By all accounts, I hope you and everyone had a good time," I said to her, knowing she probably didn't hear me.

"Hey, hey, you awake?" She wasn't responding. I lightly tapped her; then, I noticed her eyes were wide-open but glazed over. Beth wasn't an eyes-wide-open sleeper, so I knew something was up. I cautiously moved toward her and considered checking her pulse. Knowing I wouldn't feel anything with my brown gloves, I grabbed my disposable latex ones and carefully checked her pulse. There was nothing . . .

3/19/19: A New Light

It's been three weeks since Beth died. It feels so unreal. I remember how informative she was to people, how she would always be around when she was needed, and how if she seemed M.I.A. she would always pop up in the least expected minute. I waited, but she didn't, she wasn't, she's gone.

Now, my driving purpose is gone. All I have is these gloves and a sense of deep loss and reevaluation. But even that isn't enough. Beth's friends and family are still reeling like me. Funeral arrangements are in place, and the grieving process continues. I remembered being home, in these white-tinted walls and confined limited space. Just thinking, while I looked at my box of latex gloves, *What killed her?*

It couldn't have been the drugs and alcohol. Beth was usually responsible when it came to that. Well, more so the alcohol. It couldn't have been the latex; she wasn't allergic. It could've been anything, but the autopsy didn't specify any real cause of death. They noticed her whole entire body, inside and out, just shut down with no real explanation.

Being home is no real comfort other than my books, but now, I just don't feel like drowning my sorrows in fantasy literature. I often think about how I lose myself in these scriptures and forget what's fact and fiction. But Beth's demise wasn't fiction. Even if I wanted it to be.

Earlier, I decided to go for a walk, and I found myself outside near the city park. While looking at Luna and her neighbors in the ever-darkening sky, I remembered how Beth and I would always lie on the ground. I always protested, with the dirt and creepy crawlies everywhere. But her insistence got me to do what she wanted to do.

Those were the days, weren't they? I asked myself.

Touch!

Just when I thought the night couldn't be any more interesting, I saw a flurry of shooting stars. I wished that everything was a dream. I opened up and looked at my phone, and saw it wasn't a dream as I stared at Beth's obituary.

The next day, not wanting to stay indoors, I went to a combination of Barnes & Noble and Starbucks. It was always welcoming to me, especially considering it's usually short-staffed with few customers. It was my safe place, even with my fears.

Now, I typically always have my gloves and mug. I don't typically ask for anything there other than sanitizers and some book locations or special requests. I was always in good hands there. While drinking my black coffee, I contemplated if I should have gotten some Death Wish Coffee instead. *Meh! next time*, I thought, and I continued my book: *Quiet: The Power of Introverts in a World That Can't Stop Talking*.

After about ten minutes or less, I just felt a heavy burden of weight on my eyes. The tears I'd let out before came back with a vengeance. I didn't want to make a scene in a group of ten or so people. Oddly enough, I was wearing a scarf in April, not wanting to draw any attention to myself. But man, do tears have a mind of their own. Regardless of my attempts, it was futile as messages from Beth's network of folks contacted me, the vibrating notifications reminding me of the cruel fate of someone I once loved.

Shit, why now, I said to myself silently as my face started to pour.

Touch!

Unbeknownst to me, a woman walked up to me, sensing my dread. I didn't get much interaction with people as I am usually low-key, but this was certainly a cry of shame.

"Feeling the heavy rain, aren't cha?" the woman said.

I wiped my tears furiously. "No. Just had some eye crust in me."

"Didn't look that way to me."

"Yeah, well, I couldn't sleep at all recently." Usually, I would make a white lie, but this wasn't far from the truth.

"Something you want to get off your chest?"

"No, not at all. Just like to read my book in peace, please."

"Shoot. What's got your panties in a bunch? Somebody died or something?" she asked me.

Right then, I just couldn't continue as she, like my phone, kept reminding me of this tragedy. I stood up, grabbed my coffee, held my tears, and struggled to not make a scene.

"What was it? Something I said? . . . Oh shit! Oh my god, I'm a vagina!"

"I gotta go," I said to her.

I rushed out with a chink in my armor, hoping whatever incorporeal being out there would stop messing with me at this oh-so-tragic moment in my life. I knew that girl was probably trying to follow me, but I couldn't handle the reminder of the only light in my world being extinguished. I ran for what felt like an eternity.

Touch!

With droplets of tears streaming out in the wind, I remember struggling to open my car. I furiously touched my entire body, trying to find the damn keys, until I finally realized I'd forgotten them at my table. I went back inside Barnes & Noble and saw my keys thinking, *Why is today so hard to get through? It's hard every day, but more so now.*

I grabbed the keys, but noticed one of the ladies grabbed something on the ground.

Thump!

Her body collapsed to the ground like a sack of potatoes. I recall being briefly curious, but when I heard my keys jingle, I just thought, *I need to go somewhere else that's safe.*

I noticed a couple of associates rushing to the woman's aid, but I don't recall what happened afterward since I was in a panic, forgetting about reality. But reality has a strange way of mocking us at moments like these.

I was in my car rushing, and next thing you knew, I heard some more subtle thumps in the store. Maybe, my ears have superpowers, or maybe, I was hallucinating from the stress. All I knew was when I saw the lady from earlier coming out of the store, I needed to GTFO, and I did. But it didn't make me feel any better.

3/30/19: Tragedy and Tragedy

The funeral was today. I was so depressed I couldn't think about anything but Beth and the thousands of things she could have died from. Did she die from the booze, the drugs, a murder, or perhaps this was a sick joke from some unknown incorporeal being. I couldn't wrap my mind around it, but it was time to shut up and pay my respects with folks who I thought would become my in-laws at one point.

We all stood there in echoing murmurs, tears, and agonizing gloom. I tried to keep my emotions to myself, but I couldn't, as everyone could see and knew how much Beth had meant to me. I felt some happiness for a bit thinking of our good times, but mostly grief and sorrow took over me. My tears and crunched-up face showed it, as I thought about the blue corpse in front of me.

I'm not opposed to saying I thought about marriage. Especially since it was her life goal more so than my own. But ever since we'd broken up because of my tendencies, that reality or any other possibility was gone. I don't know why I thought it was a good idea, being there and being around Beth's family and friends. I knew some of Beth's friends and family, but not enough for me to say we were close or tight. They knew she meant a lot to me, but I knew she was the middle piece of this Jenga tower. Now it was collapsing, as I could obviously see in their faces, their voices, and their actions.

She was the life of the party; she would always see everyone's sides: the good and the ugly. She was the ultimate catharsis of people's lives, including mine. She was maybe touchy-feely, trying to hug and hold hands, like a magnet, and she wanted people to share their honest thoughts without bullshitting. She was the hand of an angel, and I wasn't. I would let anything go just to see her sunshine smile, like a box of Raisin Bran, return to life. What I wouldn't have done to be in her stead, to be gone

Touch!

from these heavy emotions and cynical fears of the million beasties in this dirty world.

I would've gladly been in that casket. But, I can't; I'm not the violent type. But if I was, I would've died without a final note. Maybe it was reluctance, or perhaps, it was a feeling of making peace. But, I'm far from having any type of peace as my gloves, masks, and hand sanitizers demonstrate, my arms moving six feet away from everyone. I'm just someone Beth once knew.

Beth's life was perfect, maybe not a hundred percent of the time but enough for her to say, "Life is good."

While for me, all I can do is think, *Why am I the way I am?* What purpose do I have in this life, this life I don't think I deserve. Death may not be easy for most, but inevitably, it will come. I just wished Beth lived out her clock before me, because my clock is old and slow.

The family was mourning for what felt like an eternity as everyone was hugging, crying, turning bright red, and not looking at Beth's blue body. I wanted to leave so badly, not because of the emotions, at least not entirely, but because they were flinging fluids like nobody's business.

A priest eventually spoke: "We are here to bury a beloved member of our family and welcome her to a new beginning from her end. She leaves behind friends, family, colleagues, and everyone and anyone she had an effect on. She will be missed but never forgotten. May she be granted safe passage to the kingdom. Amen!"

The priest was always good with words, whether it was because of his tongue or from some higher being anonymously called, "God." I wouldn't go as far as saying I'm a believer, but I wouldn't say God or heaven after death or prophecy isn't real. I'm just saying I really didn't take to it. I guess I can contribute that to being raised in a family of gravediggers and antique collectors. Dead bodies, death, and the human body were the norm for my folks and me, but it certainly affected my personal life. Or maybe, that's my diagnosis speaking, my medicine keeping me in check.

Either way, I envy Beth. Not for the person she was, but the fact she left so easily, while I still struggle with the complexity of this mind and body. This one that always worries, even if it doesn't make any sense.

I looked at my key chain with two bottles of sanitizers. Beth's friends and family cried and embraced, while I was far away from them under a tall, dark tree. I could still see Beth's casket as I thought, *I wish it were me, Beth. I wish it were me.*

I felt ashamed of myself for coming to a funeral wearing a surgical mask, almost looking like a less obvious widow but only lamer. It was nice to know I wasn't the only person wearing a face covering. But it felt a little off, considering most males at funerals were usually open and confident, unlike me. But maybe, that was just my own belief of the world's conception of masculinity.

Beth was slowly lowered to her final resting place. I couldn't bear to watch as I turned around, holding in my tears as much as I could. It was nearly impossible at a moment like this. I was used to seeing death, hearing about it, and smelling it, but it was too much for me to handle. I recall thinking, how bad it would be to lose another loved one.

That was when I remembered my dear Grandpa Alan: a great patriarch of my family. A man, who despite his experience and age, was like Beth full of life. He was basically one of my closest relatives. He essentially introduced me to my love of books and antiques. At one stage, I could vividly remember thinking that when he was gone, I was too. That was until I met Beth. She became my new reason to live, but now, like Grandpa Alan, she was gone. Maybe, I am gone now; maybe, I should leave and not look back.

Thump! Crash!

I heard something, and I saw Beth's ma fall into Beth's casket, into the burial ground.

I thought to myself, *Did she fall? Did she slip?*

It was so sudden I didn't know how to react other than turning around and taking a gander at what happened from afar.

Thump! Thump!

I couldn't tell what was happening. People were screaming, scattering. As if my emotions weren't already bad, they became pandemonium. My first instinct was to leave, as cowardly as that may be. But, all I knew was, stuff was getting out of hand, and I didn't want to be any more involved in a mystery than an actual, uneasy tragedy.

4/05/19: Now What?

Touch!

I remember thinking to myself that things couldn't get any worse. My ex had died; her ma died right after by unknown cause; then, a good chunk of the folks in the funeral died right after I left.

I was flabbergasted all this had happened in a short span of time. I thought this must be a joke, like in the movie *The Game*. But unfortunately, it wasn't my birthday, and no one I knew would go the extra mile for me. Plus, I didn't know anyone who had a good sum in their bank account. In other words, this wasn't a joke or a dream; this was real, and I could pinch myself all I wanted. It didn't change this cruel reality for me.

I called off from work, asking to take some time to grieve, which they approved. I remember thinking I wasn't worried about missing rent. When Beth and I were together, she always forgot, too, and it didn't help she had the tendency to spend more than we had, but because I was a kind fool, I let it slide. Now, I almost feel like I'm trying to pick up Beth's quirk even if I knew it would be impossible for me.

At some point, I went to the local community park, where I would usually hang out to clear my mind. The vast, grassy, island-like territory always made me feel like I was on the same islands from *Lord of the Flies* or *Cast Away*, but fortunately, I didn't feel alone or need to cry out for help. I always had my books and the brisk feel of mother nature and the music from her pets. I attempted to read the book *Sandcastle* when suddenly:

"We really need to find a better way to meet." It was the woman from Barnes & Noble.

Touch!

Not her! "Oh, hi. Don't mind me. I'm just reading. Nothing to see here."

"Yeah, I noticed. Just like last time, and the times before that."

"I'm sorry. I don't mean to be rude, but I was hoping just to read my book and not think about anything."

"Look, I'm sorry if I came off as a bitch from our first official meeting, and I don't mean to pry too much. I meant no harm from my comments before, but . . . is it true?"

I sighed. "Yeah. I lost someone I cared for . . . or did care for."

"I'm so sorry. I didn't know. How are you holding up?"

"As you can see, I'm trying not to think about it."

"Yeah . . . Name's Roxanne, but you can call me Roxie."

I paused. "C—Corey. Corey is my name."

She extended out her hand, but I didn't react, so she motioned for a hug now that she knew I was a grieving mess. I still didn't react.

"Not much of a touchy-feely person, are ya?" she said.

"Not really, sorry," I told her.

"How about an elbow bump?" she asked.

Reluctantly, I played along and elbow-bumped her. I don't know why she felt the need to try to socialize with me. Most would just leave me to my own devices, and I wouldn't stick out, just a tree swaying in the wind. I remembered us having a full half-hour moment of awkward silence as I continued to focus on my book. I vaguely saw her swinging her arms back and forth, like an inflatable blow-up doll but less frantic.

"So, you're really into books, I see . . ."

"Yeah, I . . . they help me escape from reality, take me somewhere else when I don't want to face facts."

"What's wrong with reality and facts?"

"What isn't wrong?"

"What do you mean?"

"If reality isn't the issue, I think it might just be me. When you're me, you worry about all the little things. Perhaps, I'm still reeling from . . ." I put my book up in my face.

"Well, at some point, you must move forward with your life. It's good you're grieving; it shows you care. It's unhealthy to keep your emotions to yourself for too long."

"So says my guidance counselor, but I wouldn't imagine you and him know what it's like to be me. Avoiding conflicts, avoiding social gatherings, not playing phone tag or games for that matter. Just a wee loner whose only paradise is the library and his bed. But now, only one of those escapes is working at all."

"Maybe not, since this is our first real meeting. You're quite the downer, no offense. And I don't know why, but I see you have a good heart deep down. Whether you want to show it or not. My intuition usually doesn't fail me."

"Well, mine is telling me I should go home."

I stood, getting ready to leave. She tried to stop me as I sheepishly avoided any real physical contact, until I stopped with a stunning realization.

"What? No—" She bumped into me.

Touch!

We noticed about twenty or more people lying on the ground. Some eyes wide open, some closed.

At first, I thought, *Is this some sort of new community game or something?*

I was in complete silence. Roxie slowly made her way over, and I don't know why, but I slowly followed along.

"Hey, are you guys okay?" Roxie asked.

I carefully walked around everyone like they were some sort of human landmines. Roxie looked at me with intrigue and followed along with my actions. I thought she was mocking me at first, but I didn't mention it. Then, I saw a man coming from the road barefoot as he ran by us. He must be a roadrunner to run that fast. Almost out of the blue, the guy ran near one of the bodies and collapsed so fast it almost seemed like he got shot by a sniper. The thing was, there was no blood, at least, not that I recall. He lay motionless near the others, and some people who'd seen what had happened.

You can essentially say I "noped" out the vicinity. I turned around in a hurry and ran to my jeep. I recall it looked like it needed a car wash, but I was in a panicked state and wasn't really thinking too clearly. I noticed Roxie was still petrified; she was moving at a snail's pace.

Feeling bad, I yelled out, "You need a ride?"

I usually would never have done this for anyone, but she didn't seem like a bad person, at least that was what my "intuition" told me. She walked over to my vehicle a little faster, and we drove. Leaving the area, I noticed why Roxie was so stunned. They were more bodies on the ground, around fifty. I don't remember the exact details, but I vividly remember seeing a woman lying on the ground on her stomach.

I don't know why, but I couldn't hear or think of anything after I saw that. I drove in the opposite direction of this unusual carnage, and Roxie called 911, as we contemplated, *What the Hell is going on!*

4/27/2019: Taking Everything in . . . Almost!

Some time has passed, and I can't get my head around this dilemma, seeing these unusual patterns, these grisly demises, especially happening to me in a run of bad luck or a curse. It's like stepping on cracks as black cats walk by. I cannot think about how all this adds up, how this sick change of pace is happening, and somehow, I'm the only one who notices anything. It doesn't make sense to me, but for the world, people go on like nothing bad has just happened. Maybe, it's because it's not them. But what difference would it make? People must hear the rumors and murmurs, but there will always be doubters and skeptics.

One day, I sat at home wondering about all these coincidences and how they could fit together. I couldn't think of a straight answer since no one would give me an answer. The cops and forensic scientists promised they looked everywhere and at everything, but no one could get a real lead or cause. Regardless of my belief or reasoning, I almost surmised some higher entity was testing us, or me.

Or maybe, I was hallucinating from lack of sleep. As my alarm could testify, it barely rang anymore. I was essentially ready for it every single time. Compare that to before when I had always been tempted to launch it across my room at 6 a.m. or 7 a.m. But, I'd been so wide-eyed, I didn't even know what day or month it was anymore.

Maybe, it was depression; maybe, it was a hallucination. Either way, I knew something wasn't right, and I wanted to know what?

Roxie and I had started talking more after our unusual first meeting and the subsequent things that happened after. Perhaps, it was more of a reluctant pity, opening this easily to her, as I was not one to open myself up much to anyone in general. Maybe, it was the fact we both essentially felt the same way when it came to these unusual mishaps, or I just needed a second opinion.

On the day I had pondered all these questions most, my phone rang, so I answered it:

"Hey, Rox."

"Hey, Corey. I just read online that similar instances are popping up on the internet and with no real clear definitive answers."

"I couldn't really do anything on my end. I'm sorry. But, I did similar research and found nothing either."

"Don't beat yourself up. This is unusual, whatever this is, but I doubt it's some sort of mass suicide epidemic the government is covering up, like the crazies say."

"I honestly find it hard to believe, but stranger things have occurred, like Ebola, swine flu, mad cow. It's probably why I turned to a vegetarian-vegan diet."

"Come on, you didn't quit cold turkey. You told me your favorite meal is a trash plate."

"Garbage plate, and yes, but that's different. They have different variants, and I choose to eat the veggie plates."

"Sure! Whatever you say, baby boy."

"Regardless of my taste buds, I still have a funny feeling something is amiss, and I'm not talking about a Stephen King novel."

"I'm with cha there. Stop by the car wash when you get the chance. I still wanted to repay you for the lift after, well, you know what."

"Yeah, I know. I'll stop by when I can."

After I hung up the phone, I scanned my apartment, just thinking, *Could this be a Stephen King novel? Like* The Shining *or* 1408*?*

Or perhaps, it was me missing some of my counseling sessions and taking a variety of medication, regardless of what it may be. I couldn't figure out the answer, but I felt like the answers were looming close. So much so, it terrified me. Because I may not like the answer.

About thirty minutes later, I headed to Roxie's friend's car wash and gas station: Sonix Mach 5. Roxie had told me her friend had something to show us at his station; he described it as a neo-noir autopsy. Curious but also needing to wash my car as well, I decided to stop by.

Roxie was alone when I got there. She basically had to service my car as she hadn't seen or heard from her friend since she got there. She told me she had tried to reach her friend's office, but he didn't respond.

"Got room for two?" Roxie stepped into my jeep, and we started moving into the automatic car wash.

The place wasn't anything I hadn't seen before, but it made things interesting. It looked like a neon cave with black lights placed all over. Once we entered the tunnel, moving forward, it felt like some sort of time vortex.

Touch!

"Hmm, flashy," I said.

Roxie was unamused, probably since she'd seen this a dozen times. I didn't show too much enthusiasm either but gave it the benefit of the doubt, especially considering I really like the sci-fi and noir genre. But something was odd. We were moving, and the lights were on throughout, but my jeep wasn't getting cleaned or at least not clean enough. The mechanism wasn't working, and there wasn't anybody around to ask for help. When we got close to the end, I saw it. A dozen folks on the ground motionless; some had their eyes open and some closed.

I thought it must've been some joke, but it wasn't. Roxie looked in disbelief as well. I'm pretty sure we were both thinking how similar it was to the park, but I alone was thinking about Beth and her folks, thinking this couldn't be coincidental. Something was different this time. The neon-black lights showed a strange glowing substance that almost looked like glow-in-the-dark paint. Or as, I personally described it, blood stains that couldn't be seen with the naked eye. It looked dry but also seemed spreadable.

Roxie got ready to open my window, and I stopped her.

"Stop! Don't touch it! I have a funny feeling here," I told her, not wanting to make sense of the situation, probably from fear. She agreed and nodded, and we wanted to drive off, but not before I had carefully looked at my, wondering if this *substance* was in it. Luckily, I didn't see anything. Nothing at all. Even on that bright sunny day. All I could see was my still filthy car.

Touch!

6/22/19: Art and Knowledge

It's been some time after the car wash incident. Roxy and I found out her friend was found dead in his office and about four or five people around the vicinity. We couldn't make out what may have caused this mayhem. I tried not to think about it, but knowing myself, I couldn't do it. I couldn't help but feel like all these deaths and unknown causes were somehow connected. I couldn't say or prove for certain, but I had a hunch. Usually, my hunches didn't let me down, minus that one time I went to a rock concert by myself and got filthy top to bottom, but not from my own actions. Metalheads sure do get easily excited.

Roxie was definitely feeling uneasy about going anywhere by herself or at least going somewhere without her lucky charm. (Ahem, me). Reluctant to play along with these games, I still allowed it, even if my hunch was wrong.

Roxie invited me to go to an art museum "for millennials," or at least that's how she described it. I remember coming over without fuss since I love museums and history, enough to say, "This should be fun."

I came by, dressed in my regular attire, nothing too flashy, nothing too big. I remember thinking the place looked like a glass menagerie inside a shopping mall. I found it interesting how few people still loved art in the community. Art didn't seem to have as much love as I would think, but then again, I couldn't really say who loved it and didn't. There was a brand-new exhibit for AIDS awareness, and it was quite littered throughout with small corridor.

Touch!

There was a piece that caught my attention for some reason. It was a sliced-off arm with a hand gesture for love. I don't know why, but I felt like it spoke more to me as an individual who was cautious with everything he touched or grabbed. Maybe, it was telling me to love everything, including my arms, or maybe, I was reading way too deep into it.

There was a sign, just like any other portraits, that said, "Please Do Not Touch," a rule I followed religiously with or without a sign. I still took a picture of it, as a reminder to always appreciate the little things. Roxie and I went to the next display, but we heard a whole lot of thumps. It was particularly audible and visible in this confined area.

She was getting ready to investigate, but my hunch told me, "to get out!"

I grabbed Roxie with my gloves and ran out toward the emergency exit absentmindedly but felt like it was a good call. Just when I was getting ready to leave, my car got jammed. I could hear the ambulance and firefighters coming closer, as I struggled to turn my vehicle on.

Just as I said, "Come on," it started, but not before the paramedics arrived.

I drove away thinking, *Why is this happening to me? What did I do?*

8/7/19: How High Can We Go?

These death tolls, these coincidences, they are getting out of hand. Summer is ending, and I feel less safe now than ever. News reports, unusual conspiracies, and the like: it's driving me nuts. I want answers, but I can't get any, not while staying home. How can I get answers when the outside world is a battlefield? One that doesn't have guns and explosions everywhere, but still dangerous.

Roxie has found some solace hanging out with me, and to be fair, I have as well. I can appreciate her sort of carefree attitude and open-mindedness, albeit she can be a bit invasive. Still she has a cute charm to her, even if I can't entirely explain or comprehend it.

Roxie invited me over to another place of her friend's, who was a freelance photographer and cannabis supporter. We stopped by his place, and it had seen better days. At least, that was how I'd put it. It was a pigsty as I carefully maneuvered everywhere like I was walking in a minefield.

His brother was asleep downstairs. We could hear his extremely loud snoring, sounding like he had sleep apnea. Roxie's friend offered us some weed, but we were more curious on what he'd found. He brought us to his weed farm, and we noticed something usual. When the UV lights were on, we could distinctly see a splatter of the same substance we'd seen before. But when Roxie's friend turned off the light, it was gone, invisible. We couldn't understand it, especially when he turned the lights back and touched the substance before we could tell him, "Stop!"

But, he was fine. We learned he was recently diagnosed with a fatal lung cancer. Apparently, he was immune to this substance. Knowing full well Roxie and I didn't have any fatal illness in us at the time, we chose to keep our distance. But when her friend's brother asked him for a hand, her friend grabbed his brother with his substance-filled hand, and his brother collapsed onto the ground.

He was dead; he was confused, but we realized that he was quite healthy. He died from this substance because he was healthy.

3/20/20: WARNING!

I'm trying, I'm trying so hard to help, but why is it so hard? Why can't people see what I see? It's so obvious, but all they can do is mask up, glove up, and buy a lifetime's worth of toilet paper they may not even need. It got bad enough tanks were patrolling the streets at one point, but now I hear this . . . *pandemic* of sorts is spreading worldwide. They don't have a name for it, or know what it is, but the death toll is astronomical. It went from a thousand to a hundred thousand to a million in the span of a couple of months, if not days, and it's still growing. It's not safe anywhere, not even in my home. But where is there to go when this substance can literally be anywhere.

Roxie and I decided to live together for the meanwhile. It didn't help that both our parents are dead, and we were too late to save them. I still think about it every single day, and it doesn't get any easier. Roxie has started wearing gloves like me, and we both carry around some black light and UV flashlights, the small kind, on our keychains. We make sure to scan every potential place before and after going anywhere, even if it isn't safe too. But, we need supplies, and getting them is another challenge for us. Trying to explain to people what we see has been impossible since most were indoors and afraid of one another.

It has become a brave new world, one that the Illuminati would maybe hate. But all we know is this is our new reality, and things are only getting harder from here on.

4/21/21: People

It's nuts out there. Murder, vandalism, theft, unionization, unemployment, and a hope for government funds that may or may not go through. This is the new norm; this is what we've come to.

At least, the world did. Roxie and I keep our distance. We stay close but at least five feet apart. We charge and bring our safety lights with us everywhere and anywhere. We send out little flyers and emails to folks in our community, and hopefully, the world, but as we've come to acknowledge, people aren't listening.

They are coming up with their own little tales and scenarios. Like mass suicide, or a government ploy, or divine intervention, and my favorite: a doomsday cult. But none really have any real validity to them. Even if it did, no one is going to come out and confess it. Just like no one will confess to being fatally ill. They say they are working on a vaccine, but Roxie and I know better. But no one will listen. So, all there is, is to survive.

4/7/22: I Don't Like This Place

What is this? What's going on? This isn't home, this isn't right, this isn't a safe place anymore. Nowhere and no one is safe. This substance is spreading like crazy, and people absentmindedly spread it like flies and mosquitoes. This is a terrible way to live if you can even call it that.

Roxie and I are at the bridge near the highway. I keep crying and overthinking, *Is this all because of me!*

A few minutes before, I spoke my thoughts aloud: "I couldn't save them. I couldn't save anyone, not even my family."

Roxie tried to comfort me. "This wasn't your doing. Besides, you saved me."

"I couldn't save Beth."

"Corey, you have to move forward; this isn't the end."

"It sure feels like it!"

"Corey, are you afraid of the world and people?"

"No, I'm afraid of this reality!"

5/22/24: 13/7 News

News just came. Several thousand dead of unknown causes.

Reading this journal after not picking it up for some time wasn't easy, but it just reminds me of how we came to be here. Roxie and I have gotten married, and we have a pair of twins, a boy named Noah and a girl called Beans. It's been like several years ever since the *substance* virus arose, but people are gradually getting the picture of what's happening.

Roxie and I live in a secure homestead out of town, and we have UV and black light everywhere in and out of our vicinity. We have a strict policy, for not just travelers, but for ourselves. It isn't easy getting the babies to acclimate to this strict guideline, but we're making it work. It's about survival now. Everything and everyone are a threat, intentional or not. We've needed to follow the rules we made, almost like our own ten commandments. But it wasn't because of just survival, but to make sure the death tolls come down.

For now, I must go back to work, in my secure booth.

Rules:
- *Do not touch anything or anyone.*
- *Must have UV or black light flashlights on hand, or at least be scanned thoroughly.*
- *Keep five to six feet away from one another.*
- *No lethal weapons of any sort. We are armed, but we mean no harm.*
- *Wear a mask and gloves. If you do not have one, we can accommodate or speak via our speaker.*
- *Inform us if you are fatally ill or have a life-threatening problem.*
  - *Spread the word to the world. Please.*

Crown of Requisite

By Dylan Arce

The Before

Tumultuous waves crashed along three massive ships that sailed the Caribbean Sea, rattling with each lash from the ruthless waters. Soldiers encased in white metallic armor came down against the wooden decks as surge waves swept along the ship's body, hitting the sails that somehow managed to stay intact. The men on the top deck tried desperately not to fall overboard, although some didn't succeed, swallowed whole by the abyss of the deep blue. The men on the lower deck made sure their *cargo* wasn't damaged, while crates of food and barrels of gunpowder slid along the oak, spilling and tumbling against one another.

Yet, none of the soldiers paid any major attention to that. They only caught those falling closest to them. Instead, they just kept their eyes on the three-dozen people shackled to each other by their ankles and wrist. Metal claws on the ends of the bindings on their chest hinged to the ship's walls attached the planks, spiked deep enough to stay stuck but not enough to puncture and let water flood in.

Most captives were men and women, but there were at least five children; only one was a boy. The rest were little girls, all about nine or younger. Their skin was a dark umber, the small patches of sun from the slatted ceiling making their skin appear golden. None of them were wearing much clothing, just loincloths around the men's waists and shaggy aprons for the women. They also had dirty blankets the soldiers had given to them, but they were bloodstained with the smell of rotten meat that swirled together with the smell from the ocean. Small traces of salt grazed the cotton, scratching the chained individuals.

Drops of water rained from the top deck onto the bottom with each hit from the ocean. The droplets slid off of the soldiers' cold steel but traveled through the bare skin of the others. Humidity had caved the lower deck, and small trickles began to perspire into glistening sweat. A clear film over foreheads, necks, chest, and backs. The rusty chains began to dampen, and more dewdrops ran along the copper-like metal.

Heat buzzed and thunder bellowed along the horizon.

"Commander Leo, we've lost a ship!" a soldier yelled from the edge of the quarterdeck.

"Don't you think I know that? We're the only ones at sea!" Commander Leo responded sarcastically but with worry in his tone.

"The storm looks to be miles long; how are we going to—" The soldier got cut off by Leo.

"Bring *them* to me at once," he said.

The soldier took no time and went to an opening to the lower deck, sliding along the floor in the process, and told the men to escort the captured to their commander. Three sets of guards stood around each chained line of a dozen captives, nine soldiers in total. The light turned from a shadowy yellow in the enclosed cage at the ship's bottom half, to a somber gray as the storm clouds grew near.

Purple bolts of lightning could be seen striking the sea, and ripples shot from the clashes. To the left, everyone could see another ship being taken by the ocean. A wave capsized over it and broke its sails, leaving only half of the wooden beam and the crew stranded. Barely moving between the up and down bounces from the current. Two more waves came, and small white glints of light came off of the ship.

Leo squinted his eyes as his men did the same, and the shimmers of white gained shapes and grew bodies, plummeting into the ocean. They flailed in the air, but before they could even think about processing what was happening, the white glimmers became a part of the black depths.

"Sir . . ." a shaken voice said. Leo turned from the quarterdeck and walked over to a tall man whose hair was entangling in the wind. He was the first in line in one of the three columns of chained bodies.

"Do you have a way to *fix* this, or are we all going to die here?" Leo asked, trying not to seem desperate but stern. It didn't really work.

Thunder continued to roar, and its sound filled the skyline. Leo stood and the man did the same, staring at

Leo's crystalline blue eyes with pursed lips, not giving a response.

"You would rather let all of us, including these kids, die at the hands of the ocean!" Leo said, frustrated as he went after a little girl who was two paces behind the man, yanking her by her hair.

She yelped in shock and pain. Her eyes glossed over as Leo dragged her to the border of the ship, pinned her face against the edge, and made her watch the ocean try its best to take them out. The heavy trail of mist rose and mixed in with the girl's falling tears. She yelled for him to stop in an unknown language to Leo, or any of the soldiers.

"Please stop. I'll do as you say, *pero* stop hurting her!" The man Leo had spoken to said in a thick accent, breaking his silence.

Leo turned and threw the girl onto the deck, letting her go in the process. Her face hit the soaked wood, making her scream in pain once again. But she stood up and scrambled to go back to the others. The other soldiers didn't put the chains back on her because when she made it back to the lineup, she clung to the woman in front of her. Her nails engraved themselves into the woman's thigh below her apron. The woman got as low as she could go, and coddled the little girl.

"So—you're gonna make the storm stop and protect the ship?" Leo asked rhetorically.

"As long as the kids aren't hurt," The man responded.

"Do you really think *you* are in any position to make an offer let alone a demand!" Leo scoffed, almost letting out a laugh.

The man didn't say anything, just closed his eyes and took a deep breath: in and out. The waves that were just commanding the ocean calmed, and the gray sky lightened. The thunder's roars became more docile, and the sun began to show.

"Fine, but only the kids get *special treatment*. The rest of you are just regular slaves. Nothing more. Also, once we get to España, you will never tell a soul about this, and if you do, this little *deal* is off!" Leo said, while directing his men to unchain the man.

The soldiers took the keys that hung on their hips and unlocked the man's wrist shackles. They didn't let his feet free from the chains, though; it would've been too much of a danger. If they let him go fully "free," that would show weakness, and although the army was pretty much helpless at the moment, their pride and arrogance stood strong.

The man continued to breathe like he had been, and his right arm began to illuminate. Patterns grew like veins, making different unknown figures that looked like fish, turtles, shells, and a sun with a face and smile. The man opened his eyes and began to bring his hands, which were parallel to each other, up and down. His pupils had gone from a dark brown to a light turquoise, resembling a shade of blue in the same family as the ones the soldiers had.

The sky cleared more and more until the sun was fully visible, and the storm was parted, like Moses with the red sea. Except this wasn't a story the people from the man's village were told by the army; this was happening right in front of their eyes.

Familiar Retribution

A wicker basket hung from my forearm as the sunlight blazed along the field. My feet soaked as I walked through the muddy ground to collect the ripe sugarcane. Every step I took, I felt my feet get heavier as the mud slushed around my legs, almost reaching my knees. I took the curved machete that reminded me of a crescent moon and had been lying on my basket, and swung along the canes gathering the billets. I could fit about five into my basket before I tossed them into the carts three men pushed and pulled around: one on the left, one on the right, and the last one either on the front or on the back.

They grunted as they dragged the cart with hundreds of billets to the mill so it could be processed to make sugar. It took the entire day to process, mill, and boil a single full cart of billets to make raw sugar.

The harvesting months were always the worst, and I dreaded the thought of having to be out working for hours, but at least, it wasn't like the adults. They had to work for days straight, with almost no sleep, just to not get beaten. And the ones who didn't do their daily set of work were taken to the stables, hit by thorned sticks and left to the starved horses. Just for their bodies to be found trampled to death or paralyzed, which made one useless. Uselessness was an excuse to be killed in the eyes of the army that regulated and watched over us.

I continued along my set path of canes and kept on cutting, collecting, and depositing the bristle-green stems onto more carts for hours until the sun began to set. From an hour after sunrise to the beginning of sunset, the horizon transitioned from a bright blue with a white glare along the center, to an orange with a subtle red underlining. Soldiers who watched from the shaded areas from the orange-red boughs of trees came to me and a few others to escort us back to the houses. Unlike how they treated the others when it was time to come home, they didn't chain us together. Instead, they just kept us at their side, walking at our pace.

It was me and two other girls, the same age as me, and a boy who was sixteen, a year older than us. There'd been another girl who was barely ten, but she got sick and didn't make it past the first couple weeks on the field. It was sad, but I hadn't known her that well. I didn't know anyone, still don't for the most part, but I've gotten along with the other kids.

The soldiers led us to the small village-style *town* that we stayed at and went back to the adults. There wasn't a fear of us running away because not only were there guards at the borders of every house. But if we managed to leave, where would we go? Into the woods alone, with nothing to defend ourselves from whatever is in it since they take the machetes away after you're done with your daily task. Or, back to the field with soldiers surrounding the area. And for the point-one percent chance we managed to sneak past them, more fields for miles upon miles upon miles. We were pretty much stranded in the middle of nowhere. It was better just to try to make the best of the little we had.

"Ramiro, can you come with me to get firewood?" I asked the older boy as he walked tiredly.

"Really, now? Can't you just do it? Or, ask Emilia and Estela?" Ramiro pleaded as he took a seat on a dead stump little mushrooms grew around, almost making a ring fully around.

"C'mon, it's faster if you and I do it than asking them," I said, trying to sound convincing.

"No, It's been too long of a day to do anything." He waved me off.

I thought about egging him on more, but I just gave up. It was wasting the precious sunlight hastily depleting. He continued to sink into the stump as I started to walk toward the trees transitioning with the weather. The harvesting season was during the fall, and the bright green leaves that encased the entire forest were now falling off like thinning hair plucked from a scalp. Little groups were carried by the breeze in passing moments. The warm leaves would flurry around the branches, soon falling to be used as kindle.

I walked through the path the village men had created with the permission of the soldiers, for easy access to the forest's shallow parts so that when the women would stay at the homes, they could easily gather berries, kindling, and piles of leaves and petals brewed for teas. The trail made my life gathering firewood easier, so I didn't complain.

The twigs on the ground snapped against my leather boots soaking in mud. I tried to watch my steps so I could pick the branches that would burn nicely, but the ones on the floor were usually too small. Instead, I broke some off the trees. I was taller than Ramiro, Emilia, and Estela, so it wasn't hard to find good sticks to burn.

I got as many branches as I could fit under my arm and went back to the village to put them in the fire pit at the center of the village. The village elders told us the center of every home was the most important part because it was the strongest point of a structure.

"If you have a strong center *Rahe,* then everything you build and make on it will be strong," I remember Ana, one of the village's old ladies saying to me.

So, they decided the fire pit was going to be the strongest point of our home. A place where we could all get together and feel a sense of normalcy since we got here. Something as normal as the feeling of being a family. Ana was like a mother to me, although the concept of maternity, of having a maternal figure, was foreign to me.

The branches filled the pit to the middle, which was enough to make a fire big enough to cook on and stay warm during the nights when it got cold out of nowhere. I swore in the day the sun would make my skin welt and boil, while at night, the winds would freeze the blisters along my hands and feet.

I dropped the last few twigs into the pit and began to forage in the bushes to find anything that could help make food. I tried to find things like wild spices, fungi, and insects. I used anything I could because anything edible could mean life or death. I also collected water from the stream north of the trail in clay bowls, from which I would strain the mud out of with a porous cloth made from hundreds of incisions with little wooden needles. It wasn't a hundred percent perfect, but it made it so we didn't get sick. While I was collecting water, I checked the traps the men had set earlier in the week. They were a pair of decently sized cones: one bigger than the other, one with an entrance in the middle. A fish would swim into the entrance but didn't know it could get out the same way, and so, it stayed trapped.

The men had set five traps, and three of them had fish inside. It was a blessing amongst the sky. There had been weeks, even months, where nothing but broken seaweed and sludge-like substances had appeared, but this week, three fish. I rejoiced at the stream and hurried back to the houses to prepare dinner.

"Ramiro, Emilia, Estela, come here, look, look!" I exclaimed as I sped to the firepit.

"How do you have so much energy?" Estela said quietly, not realizing the *gold* in my hands.

"Also, why are you yelling if it's just us? Are you trying to alert the guards?" Emilia said, backing up her sister, still not noticing.

I swear those two were never not next to each other.

Ramiro came up from his sluggish pose, still on the stump, and his face changed from a tired expression to something I've only seen on him on the days we had off. The kids were allowed two days off a month, and we would spend the whole day resting and bathing, when the water wasn't freezing, in the lake near the mill. We would all bathe together, but he would stay soaking in the water for hours, after the girls left. His eyes shut with a smile curved like the machetes we used to harvest. That same smile appeared when he saw I had the three fish.

"Cecilia, how did you—It's been months?" Ramiro asked, stumbling on his words.

"I know! But, we're not gonna question how or why. We're just going to enjoy these and savor every bite." I told him while holding the three fish by their tails.

"So, Ramiro. Can you help me now?"

"Fine, what do you need?"

"You know the wooden tent things the elders put over fire?"

"Yeah, they call them smokers."

"Well, I was thinking of smoking two fish and then using the last one as meat in a type of stew. That way, it could last longer."

"Okay, well, I'll build the smoker over a small fire because the pits are too big, and you should send *those* two to get water," Ramiro said, looking over my shoulder at Emilia and Estela.

I nodded at Ramiro and went over to the two girls gawking at each other about the fish. They turned their heads in sync when I stepped up to them. Those two were a little weird.

"Hey, can you guys go get water from the stream? I need enough to fill the clay pot."

They didn't respond, just nodded, and went together toward the forest.

They picked up the clay pot we used to make tea and boil animal blood, a form of medicine, and a few clay bowls for drinking water. Emilia and Estela were quite literally never apart, but they still got what they needed done, so I never thought that much into the idea of them separating. If it didn't make my life any worse, then why would *I* care?

As they went to get water and Ramiro started to build the smoker, I took a small flint knife we kept hidden from the guards, and started to make a slit in the two fish that were going on the smoker and put spices in them. The knife wasn't sharp enough to kill, or even heavily injure, but all the guards would see was something sharp, so it was better to not show them.

I took some roots from garlic, dandelions, and saffron, then stuffed the fish. I didn't fully know what I was doing, but I just remembered what Ana had taught me. She was the one who'd taught me everything about cooking, cleaning, and medicine. I learned how to survive from her.

As I finished preparing the fish, I went to the closest house to me. None of the houses were dedicated to a specific person. Whichever one was closest to you was usually the one you stayed at. There wasn't anything special to any of them; they were just there for us to sleep. That's all.

The smell of concrete hit my nostrils as I lay next to the doorway. I thought about how lucky we were to get some actual food instead of the regular insects and starvation. The army said they would provide rations, but after the first month, they stopped. We were never told why, but the small portions of rice and fermented beans that could soak the air with an intoxicating aroma, just stopped being given to us. Maybe, it was for the best; that forced us to learn how to live with little to nothing.

The sunlight dimmed, and it was becoming nighttime. I got up and went to check on the smoker's progress. The only light we had were the two fires at the center of the village: the pit and the fire for the smoker. The pit's fire was big enough to let you see where the walls were in the houses, but it only lasted a few hours before it shut off or the soldiers poured water on it.

The smokers' fire was next to the pit's, and on top of it was a wooden teepee. It had two layers, and Ramiro didn't use anything to bind the logs together. Instead, he made notches in the wood and hooked them together. Ramiro was always smart and crafty; he was definitely the most resourceful out of anyone in the village.

I got the two fishes lying on a bed of leaves next to the pit, still draining the spices of their flavor. They were warm from the fire but not enough to burn my hands. I picked them up and made another bed of leaves on the smoker and laid them on the lower layer. I remembered seeing Ana talking to another woman while she used leaves to cover what they were cooking. So, I did the same. But instead of a new leaf pile, I used the beds the fish had been on before and used those as blankets.

Before going to rest, I put a quick stew to boil in the pit. I got the clay pot Emilia and Estela had filled and put more of the spices, walnuts that fell right before the winter, and the last fish. I tore the last stuck into the water and cut it into chunks, letting that sit on the elevated stone in the pit. It was something that had been there before I arrived. The pit was originally just a trash hole and a place to relieve your body of its *unneeded vitamins*, but it also had a boulder that was tall in the center. So, when we decided to make the "fire pit," that stone stood alone above the crackling fire. I still got burned quite a bit, but it allowed us to boil things, so a few burns weren't too much to complain about.

All the preparation was done, and the only thing that stopped us from devouring the heaven-sent beings was time. The smoker, although effective, took hours, and there was a very good chance it wouldn't be done until sunrise. And the stew was mainly for the adults, who would be coming to the houses while we were asleep. Even if it got cold, they could just re-boil it. Although knowing their hunger and tiredness, they wouldn't even chew the fish.

I stayed awake long enough to make sure the stew wouldn't boil over and be wasted. It turned out to not be too much actual food, but it was enough for the twenty-ish portions the adults would share when they got back.

The scent of charring leaves and fish scales floated under my nose. I could feel myself salivating and the spit gathering under my tongue. *Real food,* I thought to myself. It took way too much strength, more than I'd like to admit, to stop myself from tearing the tendering fish from the leaves that encased them, and enjoying that feast all to myself, but I had to. Even though I don't remember my family, or friends, or home, I couldn't forget this was my new home, and these people were my new family. They took me in, even if they didn't have much of a choice, and raised me as their own. So, the least I could do was let them have some decent food.

Dissimulated Hero

I lay on the stiff dirt, my eyes shyly opening because of a glare that resembled light reflecting from a soldier's pristine armor through the only hole in the house: a small crack on the thatch ceiling. Sunrise already. Damn. How could hours of sleep go by like a flash of lightning?

Every day, I somehow find myself harboring that same question until the same guard, each day, bangs outside on the concrete and barges in to take me to the fields. It's the same every, single, day. Some days, I wanted something new to happen because the routine got tiring. Some of the others found relief in not having to think about what's gonna happen next, but knowing what was gonna happen before it even happens made me wonder what else was there to do? Could there be something more than the thing I've known for these past few years?

The same routine of field work, which meant collecting cane, planting crops for the soldiers to take to the city, collecting water, and cleaning for the soldiers. They would take me, Emilia and Estela, and some other women, to the barracks they had and make us clean their armor and swords. None of us knew where we were, so we didn't try anything. Besides, a guard practically had his blade to our throats at all times. Although, depending on the guard, *I* got some actual food. Little pieces of bread they would toss at me like I was a helpless bird. It was dehumanizing to say the least, but *I* still got food.

My clothes lay next to me on the side of the corner I slept on, the most *comfortable* place I could find. I slept without anything on because the "foe prisons," as the elders called our houses, didn't have any windows or major openings for air. So, it would almost always stay hot until the short winter, where I would sleep with clothes on. They sufficed for the most part. Seeing others naked wasn't an strange thing, and I couldn't care less if I saw some extra skin, but the guards didn't think the same. They saw it as improper for a woman but didn't care if it was the boys. I didn't like the double standard, but there wasn't much I could do. They had power, and I was nothing in comparison.

I put my clothes on, an oversized dress I tied in the back with tears trailing throughout. I dusted off the dirt and small pebbles from it being on the ground and waited for the guard to come.

I tried to get lost in thought, but there wasn't anything to focus on. It was strange, just my mind being blank.

A few minutes passed, and I felt the earth tremble. This wasn't familiar. I knew the sound of the two or three soldiers who would come get me, Ramiro, Emilia, and Estela, and this wasn't it. This was ten, twenty times that. It felt like a stampede of wild boars as their hooves sprinted along the land beneath them.

I went to the door, which was just a wooden plank indented into the ground deep enough to stay rooted, and hesitantly, tried to push it open. Just enough to see what was happening. With both hands, I pushed against the wood, but it wouldn't budge. It felt like it was fighting against me as I put more pressure against it. I wasn't trying to escape or even open the door to fit my body through; I just wanted to see what was happening. I took my shoulder and pushed with my hands. My feet slid on the dirt, making me lose a little balance. A little sliver of the outside world sneaked its way into my head as the door made the slightest gap of an opening.

There were a group of soldiers and some men from the village. Maybe fifteen soldiers. I couldn't tell; they looked way too similar with them all wearing the same armor and all having pale skin. But, I knew there were only three men from the village because they were the only three dark figures amongst the troops. I just didn't know who they were. The soldiers were lined up while the three guys kneeled.

I really didn't like the sight. My stomach boiled with anticipation, and my gut scratched along my abdomen leading to my chest that felt like bursting.

What did they do? Are they in trouble? Maybe, it's a good thing? Are they leaving?

My head swarmed with questions, and I was getting closer to using all my strength to knock down the door to find answers. But if they're in trouble, then I'm pretty much dead. I couldn't stand being left in the dust. The least they could do was tell everyone why they were here. But, I guess that was too much to ask from an army who couldn't even give us the basic necessities.

I paced along the four walls, until I heard yelling. A deep scream from a man. And fuck it. That scream sounded bad, and I was too agitated to continue standing. I wasn't the type of person who spontaneously made decisions, but the feeling of *having* to do something overcame my being. I was able to do something. I didn't know what, but it was gonna be something.

I took a breath and rammed myself against the door. It really hurt. There wasn't a big reaction, so I took that as a good sign. I wasn't trying to make a grand reveal. There was a big enough gap for me to crawl through. I fit my body through the opening and stayed along the side of the walls. The group was next to the pit, and I could see the smoker still holding the fish with a fire almost too small to notice in the morning sun.

I kept on crawling, and I could feel the little pebbles on the dirt dig into my feet. I didn't have shoes because that was something the soldiers gave to us.

Pain ran from my foot to my spine as a rock stabbed my left foot. I shrieked in pain, trying to cover up the squeak-like sound, but a soldier looked my way and saw me. I froze, letting the rock pierce my skin, drawing blood. I felt the warm liquid escaping my body, but I couldn't do anything. I was afraid of getting caught. But, I *did* get caught! So, what was I scared of?

The soldier's eyes burned into me, but he didn't say anything. He didn't yell or tell someone beside him, he just went back to looking at the guys.

I couldn't believe it, and my brain filled with thousands of questions. I was overcome with the sight of two guys from a gap the soldier left in the line. He wanted me to see. He wanted me to find out that the three men from the village turned into two.

"So, you're offering one of *them* instead of your own? How charitable. But, I need to make sure th—"

"Where is the other man, and why are you guys here? We haven't done anything!" I yelled, interrupting the soldier in the middle of the two villagers as I stood up.

Everyone's eyes turned and locked onto me at once. My body shivered and a jolt of fear ran from the roots of my hair to my feet, one still bleeding. Sweat began to fall like driblets from every orifice I had. The soldier attending the two men pushed past the lineup of the others and stared directly into my eyes. His eyes were a bright blue, like the sky, and his armor was brighter and cleaner than anyone else's.

I stood firmly trying to seem confident, but my foot betrayed me, wobbling and losing balance. The soldier reached to his side and placed his hand on the golden-laced sheath.

Wow, I've done it now.

The Gentlemen's Army

A small pool of blood gathered at my toes as the soldier got closer to me. He pulled his sheath off little by little, and I could start to see the gray steel of his sword. My body shivered. He continued to slowly pull his sword out, while stepping closer to me until the blade, longer than my arm, was to my chest, practically piercing it.

"You won't do it. I know you won't!" I said, bluffing.

"And why is that, little girl?" the soldier responded, moving the blade to my neck.

"B-b-because—"

"See you can't even think of a reason. Face it. You're useless."

My stomach churned as his words carved into my being. I was useless in the eyes of the army. I was nothing compared to these men in armor. But if I was *so* beneath them, why did they still keep me alive? Why keep any of us alive? If I was "useless," why was I one of the girls who cleaned their armor? I clearly had a use, and it seemed to be a good one at that, so why put me down?

"If I'm not worth anything, then why haven't you killed me?" I said, grabbing his sword and taking it back down to my chest. Was I really telling this man to kill me?

I wasn't thinking, and that was the best part. My head was clear; I don't know why, but it felt good.

"Ha, you're out of your mind," the man said, taking his sword and sheathing it.

"What are you doing?"

"I see why you want to offer the kids away, Guey," The soldier said, turning his back to me and grabbing the attention of one of the men still kneeling.

"So, is it a deal sir?" The man asked, his words shaking, while he pruned each vowel independently.

"It's a deal, but don't think this is enough to save you from any other consequences. Myself and Queen Merida will be back."

I stood at a standstill, mainly from fear and because my foot was beginning to numb from the blood loss. I tried to process what just happened, but before I could, the soldier who'd officiated the *deal* grabbed my arm and yanked me to his side. I screamed, but he covered my mouth with his hand in a thick, black leather glove. I flailed my arms and kicked my feet, but he held my arms closed with a one-armed grip on my body, and the pain from my left foot made me stop kicking.

I felt tears start to swell and fall from my eyes. I pleaded to let me go and just let me go to the field and work, but the only sounds that came out were muffled whimpers.

The two villagers stood up as soldiers escorted them to the fields, and other soldiers went to the houses. It was a group of eight men. They moved in unison and split into four groups of two. I instantly thought about Emilia and

Estela. The men said the deal involved kids, and they were the only ones left besides Ramiro.

"No, please. They won't do any good. Just take me!" I snarled, but it wasn't any use. The hand covering my mouth tightened and squeezed at my jaw. It felt like my mouth was closing in on itself as my teeth grinded against each other. The sentence turned into a collection of inaudible words.

The four groups of soldiers went to the four houses that were left, since mine was already open, and pounded at the doors in unison. There wasn't a response from three, but at the one the right of mine, came a slight push of the door. The soldiers had told us that was how we were supposed to let them know we were inside a house. The soldiers then grabbed and pulled the door from the ground. They uprooted the door with ease while I had to slam my full weight to get a gap barely big enough for me to leave.

What did I do? More importantly, who were these people? Two high-pitched cries came from the house as the soldiers dragged Emilia and Estela out.

The two girls did the same as me and kicked against the soldiers, but they were tiny girls, fighting against these giant men. They didn't stand a chance.

They tried to hold each other's hands, but the other six soldiers cut between them in a line, so they wouldn't be together. I couldn't believe what was happening. All we ever did was follow any instructions given to us. Emilia and Estela kept screaming and calling for each other, until the soldiers each grabbed a small dagger and put it to their hearts.

"Shut up, or you're gonna watch each other die."

They didn't make another sound after that.

The hand over my mouth moved to my neck. I was relieved but didn't say anything. I was too shocked to make any sound. I even tried to breathe through my mouth quietly. I could taste the sweat as I gasped for air, only able to breathe in the smell of leather.

"That's all of them, Leo," a soldier said, after coming back from checking the other houses.

"Are you positive? Did we really only have three kids?" Leo asked.

"Well, the other girl did, um . . ."

"I know about her but wasn't there a boy? Where is he?"

"He's not here sir. He's at the field. But, we can't take him. He's more of a field worker. He's improved our collection rate by over twenty percent, and he's—"

"I get it, but if something happens, it's your head on the line soldier."

"Yes, sir."

The moral part of me felt a sense of relief Ramiro would be spared, but the rest of me was pissed. All of us did the same thing as him, but he got spared from whatever the hell we were about to do and wherever the hell we were going! It wasn't right! I had a feeling in my gut it was because he was a guy.

"Why does *he* get to stay here when we did the same damn thing in the fields!" I snapped at Leo.

"Because I want him to. Problem?"

"Yes, there is. A major one! How is it Ramiro is able to get away from whatever you're doing to us? Shouldn't you just take all of us?"

"You don't get to decide what we do. You're a slave and a little gill. You don't have a say in shit. Get that through your head and stay shut. It'll help you."

I didn't respond, just stayed quiet as he said and cowardly lay against Leo's arms. There wasn't anything I could do. I was truly helpless. It felt humiliating. I was cowering with the man who was about to ruin my life.

Threat or Blessing

After walking, or in my case limping, for at least an hour, we made it to a house. It was bigger than the five concrete jail cells back at the village combined. And there was nothing around, just this massive house in the middle of nowhere. Red bricks lined the house's outside walls, and flower bushes decorated the walkway to the entrance. Two massive wooden doors as tall as Leo and the other soldiers walking alongside us were dead center of the building. Everything was so symmetrical, and the doors were actual doors, not like the panels we had. They had dark metal handles Leo pulled to let us in.

On the inside was a silver light that hung from the ceiling in a brass sculpture, which fanned out, illuminating the entire room. Two staircases on each side of the balcony led to the second floor. We stepped closer inside, and to the left was a kitchen. I saw a fireplace and pots on a shelf above it like the clay ones we had, but these were metallic with long handles. Some were flat and jet black in color.

I hobbled inside until Leo instructed me, and the two other girls, to sit on the bench in the middle of the two staircases. I couldn't be more relieved I didn't have to use my foot. It was swollen, and any pressure I put on it made a burning sensation crawl against my foot, like a swarm of wasps stinging my leg at once, over and over.

The three of us sat quietly, waiting to be told what was happening next. My back arched against the wall behind us, and I heard cracks from me stretching. Leo stood in front of us and started to begin a lecture.

"You three, young ladies, are here because Queen Merida and King Alfonso have ordered for there to be a change to your daily lives. Their orders didn't specify any of *you,* so we decided to spare you girls, since you shouldn't be doing field work. As of now, you are going to be appointed to a commander at random, and be their ward. You will be cleaning, cooking, and going to school to learn how to be a good woman. Think of it as your new life. The commander you are appointed to will be in charge of you and your belongings.

"Any decisions you make will go through him. Any changes to your body must go through him. If there are any medical problems, he will be the person making any final judgements. Also, you must behave yourself around his family and friends, as they are just as important. Lastly, if you fail to comply with any of the following rules, you will be hung at the city center, for your body to hang like a sack of meat. Don't make yourself look like a fool and behave."

I sank into the bench in disbelief. The flurry of words I wanted to yell at these men making these ridiculous changes stopped at my throat. From the corner of my eye, I saw two grins on Emilia and Estela's faces. How could they even think of smiling at these absurd demands? Surely, they couldn't be stupid enough to think this would be any better than the village? It would be the same thing but in a different environment. We wouldn't be treated any better. To these *people*, we were always going to be the servants, helpers, slaves.

Leo kept on explaining the "logistics" of what was happening, and he said we would be told who was going to be our new master tomorrow after we spent the night at the barracks. I clenched my fist at the thought of having to walk even more.

Two soldiers grabbed the pair of sisters and made them go upstairs. As they were being taken, Leo pulled me by my arm and took me to the door on the right of the entrance. His grip was solid on my wrist, and he walked fast, as if he had better things to do. I tried to keep up with his pace, but my foot opposed that idea. Leo pushed the door open, and the first thing I focused on was the enormous bed. I hadn't seen anything like it before. It had porcelain white sheets that hugged along its edges. A pillow-like blanket draped over the mattress with a symbol I recognized from the soldier's armor: a gold bird, widespread with a red sword in the middle of its body.

Leo turned to me and gestured to the bed. I stumbled as I went in front of him to make it there. I guess this was the barracks. I'd never seen the outside or any rooms besides an armory. The cold wooden floor squeaked with each of my steps until I got to the corner of the mattress and sat down. Leo shut the door as he made his way to me. The scenery was all too familiar. Trapped inside four corners with no way out, but instead of four dingy concrete walls, it was four wooden ones with paintings of some women in a red dress, her lips rouged, with her hair being just a few shades lighter than the red. I stared at the portrait, until Leo saw me.

"That's Queen Merida. She's the one who ordered for you to be my ward," Leo said, smirking.

"Excuse me? I thought it was assigned at random?"

"It was for the other two, but her majesty specifically chose me for you. I don't know why, but I'm not complaining, and you shouldn't be either. I'll take good care of you."

"I don't need anyone to care for me! Get that through your head!"

"Are you sure about that, sweetie?

Leo kneeled and took my left foot in his hand, squeezing it. I screamed, and my eyes flared. The pain was worse than anything I'd ever felt. Millions of little pins of burning steel, injecting into my heel, then ankle, then leg. It even traveled to my stomach. I grabbed Leo's arm, but I didn't have any strength, so I just cowardly placed my hands on his letting tears drop onto my thighs.

I'd never felt such a feeling of weakness. At the village, I was one of the strongest, fastest, hardworking people, but here I was truly a little girl. All it took was some pain and that allowed them to shape me into this helpless *thing* that relied on a man. Tears continued to fall even when Leo let his grip go. They weren't out of sadness, or me trying to plead, or even me trying to get him to think I was softer than I actually was. They were from the pain in my leg, but mostly frustration. I couldn't get out of what was happening, so I had two options: to either fight a losing battle and take a stand on what my heart was telling me, or live this through to survive another day.

I stared at the picture of Merida and focused on her crown. A gold circlet with three rubies on each peak. Her eyes were green, like the stem of a dandelion. In the portrait, she was alone. That stood out to me. All these guards could babble about was how women and girls were inferior to them and we should just do this and say that. Act like this to be proper. Don't do that because it'll make you look like a man. But, they took orders from a woman. Leo even said it himself. Queen Merida *ordered* him to take me as his ward.

***

The moonlight shined from the thin pane of glass on the wall, illuminating the wooden interior. I admired the sight as I lay on the bed, a blue sheen veiling the entire room. Even though the army was obviously treating us like objects for people's personal gain, the firm but soft mattress and the covers were more comfortable than the dirt floor back at the village. I reminisced on the sturdy feeling of lying on the dirt and pebbles, curled up, my elbows touching my knees. I compared it to what my life at the moment.

I was angry, scared, but comfortable and taken care of. I didn't want to give the army any credit for doing what they should've done from the beginning, and they didn't need any more validation for doing the bare minimum, but I was in a bed with better clothes than before, and my foot was able to get bandaged. They gave me good food, let me bathe, gave me soap; they even respected my privacy when I had to use the bathroom unlike anyone at the village. I set my sight on the wooden panel cut into two sections on the ceiling of the room.

What they were doing was working. I was starting to like the idea of being a ward. I would be safe, comforted. Hell, I'd even be going to school! What if Queen Merida chose *me* for a reason? What if I was something special? No more field work. No more days in the sun letting my skin burn. I would be living a better life in the city.

Every soldier always said good things about Mores. How it was free, and everyone was kind. As much as I despised Leo, what if this was my chance at a better life. I loved my family at the village because they were all I knew, but what if there was something better? Why would I sacrifice a better future for myself for them? They would want to see me live better, like I would them. I was here because of a deal the village men made with the army, they "offered" me, Emilia and Estela, and Ramiro away except Ramiro got lucky because he can piss standing up. They put us up to be taken away by the army so they could avoid something bad, so what if I did the same?

My mind was set on my goal, to make this something I could use to my advantage. I was going to sacrifice some of my humility for a better life. Even if it meant I had to bite my tongue when the army's idiocy was in my face, or submit to Leo and be his perfect ward. I was going to make the most of this. I was going to make my life better, and no one else could change that. My one chance was in a few hours. I shut my eyes letting the pitch-black take over.

Dashing Outset

  My bandaged foot sat on the cold gunpowder-gray metal of the shuttle that traveled between the village, the barracks, and the city. Emilia and Estela sat beside each other, one on each side. Before we left, the soldiers made us wear new clothes because we needed to look presentable. I guess our dirt-stained, tattered aprons, washed only twice a year, weren't acceptable to the normal citizens. They gave us white flowy dresses that hugged against our chest. A barrage of red ribbons were tied at the back, crushing our ribs to make our guts mix in with our spines. They also gave us golden necklaces with a charm, the same golden bird with a sword as the one on the bedsheets and the soldiers' armor. This was their way of branding us. This bird meant we were a part of the empire and in our case, we were their property.

  The shuttle bounced on the road, and I could feel the eggs the army practically force-fed us this morning cling to my throat. The trail to the city was two hours long, and we were only forty-five minutes in. The ground elevated and sank as the shuttle gained speed faster than anything I'd ever seen before. Through the windows, I could see we were going through the hills, and soon we would be passing a mountain.

  I'd admit the mountain range was really pretty. The fresh colors mellowed as the sun gleamed over them. Seeing the mountain tops from afar, and the faint sight of more flatlands uninhabited by sugarcane, was something nice. It felt familiar. Just living in the open with trees, flowers, wild boars, was something I recognized. I didn't remember from what or from where, but I knew I had felt this before.

While staring at the outside world and trying to enjoy all the different hues, I heard Leo's voice, which broke the vision of tranquility in the wild. His voice reminded me of what I was trying to do.

"Leo, what happens when we get to the city?" I asked, trying to seem docile and excited, but I doubt my tone let that happen.

"We will be greeted by the soldiers at the Mores's gate, and then you will be escorted by me to your new home."

"Wh—What about us sir?" Emilia asked shyly. This was the first time I'd heard either of them speak since we were taken from the village.

"As for you two little ladies, your new commanders will meet you at the gates as well, and you will then be escorted to your new homes."

"Commanders? As in more than one?" Estela said, barely forming the sentence.

"Yes, there will be two commanders, one for each of you," Leo told them, sounding over it.

"No! We need to stay together! Please, Mr. Leo!" Estela screamed, pleading as she got on her knees, begging him.

"It's already done. There's nothing I can do," Leo responded, with a flat tone to his voice.

"No, no, no! I have to be with Emilia! We're sisters. You can't do this, please!"

"Estela, he said there's nothing we or he can do. Just save your energy," Emilia said, as she hugged her sister, trying to calm her down.

"B—but, this isn't fair, and you know it isn't!"

My face became inflamed as I saw the two trying to process everything going on. Estela was right; this wasn't fair. Her and her sister were going to be put apart because of something unknown to any of us. I wanted to say something, but I couldn't find the words to match what I was feeling. Emilia and Estela's hair tangled together as they got up and sat back on the copper benches that lined the shuttle. Estela put her head on Emilia's shoulder and quietly wept. I saw Emilia try to stay strong, and I knew the front all too well. She was putting her sister first and was hiding how she felt to make her sister happy.

My heart shattered watching them. I turned my head to Leo, and his face was blank. No emotion, no feelings, no thoughts! How could he just sit there and do nothing, while these two children were breaking, a clay vase slowly cracking, just waiting to crumble into a pile of dust!

I turned facing away from Leo before the anger inside me turned into something more, and focused my attention back on the outside. The passing trees and wilting bushes flashed as we got closer to the mountain.

All of a sudden, a static and robotic voice rang from wall to wall throughout the shuttle. "Please stay seated and remain calm as we travel past Mt. Acocia."

I didn't think twice. I turned toward the other side of the shuttle, where Emilia and Estela were, so my body could be fully straight and held on to the braces on the benches. The shuttle then started to go faster and faster until it was speeding up the mountain. I could feel my soul leave my body as we continued to defy gravity. Flashes of terrain zoomed past us as we made it to the top of the mountain road. A small pause in the shuttle's movement showed the scenery and I could see the outline of Mores. It was massive.

Thousands of buildings formed groups of circles, and at the dead center, was a castle. An enormous yellowish-stone building overviewed the city. There was also an outer wall, which held Mores in a giant bubble.

I gawked and kept thinking I was in a dream because none of this felt real. Between the shuttle defying gravity and this place, something the others and I at the village could only imagine in our dreams, everything felt unreal. But, this was real. This wasn't my mind making up a fictional wonderland. I was staring directly at it. It was overwhelming. I was going to be living there. I was going to start a new life there. Mores was going to be my new home, chosen or not.

The shuttle started to move again, and my stomach started to twist into knots. We were about to go down; *Fuck me.* I clasped the metal brace warmed by my palm and prepared myself. The shuttle tottered against the peak of the road. *Really, I mean, C'mon.* It felt like the driver was messing with us.

"Please remain seated and hold on to the braces along the benches. Any injuries sustained during the duration of the ride are not admissible in any court of law in España."

Court? I'd heard about it from a few guards talking about their lives at the village when there wasn't anything to do, but I didn't know what it was. But there wasn't any time to think of that, considering we were about to plummet from the top of a mountain. The shuttle started back up again slowly, and before my heart could even beat, we were going down at lightning speed. The flashes of landscape I saw going up turned into a ball of colors that instantly went and gone.

I wanted to scream, but if I opened my mouth, my insides would pour out. So instead, I just closed my eyes and waited until it was over. I could feel my back start to go back to normal, instead of being glued to the bench as the shuttle slowed down. I didn't loosen my grip until I could fully trust we wouldn't go flying again.

Another announcement sounded overhead on the shuttle: "The hard part is now over. For the rest of the trip, it'll be a smooth ride. Please enjoy the complimentary food provided by Queen Merida and King Alfonso and relax. We will be arriving in Mores in an hour."

Hollow Inception

The outer wall met my eyes, and I could see the pattern of stone after stone and brick after brick that lined it, with thousands of intricate details I couldn't even imagine the amount of time it would take to make. Even the vines and shrubbery that grew along the wall were maintained and taken care of. Little white flowers with sun-yellow centers grew on the vines and bunches of red, pink, and orange petals covered the bushes. It seemed like Mores cared more about the greenery than anyone at the village.

I kept on staring at the wall and began to pan my vision up to the towers that looked down on the city, dozens of them lining the top of the wall. I just imagined the thought of a hundred pairs of eyes staring, analyzing, judging my every move. As if the guards at the village weren't enough, or Leo making me tell him what I was thinking at random intervals. It was seriously weird.

"We are now entering Mores. Please remain seated and allow soldiers to exit before you as you exit the vehicle. Welcome to Mores, city of Morality."

The static of the speakers cut out, and a creaking sound like metal bending and scraping together could be heard, coming from the front. When we first entered the shuttle back at the barracks, we got in from the back, so I wasn't sure if the sound was doors opening. Maybe we were beginning to crash, and we would soon just be lifeless corpses, waiting to be eaten by bugs as our decomposed bodies became homes for new species.

The thought didn't seem bad, but it didn't have the same appeal it would've had when Leo first took me. Instead, I wanted the opposite. During the trip, I kept reminding myself I would live a better life. When we were hurling down a fucking mountain, the end goal of going to a better place kept me from literally puking. It was bad. The only vision of life I could remember was at a village with nothing but sugarcane, mud, and acres of nothingness, so being *here* in a city with people and protection was a pretty big change I was going to force myself to like.

The metallic sound stopped, and the soldiers stood as the shuttle came to a standstill. Emilia and Estela were still holding each other, and along with myself, we stayed seated, just like the announcement said to do. Soldiers began to exit the shuttle in pairs of two while Leo gestured for us to get up but stay where we were. As soldiers began to disembark, Leo told Emilie and Estela to exit. They walked together, both shaking like it was a freezing winter day.

I wanted to cry for them. I couldn't imagine the pain they would feel being separated. I also couldn't find a reason for the decision.

"Leo, sir. Are you *positive* there's nothing you can do for them to be together? Please. Those two have always been inseparable. It isn't right, and you know it," I asked Leo a final time.

"I'm positive, and even if there was, you are in no place to make demands," Leo shot back at me without a second thought. Not even an um, or maybe just a no.

"Demands? I'm asking a simple question because what they're doing is wrong! And you can't be such a heartless, selfish, and ignorant bastard to not see that!" My words came out like spikes of flames.

Leo stayed quiet and ignored me as he walked to the doors.

"Really? You can't even respond. I knew I was right at the village. You *are* a coward!"

Leo did something at the door I couldn't figure out and started walking back toward me. I could see his walk start getting angry. The weight on his steps became heavy and dominating, his posture back-straight, chest-out. The same metallic grinding sound from before started back up again, and the shuttle began to move.

"Why are we moving again?" My stomach dropped to the floor.

"You're going to listen to me, Cecilia, and I'm only saying this once." His voice became deeper and bleak.

"How do you know my na—"

Leo cut me off. "I know everything about you, from your name to your birthday to your friends and 'family.' You're going to realize I know everything, and I can get any information I want about you, so here's what's going to happen. We are going to my home. You will be my ward and will do as I say. And if you don't or step out of the thin line you're on, I'll kill you and those two others myself. Also, one last thing. Learn to keep your mouth shut and bite your tongue. Even if it bleeds."

***

I began to exit the shuttle from the front doors, after a silent, grueling ride of me battling my thoughts after Leo's lecture. The sunlight beamed, and I could tell from memory the sun had just risen. It was the same feeling I would have when the soldiers would first get us at the village during sunrise. An onslaught of emotions and potential comebacks swirled in my body, but I reluctantly behaved. If I was going to at least try to have a better life, then my pride needed to take a back seat.

Leo followed behind me as we stepped across the road that the shuttle took. Apparently, this was one of many shuttles that railed across the city. When people had to travel long distances, they would take a shuttle to speed up the process. The shuttle we we'd been on was originally supposed to make a brief stop at the Mores' outer gate and then go back to its original path, but the driver made an exception for Leo.

A path to a house, about half the size of the barracks but with a decent-sized yard, was in front of Leo and me. It was made from the same bricks as the outer walls but with less intricacy. The roof was made of a dark wood stripped in a beige color. We walked along a short stone walkway and made it to the door. It was similar to the one at the barracks, but instead of a dark metal, this handle was a red copper. Leo pulled the handle and opened the door as he sent me in.

The Place to Be

"Maria come here, please," Leo announced, his voice projecting on the lavish wooden walls, which had paintings of him and a bunch of soldiers. Leo stood out among them. His armor in the picture was a bright white silver with the golden insignia of Mores along his upper body. The wings draped across his shoulders led to his chest and his breastplate. He also had a black sword with a red lace around its sheath on his waist satchel. The other soldiers had smiles across all their faces, and I could see this was a moment where Leo was bathing in glory. His smirk almost disgusted me with the realization that it was a front, at least to me.

A woman came up from steps that lead to a lower part of the house. She had straight blonde hair with even more crystal-clear blue eyes than Leo. Her dress was lilac with pink cross details symmetrically lining the hems on her waist, and a white crucifix at the center of her chest on a necklace. Her exposed skin was also paler than Leo's, but her cheeks were a pink that blended with her natural skin color Her lips were a fiery red that mixed well with the rest.

"Maria, this is Cecilia, and she will be assisting you and I with anything necessary. She is also going to be living here and attending school in the city," Leo said as if I was their new child.

"That's wonderful. I'll have someone when you're in battle, but Leo why did you bring one of *them?*" Maria asked Leo with a condescending cheerfulness in her high-pitched voice.

"Queen's orders, Maria, and besides, she'll be more useful with labor since she was in the fields, even if she isn't a boy."

"Fine, but you're going to have to earn your privileges, starting with your bedroom."

Maria started explaining to me what I would be doing while Leo was gone doing his duties as a commander in the Mores' army. I would be cleaning, learning how to cook "proper" food and how to sew, doing laundry, maintaining a garden, and running errands in the city.

I was in utter shock. She wasted absolutely no time with the explanation and told me today would be my first day. No time to prepare or even breathe, straight into being a ward. Although it felt more like a personal servant, I guess the two were interchangeable.

Leo went to his chambers at the west end of the house, and Maria and I started our first day together. First, we went to the kitchen and began preparation for lunch and dinner since Leo didn't eat breakfast. Something to do with the army's rules. She laid out an assortment of new fruits and vegetables like nothing I'd ever seen. Maria made me learn each of their names and uses. We had bananas, plums, apples, peaches, apricots, onions, tomatoes, and potatoes. At the village, we only got what we could find, and we never found any of these.

Maria showed me how to cut the fruits into cube-like pieces so they could be mixed into other meals for nutrition, while the vegetables were going to be cut into more finely so they could fry easily. She taught me by grabbing my arms with her behind me and placing a sharp knife in my hands.

I felt like I could overpower her if I tried hard enough. The handle of the knife warmed up as my grip got tighter. My knuckles flexed. I could do it. I could kill her. I raised the knife, with a swiftness I– I cut into the onion on a wooden cutting board. She didn't deserve to die. If anything, Leo was more punishable by death than her, but neither of them had done anything severe to me. They were just doing what they were told from the higher-ups. If I ever got the thought of changing the system in place, or even getting revenge, my first target would have to be the King and Queen. Straight to the source of the problem.

We cut pretty much anything green—like for like three hours, before we got to the next part of me learning to be a Mores' lady. Next was laundry, which I was familiar with. We cleaned Leo's four suits of armor and washing some of Maria's dresses. There were two buckets by a small pond of water in the backyard of the house. These people had money. One of the buckets was filled with clear water, and the other with water and a soap, turning the water into a milky white.

We dunked the dresses in the pond to get them wet, put them into the soap bucket, and scrubbed. I scrubbed vigorously until Maria said to stop; then we put the dress into the other bucket to rinse the soap off. Once the dress was clean, we would hang them on thin wires strung from two poles. The stream of wind would flow in between the almost dozen dresses we'd hung, and I could see the water start to dry.

While the dresses were drying, we also attended to the garden and made sure the weeds were cut, and everything was growing normally. This also wasn't new to me because it was how I would get food at the village. I'd taken care of any crops that grew in the forest. After all, how else would I get food?

The final thing we did was go to the city and pick up a few materials needed in the house. My body couldn't keep up with the pace this woman was going at. It was literally my first day. Less than twenty four hours in the city and I was already on my second shuttle. It took less than thirty minutes to get to the shopping capital of Mores.

During the ride, Maria talked me through how the shopping center worked. It was next to the financial district of España, Pecunia, and all we would be doing was going to three specific places. Our first stop was to get fabric so Maria could teach me how to sew, the second was to get more food, and the last was to pick up any mail the army had sent to Leo.

The first two stops took almost no time at all, in and out, even though the centers were full of people. Walking through the aisles of fabric walls, I felt stares and judgment seeping into my skin, burning my pores. The same feeling had been at the market as well. But, the worst part happened at the mailing hub.

The sign at the doors stated it was "Militia only." I asked Maria if I was allowed to go in, and she told me it was fine because I was with her. But, she wasn't in the army I questioned. She walked in with her hand on my wrist and told me because she was a commander's wife that she had certain rights.

As soon as I stepped foot into the hub, everyone instantly turned to me like I was a target. My heart dropped. I started to sweat and could hear the comments about me. It was like I was a *thing*, instead of a person. I was this woman's property. We walked to the counter, and Maria got Leo's mail without an issue. I almost felt relieved it was a quick process, but before we left I heard the clerk behind me:

"Useless Morena."

I didn't understand what it meant, but I knew it wasn't something good. I wasn't that naive. Maria looked back at him but didn't say anything, and we kept walking. Maria then let go of my wrist and grabbed my hand instead.

"You've earned your room, Cecilia."

***

I sat on a chair in the corner of my new room and stared out the window. Ever since the night at the barracks, this was my new way of trying to gather my thoughts. I kept on replaying the guy's phrase, "Useless Morena." What did it mean? I tried asking Maria on the shuttle back, but she avoided the question or just stayed quiet, and I didn't bother asking Leo.

Something in my gut told me it somehow wouldn't end well. I knew I wouldn't be treated fairly or even decently from the very first time Leo called me useless. But, I still wanted to know what they were saying. The murkiness of the situation just made it worse. I felt like if I could prepare for the insult or know vaguely what they were saying or what they wanted to say, it wouldn't hurt as much.

Dark spots started to show on the lap of my dress, like little puddles of tears. I tried to breathe but the ocean of defeat entombed my lungs. I started to gasp, and a hoarse breath escaped my throat. The weight of existing in this city came down on me like a roof caving in. How could I possibly think I could make this my new home when everyone else just sees a dirty village girl? No matter how many fancy dresses I wore or golden necklaces hung from my neck, these city people would just see a slave girl who got lucky. This wasn't the place I wanted it to be, it was the exact same thing as the village but in a new form. I was still an object someone owned. The only difference being, I was alone.

Needed Alive

I sat on the steps of the basement and waited for Leo to finish putting his undergarment on. He made it pretty clear I wasn't allowed to see any of his *natural features*. I couldn't care less, but if it meant I got a small break, be my guest. The basement was pretty much a replica of the "houses" at the village, a small concrete room with dim lighting. Leo called for me, and I stepped into the room where he was in. Four suits of armor were on four mannequins that stood on the wall farthest away from the room's entrance. They were all the same armor sets; it just looked like some of them were used more than the others.

Leo decided on one of the four, and I started putting his armor on for him. It was a bit dehumanizing, but I just stopped myself from laughing as I was doing it. I mean seriously. This grown-ass soldier, not soldier, commander, was making a fifteen-year-old put his armor on for him. That in my "useless" opinion was pretty pathetic. I finished putting on his armor and wiped it with a damp rag to make sure it was clean.

"If it doesn't gleam and shimmer under the light, it isn't clean enough," Leo told me before I began.

After Leo made sure his armor was good enough for the mortal eye to see, we made our way back upstairs and to the kitchen. Although Leo didn't eat breakfast, Maria and I still did and because I was helping Leo, I got out of kitchen duties. A plate of eggs with some cut fruit and slices of fresh bread sat at the table waiting for us to return. Maria and I waited until Leo was sitting, and he had his glass of water before we could sit and eat. While we ate, Leo opened the mail we'd picked up yesterday. His reactions weren't big, mostly some complaining about army standards and having to do paperwork, but one letter caught his and Maria's eyes. Although Maria picked up the letters, she didn't go through them. The letter that got their attention was in a white envelope with a red and yellow border, and a black wax seal with the outline of the Spanish insignia. I really was getting tired of this damn bird. It was on everything.

Leo opened the letter carefully like picking a rare rose from a garden, not wanting to damage it. He read it closely, paying attention to every character on it. Maria stopped eating and I could see her put all of her focus into her husband.

Seriously, what is so important about this letter? I thought to myself as I continued to chew on the peach slices left on my plate, savoring the flavor like it was my last meal.

"Well, what does it say, Leo?" Maria asked hesitantly.

"I—I need to leave at once, and Cecilia is coming with me!" he responded as he rushed to pull me up from my chair and to the front door.

I nearly choked trying to get the last chunk of food down my throat. Maria was surprised at the sudden rush, but she didn't try to stop him. She didn't even ask any other questions. She just stood, dutiful, after saying she loved him. I guess that's what Mores' love was like.

At the village, no one had a chance to keep a relationship. The soldiers would beat anyone they thought were together. The only time any *personal* contact was allowed, was when the soldiers forced the women to procreate. When they would see the elders starting to fade in condition, they saw it as time to start a new life. The worst thing about it was when the women were picked at random to make babies, the soldiers would get to plant the seed. There were times, when I was about twelve and thirteen, I could hear glass-breaking screams of women as the soldiers they were with raped them in the houses.

I could only imagine what it was like. Their white, disgusting bodies on yours as you yelled, kicked, clawed, and scratched until your nails pierced their skin, but they still didn't stop. After using all the energy you could give, you just stared at the concrete walls counting the second until it was done, to then carry their child for nine months. It was something no one ever talked about, but we all knew. How could we not?

Leo and I waited for a special shuttle only for army members, and I thought about his and Maria's relationship.

"Leo, do you love Maria, or are you using her?" I asked. I wanted to know if he shared the loving sentiment Maria showed because knowing he was a commander, he couldn't be clean from the atrocity done to women at the village.

"My relationship with my wife is none of your concern."

"Then, why respond instead of keeping quiet?"

There wasn't a response.

"Nothing to say. Fine, be like that."

I didn't understand why he couldn't just respond with an actual answer. I would be spending the rest of any future I had being at his beck and call. The least he could do was not be a dick. The rest of the wait was silent, and it was agonizing.

My mind just started to come up with questions about why Leo was taking me with him. It seemed like he was about to handle some army business, but I was here. Did he need me to do something for someone else, like a favor for a favor? He'd get something, and in exchange, the other guy would get me for a day. Leo did a pretty damn good job establishing I was more of an object than human, so it wouldn't be that strange. Or, what if I was a sacrifice of sorts? Some inner-city scheme that involved a sacrifice to keep something at bay or make something happy. I didn't know at that point my brain was just making things up to keep me from boredom.

After an hour of waiting, which we could've just spent in the house, a black shuttle came. The regular shuttle was a blueish-gray, but this one was midnight black with gold accents. It was actually very nice to look at. The doors opened, and the inside was lavish. White-padded seats instead of benches, windows that sheared into a black ombre to fade in with the walls. The floor was the same gray metal as the regular shuttles, but at the center was that, damn, bird!

I'm sick and tired of seeing this symbol everywhere! It haunted me, like my shadow, following me wherever I go.

Leo and I sat in the first row of horizontal seats separated into two sections by a walkway in the middle: three seats on the left and three on the right. I sat a seat away from Leo, on the inner seat, leaving the gap because he wasn't comfortable with having me so close. How *dare* he be seen sitting next to his "ward" that had brown skin instead of white?

I didn't care. I didn't want to be next to him either or here in the first place. I would've been better off at the house learning more basic chores, but no. I had to be dragged out by Leo because of a letter.

The shuttle began to move, and every so often it stopped, and more soldiers got on. Their armor was like

Leo's: bright, white, and clean. I was in the same white dress given to me, so at least my clothes didn't stick out. As they got on, I could feel their eyes dart toward me. My clothes matched, but I was still the odd one out. A black sheep in a group of ascending doves.

They snarled and made noises of disgust, each like pin needles digging themselves under my skin. When Leo made comments, I shrugged them off as best I could. I was a bit used to it. But when it was these strangers I'd never even spoken a word to, it hurt so much more. They didn't even know my name, but they had enough information to make a judgment on something I had no choice over.

***

I stood up from my seat and followed Leo as we got off through the back exit. Another shuttle ride finished. As the shuttle began to drive away, I looked around to try to find out where I was. The castle! I was at the literal castle of Mores, the one I could see from the mountain. The same yellow building. Why were we here? No, not we, why was *I* here? I get Leo because his important commander business but me! At this point, being a nobody in the eyes of this society would be a favor.

"Follow me, Cecilia, and move quickly," Leo said as he walked to the small bridge just before the jaw-like entrance of the castle. I trailed behind Leo trying not to trip on my dress. The bridge was above a big creak that had a stream that rushed along it. The sound of the water and a small waterfall traveled through the air. I could see little shadows of fish swimming, and boulders lined a border on the sides of the stream. I continued walking on the stone bridge trying to calm myself by breathing in the mist from the water. As we finally made our way to the entrance doors twice as tall as Leo's, a soldier in baggy gold pants, a tight red shirt seen through the holes of the chainmail over it, and a white overcoat pinned on his shoulder came from behind the doors to greet Leo.

"Commander Leo Bastelio. What brings you to the castle?" The man asked with an angry friendliness.

"Juerio. I am here to meet Queen Merida."

My face turned as white as Leo's. He was meeting the Queen, and he brought me! It was day two of me being in the city, and I was already on my way to meet royalty.

"Really, Leo? If you wanted to get away from your responsibilities, you could've just said that. It's not like it's the first time you've done this," Juerio said, chuckling.

"Juerio, this is serious!" Leo took the letter from his satchel that hung from his hip and shoved it in the guard's face.

"I—I— I'll take you at once sir." Juerio's expression turned serious. He opened the doors and started escorting Leo across the halls.

I followed the two men because what else was I going to do, stay at the gates. The tunnels of hallways were dark oak with windows spread out evenly and sheer beige curtains on their sides. The floor was also wood but a lighter shade of oak; it almost matched my skin. There were also crystalline lights ingrained into the roofs of the hallways. They illuminated the hallways in a way that was like natural sunlight.

As we walked, my body felt heavy like someone was on my back. My steps became sluggish, and the two men noticed but didn't say anything. Usually, Leo would tell me to "Hurry up," or "Keep up with the pace," but he kept quiet and followed Juerio. Something was wrong. I knew something was wrong. There was someone or something doing this to me.

"Leo, something's wrong. I can barely walk," I said, as I slowly went to the wall to try and sit.

"What do you think you're doing little girl? Stand up immediately!" Juerio said, barely managing to not yell his brains out.

"Cecilia, get up, now!" Leo said as he walked toward me.

Leo grabbed my hand and tried to force me to stand, but when I managed to get up, I just fell back down as if my legs were turning into puddles.

"Leo, get it to move before we're spotted by other guards," Juerio said, while making his way to me.

Wow, *it*. First "little girl," and now "it." I had a feeling Juerio wasn't too fond of me being here. If only my legs would work so that I could get out.

"Cecilia, this isn't time for games. Get the fuck up!" Leo shouted at the top of his lungs, his rage bouncing off the walls.

"I'm trying! I'm not doing this on purpose Leo!!"

In a flash, I could see Leo's hand raise and start to make its way to me. I tried to block, but I wasn't fast enough. Rumbles of footsteps trembled the floor as my body shook. Time slowed as the figure of Leo's hand became bigger and closer.

A hard sound like a slab of meat hitting the floor echoed. My face instantly inflamed. I screamed, but Juerio quickly put his hand on mine from behind. A pain like stinging hornets dug into my check. My eyes filled with tears as I tried to pull Juerio's hand away. He wouldn't budge. I tried biting his hand, but all I ended up doing was licking his palm. Juerio immediately pulled away. His face plunged into a pungent disgust. From my liquidy vision, I saw more men in the same clothes Juerio had coming from the corner of the hallway.

"Stop. Why are you all in the castle? Who has permitted you access?"

"Relax. He's with me, and the girl is with him," Juerio said in a fake confidence. He sounded nothing like he did when it was just Leo and him.

"You can't give access to the premises guard, so why is *he* here?" The man at the front line of the swarm of guard asked.

"I have a letter from her majesty to meet her at once," Leo explained. "Her majesty requires for me to bring her. I don't know for what, but I do know it was urgent as the letter was directed to me personally and not Captain General Francisco. I apologize deeply for the lack of communication and for the disturbance, but I must meet her majesty at once."

The guard looked at Leo and told him to give them the letter. Leo complied, and the guards certified the legitimacy of the letter. They carefully analyzed every micro-detail of it and at the end decided it was of actual importance.

"Follow us sir."

"There is another issue we face, though. *She* isn't getting up from the floor," Juerio complained, forgetting the fact this wasn't my choice.

"I'm not refusing to get up. I literally can't move my legs, and I don't know why."

"Mm-hm, okay. Wait one moment." The guards started to whisper, and one left for a few minutes.

What were they doing now? Another punishment because my legs decided to not function! The man came back with a chair that had two wheels attached to it.

"Seeing as you are needed for this meeting, we need you to be mobile. Sit on this, and a guard will escort you to and from the Queen's chambers."

Huh? This wasn't something I was expecting from people close to royalty; they were being nice. Well, I didn't know if it was *being nice*, but they were treating me like a person. It felt good to be met with basic decency, but I wasn't going to give them any thanks. This was what should always happen. Even if I wasn't handicapped or a slave or a girl, I and everyone else who didn't fit the Mores' standard, should be treated like a human.

I held my dress from entangling with the wooden wheels of the wheelchair as we made our way to the Queen's chambers. Leo was in the front of the group with the head of the royal guard, Carlos. He was as tall as Leo with a different uniform than Juerio. He had skintight, black pants and a red button-up shirt that showed off his muscles. He also had a white trench coat that looked like it was supposed to be buttoned up but wasn't.

He and Leo seemed to be having an important discussion, but I couldn't hear what they were saying. The man pushing me around, Pilar, was actually being friendly and trying to make conversation. He asked me questions about the village, how I was adjusting to the city, and some of my favorite things to do. I kept my answers brief and simple. I didn't know who this guy was and him being so interested in me set off alarms. How could I be sure he wouldn't go to the village and take more people. I couldn't take any chances. He was disappointed I didn't play into his conversations, but that wasn't my problem. If he wanted to talk to someone, he had every person in Mores, not me.

We reached the Queen's chamber, which was guarded by actual soldiers like Leo. They had their swords in an X formation, one on top of another, blocking the door. Leo greeted them and immediately showed them the letter. They stood their ground until Carlos signaled them to let Leo and me through. Pilar pushed me to the door, then gave the handles to Leo. He couldn't enter the chambers as he wasn't on the letter. Leo grabbed the handles, and we started to move inside.

Independent Analysis

The Queen's chambers were probably the most expensive part of the castle. It was covered in gold. Gold vases, statues of birds, flowers, and golden silk as the curtains to the massive windows. The yellow mellowed out the harsh black and red furniture. Every step Leo took was cautious and hesitant. Was he scared? It felt like we were approaching a lioness in her den.

As we walked through her chamber hallways, I felt my body get heavier. Some of it was from the shock of one person having a house inside of a castle as their chambers, but most of it was the same feeling I had before. Only this time, it wasn't my legs; it was my entire body. It felt like a pile of bricks sat on my lap and shoulders. There wasn't any pain that came with it, just the pressure.

After traversing through the Queen's quarters, we made it to a door labeled, *Private Court of Mores.*

Huh, we were going to court?

I guess that wasn't too bad. I still didn't really know what court was, but I didn't think it involved physical pain, so that was at least a plus. Leo opened the doors and pushed me into the room. It was, again, massive! This castle had like seven-hundred houses inside of it. This room had a bunch of chairs, and a few benches made an upside-down U-shape, with the middle having seats elevated from the rest.

The lights in the room were a bright snow white, and their glare blinded me. I couldn't even move my arms to shield my eyes. As soon as I could focus, my vision, I saw a bunch of soldiers sitting along the benches and a lady with big red hair dead center of the elevated seats. The picture of the woman at the barracks instantly flashed into my memory.

"That's Queen Merida," I remembered Leo saying.

My heart almost came flying out of my chest. I knew she was going to be here, but seeing her so close and having so many questions made my heart palpitate a hundred beats per millisecond. Her face was almost identical to the one in the painting. It was only a bit darker in person. Instead of bone white, it was almost beige.

She sat tall with her hair in a beehive with a fan in her hand that she gracefully held and used to cool herself down. Her fingers twirled around the golden, sparkly fringes that flowed along the fan's handle.

Leo kept punching me until I was in the very middle of the room. I moved my head to look around me, and my mouth went dry, and my heart went from lightning to snail speed. I saw dozens of pairs of eyes, on both sides of me, stare into my soul. I quickly turned to face the ground, but an alarming voice caught me off guard.

"Please rise for the honorable judge, Merida de España!"

I remained seated because everything under my neck decided that today was the day not to work. The stares before turned into infuriated gasps and snarls.

"How can you just sit while Her Majesty is in your presence?"

"This is more than disrespect. This is a crime!"

"Just as expected from one of *them*. How are they even allowed in the castle?"

More and more insults and snarky remarks kept fluttering throughout the room's walls, bouncing from person to person and digging into my ears.

"Silence!" a commanding yet feminine voice said.

I looked up at the Merida, and she was standing with her fan in both her palms; the handle in one and the actual cloth in the other. From my view, she had a red dress on with the Mores' insignia on the bodice as the centerpiece. It was simple, but it made a statement. Her energy was like Leo's but far more so. She knew she had power and was in control and didn't have to prove it.

Looking at her command a room of soldiers, with a simple word, made me more curious than I'd been in my life. I wanted to know how she got to this position. Being queen was just having a title, but with Merida, I knew she had more than a title; she had presence and respect from her people.

The room went silent, and Merida sat back down and started talking.

"Commander Leo Bastelio of the Seventh Battalion of Mores, you stand here today to inform the council of your discoveries while traversing through the sea. Is that correct?"

"Y—Yes, my Queen. That is correct."

"Very well. You may start your testimony."

"During my travels to the Island of Gold, we encountered many turbulences while sailing. Some of such are heavy storms, lightning striking at rapid places, and sinkholes in the ocean. Um, whilst some of these may be natural, it was nothing like the past expeditioners recorded in their logs. As we made it to the island, we were greeted by more of the people, which we know are called the Tainos.

"They were resourceful, but no doubt they were cautious of our presence. After gathering resources such as gold, native agriculture, fowl, and different fabric-like materials, we made our way back to the three ships. Along with the materials, we also had three-dozen captives waiting to be loaded. Once back on sea, we ran into a tremendous storm that dwarfed any other we had previously encountered. It's a miracle any of us even made it out alive. Although I and my battalion made it out alive, I can't say the same for battalions two and five of Tanix and Sereno.

"I deeply apologize for the death of my brothers, and I will continue to mourn their death every day, for the rest of my life."

"Thank you for your report, Leo. This will be logged into the royal record of Mores along with España's imperial archives of its Army. As for you, I don't entirely believe your story. How is it the slave ship was the only one that managed to escape, in your own words, a tremendous storm? So, Leo, explain to me in full detail of your escape from the storm."

"Uh, well, some of my men informed me of Commander Tanix's ship being out of sight, and when I went to the edge of the deck to try and scope it out, I saw glimpses of soldiers falling into the ocean. I immediately checked the other side of the deck to begin to signal Commander Sereno, but I was too late, his ship was being sucked into the ocean as the waves began to tear it apart. My men and I watched as the sail rod was torn in half.

"I knew we would be next if something wasn't done, so I called all of my men on deck, and we began to sail the ship past the storm. There were moments where I didn't think any of us were going to make it out alive, but my Queen, it is truly by the grace and miracle of God we did, and that is the truth."

As Leo finished his testimony, a flood of memories came back to me, surging through my head. Flashes of white light with a terrible pungent smell like salt with rotting flesh. A scratchy sensation along my body with my hair being pulled. My chin being grabbed and squeezed until I made a face like I had tasted something disgusting. Then, I saw a man with the same skin as mine and long, jet-black hair swishing along the wind's currents. He stood at the edge of a wooden floor with an almost turquoise radiance, clearing the sky until it went from a somber dingy purple to a tranquil light blue.

"Hmm, very well, Commander. I thank you for your service to Mores, and w—"

"Wait!"

The crowd went berserk as I cut Merida off.

"Merida, that's not the truth. I remember being there. I remember the man who saved us, and it definitely was not Leo."

Leo was furious, and so were the other soldiers. How dare I call this hero a liar!

"Order! I demand order at once!" Merida yelled, making everyone halt.

"Now, what is your name, girl?" Merida asked me in a calm voice.

"I—my name is Cecilia. But that's not really impor—"

She cut me off. "Now, now, Cecilia. Relax. You will have time to make your statement, so there is no need to rush."

"Okay, so will you let me finish?"

"I shall in due time."

"What does that mean?"

"It means you will have a chance after this evening. For now, we shall recess so that—"

I cut her off this time. "No, I'm going to say this now. Leo is lying. He was willing to let all of us die, and if it wasn't for a man called Guey, who parted the storm, using something, we would be dead. So, go ahead and treat this bastard like a savior, but in reality he is a weak, lying, coward who got lucky."

"You lying rat. I will have your head!" A man's voice said from the crowd.

"Stop him at once, guards!" Merida shouted.

The soldiers at the sides of Merida pounced and apprehended the guy, who was still unsheathing his sword, in less than a few seconds. My face was aghast, and I hadn't realized what just happened.

"Send in the royal guard to put this man in holding. As for you two, come with me. Court is adjourned."

Leo started to push my wheelchair as we began to follow the Merida. Her long dress swung side to side as she walked.

Merida brought me, Leo, and her two guards, to a private room. It was the first thing in the castle that wasn't decorated to a lavish degree. It was just a basic room with a table in the middle, some paintings, and two little stone statues, one of a hummingbird and one of a frog, sitting on the windowsill. Merida sat us down, Leo and me on one side, and her directly across from me, staring at me with longing eyes. Her emerald green irises met and stayed locked on mine.

"Leo, would you be so kind as to exit this room for a few minutes? Cecilia and I need to talk," Merida said.

"Um, O—okay," Leo responded quite plainly.

"Excuse me?"

"Apologies. Yes, my Queen," Leo said, correcting himself.

One of Merida's guards brought Leo out of the room, and it was just the Queen and me. I guess for my second day in Mores I wasn't doing too bad in the things-that-I-couldn't-believe-happened category.

"Okay, Merida, let's just get the bullshit out of the way. Why did you want me here, and why do you want to speak to me alone?" I wanted to have an actual conversation. I wanted answers.

"I guess it would be pretty un-like you to call me Queen, wouldn't it?"

"You're just another person to me. Are you that much of a narcissist you require acknowledgment through the title of Queen?"

"But I have to say, you're just like *him*. It's a shame he died before you could meet. I feel like he would've liked you."

"What are going on about?"

"You're smart, quick-witted, and it seems like you don't like authority. Definitely *his*."

"Who's *him*?"

"Ha ha, your father, Cecilia. I knew him well. You can say him and me were somewhat friends."

"Lady, what the hell are you talking about! For all you know he could've been some random person. How can you know that you're talking about is my dad?"

"Cecilia, I helped get you here because you were his."

An Indescribable Truth

Hearing the Queen of España say she knew my father was a laughable situation. I wasn't what I thought would happen when Leo brought me to the castle, but here we were. A mother, a father, and such figures were all concepts I hadn't fathomed in my life. I didn't know what it meant to have a mom or dad, and I definitely wasn't thinking of becoming a mother. The village taught me that ultimately all that did was hold you back. The mothers were put into this specific box of being helpless without a man, even though they were the ones who went through the torture of birth, not to mention actually raising and taking care of the child. It was yet another anomaly that made no sense, but people believed because *the men said so.*

"I thought I said no more bullshit, Merida. First you order your army to take me from the village to be a servant to an asshole of a commander, then you feed me this garbage. You're saying you sent soldiers to get me because you knew my dad! How much of a gullible idiot do you take me for?"

"Cecilia, give me a moment to explain to you what happened. I know there's a part of you that wants to at least hear me out. You're young. What fifteen, maybe sixteen? And you've only been in Mores for a couple of years. Let me tell you your father's story."

She was right that I wanted to hear her out because what if there was the slightest bit of truth in her story. What if she actually knew my dad? I could learn more about myself. I wasn't hearing her out to give her validation of me needing her; I was hearing her out because I needed to do it for myself.

"Fine, go ahead. I'm listening."

"Your father, Christopher Columbus, was an explorer from the day he was born to the day that he died.

He and I knew each other since we were both children, maybe six, or seven. He would tell everyone in our town, in Mores, about how he found the most random things. There was one time he made a fuss that no one listened to his story about finding a unique stick with special markings, which were somehow rare. But anyway, we were raised in Mores, and both got noble titles.

"He was a soldier who made his way to commander and then to a new position, Head of International voyages. He was in charge of every voyage that had to do with new land outside of our known allies. And as for me, I made my way up from a ward like yourself to a maiden of King Helio. Then I married Alfonso, and now I am here.

"Christopher made a name for himself in España and that allowed him to make decisions, such as the collection of islanders like yourself. Christopher wanted to take people from the islands he'd *found* and make them work for the empire. I wasn't too fond of the idea, but I couldn't do anything. I was only a wife to a prince with a say in official matters. It came to a point where Christopher was abusing his power and using the advantages he was given to make other people's lives a vicious cycle of torment and torture.

"But, I'm getting sidetracked. Your father was a good man until he wasn't, and it's because of him you are here. And it's because of me, you are being treated decently. As soon as I heard the truth of what happened during the voyage of your collection I knew I could keep you somewhat away from a bad life. Cecilia I wish I could do more, but my hands are tied. The empire would get suspicious if I didn't keep the policies of the Collection

Order in place. Your people have made España's life easier, and they would fight with their full might to keep it that way."

I listened to every word Merida had to say, and I still didn't believe all of it, but she wasn't making it all up. I knew that much.

"I'm assuming you're still not convinced?"

"Is there a way to prove any of this? Maybe then, I'll be more convinced."

"There are the royal archives of Mores, which note every soldier appointed to the army, including Christopher. But I'm afraid, I can't let you access them. Still, there is another way. The Chief of Alchemy, Roberto, can do a simple test of your blood to test it with Christophers."

"Isn't he dead? How would you have his blood?"

"Along with many written archives the empire keeps, they also have small vials and swatches of every person's blood for those with titles. For example, any soldier promoted to commander must give a blood sample."

"Okay let's do the test, and if you are right, what happens next?"

"Well, there's not much I can do besides send you back to Leo unless you join the army. Which is not going to be easy considering your gender, but it can happen. And I'm not saying to cause trouble, but if you're *lucky*, you can change your father's system."

The thought of joining the army made my heart ache, but the fantasy of inciting change, especially if one of my creators was the reason for the system that brought so many people pain. I could help Ramiro, Emilia, Estela, Ana, all the women forced to conceive, and all the men worked to death. They could all live a better life if I sacrificed mine. That was something I was willing to do.

Ancestral Expense

Merida ordered her guards to bring back Leo and to escort us to Roberto's lab at the west end of the Castle. Merida said she couldn't accompany us because she had work to do but her guards would protect us, more specifically me. It would be a short journey to his lab because it turned out we were in the east wing of the castle. Merida explained the route to the lab, and in the process, gave me a picture of the layout of the castle's main floor.

The east side of the castle was for Merida and her court system. It was also for the royal garden. The middle of the castle was used as walkways, and tunnel hallways connected everything together. The west end was for Alfonso, the King of Mores. It also had the Mores' archives and another royal garden.

Merida's garden was for looks with pretty flowers and bouquets, while Alfonso's garden was for using vegetables, fruits, and medicinal herbs.

As we started to make our way to the lab, I noticed that Leo was no longer pushing me. One of Merida's guards had taken over the job of making me movable. His hands were covered by black metal armor. Unlike any other soldiers, these two were in full head to two solid black and silver metal. They didn't have leather gloves; instead they had metal ones that bended with their fingers. I didn't even know that was possible! He also didn't try to make any awkward small talk. Just pushing me in silence.

I turned my head to see Leo behind me. He was walking aimlessly, following Merida's other guard, who was in front of him and beside my wheelchair. I realized that Leo didn't know what was happening at all. He had no idea about the news that Merida dropped onto me. What would his reaction be? Would he be mad? Would it somehow change his opinion on me? Maybe this would be my chance to be treated better? If people found out that one of their country's so-called heroes had a daughter and that it was me, they would value me, right? It would turn me into a star of contradiction; here's this slave girl who just happens to be a "good guys" daughter. But I would have to uphold his image and values. I would have to live in his shadow as a reflection of himself. There wouldn't be any more Cecilia, there would only be "She's a Columbus".

We kept on trailing across the castle and made it to an impasse with a group of soldiers. Leo asked what they were doing, and they didn't respond.

"Soldiers, why are you blocking the path to this wing?" Leo asked again.

"We are members of the ninth battalion of the army of Mores under Diego Sanchez."

That's all they said. That was their answer to any question or response to any statement. Those fifteen words were seemingly all they knew.

"Can you step aside? We need to pass." I said.

Silence.

Of course, because when it's Leo he gets a response, when it's me I get not a damn thing.

"Move", Merida's soldier said in unison. They're voices were identical. Deep and unnerving.

Without hesitation the members of the battalion moved with their heads facing the floor. You could almost see their sweat start building on their foreheads. These guards were no joke. I'm guessing that the only people that Merida is with all day every day, so they have almost as much power as her, respectively. Even after we passed the men, they still looked down, not moving an inch.

We continued our "adventure" of venturing through the castle's maze-like pathways. It was– quiet to say the least.

***

After the much too long journey we made it to Roberto's lab. He had a massive "DO NOT DISTURB" sign on the door. I told the guard to push me closer to the door so that my arm could reach it. He complied, surprisingly, and once I was close enough, I knocked furiously. Just enough to make him visibly furious when I see his face. Angry mumbling could be heard coming closer and closer. The wooden door swung open, and Roberto's blue eyes looked to be bulging from his face. Even his stubble seemed to be standing with anger.

"How long is it going to take for a blood test?"
"Who the hell are you?" Roberto said with an attitude like I was breaking into his house.

"Literally no one, unless the blood test proves otherwise, which I'm hoping it doesn't."

"Leave me alone and go back to your field *Morena*"

"These are direct Queen's orders, you should reconsider Sir, Roberto." The guards said.

"Don't you even dare threaten me with your bluffs. You get five minutes."

Leo and one of the guards stood outside of Roberto's room while me and the other guard followed him inside his lab.

His lab was messy but organized at the same time. Piles upon piles of papers messily stacked, but herbs and flowers organized by color and height. A mortar and pestle seemed to be at every corner with whiter powder in each. I looked crystalline but really fine. As we dove deeper into the lab, I began to see a blurry wall of red with a white lines that separated it into sections. Getting closer to the wall the shapes cleared up and the white lines turned into small cut slips that had names written on them and the wall was actually the vials of blood in little compartments. Everything was ordered alphabetically. I skimmed the wall until I saw *him*. A piece of *him* was right there, in my line of vision. It was one of the strangest things to think that whatever was in that vile and what was in my body could possibly share the same traces of DNA.

Author's Bios

Rashmond Lopez is a twelve-year-old sixth grader who likes to play and watch football and basketball and play with his one-year-old dog, Lee. His favorite football team is the Minnesota Vikings, and his favorite wide receivers are Randy Moss and Justin Jefferson. He has four brothers and one sister. Math is his favorite subject because he likes to work with numbers and enjoys problem-solving.

Royalty Harvey is 13 years old and the only girl of five siblings. She loves to write, and sing, but her passion is dance because that's what she's very good at. When writing something, she does so with the intent of people knowing that even though life is hard, she is still getting through it with the help of her family and herself. She is currently taking honors classes which will lead to early graduation and acceptance into good college. Royalty speaks her mind, is happy when others are, and loves to take pictures.

Jemeah Scott (Jemeah Scott) is an 18 year old native of Rochester, NY. She is a recent graduate of Penfield High School and a member of the National Society of High School Scholars (NSHSS) who loves to learn new things. She is down-to-earth, eclectic, marches to the beat of her own drum, and aspires to a life of creativity

Author's Bios

and happiness. She enjoys drawing, painting, crocheting, bookbinding, sewing, reading, and writing. Her favorite dessert is apple pie with vanilla ice cream.

Kenneth Santiago is a Rochester, NY native. He is a writer, aspiring director, actor, comedian, an avid nerd and fanatic. He hopes to get his ideas from pen to paper and distributed them so he can help others with similar interests. Kenneth also hopes to make an impact in the fields and genres he holds dear. His life goal is to see the world and make a stable and healthy living.
"Life is too short to take everything seriously, so just laugh," is his personal motto.

Dylan Arce Carrion is a 16-year-old, up-and-coming author and anarchist, who decided that writing books is fun. He started writing as a way to cope with bottled-up feelings and now writes worlds with systems of change that he wishes could be implemented in our current society. Be on the lookout for the full release of Crown of Requisite by Spring 2023!

Nhaziah Bedell-Scott is 12-years old. She enjoys watching TV, talking with her little brother, playing video games, talking to her friends, and getting fresh air. Nhaziah also plays the violin, the trumpet, and lacrosse.

Gregory Harvey is a 14-year-old author.